There are many in our world who have the ability to write, however, there are special ones who have the *gift* of writing. Paula Parker is one of those with a gift. Thank you, Paula for sharing the gift of *If I Perish: A Queen's Sacrifice*. Thank you also for the incredible amount of research on cultures and customs that elevates the reader's understanding. I sat mesmerized as I followed the lives of these characters that I have read about for many years. I laughed, cried, cheered—for or against. No one should let this book pass by without it becoming a part of their library. It will be a favorite for years to come.

~Donna Williams, Co-Founder
EPIC Ministries, Inc.

On the copyright page of her new novel, *If I Perish,* author Paula notes that she has *endeavored to be respectful to all persons, places, and events presented in this novel, and attempted to be as accurate as possible. Still, this is a novel, and all references to persons, places, and events are fictitious or used fictitiously.* While this is a novel, Paula's humility and earnest respect for the source material is evident in the diligent research that flows off of every page. I felt transported back to the Persian Empire in the ancient days of Queen Esther. Though I have only a meager knowledge of that time period, everything felt so right with characters who were authentically from that era—not modern day characters playing dress up. Their speech, thoughts, manners—everything rang true to the history they belonged to.

The story of Esther is familiar to Jews and Christians; at least the bare bones of the story. Paula's respectful and creative novel brought the story alive as a dramatic epic. Knowing the story, I was still compelled to turn the page and discover what happened next! Her gift of weaving fact with fiction to further illllustrate a Biblical history has achieved a higher level!

I have read and love all of Paula's Biblical novels and can't help but think each the best one she has written to date—yet it is true, those who diligently work at their craft continue to achieve more mastery in it.

If I Perish reflects that artistic mastery in Paula's writings. When you open the book, you step back to the time of King Xerxes, discover what life was like for Jews and Persians alike. The drama and intensity is brilliantly combined with scenes that bring a tear or light hearted laughter. You'll catch a glimpse of what it might have been like to be an orphaned by a brutal mass murder, to be ripped away from your only surviving family member, to be being brought before a King whose whim determines whether you live or die, and ultimately having the weight of saving your entire nation cast upon your shoulders with nothing exept your enduring faith that God is with you—even it if means you perish in the process.

If I Perish will leave you breathless as you reach the end and suddenly realize, it is not a statement of resignation, but of Faith.

Tracy H Sugg, Sculptor
Fine Art Bronze & Monuments

How wonderful that Paula K. Parker has delivered yet another biblical era masterpiece, even surpassing her well-crafted and captivating *Sisters of Lazarus* series. Once again, this gifted writer takes her readers back more than 2,000 years, deftly weaving into the narrative enlightening historical information while never losing the flow of the story. Thank you, Paula, for portraying Mary and Joseph as living, breathing human beings who willingly accepted the greatest responsibility of all time.

~Marian Rizzo
award-winning author of *The Leper*

Most of us are familiar with the story of Mary as told by the Sunday School play each Christmas. A neat and clean version with little hardship or doubt. Paula Parker pulls back the curtain and shows us what may have really happened for Mary and Joseph. Paula's meticulous research gives historical and cultural details for more realism. A retelling of this important story to give all readers, believers and non-believers alike, a new appreciation for Jesus's parents.

~Susan K. Stewart
author of *Donkey Devos: Listen When God Speaks*

In *The Carpenter and his Bride* Paula Parker reveals an ancient world and culture that, because humans are involved, is relatable to our own today. Mary and Joseph: just a boy and a girl who one day fell in love, having no idea of the journey God had laid ahead of them. But that's not where it stops. As with all God-stories, this is only the starting point of an amazing adventure!

~Mary-Kathryn
internationally acclaimed recording artist

I just read the last word of *Glory Revealed: Sisters of Lazarus, Book 2*. I remain mesmerized by the world Paula Parker's words evoked. I feel as though I visited the family of Lazarus and experienced the final, earth-bound days of Jesus along with them. To sum up my reaction, I have only one word: masterpiece! Or in this case, the Master's peace is all over this book! I highly recommend this book to any who wish to rekindle their first love with the lover of our souls, Jesus of Nazareth, the Messiah, the heavenly bridegroom awaiting His bride.

~Brenda Noel
Audie Award-winning production supervisor of
The Word of Promise: Next Generation

In today's modern world value and self-esteem issue abound. It's as if a cruel joke has been played on humankind whereby the traits that are really valuable have been diminished and the outward, temporal things have been inflated beyond measure. As I read *Beauty Unveiled: Sisters of Lazarus Book 1* I saw this reality in a new way. I traded my 'I'm not worth much' tag for 'I'm extremely valuable to God.' This book is captivating—I couldn't put it down—and brings to life that which is most important.

~Monica Schmelter
General Manager, WHTN-TV

In *Beauty Unveiled: Sisters of Lazarus Book 1*, Paula K. Parker pens a riveting story of love, longing and faith. Parker's novels bear the profoundly satisfying mark of her gift as a playwright. She combines masterful storytelling with well-crafted dialogue. The result is a cast of Biblical characters fresh and human and real.

Through the eyes of Lazarus, Mary, and Martha the reader eagerly connects with three siblings from a normal, dysfunctional family. Gone are the dusty, unapproachable characters of Sunday school. Set in Bethany, 2,000 years ago, Parker breaks the time barrier with her brilliant use of cultural detail. The veil lifts, and we are brought face to face with flesh and blood people who jump off the pages and into our 21st century world. We resonate with their struggles, dreams, delights, disappointments, and the unpredictable ways God continually touches the human heart. Thank you Paula for giving powerful new voice to another ageless story.

~Bonnie Keen
Dove Award winning recording artist

Having thoroughly enjoyed the first two books in this series, B*eauty Unveiled* and *Glory Revealed*, I was more than excited to hear that Paula would be completing the trilogy with *Grace Extended*. I was then deeply honored to be given the opportunity to get a first look at the anxiously awaited manuscript. Oh my—it did not disappoint!

Though it may sound strange, I have to say, *Grace Extended*—in my opinion—is more painting than book. Vibrant strokes of beauty, pain, loss, and betrayal kiss the gently muted hues of love, forgiveness, and ultimately, redemption, creating something so real you want to reach out and touch the virtual landscape. Paula's skillful mastery of word and (seemingly endless) knowledge of period, language, histories, and human nuance, add depth, texture, and breath to the page, making you read a little faster than intended, so great is your need to see what happens next.

From beginning to end, I found myself drawn deeply into her expert brush work, and in the end felt I had been left with something quite breathtaking. I genuinely wanted to stand back, hands clasped behind my back and quietly ponder—as one might in the Louvre when spending time with a work they love and are reluctant to leave.

When I closed the book and stepped away, my final thought was—Monet's *Water Lilies*...in word. Simply lovely.

I cannot wait to see her next work.

~Barbie Loflin
Executive Pastor, Springhouse Church
author of *I Wish Someone Had Told Me*

IF I PERISH

Also by Paula K. Parker

The Sisters of Lazarus Trilogy
Beauty Unveiled
Glory Revealed
Grace Extended
The Carpenter and His Bride

with G.P. Taylor
YHWH
Yeshua

IF I PERISH

A QUEEN'S SACRIFICE

PAULA K. PARKER

WordCrafts

Scripture quotations are either paraphrased by the author or taken from The Holy Bible, New International Version® NIV® Copyright © 1973, 1978, 1984, 2011 by Biblica, Inc. Used with permission. All rights reserved worldwide.

Published by WordCrafts Press
Cody, Wyoming 82414
www.wordcrafts.net

For Mike.

"Silence in the face of evil is itself evil:
God will not hold us guiltless.
Not to speak is to speak.
Not to act is to act."

~Dietrich Bonhoeffer

Part One
She Was An Orphan

Chapter I

8 Farvardin
Third year of the reign of Xerxes,
King of the Medes and the Persians

Hadassah dropped the sprigs of parsley into the basket half-filled with herbs. *So few left,* she mused. She pressed a hand against the lower part of her back and straightened just high enough on her knees to glance over the stone wall toward the house across the field. The only movement was from peacocks strutting around the yard. Their irritating squawk—a stark contrast to their beautiful plumage—would give alert of someone's approach.

Drawing in breath, she sat back and lifted her face upwards. Overhead, clouds like fat fluffy sheep waiting to be shorn gamboled in the azurine sky. She watched several doves swooping down to snip leaves and grass to carry back to build their nests. In the distance, the sky over the royal capital of Susa roiled with hawks and falcons. She recognized some by their *flap...flap...glide* pattern, and others by their hunting pattern; folding their wings and shooting arrow-like toward the ground, to soar up again with—she knew, although too far away to see—prey clutched in their talons.

Yet, even without seeing their wing pattern, from this

distance—Susa was two leagues away—Hadassah still knew these were birds of prey. Today was the last day of *Norooz*, the five-day festival honoring the beginning of the Persian year and the coming of Spring. Celebrated across the Empire, during these days, people feasted, danced, and gave gifts. In the Royal Citadel—the Palace of the Persian Kings—King Xerxes, his nobles, and honored guests celebrated with feasts, with displays of athletic and military skills, and with hawking and falconry in honor of Tishtar, the Persian goddess of rainfall and water.

A celebration of life.

Drawing a shuddering breath, her eyes misting, she adjusted the folds of her brown wool tunic under her knees. She tightened her cloak and pulled one side of her head covering across her nose, tucking it above her other ear. Even with the signs of Spring's coming renewal, the Winter's chill lingered in the air and in the ground where she knelt.

She pinched a faded flower from a basil plant, she held it to her nose and breathed. Even withered, she could smell the hint of freshness. Crushing the dried blossom, she carefully removed the seeds and dropped them onto the cloth in her basket and tossed the withered plant on the ground.

She looked around; even with the celebration of Spring, there were no signs of life in this garden. Weeds crept over the stone wall to mingle—and in some places strangle—the plants. In years past, on this day, the herbs would have sprouted, unfurling new leaves to the sun. The leaves she gathered today were from plants withered due to neglect.

Maman would have been upset to see the garden this way.

Although she had plenty of servants, her mother would spend time each day—regardless of the season—amongst their gardens of vegetables, fruits, herbs, and flowers. Hadassah closed her eyes, picturing her mother—dressed in old garments with a thick shawl wrapped around her head and shoulders—facing the coldest day to tend the gardens.

As a child, Hadassah helped her mother with this garden, carrying amphorae of water to pour on the soil near each plant; wrapping strips of cloth around the plant's base to protect it from Winter's icy touch; removing diseased leaves; or attacking insects that threatened the plants.

Once Maman was certain every plant was cared for, she would place a thick cushion she had woven—white with red foliage—on the marble bench in the middle of the garden. There they would sit, snuggling for warmth, eating handfuls of almonds Maman brought from the house, and talking about their completed task.

"Was this not satisfying?" Maman would ask.

"It was hard," Hadassah remembered complaining once.

"What does Baba tell you?"

She sighed. *"'You can do hard things,' But, Maman, some things are really hard. I do not mean tending the garden or working in the house. Those tasks are tiring, but other things are hard."* She laid a hand on her stomach, *"When my stomach feels as if I am being stomped by an elephant or gurgling like a whirlpool,"* she moved her hand to her head, *"when I feel dizzy and I faint; those times are hard. Sometimes, it feels…"* her mouth drooped as she whispered, *"it feels as if I will perish."*

Her mother laid an arm over Hadassah's shoulder, pulling her close. *"Trust me. Trust your baba. Trust Yahweh. Remember the patriarchs."*

Growing up, she loved hearing the stories of the patriarchs. Father Adam and Mother Eve in Yahweh's garden. Joseph sold into slavery by his brothers, spending all those years in prison, only to be appointed second to Pharoah, and ultimately saving his people from starvation. Moses removing his sandals before Yahweh in the burning bush, leading the Jewish people through the sea and to the Promised Land. David going from tending his father's sheep, to slaying Goliath, to becoming King of Israel.

When her parents taught her these stories, she would invariably ask, "Why?" Why would Yahweh allow the patriarchs' suffering and—in some stories—their death. *"If they perished, would they not just go to Abraham's bosom?"*

"Hadassah, you have seen Kaufa help your baba lift stone and marble." Her mother pointed to one of their servants, muscles rippling as he lifted a rock to build the wall around the garden.

"Yes," she nodded. *"Baba let me try lifting one, but I could not. It felt as heavy as a mountain. Kaufa is strong."*

Mother smiled. *"Kaufa was not born strong. He began by lifting one small rock, then a heavier rock, then eventually a tree trunk. By lifting heavier things, he has grown stronger.*

"It was thus with our patriarchs. Each time they faced harder challenges, they grew stronger in here," she tapped her chest, *"in their spirit. If they overcame, it was because Yahweh was helping them win a great victory. If they perished,"* Mother reached up to tuck a raven-black curl behind her ear, *"it was because Yahweh was calling them to the bosom of Abraham. When we face hard times, we must remind ourselves of the patriarchs. If we overcome, it is a victory, a gift, from Yahweh. Remember this,"* Maman had touched her nose, *"whatever you do in this life will remain after you are gone.*

"And you were a gift," she smiled. *"Just as Isaac was a gift from Yahweh to his parents Abraham and Sarah, you were a gift from Yahweh. For many years, your baba and I prayed, pleading with Yahweh for a child. Yet our prayers were never answered. Until you."* She pointed to the Evening Star twinkling through the clouds. *"You came when the night sky was brilliant with stars."*

"That is why you not only named me Hadassah, but you also called me, 'Esther.'" Hadassah bounced on the marble bench, repeating the story she heard many times. *"Because 'estra' is the Persian word for 'star.'"*

Her mother laughed, bending down to kiss her forehead. *"Yes, it is. Your baba and I thought we would perish for want of a child. It was hard. However, at the right moment, Yahweh gave you to us. You are the brightest star in our lives.*

"We have faced challenges. We know when we face them again,

Yahweh will be with us. And one day, if we perish," her mother shrugged her shoulders, "*we perish. But then Yahweh will take us to Abraham's bosom.*"

From that day, whenever Hadassah complained about something as being hard—either household tasks or the pains from her churning stomach—her mother or father would ask, *"And if this is so hard that you perish…?"* to which she would reply, *"If I perish, I perish."*

Hadassah lifted a hand to wipe away the tears pooling in the corners of her eyes and looked toward the center of the garden, where four tufts of dead grass were the only indication of the bench ever having been there. *I wonder where the bench is now?* Her father—a sculptor as well as a master builder—carved the bench from white marble as a gift for her mother. Maman loved it and promptly set to weaving a white cushion with red flowers and twining vines, to place on the bench. Each morning, she would come to sit there. She claimed it was her favorite place. *"It just feels peaceful."*

When her father pointed out that the red in the red and white designs on the cushion was the color reserved for the Royal Court, her mother shrugged. *"What are the chances King Xerxes will ever see this bench, much less this cushion?"* Lifting her black eyes to her husband's olive-gold ones, her mother added haughtily, *"If you recall, Abihail ben Shimei,"* addressing him by his full name, *"we are of the tribe of Benjamin and descended from King Saul."*

As the author of Proverbs wrote, Baba's creative skills brought him before great men. Many wealthy people in Susa commissioned her father to build their homes. It even brought him before the King, who had commissioned him to work not only within Susa, but also within the Royal Citadel.

Baba also designed and oversaw the building of their own home. Using stone the color of cream and patterned after the houses he constructed for the nobility in Susa, their house was wide as it was long. Arched windows were set deeply into the exterior walls to provide a shield from the sun. Scrolls and leaves were carved into the lintels over the main door in the front and the smaller door in the back that led to the cooking area. Being too far to bring water from the well in the center of Susa, her father also dug a well to supply water for their house. Inside, frescos of palm trees, ferns, and pomegranates decorated the walls, the colors echoing the red, gold, and green of the intricate mosaic tiles on the floors throughout the house. In the center of the house was a large courtyard with a small ornamental pool. Around the court-yard, Maman placed benches and small tables with pots of fragrant flowers nearby to create peaceful spots for their family and guests.

Their home also had two things not commonly found in other houses. Father designed a *yakhchal,* a tall, ceramic, domed structure, with a storage space beneath the ground where great blocks of ice were placed next to shelves and baskets that held their food and wine. Next to the yakhchal was a large tower connected to their house, and beneath the tower's roof were windows with vertical slats. Known as the *bagdir,* the wind catcher, Father designed it to help cool the house.

"How can a tower cool air?" she asked Baba.

"There are many things that contributes to the cooling," he said. *"The way I designed the layout of the house, the direction the tower faces, the slats in the window, how many windows are in the tower, the design of the blades not only in the window but also throughout the tower, and the channels and vents throughout the house."* When he noticed his daughter's confused look, Baba smiled and pointed to the tower of the bagdir. *"The air is caught by the slats in the windows in the tower. It is funneled down the tower to pass through a channel in the yakhchal, where the air is cooled before being sent through a series of smaller channels to vents in the rooms in our house."*

The wind being drawn into the bagdir not only cooled the house but also attracted birds each Spring to build their nests in the tower. Even from this distance, Hadassah could hear the echo of chirps inside the bagdir.

The yakhchal and the bagdir not only made their home unique among the houses in Susa, but they attracted more business for her father. These also brought offers to purchase the house, which he refused. "This is my family's home," he always explained.

This, the house where she was born and grew up, was on the other side of the stone wall.

"*Kokoko!*"

Hadassah stood and turned in one fluid motion, her heart pounding in her throat. She was of average height, but she still crouched so as not to be seen over the stone wall. Glancing around, she placed her feet carefully, side-stepping until she stopped behind an ancient walnut tree. She set the basket on the ground next to a thick branch. She picked up the branch, propping it against the tree and, hands splayed against the wide trunk, leaned to the side until she was just able to peer over the wall, toward the house.

In the yard, the peacocks were rushing about, wings folded against their bodies, squawking, "*Bu! Pe! Bu-girk! Pe-girk! Khok! Kokokkokoko!*"

Someone was approaching.

The last time she heard those peacocks squawking was on this very day, one year ago. *An entire year. How can it be a full year since the worst day of my life?* Eyes wide, her hands cupped against the tree, she began softly closing each finger against the trunk, moving in rhythm to her heartbeat, quietly humming a wordless prayer. This calmed Hadassah, but it did not prevent the memories that haunted her every moment—both waking and sleeping—from flooding back.

It was a year ago today. While the Persians celebrated the last day of Norooz, she went with her cousin Mordecai ben Jair to the house of Natan bar Chanan.

Of an age with her father, Mordecai was trained as a *Gyah Pezeshk*, a physician who treats the sick using herbs and plants, and as a *Mantreh Pezeshk*, a physician who used holy words and prayers to cure patients suffering from conditions which would not

9

respond to herbs and other medicines. This treatment consisted of talking with the patient to determine their needs, followed by reading from Holy Scripture, and praying over the patient, while soothing harp music was played to console and calm the patient.

When Hadassah was young, Mordecai's combination of herbs, Scripture, prayer, and harp music helped ease her stomach disorders. When she was older, she expressed interest in learning to play the harp, not only to help her own discomfort, but to help others. She proved to be a gifted harpist and asked to accompany her cousin whenever he visited the sick.

One year ago today, she accompanied Mordecai to Natan's to treat the man's elderly mother, Naibam bat Reuel, who could not breath easily. While Mordecai burned frankincense and mixed herbs into a tonic, Hadassah held her harp and sat next to the elderly woman. Plucking the instrument's strings, she noted how Naibam responded to the music. When she noticed the elderly woman relax, Hadassah used those strings to play a soothing melody, while Mordecai repeated Holy Scriptures over Naibam. After Naibam fell asleep, Mordecai left the tonic with Natan and arranged to return the next day.

They were about half a league away from home when they heard the peacocks squawking. When she opened her mouth, Mordecai grasped her upper arm, swinging her to face him. Placing a finger against her lips, he shook his head. "Make no sound," he breathed.

"But Cousin!" she whispered, her stomach tightening. "The peacocks have never screamed like this. We have to make sure Baba and Maman are alright."

"We will, but we much approach quietly. We do not know what...or who...we will find." He raised his eyebrows significantly. "Do you understand?"

A scream rose up from her belly, but she suppressed it. She could feel it even now, crouching in the base of her throat, like a tiger waiting to pounce. She nodded.

"Do as I do," Mordecai whispered, sliding his hand down to grasp her hand.

She held the harp against her body with her free hand as she followed him step by careful step through the woods and across Maman's garden to crouch behind this very tree.

Although they were cautious to not make noise, there was no need. The peacocks' squawks would have covered their footsteps. But the birds' squawking did not cover the cacophony of a struggle; angry cries, *thuds*, terrified screams and pleas that rose and then stopped, groans, *thuds*. Then no cries or screams; only *thud…thud…thud*.

"Enough!" A man's voice commanded. "Teresh! We must go."

The *thuds* stopped. "As you wish, Bigthana!" another responded. Laughter accompanied by the musical ring of a blade slipping back into the scabbard. The crunch of boots walking across the grass. When they heard horses' hooves against their gravel walk, Mordecai drew her down.

When the horses' gaits faded, Hadassah tried to stand but was held fast by Mordecai. "Let me go!" she hissed, twisting her arm, trying to pull her hand from her cousin's grasp. "Maman! Baba!"

"Hadassah!" he tightened his grip. "Stop!"

She froze, staring at her cousin.

He leaned toward her ear, "Stay here," he whispered, "I will check." He stood, handing her his leather bag which contained pouches of herbs and tonics, as well as pieces of parchment and writing implements for making notes about his patients' care.

Setting the harp on the ground by the tree, she took the bag and slung it over her shoulder. Leaning against the tree, she watched as he crept to the edge of the wall and rose up enough to peek over. He clapped a hand over his mouth before turning to her, his eyes wide with horror. Lowering his hand, he mouthed, "Come. Bring my bag."

Crouching as she saw Mordecai do, she ran softly to his side. "Maman? Baba?" she whispered. "Are they…"

11

"Hadassah," he interrupted, "they are hurt."

"Hurt!" she gasped. "We must help them."

"We will help them, but," he placed his hands on her shoulders, tears filling his eyes, "you must not cry out. We do not know if all of *the other people* have left."

She followed him along the stone wall to the wooden gate and turned, looking toward her home. She clapped her hands across her mouth, tasting blood as she bit her lips to keep from screaming.

The yard near the house was strewn with bodies; some moving, others still. She recognized Kaufa; their cook Adah; Bityah and Leah, their maids; and Elon and Barukh, the young men who helped Kaufa in the yard and fields.

Mordecai ran to the nearest, Kaufa, and knelt, gently turning him over. Kaufa moaned and wheezed as he tried to draw breath. His tunic and robe were torn, drenched red as blood poured from the gash across his chest.

"Stay still, Kaufa," her cousin said. He removed his brown turban, wadded it, and pressed it against the gaping wound. "Hadassah, hold this…"

She paid no heed, running toward the front door where her father was embracing the limp body of…

"Maman! Baba!" Hadassah threw herself down next to her parents. Ripping open the leather bag, she dumped out the herbs. "Baba…Baba! We are here. Please lay Maman down. Mordecai will help her. I will help her. Please, please. Baba…let us help her."

Her father did not respond. "Atarah." He held his wife closer, rocking her. "Atarah. *Beloved*." He lifted a thick lock of hair covering her face, revealing a gaping wound across her throat. Her eyes were opened, still, focused on nothing. "Beloved?" Her chest did not move. "No. Atarah! No!" He threw his head back, as a moan rose from deep within, erupting from his lips as a sobbing wail. "Nooo….!"

"No! Maman! No!" Hadassah threw her arms around her parents, rocking and shrieking, "Nooo! Maman! Do not leave us!"

12

"Abihail...*cousin*," Mordecai knelt next to them. "Please let me help Atarah."

Hadassah's father only shook his head. "It is too late...Atarah is...*gone*," his voice cracked with another deep wail. Lifting her head, he kissed her lips. "Do not despair, Beloved. I will join you soon."

"What?" Hadassah cried, gripping her stomach. "No! Baba!"

"Abihail, let me help you," Mordecai grasped his cousin's arm. "Where is your injury?"

Her father tenderly laid his wife down on the ground. He grimaced as he removed his sleeveless robe and handed it to his daughter. "Here, Hadassah. Cover your maman. I must speak with Mordecai."

She took the bloodied robe from her father's trembling grasp and turned to lay it across her mother's body. Lifting the edge of her own robe, Hadassah wiped the blood from her mother's face and kissed her cheek as she whispered, "I love you, Maman. I love you."

"No! Abihail!"

Hadassah turned to see Mordecai, shaking his head, his eyes wide. "I cannot."

"Mordecai," her father's breathing grew labored, "you must."

"What?" she asked. "What is it?"

"Hadassah," her father wheezed, "you and Mordecai must leave."

"Leave?" She shook her head. "No!"

"You must...leave," Her father lifted a hand to her cheek. "Always remember...your maman and I prayed...Yahweh answered our prayers...you were our estra...the brightest star in our lives."

"No!" She shook her head. "Baba! We must tend your wounds." She thrust a hand toward their servants. "We must tend Kaufa and the others."

"You cannot."

"Abihail," Mordecai said, "you will die."

"I must die," Baba lifted a weak hand toward the others lying on the ground. "They must die. You must leave."

13

"No! I will not leave you." She sobbed, laying her head on her father's chest.

"You cannot stay. Remember…you can do hard things." His fingers trembled as he grasped Mordecai's sleeve. "You must dress Leah…in one of Hadassah's tunics…as the daughter of the house… and then you…*must* leave. *They* are going to tell *him*…when he returns…If we…are gone…they will believe—*he* will believe… we still live…they will hunt…for us…for you," his eyes slanted toward Hadassah, "for her. Take care of her; you are now her kinsman-redeemer."

"Abihail, I do not understand," Mordecai said. "Leah is dead; why do we need to change her clothing? No. Once we have helped you all into the house, once we have dressed your wounds, then I will report this crime to the *Pasvar*, the official in charge of keeping the peace in Susa."

"The Pasvar…will do nothing." Baba's lips were tinged blue.

"No, he will help," Mordecai squeezed her father's hand. "I will report it myself. The Pasvar will send his officers to arrest those *Amalekites,*" spittle flew from his lips as he spoke the worst curse a Jew could use, "who attacked you."

"No…you must not…report this," her father grimaced, "but you…are right," his breath grew ragged, "about…who…"

"What?" Mordecai eyebrows arched in confusion, then his expression hardened. "*Amalekites?* You do not mean…?"

Abihail lifted a finger. Mordecai lowered his ear to his cousin's mouth.

"Haman…" Baba sighed, breath leaving his body.

Chapter 2

Tears fell over Hadassah's hands as she strummed a song against the tree's trunk—knowing which harp strings she would have plucked—quietly humming her pain.

"My soul is weary with sorrow," her voice barely a whisper. "My flesh and my heart fails…weary with sorrow…my heart fails."

The words from King David and from the prophet Asaph painted her anguish. Hadassah repeated the two phrases over and over, keeping beat with her heart and echoing the sadness she still felt. *It has only been one year.* She switched to words from the wisdom of King Solomon.

"It is a time to weep. It is a time to die. A time to weep…a time to die…a time to weep…a time to die…"

Maman, Baba; I wish I could be with you. Stop! She chided herself. *Do not allow your sorrow to diminish Maman's and Baba's sacrifice. Pray something else.* During the last Sabbath meeting, Rabbi Omar bar Anaiah read from the prophet Isaiah. *"He has borne our grief and carried our sorrow."* The Rabbi confessed to those gathered he did not know *who* the prophet meant had borne our grief or sorrows, but Isaiah's words brought comfort.

"He has borne our grief and carried our sorrows. He has borne our grief and carried our sorrows." Without thinking, she changed two words, *"You* have borne *my* grief and carried my sorrows." For her, playing was a form of praying. "You have borne my grief and carried my sorrows."

"Beautiful words."

She grabbed the branch, lifting it above her head as she whirled.

"Hadassah!" Eyes wide, her cousin raised his hands in a sign of surrender.

"Mordecai!" She dropped the branch, and bent over, gulping in air. Her heart pounded in her ears. "Forgive me. I did not hear you approach."

"I am sorry I startled you," her cousin grinned, "but I am glad to see you remembered to keep a cudgel near you."

"I am sorry for lifting it against you." She turned to lean against the tree. "I was…distracted."

"I could tell." His grin dropped, his eyes misting. "Your song was…comforting."

"Not at first." Lifting a hand, she swiped at the tears on her cheeks. "I have never lost someone this close to me and in such a manner. I did not realize the pain would linger." She looked away from her cousin, gazing over the field toward her home. "Everywhere I look, I see them."

He placed a hand on her shoulder. "As our Grandmother Elisheva—may her memory be blessed—always said, 'Grief is like a splinter deep in every fingertip; to touch anything is torture.'"

A smile hovered around the corner of Hadassah's mouth, and then was gone. "I wish I had known her." She took a ragged breath. "I miss Maman and Baba, may their memories be blessed."

"I know you miss them, but you can see your mother every time you look in your mirror." Mordecai lifted a hand to cup her chin. "You are twenty, the age your mother was when you were born. You look like her." He grinned. "Except for your eyes. You have your father's unusual eyes."

Her lips thinned into a tremulous smile. She grew up wanting to look like her mother. With soft curves, golden skin, and thick black hair that waved above delicate features, Atarah bat Ishvi was considered a beautiful woman by all who knew her. A little above average in height, Hadassah could have been a copy of her mother except, as Mordecai noted, for her eyes. Whereas her mother's eyes were onyx, Hadassah's almond-shaped eyes were like her father's, the hue of a new olive; dark green with a hint of gold.

"Baba always said I took the best of Maman's features. I wanted so much to be like her; to marry a Jewish man who loved Yahweh and loved me. To live in this house, and one day have children. But now..." she shook her head and looked up at her cousin. "You look much like Baba," she smiled, "the same height, the same curly hair, the same strong brow and angular jaw."

Mordecai laughed softly. "The only *strong* aspect of my looks are my brow and jaw." He stroked his beard—with as many streaks of white as black—flowing onto his cream tunic. "I am a physician, he worked with stone and wood. I told Abihail once while he might have the strength of Samson, I had the wisdom of Solomon."

Hadassah laughed, ending in a ragged breath. She looked at the garden, the fields, the house. "I still remember that day...a year ago...seeing Maman, Baba...the others." Her eyes hardened. She shook her head, blinking away the sheen of tears in her eyes. "Why, Mordecai?"

She straightened. "Why did Haman pur Hammedatha send those men to kill my parents and our servants? What did Maman or Baba do to anger the *Hazarpatish*," she spat, "the Commander of The One Thousand Immortals, the King's personal bodyguard? He has wealth and power." She thrust a hand toward the direction of Susa. "No one may even enter the King's presence without the Hazarpatish's permission. Kaufa, Adah, and our other servants did not know him. They rarely went to Susa and would have mentioned if someone pointed Haman out to them. Why? Why did he want them all dead? Why did he take our home?"

"I do not yet know," Mordecai's brows lowered, his lips a thin line, "but I will learn. For now, we must go." He pointed toward where the sun had slipped halfway to the horizon. "Haman and his household are in Susa, celebrating with King Xerxes and Queen Vashti, but their servants will be returning soon. This house and land are isolated; only someone associated with Haman's household would be traveling on the road leading to or from here.

"I left Deagah ben Caleb's donkey and wagon on the other side of the woods," he pointed toward the stand of trees on the far side of the garden. "Even with a wagon, it will take us time to get back to town. Were you able to gather the herbs we needed?"

"Some," she bent to pick up the basket, "but not all."

"These will have to do." He lifted the cudgel, took her arm, and began walking across the garden. "Tonight begins the Sabbath. After our evening meal, we will sing a prayer in memory of those we have lost. But Hadassah," he stopped and turned, looking fully at her, "this I vow; I will discover why Haman committed these atrocities, and I will see him punished."

CHAPTER 3

Walking through the Palace away from the Corridor of the Royal Residence—the only access to the Private Residence, which included the King's Private Apartment as well as the apartments for Queen Vashti, the Queen Mother Atossa, and Crown Prince Artaxerxes—Haman's steps echoed on floors inlaid with intricate mosaics in gold, green, blue, and red. Eyebrows bristling, he chewed his lip in deliberation, ignoring the wealth displayed in gold and silver vessels on tables placed beneath walls decorated with paintings of the various Kings of Persia, designs of the *Shahbaz*—the royal falcon, representing the strength and aggression of the Persian Empire, and of the *Lamassu*—the deity in the shape of a flying lion—along with paintings of the Army and the blue waterlily, all set between massive columns topped with the forms of kneeling bulls.

He passed servants arrayed in simple white tunics and trousers, hurrying on quiet, slippered feet, carrying baskets of linens, trays holding silver amphorae of wine and golden goblets, trays of food, or other items required by the King's guests. Seeing Haman, the servants stopped, backed against the walls, and bowed their heads. "Sir," they whispered, averting their eyes until the Hazarpatish passed.

He also passed members of The One Thousand Immortals,

Warriors selected from the Ten Thousand Immortals—the core group of the Persian Army—to be part of the King's personal bodyguards. Dressed in clothing similar to his—elaborate saffron-colored tunics and trousers, caps trimmed in gold—each Warrior stood at stiff attention, long spears with a silver blade and pomegranate insignia held upright, the butt resting firmly on the toe of his pointed shoe. The Warriors noted Haman passing, eyes flicking toward him, before returning to watch the corridor. Haman did not expect them to further acknowledge him when they were on duty, watching for potential harm to the King and his family.

Passing the Court of the Throne Room, Haman opened the door and entered the bedchamber assigned to the Commander of The One Thousand.

Flames dancing over lamp stands placed around the room gave off the scent of perfumed oil. The walls were covered in tapestries depicting the conquests of the Persian Kings. Along one wall were intricately carved chests for storing his clothing and a wash-table holding a bowl, an amphora of water, a bar of soap made from olive oil and rose water, along with several folded linen towels. The bed was against another wall: a thick pallet, covered in fine linens and placed on top of a wide, finely carved wooden frame. A table next to the bed held a silver amphora of wine, beaded with condensation, and two golden goblets.

On the wall by the bed hung his armor; a bronze helmet trimmed with gold, and a breastplate of golden scales beneath a red tunic. Next to his armor was an array of weapons; several battle-axes, long bows with quivers of arrows, swords of varying length, and his long shield. Haman carried a short, double-edged sword from a tooled leather belt on his right side. For those who did not know the Hazarpatish by sight—tall, his physique hardened from years of battle, dark eyes, hooked nose, a frown in a black beard with streaks of gray—wearing this weapon as he did identified him as one of the King's most trusted officials.

On the far wall of the room stood a wide table and bench

made of polished ebony. It was at this table Haman would sit to write his reports for the King.

Now his reports, along with a stack of blank parchment and his writing implements, were in a basket on the floor. On the ebony table stood a large mirror with a polished bronze surface reflecting the frowning countenance of his wife, Zeresh. Behind her stood Rauxshna, Zeresh's personal maid, comb in hand.

As he shut the door, the young slave girl turned, stepped to the side of the table, eyes wide as she bowed, whispering, "Sir."

"You may leave, Rauxshna," his wife snapped. "Come back to dress me for the morning meal."

"Yes, Lady," the girl set the comb on the table, bowed to Zeresh, crossed the room, and bowed again to Haman. He noticed her eyes were reddened and a bruise forming on her cheek. Her gaze lowered, she skirted around him to slip out of the room, quietly closing the door behind her.

Haman crossed the room to the table. Lifting his wife's hand, he kissed it. Even though he had not seen her in weeks, this was not the time for more intimate affection. Being the Hazarpatish required his constant presence in the Palace or wherever the King happened to be. When Haman did return to their home, it was never for more than a night or two.

"I did not expect to see you so soon." Zeresh withdrew her hand to open a small bronze tube of kohl. Picking up a thin stylus, she dipped it in the tube and—gazing at her reflection—drew a line of black kohl along her lashes. "Did the King conclude the men's festivities for the day?"

"No; My Lord King needed a time to," Haman grinned, "refresh himself. I left fifty Immortals guarding him." He walked to the side table and lifted the amphora. "Wine?"

"Yes."

Haman poured wine into the goblets. "Where are our sons and daughter?"

"Our younger sons are with their older brothers in the city, celebrating the New Year." She set the stylus down, examining her eyes in the mirror. "I saw them earlier this morning. They all had already been drinking so much, tomorrow they will feel as if their heads were bludgeoned with a battle mace."

Haman snorted. "I know how that feels." He crossed the room to hand Zeresh a goblet. "Where is Navjaa?" His eyes thinned, eyebrows slanting over a hooked nose. "Certainly not amongst her brothers' friends? Not only would that be inappropriate, but it might destroy our plans."

"Be calm. She is with Dalphon. Our eldest son recognizes it is his responsibility to protect his sister. They said something about going to the Citadel Marketplace before returning home." Glancing at the mirror, she studied her reflection, tweaking an errant curl, drawing the tip of her little finger beneath her rouged lip. Nodding, she turned to take the goblet. "What about you? What about today? What has happened?"

"Nothing." Haman took a drink.

Zeresh's brows slanted downward. "Nothing?" Her voice was shrill. "You and the—" she stopped at Haman's glare. He jerked a thumb toward the door beyond. She continued in a whisper, "You invited six of the most powerful *Shathapavans*—provincial governors—in the Empire to our home to plan."

"Yes."

"You...*arranged* to...*get* a home that is isolated. We are not farmers, I did not wish to live outside the walls of Susa, yet *you* insisted. You said the location of the house would prevent people from seeing so many important men coming to our home."

"It does."

"You and the others planned for months. Here we are, at the last day of this *interminable* feast, and you say *nothing* has happened?"

"Yes. Nothing has happened." He took a deep drink. "We have watched for the last six days of this feast and before that time. While you stayed here, I traveled with Xerxes for one hundred and eighty days as he escorted his Shathapavans, his nobles, his generals, the magi—all the important citizens across the Empire— pointing out the vast scope and wealth of the Persian Empire and the strength of his armies. All to reassure these people and garner their support for his invasion of Greece."

Since he ascended the Throne three years prior, King Xerxes had suppressed revolts in Egypt and Babylon. Last year, just as the rainy season came with the month of Mehr, the King began this celebration tour. The King had escorted his nobles and military leaders to view his Empire. In each of his capitals—Ecbatana, Persepolis, Babylon, and now Susa—the tour had included sporting events and feats of military strength similar to those of Athens and Sparta. It ended with week-long feasts in each city, where wine and food were served day and night. Tonight would end the celebration here in Susa.

Haman laughed. "This morning, Xerxes had a Royal Scribe read the number of Persian Warriors, chariots, horses, and weapons. Afterwards, the King boasted," Haman pitched his voice deeper, "'Persia has all of this, but *I*," he lifted a fist above his head, "*I* will conquer Greece with my archers alone.'"

"And the lingering Noorz festival?" Zeresh set the goblet on the table and opened an ebony box. Gold, silver, and precious jewels glinted in the light. Lifting a golden collar set with rubies, she secured it around her neck. "After such a long tour of the Empire, why prolong the New Year celebration?"

"The King told me he wanted one more feast to allow his guests time to think about what they had seen," Haman took another drink. "He also wanted them to consume as much food and wine as possible. He wants everyone drunk, so when he asks for their decision, no one can lie."

"Lie!" Zeresh's brows arched. "Does the King truly think someone would risk execution by committing such a heinous crime, especially in his presence?"

"Possibly," Haman shrugged. "At the beginning of this

morning's feast, he offered praise to Ahura Mazda, the creator and great god of truth and order. King Xerxes had the Royal Scribes read something his father, Darius the Great, had once said. '*As the representative of Ahura Mazda, the King of Persia is the friend of right and truth. He is also the enemy of the man who speaks lies.*'"

Zeresh shook her head, slipping golden bracelets on her arms. "As if anyone within the Persian Empire needs reminding that speaking lies is an act against Ahura Mazda and punishable by immediate death."

"I know Agarbayata, Jata, and the other Six wish one of the seven *Azam*—the King's personal advisors—would be caught in a lie. They frequently counter any advice given by The Six with unbelievable, foolish advice. Being the King's companions since childhood does not make one a wise advisor. They left the banquet with Xerxes; he called for more wine to be brought to the Royal Apartment.

"Enough of the King's feast for the men," he sliced his hand through the air. "What happened during Queen Vashti's feast for the women?" He crossed the floor to sit on the bed.

"The same as the King's feast for the men," Zeresh shrugged. "The Queen complained from the moment she entered the Court-yard of the House of Women."

"She is the *Shahbanu*, the King's Lady," he said, leaning back against a pillow. "One would think she would have nothing of which to complain. However, I know from experience that is not the case." He shook his head, adding in a bored tone, "What were her complaints today?"

Zeresh sneered. "It would be briefer if I told you what she did *not* complain about." She lifted her hand, fingers spread, and touched her thumb, ticking off each item. "Vashti was tired of trav-eling around the Empire with the King for these last one hundred and eighty days. She complained," Zeresh lifted her nose, frowning, pitching her voice higher, "*Even in a curtained palanquin, it was not comfortable to travel all day. When we were not near one of our*

Palaces, we slept in tents. The air was close and dusty. These conditions are not good for my complexion. When we ate, the slaves could not keep the bugs away from our food. It was so boring."

Haman sighed. "I have heard these complaints from her many times over the past one hundred and eighty days."

"Who has not? There is more." Zeresh touched her second finger. "Vashti added it was made worse by Xerxes insisting the *Puora Vaspuhr*—the Crown Prince—Artaxerxes, ride in the palanquin with her." Zeresh wrinkled her nose. "Vashti said, *'He is such a noisy child.'*

She shrugged her shoulders, "I agree with Vashti about traveling, which is why I choose to stay home when you travel with the King, especially to war. Vashti mentioned several oils and beauty treatments I wish to try." Zeresh touched her third finger. "She also complained about the *Malekeh Jahann.*"

"Vashti complained about Malekeh Jahann Atossa," Haman sat up, his eyebrows arching, "the *Mother of the World?*"

Zeresh nodded.

"What did she say about the King's Mother?"

"Vashti complained of Xerxes favoring his mother over her. She said, *'After all, I am his Shahbanu, the Queen, his favorite wife, the mother of his heir. I should sit on the Throne next to him; not..."'* Zeresh dropped her voice, as if she could be heard through the thick door, *"'an old woman.'"*

Haman gasped. "She said that?"

Zeresh nodded. "From where I sat, it was obvious that Vashti's comments shocked all those present—women, servants, and eunuchs."

"As they should."

"The question is; will Vashti's comments raise questions?"

"Xerxes has said nothing of it in my presence," Haman drank the rest of the wine and set the goblet on the side table. "There is an old contention between her and Xerxes. She has often claimed he chose her to be his Queen, not for her beauty, but because she is General Otanes' daughter. From what Otanes has said to me, Xerxes has spoken to him about Vashti's apparent lack of affection and care for Prince Artaxerxes. As Vashti's father—and the Prince's grandfather—it is understandable that the General of the Persian Army would be concerned not only for Artaxerxes' safety and care, but also that the Empire be intact when the Prince ascends the Throne of Persia."

The General had been Haman's commanding officer for fifteen years. While King Darius prepared to lead expeditions to expand the borders of the Persian Empire, the General had recommended the King appoint Haman to become one of The One Thousand Immortals, to protect the Royal Citadel and his heirs, including the then Crown Prince Xerxes. When Xerxes ascended the Throne, the General suggested the new King appoint Haman to become the Hazarpatish, the Commander of The One Thousand. Xerxes took his father-in-law's advice.

"Nonetheless, at this point, I do not believe Vashti's complaints would be considered treasonous." Haman stood. "Watch and listen. Listen to Vashti; listen to what the other women say. I will also keep watch during tonight's feast for the men. If the opportunity presents itself, I will speak with the *others*.

"Nor do I think Xerxes will decide within the next few days. There should still be time for *something to happen* we can use to our advantage." His forehead wrinkled as he stroked his beard. "Hmmm...should an opportunity present itself and Xerxes sends a servant, and not me, to speak with the Queen, I will have the servant give you this message, 'Tell my wife there is a beautiful sunset; it reminded me of her.'"

She nodded. "That is good; I will watch." She closed the jewelry box and stood to face her husband. "Now, I must go. It is nearly time for Vashti's final banquet." She extended her arms to each side. "Well? Am I presentable to dine with the Queen?"

His wife of twenty years, Zeresh dokhtar Tattenai did not look alike a woman who had borne one daughter and ten sons, including a set of twins. Of average height, with a voluptuous figure, her face was a perfect oval with full cheeks and lips, a refined nose, and sharp brows above onyx eyes. Only a few wrinkles lining her smooth olive skin hinted that she was almost forty years old.

He stepped closer, drawing her into an embrace. "You are still the most beautiful woman in the Persian Empire."

She smiled, a provocative look under thick lashes. "Even more beautiful than Vashti?"

"Ah, my wife," his smile was slow and warm, "compared to you, Vashti is," he leaned in closer, whispering in her ear, *"zesht."*

She gave a peal of laughter. "Ah, what would King Xerxes say to hear you pronounce his Queen as *ugly?*"

He grinned as he escorted her to the door. "As the King only speaks truth, he would agree with me."

She smiled, sliding her hand across his chest. "Come back soon and speak more of my beauty." She turned and walked down the corridor toward the Courtyard of the House of Women. It was there Queen Vashti would hold tonight's banquet for the wives of the men feasting with the King.

Haman grinned as he watched Zeresh, her hips swaying as if dancing beneath a robe of pleated blue linen embroidered with gold threads and sparkling with gems. She *was* beautiful. After twenty years of marriage, he knew not to suggest—nor even consider—anyone as more beautiful; not even the Queen.

He recalled the bruise forming on Rauxshna's cheek and wondered what the maid had done to offend his wife. Certainly she would not speak of Zeresh as, "*almost* as beautiful as Queen Vashti." The last slave who made that mistake was now lying beneath the earth on the far corner of their land. He smiled; it was one of advantages of owning a home with large property outside the city walls of Susa. Not that anyone would notice the girl's absence. After all, she was only a slave.

Chapter 4

"It is interesting the King chose this year to display all his wealth and might," Deagah ben Caleb whispered to Mordecai as he measured out the wheat. "Rumors abound he is trying to raise support amongst his nobility to invade—and recapture—Greece."

Mordecai and Hadassah had gone to Deagah's shop to return the donkey and wagon. She was in the family courtyard, visiting with Deagah's daughter—and her friend—Miriam. Mordecai was trading cinnamon, parsley, cloves, garlic, saffron, and fragrant oils with the merchant for honey, grain, and olive oil.

Shorter than most men Mordecai knew, yet wider than all, Deagah wore a brown turban to hide his baldness and trimmed his white curly beard in the square-cut style favored by the Persians instead of the longer, untrimmed beards favored by other Jewish men. His cream linen tunic reached his knees, revealing brown trousers and pointed shoes. Deagah often confided to Mordecai that he wore these garments, "to hide amongst the Gentiles."

"I must engage them in commerce," the merchant said. "Thus, I need to make them feel comfortable around me. *Yet*," he laid a finger alongside his nose and dropped his voice, "I do not wish to stand out. Ahhh…" he turned and bowed his head as two men dressed in saffron-colored tunics entered the shop. "Sirs, welcome to my humble shop."

Mordecai was not offended at Deagah cutting off their conversation to address the newcomers. Wearing sash-like harnesses which held weapons over their tunics identified these men as part of the King's One Thousand Immortals.

"How may I serve you?" Deagah swept his hand wide, indicating the shelves around the room. "The House of Deagah has spices, honey, oil—for both cooking and lamps—all manners of foodstuffs, balms and other medicinal supplies, supplies to care for your clothing, your weapons, your saddles, and your horses. For your wives, we have cooking pots, dishes, fine fabrics, costly apparel, ivory, ebony, gold, silver, and precious stones. Pardon, Sirs," he said as three women wearing pleated linen tunics and glittering jewelry entered the store. "Yintl," he turned, calling, "we have more guests. Welcome Ladies," he spoke to the women. "My wife will help you in a moment's time. Now, Sirs," he turned back to the Warriors, "what may I show you?"

The curtain at the back of the room shifted as Yintl bat Azarel—a short woman with a thick white braid, dark eyes, and a large smile—walked from their supply room, crossed to the three women, and bowed as her husband had. "Welcome, Ladies," her voice was soft. "We are honored to have you come to the House of Deagah. What may I show you?"

"Sirs," Deagah opened a small container and extended it to the Warriors, "this wax will clean and condition your saddles. I doubt you would find better saddle wax anywhere in the Empire or in the world." He laughed. "Not that wares from foreign countries match the quality of Persian goods; am I right?"

"This is from the Far East. It is called *silk*," Yintl spread a length of shimmering fabric across the table. "Feel it. Garments made from this fabric would look beautiful anywhere, even to a banquet in the Royal Palace, as I am certain you ladies have had the pleasure to experience."

Mordecai watched his friends tend their customers, offering different items for inspection, pointing out the superiority of their wares. After the customers selected what they wanted, they settled into the rhythmic barter, offering, countering, reoffering, discussing, and offering again, until a price was agreed upon and the transaction completed. After taking the customers' coin and wrapping up their purchases, Deagah and Yintl escorted them to the front door, with unending comments on the beauty of the day, the excitement of the New Year's celebration, and the hope the customers would not only return to their shop but would tell their family and friends about the House of Deagah.

Deagah was a merchant of great repute, buying products from the caravans that traveled beyond the reaches of the Persian Empire. Unlike other merchants who had a small booth or tent in the Susa Marketplace in the center of city, Deagah and Yintl owned a building—that was both a home and shop—in the Citadel Marketplace in the northern part of Susa, near the Royal Citadel.

Built of cut stone, the cream façade of the two-story home was carved in white floral swirls, set with one large window next to the front door. The main room on the lower floor was large, with walls of smooth clay and the floors tiled in alternating squares of blue, yellow, and cream. Bare of decorations, the walls had shelves to hold their merchandise and tables to hold the items the customers wanted and to complete the sales. Tall oil lamps were placed in the corners and on either side of the large window. Through the curtained opening at the back of the room was a storage area for more merchandise and a small corridor that led to a courtyard in the back where Yintl and Miriam would prepare meals and their family would eat. Alongside the back wall of the house were stairs that led to second floor, where was located their bedchambers and a large room for gathering during inclement weather.

After escorting the Warriors to the front door, Deagah returned to Mordecai. "Is there something more I can do for you, my friend?"

"Do you have something cool to drink?"

Deagah lifted white brows. He glanced over his shoulder where Yintl was finishing wrapping the purchases of the three ladies before dropping his voice. "I have something refreshing in the yakhchal. Come."

Mordecai followed Deagah across the store, through the curtained opening, to where Deagah's son Kalev was restocking the crocks of honey.

Kalev turned and bowed his head. "Greetings, Mar Mordecai ben Jair, peace be on you." Taller than his parents, he had his mother's eyes and his father's easy smile set in a chiseled face.

"And on you peace, Kalev ben Deagah," Mordecai returned the traditional greeting.

"You are almost finished stacking the crocks of honey?" Deagah asked.

"Yes, Father. Once I am done, I thought to go to the courtyard and—"

"Once you are finished with the honey, you can sweep the front walk of the shop."

"Yes, Father," Kalev's countenance drooped.

Deagah exchanged glances with Mordecai before adding, "Your sister has prepared honey cakes for our guests. If you hurry, I am certain she will have extra to share with you."

Mordecai bit back a laugh at the young man's sudden grin.

"Yes, Father, I will hurry." Kalev placed the last two crocks on the shelf, before reaching for the broom and hurrying from the room.

Deagah smiled at Mordecai. "Kalev is a good son, and a hard worker."

"He is," Mordecai stroked his beard and grinned at his friend. "It also appears he loves honey cakes."

Deagah nodded, "Especially when Miriam makes them for *special* guests."

Both men stared at each other before breaking out in laughter.

"Truthfully, for months now Kalev has wanted me to speak to you about Hadassah," Deagah laid a hand on Mordecai's shoulder. "He realizes the traditional period of mourning is a year, but in her situation, we expect it to last longer."

Mordecai nodded. "You speak truth. However, I do not think her grief will end until *Haman*," he turned and spit, "is made to pay for his crimes."

"I will keep my ears open for any information that will help you," Deagah said. "While Yintl and I want grandchildren, we do not wish to hurry our children into marriage."

"Abihail and Atarah—may their memories be blessed—felt the same about Hadassah."

"Come," Deagah smiled, "let us get your cool drink." He led Mordecai down the corridor, to the courtyard, where laughter and soft music floated on the wind. Hadassah was showing Miriam how to play the harp. Of an age with her friend, Miriam was short, with smiling brown eyes, and a thick black braid that hung to her waist.

"Miriam," Deagah said, "I am going to get something cool for Mordecai."

"Yes, Baba. And Mar Mordecai, the honey cakes are nearly finished. I hope you and Hadassah will stay long enough to eat some."

"I would never pass up your honey cakes, Miriam. Once we are finished, Hadassah and I will go home." He glanced upwards, where the sun sent shafts of gold in the afternoon sky. "We will have enough time to prepare for the Sabbath."

Hadassah nodded. "We are almost finished with Miriam's lesson."

The men walked to the far side of the courtyard where was located the door for the yakhchal. Several years before, Deagah commissioned Abihail to build the cooling chamber to protect foodstuffs, wine, and other items for their store and for themselves. Next to the door was a small table with a few small oil lamps and flints. Lighting a lamp, Deagah opened the door and gestured for

Mordecai to precede him. Holding onto the rail built into the interior wall, the men descended stone stairs to the lower area.

Walking past great blocks of ice and shelves holding food and wine, the men went to the far wall. Deagah handed the lamp to Mordecai before slipping his hand into a crevice in the stone wall and pulling. After a moment, a small portion of the wall moved, opening to reveal a room beyond.

When Abihail had built Deagah's yakhchal, he had discovered a labyrinth of caves. After conferring with the merchant, he carved a block of stone that—once set in place—looked like part of the cave wall, masking the door, and hiding the labyrinth beyond.

Deagah took the lamp and led Mordecai to a shelf on the far side, which held a number of small chests. Mordecai lifted two of the chests from the shelf, set them on the ground, and knelt to open the lid of the closest one. Gold coins glinted in the lamp light.

The Jews in Susa did not trust the magi, who not only conducted the religious practices for the Persian gods, studied the sciences, and taught some of the lessons for the Crown Prince, but also oversaw the banking for the Empire. Instead of taking their money to the Gentile-run banks, the Jews in Susa carried chests filled with their coins, jewels, and other precious items to be stored in the caves beneath Deagah and Yintl's store.

To those who were not Jewish, Deagah might appear foolish, but his friends and family knew him to be a wise and cunning man. He was descended from Caleb, the man Moses chose from the tribe of Judah, who—along with eleven other men—were sent to explore the land of Caanan.

Deagah considered himself a copy of his ancestor, listening while talking, always gleaning tidbits of information while conducting business. Beyond being cunning, Deagah was trustworthy, never charging more than an item was worth, not even to Gentile customers. He and Yintl were known for their compassion, often reducing the price of items for the poor. It was these qualities that made the Shushan Jews trust him to store their wealth.

"Do you think any of the Persians suspect this room?" Mordecai asked.

Deagah shook his head. "If they did," he grimaced, "I do not doubt they would consider this," he gestured to the room, "a lie and would have executed me by now."

"When you face that prospect," Mordecai sat back on his heels and looked at his friend, "why do you stay? You know what Haman's men did to Abihail and Atarah and their servants, may their memories be blessed. Why do you and Yintl and your family stay in Susa? When Cyrus the Great was King, he allowed the Jews to return to Jerusalem. They are rebuilding the city as well as the Temple of Yahweh. Why do you not return to the land of our fathers?"

"Who would care for our people; who would provide for those who cannot afford food?" Deagah spread his hands toward the vast array of boxes. "Who would protect the money our people store here? Would I like to go to Jerusalem? Yes! Yintl and I would love to see the land of our ancestors, we would love to offer sacrifices in the Temple, but we will not. Our family remains in Susa, to help those who cannot afford to return to the land Yahweh gave to our ancestors."

"I pray Yahweh will honor your care for our people."

"Beyond that, Susa is our home. My parents were born in Babylon and their parents were born in Jerusalem, but Yintl and I were born here. Our children were born here, not in Babylon nor in the City of David.

"What about you?" the merchant asked. "After what happened to Abihail and Atarah, may their memories be blessed, why do you and Hadassah stay here?"

"My reasons are similar to yours. My ancestors were born in Jerusalem and my parents in Babylon. I was born in Susa. If I leave here," Mordecai said, "who would care for my patients, especially those who cannot afford a Persian physician? Even those who have the money, what Persian physician would speak the Holy Words of Yahweh over them?"

His beard drooped in a frown. "Before Abihail died, he commended Hadassah to my care. I have spoken to our Elders. As her kinsman redeemer, she is now my adopted daughter." He indicated the opened box of coins in front of him. "This one box of coins is only part of the inheritance Abihail and Atarah left their daughter. She is not only a wealthy woman, but also beautiful.

"She has told me many times all she wants is marry a Jewish man who loves Yahweh, who follows the Law given to Moses, and who loves her. She hopes one day to be a mother like Atarah was to her. If your Kalev had not expressed an interest in her, I do not doubt there would be other men who would. Her wealth and beauty will draw many men seeking her hand in order to win her and her fortune, but not necessarily her heart.

"I will do whatever I can to protect Hadassah and her inheritance. I am pleased to know your Kalev is drawn to her; I believe he would be a good husband. Seeing her happily married will bless Abihail and Atarah's memories."

Mordechai closed the lid of the box and pulled the second box over and opened it, revealing his own coins. Reaching into the folds of the wide cloth sash wrapped around his waist, he withdrew a pouch and loosened the leather ties wrapped around the top. After filling the pouch with coins, he tucked it back into the sash.

"Abihail's skill as a master craftsman brought him before Darius and Xerxes. He told me he often spoke of our people to the Kings. He chose to stay in Susa to be an advocate for our people, as you and Yintl chose to stay to care for our people, as I chose to stay to care for my patients.

"For an unknown reason, Haman pur Hammedatha sent men to kill Abihail, Atarah, and their servants." A frown creased Mordecai's brow. "The Hazarpatish did not follow the law. He did not have the Superintendent of Police arrest them, nor did he take them before the judges to bring charges against them. He sent armed men to slaughter them. Hadassah and I were not allowed the comfort of washing, anointing, and wrapping the bodies of her parents and their servants and burying them in the tomb of our fathers.

"It has been one year since Haman," he spat, "murdered our loved ones and took their home. I have yet to learn why he did this, but this I vow." He stood and reached up to remove his head covering. He laid his right hand, fingers splayed, on top of his head. "Before Yahweh, I vow never to acknowledge Haman nor his authority. I vow to not stop searching until I uncover the truth and see that cursed Amalekite punished for his atrocities."

Chapter 5

The sounds of slapping and grunts echoed across the cooking area and courtyard in the back of Mordecai's house. Hadassah's clothing, hair, and face were covered in flour, as was the dough on the table in front of her.

Before last year, in addition to maintaining gardens, Maman had been teaching her the skills necessary to run a house. Hadassah learned most of them, but baking bread was a skill she had not quite mastered.

Bread was a staple in every home, yet making it was one of the hardest things to master. It begins with properly grinding the grain into flour; mixing the right amounts of flour, seasonings, liquids, and leaven; kneading the dough, shaping it, and finally baking it. A wrong step along the way, inaccurate amounts of ingredients, too little—or too much—kneading, and the bread is ruined. Only when it is removed from the oven can the cook know if she has been successful.

Her frown and the punches to the dough on the table before her were evidence of her determination not to give up.

"You uncircumcised Gentile!" She balled up a fist and punched the dough. "You send armed men to my house!" Another punch. "You attack Maman and Baba!" She flipped the dough and punched again. "You killed our servants!" Taking the dough between her hands, she squeezed. "How would you like to struggle for breath," she tightened her grip until the dough split in half, "until your life's breath leaves your body and you die?" She continued squeezing until the dough was divided into smaller balls of dough. Placing the dough in a bowl, she moved from the preparation table to the baking oven.

Located in a courtyard at the back of Mordecai's and her house, the cooking area had shelves for storing food, several tables for preparing food, an open fire pit, and a baking oven. Shaped like a fat amphora that reached the height of her waist, the bread oven had a large opening on one side with a flat stone to cover it when not in use.

She picked up an iron rod, one end wrapped in thick cloth, to shove aside the covering to the oven. Inside, flames danced above the red coals. After adding a few more pieces of wood to the fire, she knelt by the oven and set the bowl on the ground. Lifting the balls of dough, she flattened them between her palms and slapped them onto the walls of the oven. While the bread baked, she went back to the shelves to get a large tray and a cloth. When the top of the dough set and the edges browned, she lifted the baked bread from the oven to the tray and covered it with the cloth.

She walked to the worktable and dipped a cloth into a bowl of water to wipe her face and hands and swipe at the flour on her garments. She set a large pot of water over the coals; after they finished the evening meal and the reading of the Holy Scriptures, she and Mordecai would both want to bathe in anticipation of the Sabbath.

The home she shared with Mordecai was located near the Susa Marketplace, far from the Royal Citadel. Walking from Deagah's home, they would pass by the Great Gate leading into the Citadel, with two heavy columns supporting a roof. On the street side, the entrance of this gate was flanked by two statues of Darius, twice the size of a regular man, on a base two cubits tall. Each statue was of the late King, dressed in his royal robe, standing with one foot advanced and one arm held against his chest. On the folds of his robe was an inscription in three languages,

Here is the stone statue
which Darius ordered to be made in Egypt,
so that he who sees it in the future will know
that the Persians holds Egypt.

On the base below the statue was an inscription,

King Xerxes says: By the grace of Ahura Mazda,
King Darius, my father, built this portico.

Hadassah remembered when Baba received a royal summons from the former King Darius. Baba had let her see the parchment scroll, with the request to come to the Royal Palace, and sealed with the King's seal; a winged bull with the head of a bearded man wearing a crown. He had helped her read the words. Unlike other parents, Baba and Maman felt it important their daughter could read and write not only the language of the Holy Scriptures, but also the language of Persia.

The morning he was to go to the Royal Citadel, she and Maman helped him select his clothing, and waved him off, wishing him favor, and urging him to remember details of the Palace, the King, and the meeting. When he returned, after quenching their thirst with a brief description of the Palace—which seemed impossibly gigantic—Baba told them why the King had summoned him.

"King Darius had seen samples of my work around Susa," Baba had said, "from the homes of some nobles, to buildings for merchants such as The House of Deagah. He had also seen some of the sculptures I did around the city. The King was kind enough to compliment my work and offer me a commission to work on some royal projects around Susa."

The Great Gate leading into the Royal Citadel was one of the first royal projects Baba worked on. King Darius wanted it to look similar to the Gate of All Nations in Persepolis, but without the colossal bulls placed on either side. Whenever she passed the gate, Hadassah would look for her father's master builder mark; a multi-pointed Persian star with the Hebrew letter A in the center. After that, wherever she went in Susa, she looked for her father's mark.

These royal commissions led to others from the new King. When King Darius died and Xerxes ascended the Throne, he followed in his father's footsteps, commissioning her father to continue working on various royal projects around Susa. Whenever she walked passed any of these projects and saw his mark, she felt her father's nearness.

The house Mordecai had purchased was not one of her father's projects. "Until we know why Haman ordered the death of your parents and servants and took your home, we must live modestly and not draw attention to ourselves."

Built from thick stone similar to the other houses in this section of the city, nothing about their house suggested it was the home of two of the wealthiest Jews in Susa.

Lifting the tray of bread and another of fish, she walked into their house and down the corridor. Passing their sleeping chambers, she paused at Mordecai's room, where he was refilling a large dome-shaped lantern designed with a handle to be carried rather than set on a lamp stand. He refilled this lantern every day, in the event he had to attend patients at night. The lantern had two separate parts; the top was shaped like a cone with holes placed around its surface and slid over the bottom part which held a bowl for the oil, a wick, and a handle for carrying the lantern. Every night, Mordecai would refill the oil and insert a thick coil of wick. The dome would protect the flame from being blown out by winds.

"The evening meal is ready," she said.

"I will come." He picked up the lantern and joined her.

They walked to the front room in the house. Used for meals when the weather was inclement, the room stretched the full width of the house. The walls were covered in smooth clay with lamp-stands in each corner; the floor a simple tile. Along one wall was a taller, narrow table with several stone jars that held water and wine. In the center of the room was a low table with thick cushions beneath. It was here she and Mordecai—and their occasional guests—would recline for meals.

Tonight, as every Sabbath, the table was set with their special dishes and most comfortable cushions. When she was a child and had asked why they prepared their house this way each Sabbath, Maman answered, "We must prepare our house as we would prepare for a bride for her wedding. You have heard Rabbi Omar explain that the Sabbath is special and to be treated as a bride or queen."

While Mordecai placed the lantern near the door, she set the trays of bread and fish on the table next to a bowl of vegetables and another of grapes and crossed to check the stone jars. "We have enough wine for this Sabbath," she said, "but we will need to get more for next Sabbath." She filled a small amphora with water and another with wine and carried them to the table. After Mordecai joined her, she covered her eyes as he spoke the blessings over the Sabbath meal.

"Blessed are You, Yahweh, Lord our God, Ruler of the Universe, Who brings forth bread from the earth.

"Blessed are You, Yahweh, Lord our God, Ruler of the Universe, Who creates the fruit of the tree.

"Blessed are You, Yahweh, Lord our God, Ruler of the Universe, Who creates the fruit of the ground.

"Blessed are You, Yahweh, Lord our God, Ruler of the Universe, Who creates varieties of nourishment.

"Blessed are You, Yahweh, Lord our God, Ruler of the Universe, at Whose word all came to be."

She joined him in speaking, "Amen," before Mordecai continued with a portion of the Proverb written by King Solomon that began, *"A wife of noble character who can find? She is worth far more than rubies."*

She had heard her father—and now her cousin—speak this passage at the start of each Sabbath. It was one of Baba's favorite Scriptures. Not only did he quote it each Sabbath, but he would also frequently include it in their evening prayers, ending by saying, "I am certain when King Solomon wrote this, he was describing your maman."

After they washed their hands, she filled their plates with bread and fish, while Mordecai poured wine and water into their cups. After selecting the vegetables and grapes, they settled down to eat.

Mordecai tore a small piece of the bread and put it in his mouth. "Ummm…" his eyes widened, "this is delicious. Your baking skills are improving." He grinned. "How many times did this dough take *someone's* beating?" They had agreed never to mention Haman's name during meals—or before and during the Sabbath.

Ready laughter sprang to her eyes. "More than usual." She took a bite. "Mmmm…I should remember this. The extra beatings softened the dough."

"Your maman would be pleased with this bread."

"I think she would." She nodded, her lips drooping as tears sparkled in her eyes.

"Cousin," Mordecai laid a hand on her forearm.

She shook her head, "No." She lifted a cloth napkin to wipe her eyes. "No. I will not allow my tears affect the Sabbath nor diminish Maman and Baba's memory." She blew out a deep breath. "You are right, Cousin. I think Maman would be pleased with this bread." She lifted a piece and took another bite.

Mordecai resumed eating. "Your parents would be proud of you," he smiled gently.

"I hope they would be proud. My desire is to be like them. If the Holy One allows, one day I make bread for my husband and our children and tell them about my wonderful parents," she laid a hand on his arm, "and you."

"With your beauty and your gentle nature," Mordecai picked

up a piece of cheese, "I am certain one day you will have a husband." He took a drink of water. "I saw Kalev ben Deagah at the
shop today."

"I saw him too." She put more grapes on her plate. "He was
helping his parents in the store."

"How old is he?" Mordecai took another piece of bread. "I do
not remember."

"I believe he is twenty-two," she lifted a napkin to wipe her
mouth. "He is three years older than Miriam, and I am one year
older than her."

"Deagah ben Caleb tells me Kalev is a hard worker, learning
what he needs to know to one day take over the shop."

"He will be as skilled a merchant as his father." She bit into
a piece of cheese.

"He will also be a good husband."

She agreed. "I am surprised he is not already married. Most
young men his age are already husbands and fathers."

"Deagah tells me Kalev is interested in a young woman and
has been…waiting…for her."

"Truly? What is he waiting for her to do?" She poured more
water into her cup.

"To reach the end…of her mourning."

Hadassah's eyes widened, as awareness shot through her like
a wandering star in a dark night sky. She looked at her cousin,
who was grinning. Her heart flew up in her throat and beat there
wildly. She realized her hand holding the amphora was trembling.
She carefully set the container on the table, clasped her hands, and
looked at her cousin. "Cousin, are you saying…"

"Deagah told me Kalev is interested in you."

She stared at her hands.

"Cousin…Hadassah," the laughter left Mordecai's voice, "look
at me."

She lifted her golden-green eyes to his face.

"You have told me many times you dream of one day having

43

a young Jewish man—who loves Yahweh and cares for you—to be your husband. That does not mean you have to marry the first man who fits that description. Deagah is my friend."

"Miriam is my friend," she heard her words echoing in her head.

"Our friendships with Kalev's family do not matter in this situation. When you marry, it should be to a man of your choice, not anyone else's choice. Deagah only told me of Kalev's interest, he did not present a proposal of marriage. What I want to know is, should Deagah present Kalev's proposal of marriage for you, would you want me to accept it?"

She stared at her cousin as thoughts rushed about her head like bees around a hive. *Kalev ben Deagah is…interested in me?* The words seemed foreign. *He might want to have his father speak to my cousin and present a proposal of marriage for me?*

She was past the age when most Jewish girls married. Her parents had not pushed her to think of marriage. "We waited so long to have you," Baba had said, "we are not in a rush for you to marry and leave home."

That did not mean she had not thought about marriage. She had grown up in a home with parents who loved each other; she wanted what they had. As Mordecai said, she wanted to marry a good Jewish man who loved Yahweh and followed the Law given to Moses. She wanted a husband who loved her, or who at least felt affection for her. Many of her friends had been told by their families, "Marry for a husband and a home; love and affection can come later." Her parents had prayed for her, had waited for her, had been the best parents. She wanted her children—should Yahweh bless her with them—to have that same experience.

Kalev was a hard worker and learning what was needed to one day take over his father's store. Miriam spoke of him being the best of brothers. She had seen him with their friends; he was kind and pleasant to everyone, even to Nehemiah bar Hakaliah, the outspoken son of the goldsmith. During Sabbath services in the synagogue, Kalev's participation in the worship and in listening to Rabbi Omar's teachings showed a devotion to Yahweh and the Holy Scriptures.

Beyond the important matters, she smiled, Kalev was a handsome young man.

He was everything she wanted in a husband.

All that flashed through her mind in the time it took for her to draw another breath.

"Hadassah? Hadassah."

She turned to look at her cousin.

A frown gathered on Mordecai's face, his gaze unwavering. "I ask again. Should Deagah approach me with Kalev's proposal of marriage for you, do you want me to accept it?"

"Yes," her voice echoed in her ears. She nodded, smiling. "Yes, Cousin. I want you to accept Kalev's proposal for me."

CHAPTER 6

The rest of the evening passed as quickly as a Spring rain. After Hadassah cleared the table and stored the bread and food—she had made extra to eat after tomorrow's Sabbath meeting—she brought back two pitchers of steaming water for their baths. She set them on the back table before joining Mordecai to listen as he read from the Holy Scriptures.

She tuned her harp as he opened a scroll. Most Jewish families did not own a copy of the Holy Scriptures, but as Mordecai was a Mantreh Pezeshk, Rabbi Omar had arranged for her cousin to make a copy from several scrolls from the Holy Scripture. While she played soft chords and runs on her harp, Mordecai began reading from the writings of the Prophet Isaiah.

"Why do you complain, Jacob? Why do you say, Israel, 'My way is hidden from the Lord; my cause is disregarded by my God,'?

"Do you not know? Have you not heard?

She smiled at the opening verse. Even though she did not understand most of the prophet's writings, she loved the beautiful phrases. She changed the music, building in soaring chords, as her cousin continued.

"The Lord is the everlasting God, the Creator of the ends of the earth. He will not grow tired or weary, and his

understanding no one can fathom. He gives strength to the weary and increases the power of the weak. Even youths grow tired and weary, and young men stumble and fall; but those who hope in the Lord will renew their strength. They will soar on wings like eagles; they will run and not grow weary, they will walk and not be faint."

After singing a hymn of praise to Yahweh for the blessing of family, she and Mordecai covered their eyes and spoke the *Shema*, considered the most important part of the day:

"Hear, O Israel: The Lord our God, the Lord is One. Love the Lord your God with all your heart and with all your soul and with all your strength. Amen."

Generally, they would spend the rest of their evenings together talking about events among their friends, laughing over memories of happier times, and eating sweet cakes and fruit. The night before the Sabbath always ended early, in order for them to bathe and prepare for tomorrow's meeting at the synagogue. Carrying their pitchers of water in one hand and a lamp in the other, she and Mordecai went to their bedchambers.

The wooded furniture in her room gleamed from diligent care. The walls were covered with tapestries Mordecai had purchased from Deagah's store. One on wall was a wooden chest that held her clothes. Next to it was a table with a bowl and pitcher for washing and a comb for her hair. A small table was next to her bed, a thick pallet on top of a wooden frame and covered in linens, also purchased from Deagah's store.

Crossing to the side table, she set the lamp down before moving to the wash table, where she poured the steaming water into the bowl. Removing her garments and setting them aside for laundering, she washed her face and body before leaning over the bowl to wash her hair.

After washing and rinsing her hair, she patted her body dry with a linen towel before using it to rub her damp hair. She opened the wooden chest and lifted out undergarments and her sleeping tunic. Slipping on the clothes, she picked up the comb, sat on her bed, and began working the comb through her dark tresses. Once she had combed out the tangles, she braided her hair and tied a small ribbon around the end.

She slipped between the covers on her bed and blew out the lamp. After fluffing her pillow, she closed her eyes, but sleep eluded her as thoughts chased each other like children playing a game.

Kalev is interested in me, she smiled into the darkness.

She had often overheard women and girls—in the marketplace, or after Sabbath gatherings— discussing marriage. The girls would nod their heads, slanting glances toward the unmarried men. Giggling and simpering, they would discuss the men's features, their skills, their strength, their potential as a husband as one would consider an item to be purchased in the marketplace.

Amongst their people, marriages were arranged by the parents of the bride and groom. Most were little more than business contracts, where family position and possessions carried greater weight than character and affection. The young couple had no voice in the matter and often were informed of their upcoming betrothal by their parents.

Although rare, there were marriages based on affection and love, as her parents' marriage had been. This is what she wanted and prayed for; a marriage where she and her husband preferred each other; cared for each other; *loved* each other.

Kalev is interested in me. Her smile widened. Then her smile faded. *This is not how I wanted it. It will be hard to face it without Maman and Baba. I love Cousin Mordecai dearly, but it will be hard not having my parents with me to celebrate my marriage.*

"Stop!" She whispered to herself. "Maman and Baba are with Yahweh in the bosom of Abraham. Their memories will always be with you. Remember what they taught you about facing challenges, *'If I perish.'* They would want you to rejoice in a godly husband." She filled her lungs, blew out the air and whispered into the darkness,

"Maman...Baba...Mordecai says that Kalev ben Deagah

is interested in me. Me! Your Hadassah—your estra, your little star—might become a bride. I will part of a true family and not an object of pity."

As a child, she had always noticed that other children her age had siblings. These families seemed filled with love and laughter. While she loved her parents, and Mordechai, she had often wished she had a brother or sister, to keep from feeling…different…from other families. If she married, she would be part of a larger family.

If Kalev were truly interested in her, Deagah would approach Mordecai with his son's proposal of marriage. Her cousin and Kalev's father would discuss the advantages of the possible union, including the *mohar*, the gift given to the bride's family. Traditionally there was no set amount; it depended upon the social standing of the families. The gift was money or something of equal value to compensate the bride's family for the loss of their daughter. The main purpose of the mohar, however, was to provide the bride with support should she become widowed. For Hadassah, the mohar would satisfy tradition only. Mordecai had told her about her parents' wealth stored in the labyrinth of caves in Deagah's yakhchal, waiting for the day she married.

Once Mordecai was satisfied with the details of the mohar, he and Deagah would seal the agreement with a toast of wine. The betrothal ceremony would take place a few days later to allow Mordecai time to prepare a celebration feast.

During the betrothal ceremony, Mordecai would send for her to allow Kalev to proclaim his affection for her and his desire for her to become his bride. Her parents had told her—as now her cousin did—when a marriage proposal was offered for her, she would have the right to accept or reject it.

If she accepted the proposal, Kalev would give her a gift. For couples who were poor, it would be ten coins from the mohar. Because of their families' wealth, Kalev would give her a ring, saying, "Behold, you are consecrated unto me with this ring, according to the laws of Moses and Israel."

The betrothal ceremony would conclude with a toast of wine, after which his father and her cousin would further discuss the marriage contract, the size of the dowry, as well as the details of the wedding ceremony.

The wedding ceremony would take place after Kalev prepared a room for them in his father's house. This generally took about a year. Until that time, their betrothal was binding. Although they would not live together during their betrothal period, a bill of divorce would be required to sever their union.

Even though she and Kalev would be considered husband and wife, before their wedding ceremony, they would not be allowed to be alone for more than a few moments, and certainly would not have intimate relations. Whenever they were together, one of his parents, Mordecai, or another older family member or friend would be present to provide supervision for them.

While Kalev built their room, she would prepare her bridal garments as well as gather—or make—the things she would take to her new home. Each day, she would wait expectantly for the sign he was coming for her.

There would be no specified time of day for Kalev's coming. Within their community, it typically took place at night, when the workday was finished and all the family and friends could attend the celebration. At that time, Kalev, and the friends he chose as attendants, would come to her home.

Although his coming was *supposed* to be a secret, Mordecai and the friends she chose as bridal attendants would know when it might be. They would be watching, and when they saw Kalev coming with his friends, they would announce, "Your bridegroom is coming!"

At that point, she would stop whatever she was doing to prepare. Her friends would help her don her bridal garments. She would wear her hair loose with gold and jewels braided into the lengths. A long veil would be draped over her head and a crown set on top.

Once she was ready, Mordecai would lead her to either the

main room of their house or—if the weather were pleasant—to sit on a bench outside. There—dressed like a queen—she, along with Mordecai and her attendants, would wait for sight of Kalev.

He would be dressed like a king, with a crown on his head. His friends would be carrying torches or playing tambourines and other musical instruments.

Before leaving her home as an unmarried woman for the last time, Mordecai would give her a blessing. "You are your parents' daughter, and you are my daughter. May you become the mother of countless thousands and may your children's children's children rule over the nations."

Kalev would escort her to his house, with Mordecai and her attendants preceding them, scattering parched grain along the path, while Kalev's attendants played their instruments and danced. As they walked through the streets of Susa, their guests—all carrying torches—would join the procession.

Once they arrived at Kalev's home, her attendants would take her aside and straighten her hair and garments. Making sure her face was covered by the opaque veil, they would take her to Mordecai, who would lead her to the courtyard where a canopy was set outside under the stars.

There Kalev would be waiting for her. Standing by each other's side, they would listen as Mordecai and Deagah spoke the blessings that would join them as husband and wife.

Then the wedding feast would begin. Seated at the place of honor, they would be reign as king and queen of the day. They would praise Yahweh for His blessings and would laugh at the riddles told by the steward of the feast and acknowledge the compliments paid to them.

At one point during the wedding feast, Kalev would escort her to their wedding chamber. While their guests continued celebrating, they would consummate their marriage.

Maman, Baba, if all goes well, she thought as she slipped into sleep, *before one—or at the most two—year pass, I will be a bride.*

CHAPTER 7

Haman suppressed a smile as he watched the King's guests enter—eyes wide and jaws slack—into the Courtyard of the Garden. For many of the guests, this was their first time to enter the Royal Citadel of Susa; for everyone, it was their first time to see this particular hall.

King Darius—Xerxes' father and he who was known as *the Great*—had started the construction for the Citadel in Susa, patterning it after the one in Persepolis. King Xerxes, upon ascending his father's throne, continued the work on the Citadel in Susa. Before beginning the 180-day tour of his Empire, Xerxes left instructions that the Courtyard of the Garden was to be finished before he returned with his guests for the Norooz celebration.

More audience hall than garden conservatory, the surface of the Courtyard's mosaic pavement of porphyry, marble, mother-of-pearl, and other costly stones totaled over 20,000 cubits. Thirty-six marble columns, each measuring forty-three cubits high—and crowned with a capital in the form of two kneeling bulls—held up a ceiling forty-six cubits above the pavement. The Courtyard had hangings of white and blue linen, fastened with twisted cords of white linen and costly purple and secured to the marble columns by silver rings.

Surrounded on three sides with porticos, in the center on the fourth side of the Courtyard was a raised dais upon which stood an intricately carved table and eight chairs for the King and his seven advisors to sit during the feast. Four Immortals—handpicked by Haman—stood on the four corners of this dais; Haman would stand behind the King's right shoulder. As found throughout the rest of the Palace, the walls of the Courtyard were decorated with colorful glazed brick panels of Lamassu, winged bulls, blue water-lilies, and—lest a guest forget whose home this was—The One Thousand Immortals in full battle array.

Perfumed smoke wafted from torches placed around the Courtyard. From one end of the hall to the other were couches of gold and silver set before low tables draped in linen. On each table, intricately carved dishes and goblets in gold and silver glinted in the torchlight.

The Courtyard buzzed as the King's Shathapavans, nobles, magi, and officials made their way to the tables. Servants stood ready to offer refreshments for the 1,000 guests attending the feast. Xerxes had ordered food and wine from around the Empire.

"The King wants each guest is to drink without restrictions," Haman had relayed Xerxes' desire to the Steward of the Banquet, "and to drink whatever wine he wishes."

There were two reasons for this generosity. The King wanted to show his guests the vastness of his wealth as well as his liberality. The other reason he wanted every guest to drink all they wanted was—as Haman had told Zeresh earlier— a drunk man could not lie.

Haman had inspected the Palace kitchens and wine cellars earlier that morning. Poison was an assassin's easiest weapon; dozens of tasters stood ready to carry and sample each dish and wine presented to the King.

"Greetings, Hazarpatish."

Haman turned and bowed his head to the tall man entering the Courtyard. "Greetings, General Otanes zad Avajata."

Older than Haman by more than a decade, the Supreme

General of the Persian Army carried himself as the seasoned Warrior he was. Wearing garments similar to Haman's—elaborate saffron-colored tunic and trouser, pointed shoes, and gold-trimmed cap—the senior officer did not follow the fashion of many Persian elite; he refused to use dye to cover the white streaks throughout his black curls or square-cut beard.

"How did you find Prince Artaxerxes?" Haman asked.

"My *Pesarbozorg*—grandson—is fine," a smile lit the general's eyes and then quickly faded, "even if his mother pays little attention to him. He is spending the evening with Queen Atossa dokhtar Cyrus."

Haman's eyes widened. "I did not realize the Malekeh Jahann would be caring for her Pesarbozorg this evening. I thought the King's Mother would be attending Queen Vashti's banquet for women."

"I spoke with Queen Atossa when I went to see Artaxerxes; he was in her chambers. From what the Malekeh Jahann told me, she had planned to attend," the General shrugged, "but she changed her mind. She said she preferred spending a quiet evening with her Pesarbozorg over a noisy banquet with *squawking pea-hens*." He lifted his hands in a sign of surrender. "*Her words*, not mine," he grinned, "although I agree with her.

"I was able to see Artaxerxes for a few moments. He was pleased with the new hawk I gave him for the celebration of Norooz. He is training with the magi and is already showing skills in matters of war, law, statecraft, and Ahura Mazda. After his twelfth birthday, he will begin training with the Army. I, along with the King's three brothers, will oversee Artaxerxes' military training. He will be a fine king one day," he looked toward the empty dais, brows slanted over a hawk-like nose, "as long as the Throne is not..." his voice dropped to a whisper, "lost through foolishness." He drew a deep breath and looked around the room. "Have the *others* arrived for the evening banquet?"

Haman gave a half nod, his eyes slanting toward the table

in front of the King's dais. There, a group of six men—dressed in
in linen tunics and trousers in rich hues, golden pointed shoes,
gems glittering on their chests, fingers, and turbans—were talking
with those around them. Their dress—and their proximity to the
raised dais—identified them as Shathapavans of the most powerful
satrapies—provinces—of the Persian Empire.

When Cyrus the Great—Xerxes' grandfather—overthrew
Babylon, he became ruler of the largest Empire the world had ever
seen. Due to the vastness of the Persian Empire, Cyrus divided the
governing of the Empire into twenty-six regions called satrapies.
By the time Xerxes ascended the Throne, the Empire had 127
satrapies. Each of these regions was governed by a Shathapavan
who levied and collected taxes, cared for his region, maintained
the peace, punished criminals, and trained Warriors for the King's
miliary campaigns.

Several of the six Shathapavans lifted a hand toward Haman
and the General, beckoning to them and indicating their table.

"Come," the General lifted a hand in response. "Let us greet
the King's most devoted Shathapavans before tonight's feast begins."

Haman turned to the Immortal next to him. "Teresh pur
Ashoor, let me know when the King is approaching."

The Warrior nodded, his dark eyes studying the crowd. "Yes, Sir."

Haman extended a hand for the General to precede him.
Winding their way amongst the tables, pausing now and then to
greet various guests, at length they arrived at the table of the six
Shathapavans, who were discussing the weather, their families, the
New Year's celebration, and various business ventures.

"Greetings, Shathapavan Jata," Otanes exchanged nods with
the King's governor in the satrapy of Lydia.

The greetings continued around the table with the other Shathapavans: Agarbayata from Persepolis; Zurakara from Cilicia;
Arika from Ecbatana; Drauga from Parthia; and Bagadata from
Ionia. When talking privately with Haman or Otanes, the King
referred to these men as, "The Six."

These men ruled over their own satrapy with considerable autonomy. As long as they were loyal to the King and brought their satrapy's annual taxes to Persepolis—the largest and most northern of the four capitals of Persia and location of the imperial treasury—the Shathapavans lived as they wished, each owning several estates and palaces and having many servants and advisors.

However, the wealth and power of The Six came with a price. It was these men Xerxes expected to not only approve his plan to recapture Greece, but to contribute the most Warriors and money to fund the campaign. This meant depleting their own treasuries as well as reducing the number of Warriors needed to maintain the peace in their own satrapy.

The problem these men faced was not necessarily the King, but the King's Azam.

Three years prior, when Xerxes had ascended the Throne, he altered his father's title from "King of the Babylonians, the Persians, and the Medes," to "King of the Medes and the Persians." Xerxes did not seek the advice of The Six. His decision to remove "King of the Babylonians" from his title was made after speaking to a group of young men who had been his friends when he was the Crown Prince.

Babylon was one of the most powerful satrapies in the Empire. This insult was the impetus for these men sitting at the table—through General Otanes—to reach out to Haman and ask for a meeting.

"Preferably away from the Palace," Otanes had added when he approached Haman over two years ago. "These men wish to gather in private, where no one will see them and wonder what they are doing. Do you know of such a place or," the General added, "can you acquire such a place?" His gaze was direct and unbending. "The Six said to let you know it will be of...*benefit*...to you."

Otanes' words piqued Haman's curiosity. He believed Otanes— as Xerxes' Supreme General as well as being his father-in-law—was loyal to the King and would not be part of anything that would potentially harm Vashti or Prince Artaxerxes. Yet, as Commander of The One Thousand, Haman knew he could not dismiss potential plots against the King. Xerxes was the only King of Persia who had inherited the Throne. Even his father Darius had become king as a result of a conspiracy between six Shathapavans who had plotted to kill the recently crowned Bardiya, who had succeeded Cyrus the Great.

Haman realized until he heard these men's thoughts, he would not know whether they were planning a celebration to honor the new King...or a plot to kill him. Either way, he needed to be a part of it, to make certain the results benefited him.

Haman nodded to Otanes. "Give me time. I will find a location."

Finding a location proved harder than he anticipated. Most Persian nobles lived within the walls of Susa; the homes outside of the city were poor farms. While acquiring one of these farms would not be difficult, Haman would not deign to invite The Six to such a place.

The challenge continued until the day Abihail ben Shimei was summoned to the Palace.

During the reign of King Darius, Haman—then one of the Ten Thousand Immortals—had no contact with the men who designed and built the monuments and buildings throughout the Empire. Within days of ascending the Throne, Xerxes summoned Abihail ben Shimei, the man who had been one of the artists and master builders his father had hired to build the monuments and buildings in Susa.

Part of Haman's responsibility as Hazarpatish was to question anyone who entered the King's presence, even those of the King's own family. Once Haman had ascertained Abihail ben Shimei was nothing more than a master builder, he escorted him through the two courts and into the Throne Room. Bowing to Xerxes—bending from the waist, his right hand cupped in front of the lower half of his mouth—Haman returned to take his position at the door; there, he would divide his attention between watching the two courts leading to the Throne Room and listening to the conversation. Not for memory's sake—the Royal Scribes chronicled all the King's public conversations—but to listen for potential threats.

"You are Abihail ben Shimei," Xeres had said.

"I am, My Lord King," Abihail had copied Haman's bow, only much lower, as his status as a master builder did not carry the weight of the Hazarpatish.

The interchange between Xerxes and the master builder sounded innocuous, beginning with the King mentioning the projects Abihail ben Shimei had built.

"I have seen many homes of my nobles throughout my kingdom," Xerxes had said, "but none are as beautiful as the ones you designed here in Susa."

"I am honored you think so, My Lord King," Abihail bowed.

"I am told your own house is as beautiful, but I am not familiar with it. Where in Susa is it located?"

"My Lord King, my home is not within the walls of Susa," the builder had said. "My wife wanted a home away from the city as she prefers the peace of the country with land to grow flowers and food and to raise animals. We purchased property two leagues outside of the city walls to build our home."

"It sounds peaceful. I would like to see your home."

"My Lord King," Abihail had bowed again, "my wife, Atarah bat Ishvi, and I would be honored to have you come to our home."

"I will have the Hazarpatish arrange it," Xerxes said. "Now, as to the purpose of this summons. I wish to commission you for several projects within Susa. One is the Gate my Father, King Darius, started at the entrance to the Royal Citadel; his desire was for it to be similar to the Gate of All Nations he had built in Persepolis. I would also be interested in learning more about this *wind catcher* you have designed. There are several rooms placed within the Palace that would benefit from such an addition, beginning with the Royal Apartments."

"My Lord King," the master builder bowed once more, "I would be honored."

CHAPTER 8

Over the next several weeks, the King was in a council of war with his generals concerning the upcoming campaign to crush revolts in Egypt and Greece. During one of these days, Haman left a contingent from The One Thousand to guard the King while he rode out to arrange for Xerxes and Vashti to visit the home of Abihail ben Shimei.

As he approached the house, Haman realized this would be a perfect location for meeting with General Otanes and The Six. The house's distance from Susa would shield any private gatherings of these men from curious eyes. The beauty of the house—its exterior almost palatial in appearance—would not only satisfy the tastes of the King and Queen Vashti, but also the General and the Shathapavans.

A servant escorted him into the main courtyard where he found Abihail ben Shimei and a woman—Haman assumed it was the man's wife—waiting for him.

"Greetings, Haman pur Hammedatha," the master builder nodded, a hand on his chest, "peace be on you. Welcome to our home."

Haman returned the gesture. "Greetings, Abihail ben Shimei."

"May I present," Abihail extended a hand to the woman standing next to him, "my wife, Atarah bat Ishvi."

Haman controlled his eyes from widening at the sight of the beautiful woman. He knew he would not mention meeting Atarah bat Ishvi to his wife; Zeresh would not tolerate his appreciation of another woman.

"Greetings, peace be on you. Welcome to our home," the woman said. "It is an honor to meet the Hazarpatish."

"Greetings, Atarah bat Ishvi," Haman said. "The honor is mine."

"Please be seated," Abihail gestured to a low table with thick cushions beneath. "My wife has prepared food and drink."

"Thank you." Haman sat opposite Abihail.

Atarah offered a plate of warm bread and bowls of cheese and dates. After pouring wine from an amphora beading with condensation, she excused herself. "I will share a meal with our daughter while you men have your conversation."

Haman watched as she left the courtyard. "You have a beautiful wife."

"I am blessed with my wife and my daughter." Abihail took a drink. "Both are worth far more than rubies. Are you married?"

"I am. My wife, Zeresh dokhtar Tattenai, and I have ten sons and one daughter. You have a daughter; do you also have a son?"

"No," Abihail shook his head. "We lost several babies before having our only child, Hadassah."

"That is sad."

"It was hard, but Yahweh blessed us with a daughter who is as beautiful and gifted as her mother," Abihail smiled. "For that, I am thankful."

"Yahweh?" Haman lifted eyebrow. "You are Jewish?"

"We are of Jewish descent, but my family is Persian, as our family has been in Persia since King Cyrus defeated the Babylonian Empire." He lifted his chin. "We are of the tribe of Benjamin and descended from Kish, father of King Saul, the first King of the Jews."

"Like you, I am also descended from royalty," Haman lifted his chin, "and I believe our ancestors were acquainted. My family

61

is descended from Agag, King of the Amalekites. Perhaps you have heard the story of the *meeting* of King Agag with your King Saul?"

Abihail's eyes narrowed. "I have heard of several times when our ancestors *met*. After Yahweh freed my people from Egyptian bondage, Pharaoh took his Army and followed to where my people were encamped next to the Great Sea that bordered Egypt." He smiled. "Yahweh was on our side, drowning all the Egyptian men and chariot horses in the sea. Our people rejoiced over Yahweh's protection from the Egyptians and our other…*enemies*." He took a sip of wine and set his goblet down. "But that was generations ago," his smile tightened as he looked at Haman. "What is that to us?"

Haman knew of the *enemies* to whom Abihail was referring; they were his ancestors. He had grown up hearing his father and grandfather tell stories the Amalekites, the mighty nomadic nation that dominated the region near the Great Sea which bordered Egypt.

His ancestors had learned of the defeat of the mighty Egyptian Pharaoh and his Army at the hands of an army of former Jewish slaves. The Amalekite leaders sent spies to confirm this story, with the idea of taking advantage of Egypt's weakened state. The spies came back with the confirmation that, yes, Egypt had been defeated, but there was more. Between the Amalekites and Egypt, near the city of Rephidim, walked a long line of the former slaves. Their young, strong men, armed with weapons, led this line. At the end were not only the weak, the weary, and elderly, but also wagons filled with the spoils of Egypt. Instead of attacking the armed men, his ancestors had chosen to go after the spoils of Egypt.

"What did it matter if the children and the aged were killed?" his grandfather had asked.

"It mattered not," his father had added. "After all, they were slaves who had attacked their former master."

His father and grandfather had other stories of the enmity between the Amalekites and the Jews, including the time this King Saul and his Army attacked the city of Amalek. Haman's grandfather said their family was away on a hunting expedition when the Jews set up an ambush in the ravine outside the city. The Jews killed almost every person and every animal inside the city walls; with the exception of King Agag. For some reason, Saul did not kill Agag but took him captive and kept the best of the sheep and oxen. King Agag thought he was going to be spared; until a Jew named Samuel arrived. After condemning King Saul, this Samuel killed Agag.

As a boy, he would ask, "Why do I need to know this? It has been nearly forty generations since our ancestors attacked the Jews at Rephidim and fifteen generations since the Jews attacked Amalek and killed King Agag."

His grandfather would spit, adding, *"Hate and Revenge are twin wolves; they never perish and they are always hungry."*

All of that flashed through Haman's mind in the time it took to set his cup down on the table. "You speak truth, Abihail ben Shimei. Those things happened a long time ago." He returned the Jew's tight smile. "What is that to us?"

After walking with Abihail around the house, the gardens, and the full extent of the property—noting the number of doors and windows, as well as potential places assassins might hide, Haman said, "I will give this report to King Xerxes. He is going to be away from Susa for a while; I will arrange for him to visit your home before he leaves."

"We will be honored to have the Lord King come to our humble home."

Haman mounted his horse, his gaze sweeping across the home and estate. "You have a beautiful estate. Do not be surprised if the King offers to purchase it."

"I hope he does not make an offer," Abihail smiled, "as I would reject it. I built this home for my family. I would not be willing to sell it, even to the Lord King." He lifted a hand, palm forward, "Farewell, Haman pur Hammedatha. Peace be on you."

Haman nodded as he gathered the reins and turned the horse.

"Farewell, Abihail ben Shimei." He squeezed the horse's ribs and moved forward.

As he rode down the long road toward the gate at the edge of the property, Haman again noted the beauty of the house and its land. *It is too bad you would not sell it to the King,* he snarled. *It would have been easier.* The King was generous with those closest to him. After a few months, Haman would have arranged for *someone* to suggest that Xerxes give this property to his Hazarpatish. *Now, I will have to* arrange *for something to be done.*

Haman began noting which trees and plants he would remove, as well as that white marble bench with a red cushion in the garden. There was no need for it, as Zeresh did not care for gardening nor sitting out of doors.

When he arrived at the Royal Stables, he swung down, handing the reins to a servant. Walking into the Palace and turning toward the corridor leading to the King's Private Apartment, he noted Bigthana tabar Farrok and Teresh pur Ashoor standing guard. After listening to their report concerning the King's safety, he nodded. "Good, good."

With a quick glance down the corridors, he stepped closer to the guards. "I must speak with the King now," he whispered. "When you are finished with your duties, come to my bedchamber. I have a special…*task* for you."

Walking toward the King's Private Apartment, Haman thought, *Grandfather was right,* he thought. *Hate and Revenge never die; they are always hungry.* He smiled—and not pleasantly. *It is time to release the wolves.*

Chapter 9

After bidding Hadassah a good night, Mordecai opened the door to his bedchamber.

His room was similar to his cousin's; the only difference was a was a long, low table near the window with a thick cushion beneath. On top of the table was a stack of scrolls, blank sheets of parchment and papyrus, and writing implements. This was where he would sit and read the Holy Scriptures, write notes about his patients, or make notes of personal things he wanted to remember.

He crossed to the long table and set the lamp down before setting the pitcher of water on the wash table. He removed his sandals and garments and moved to the wash table to wash his face, body, and hair. After he patted dry with a linen towel, dressing in a sleeping tunic, and combing his hair and beard, he crossed to sit at the low table with the scrolls.

Laying both hands on his head—although not required by the Law Yahweh gave Moses, he never prayed with his head uncovered—he spoke the blessing over the reading of the Holy Scriptures.

Blessed are You, Yahweh our God, King of the Universe, Who has sanctified us with His commandments and has commanded us to engross ourselves in His Holy Scripture.

Yahweh, our God, please sweeten these Holy Words in our mouth.

May I, my cousin, and all Your people know Your Holy Name and study Your Holy Scriptures for its own sake.

Blessed are You, Yahweh, Who teaches these Words to His people.

Blessed are You, Yahweh our God, King of the Universe, Who selected us from all the peoples and gave us His Holy Scriptures. Blessed are You, Yahweh, giver of Your Holy Words. Amen.

He lifted a scroll of the Holy Scriptures and untied the ribbon securing it; this one contained the psalms, most written by King David. He unrolled it and scanned the words until he came to where he had stopped reading the night before.

"Praise the Lord, my soul; all my inmost being, praise His holy name. Praise the Lord, my soul, and forget not all His benefits—who forgives all your sins and heals all your diseases."

He was drawn to the Scriptures that proclaimed Yahweh as a healer. Not just because he was a physician, and Hadassah suffered with stomach disorders, but because they showed the tender love and care Yahweh had for His people. Mordecai smiled. "Thank you, Yahweh."

He continued reading until he came to the psalm:

He sent out His word and healed them and delivered them from their destruction."

A frown creased his brow. While this Word of Yahweh held the promise of divine healing, the words, *"delivered them from their destruction,"* were ominous, portending a dire event.

"Yahweh," he prayed, *"our people have gone through much. Hadassah and I have gone through much. There is the hope of a marriage for her. Please do not let us face any more tragedies. Let our lives be at peace."*

He re-rolled the scroll, tied the ribbon around it, and set it aside. He stared at the flame dancing over the lamp, pondering, and then stood and moved to the chest that held his garments. He opened the lid and reached into the bottom until he found a small box, which he carried back to his table. He opened the box and lifted out another scroll; the note Abihail had written over a year ago. The papyrus was creased and torn in places, mostly from being folded and shoved into the soft sash Kaufa wore around his waist.

Filling his lungs, Mordecai exhaled painfully. Like Hadassah, even after a year, remembering that time still caused a deep ache in his heart and soul. Unrolling the scroll, he saw the ink was beginning to fade. *Even if all the words fade,* his eyebrows pinched together, *I will never forget.* Lips drawn in a thin line, he re-read his cousin's note.

> *Mordecai, I know you will say this is nothing, and I pray to Yahweh you will be correct, but I must caution you.*
>
> *As you know, the Hazarpatish came to our house today to arrange for King Xerxes and Queen Vashti to visit. During our conversation, I mentioned Yahweh blessing me with Atarah and Hadassah. He questioned my speaking the name of the Holy One and asked if we were Jewish. I confirmed it, adding that we were of the tribe of Benjamin and related to King Saul. I asked if he had heard of Saul.*
>
> *He told me he had, adding that he was Amalekite and a descendant of Agag. After a brief retelling of our ancestors crossing the Great Sea and Yahweh defeating our enemies, nothing further was said about that time, save for mentioning that it mattered not what happened generations ago.*
>
> *As I showed him our house and grounds, he complimented our home, stating that I should not be surprised if King Xerxes wants to purchase it. I replied I hoped the King would not make that offer, as I would have to turn it down, explaining this was the home I built for my family.*
>
> *He said nothing more about it, but the look in his eyes concerned me. As Hazarpatish, he has the King's ear; who knows what he might say?*
>
> *You are our only living relative. Our people's tradition states that, should something happen to me, you would be Kinsman-redeemer for Atarah and Hadassah. You and I need*

to meet soon to discuss my finances, the care for my wife and daughter, and what I have set aside as a mohar for Hadassah.

I wish to take a step further and name you as Kinsman-redeemer before our Elders and have it written in a document; I will speak with Rabbi Omar this week about it. Once the document is completed, I will put it in the chest of my money in the caves beneath Deagah's yakhchal.

Although he said or did nothing, I do not trust Haman. I do not think it is likely you, Atarah, or Hadassah will ever meet him; should that happen, guard what you say in his presence. He has hungry eyes.

CHAPTER 10

"Greetings, Hazarpatish." Shathapavan Agarbayata of Persepolis stepped next to Haman. Even dressed in rich raiment, with heavy jowls and brow, Agarbayata looked as if he were a tradesman rather than the governor of the largest of the four Persian capitals. Glancing around, he lowered his voice. "Thank you for inviting us to your home."

Haman slanted a glance toward the dais; none of The One Thousand were close enough to hear. "You are welcome. I was pleased to have you and the others come to my home."

Arika, the Shathapavan of Ecbatana, another of Persia's capitals, joined them. Like, Agarbayata, he wore rich garments and had heavy white streaks through his hair and beard. "I believe our discussion was of value. We," he extended a hand toward the other members of The Six, "are agreed we need to convince the King that launching a campaign against Greece is not in the best interest of the Empire." He glanced toward the long table on the dais. "The King's *advisors* are young; they think of war and glory and destruction and not of rebuilding our cities and regions."

"Rebuilding our satrapies will take time and money," Agarbayata said. "Haman, you mentioned money from another source. Have you secured it?"

As part of preparing for the King to visit Abihail ben Shimei's

69

home, Haman spoke with the magi who oversaw the banking in Susa to determine if the Jew had any large expenditures. He was surprised to learn the master builder did not have an account with their bank. Upon further questioning, he learned that no Jew stored their money with the magi.

Haman wondered if—due to its location outside the city walls—the Jews in Susa kept their money at the master builder's home. After moving his family into the house, he searched throughout the estate, knocking on every panel of wall, stomping on every handsbreadth of flooring, digging in the yakhchal, and nearly fell out of the bagdir, looking for a cache of money. He found nothing.

"Not yet. I will continue looking for the money and for opportunities to *encourage* the King to listen to your wisdom," Haman said.

"I know you will. Praise be to Ahura Mazda that Xerxes' interminable tour ends with tonight's feast. But enough talk of governing," Agarbayata sliced the air with his hand. "Arika and I saw your son Dalphon and your daughter, Navjaa, in the Citadel Marketplace today," he smiled. "Dalphon mentioned his five younger brothers are training to become one of the Thousand Immortals."

"They are," Haman nodded. "As with the other sons of Persia, they began their military training at age twelve. I have been overseeing their training."

"No doubt, with your oversight, they will be selected to guard Xerxes," Arika said. And Navjaa; she is a beautiful young woman. I imagine you are deluged with young men wanting to marry her."

"Her mother and I have someone in mind for Navjaa." A smile hovered around Haman's mouth.

"Ahh…" Arika smiled, "anyone we know?"

"Yes," Haman gently tilted his head toward the dais.

The two older men's eyes widened.

Haman lowered his head in a single nod.

"Truly?" Agarbayata asked. "Does Navjaa know?"

"She does. She is," he smiled as a memory of recent events crossed his mine, "...*most anxious.*"

Xerxes' entourage for the tour of the Empire arrived in Susa two days before the Noorz celebrations were to begin. The King had told his guests to rest and recover from their travels. After seeing the King and Queen settled into their personal apartments and listening to the report from Artabanus tabar Mithradata—his lieutenant who had stayed in Susa to oversee the protection of the Royal Citadel—Haman rode home.

He gathered with Zeresh and their children for the evening meal. After discussing all that had happened while he had been gone, the conversation turned to their plans for the future. From his youth, Haman had sought ways to advance himself, and later, his family. He listened to his younger sons' report on their training, giving advice where needed.

Lifting a goblet of wine, he turned to his daughter. "And you, Navjaa? What have you been doing?"

"Nothing." She tucked a stray lock of hair behind her ear. "What is there to do out here, away from Susa?" she pouted. "Pedar—" Haman and Zeresh always insisted their children address them formally, "—did you speak of me to King Xerxes?"

At eighteen years of age, his only daughter was a copy of Zeresh. Slightly taller than her mother, Navjaa's black hair cascaded over her full curves. Her rosy cheeks, onyx eyes—framed by thick lashes—and pouting lips were set in an oval face.

"Queen Vashti was with us," Haman said. "You were not mentioned beyond the King and I speaking of our children."

"I am not a child. I am a grown woman." Her pout deepened. "My friends are all getting married. I do not wish to be the last one without a husband."

"Navjaa, if Pedar and Madar's plans come to fruition," Dalphon said, "you will not just have a husband. You will be married to the King."

"You need to learn patience," Parmashta, Haman's second son, reached for another piece of bread. "As one of the King's wives, you will need it to have the power to influence him."

"I will be able to," her pout turned to a slow smile, "…influence the King."

"Enough!" Zeresh snapped. "Navjaa, we will speak later; you need to learn influence does not come from pouts and curves."

"With her mother's beauty, and her father's wisdom," Agarbayata said, "she has the potential to be a…persuasive…wife to the King." He stroked his beard. "She would be of help to our plans."

"She would, indeed." Haman noticed Teresh weaving his way through the crowds. "If you will excuse me, I must leave. The King will arrive momentarily."

He joined Teresh and walked back to the door where Bigthana was waiting. After discussing the final details for guarding the King, Haman glanced around before stepping closer and lowered his voice. "You two did a good job…*investigating* the murder of the Jew and his family."

Within days of visiting with Abihail, Haman had left with Xerxes to go to Persepolis to speak with Agarbayata about the Egyptian rebellion. During that time, Haman received a report from Teresh and Bigthana that the Jewish master builder, his family, and their servants had been found murdered. On Xerxes' behalf, Haman insisted the Superintendent of the Police do a thorough investigation; however no evidence was found to convict anyone of this crime.

Haman had casually mentioned to King Xerxes how sad it was that Abihail had no living relative. "I do not know what will become of his home. I wish you had been able to see it, Lord King; it is a beautiful house," he said, "such as my wife Zeresh would love."

"You shall have it," Xerxes had said.

"What?" Haman managed a surprised look. "My Lord King, I do not understand."

"You have been persistent in corresponding with the Superintendent of Police," Xerxes had said, "doing what you could—even this distance from Susa—to find those responsible for this crime. Without an heir, the master builder's land and house becomes the property of the Empire. I do not need another house. I am giving it to you as a reward for your diligence." He smiled. "I am certain Abihail ben Shimei would agree with me."

"Thank you, Hazarpatish," Bigthana said. "We did as we knew you would wish."

"I will see you," Haman glanced around, "are rewarded for your efforts."

"Thank you, Sir," Teresh said.

A fanfare of trumpets, followed by the sound of feet echoing in the corridor, silenced them. Turning back to their position, the two Warriors snapped to attention, long spears with a silver blade resting on their shoe.

Haman strode to the center of the Courtyard of the Garden and turned. Nodding, the Immortals around the Courtyard lifted their spears and thumped the butt of their weapons onto the mosaic pavement, silencing all conversation.

"All hail His Imperial Majesty," Haman's voice echoed across the room, "Xerxes the Great, King of the Medes and the Persians."

Chapter 11

Across the Courtyard, all the guests bowed, cupping their right hands in front of the lower part of their faces, as a *sadfarbod*—100 Protectors of Glory from The One Thousand Immortals—marched through the door. In the center of the armed Warriors was King Xerxes Kiapur Darius, the ruler of the Persian Empire.

The King stopped when he reached Haman. The Hazarpatish bowed and stepped back, leaving the King in the center of the Warriors.

While those of rank and wealth at the feast wore garments made of linen, sewn with gold and silver threads and jewels, the King's Royal Court robe was constructed from a large piece of silk. Dyed with expensive colors and adorned with elaborate embroidery of golden thread as visual reminders of his power and wealth, it was draped over his body and secured around his waist by an intricately tooled leather belt. The court robe, the silver collar with the imperial golden Shahbaz, his golden pointed shoes, the Imperial Signet Ring on his right hand, and the Crown of the King of Persia set on shoulder-length black curls marked Xerxes as ruler of the greatest Empire on earth.

The King turned slowly, dark piercing eyes surveying his guests, full lips frowning in the midst of a square-cut beard.

"Greetings…"

The King's first word, his voice deep and resonate, carried across the Courtyard of the Garden. All present lifted their heads to look at the King, their hands remaining in front of their mouths.

"…to the Shathapavans, to all the nobles of our great Persia, to our magi, to General Otanes, and the Hazarpatish," he looked at his father-in-law and Haman, with a slight smile, "and to my Warriors." He extended his arms to each side. "Welcome to the Courtyard of the Garden."

The room erupted in applause and cheers. Xerxes smiled, clearly reveling in the adulation, before patting the air to silence the people.

"For one hundred and eighty days, you have traveled as my guest across our vast Empire. You saw the four imperial capitals of Ecbatana, Persepolis, Babylon, and now Susa, each with beautiful palaces, buildings, roads, canals, and centers of commerce." He extended his arms to each side, "You saw the number and strength of the Persian Army."

Another round of applause echoed. Haman, General Otanes, and The Immortals around the King and across the Courtyard lifted their chins, until Xeres once again silenced his guests.

"Celebrations were held in each of my four capital cities, with displays of athletic and military skills, with hawking and falconry, and ending with feasts lasting for a week."

More applause.

"We have ended the tour here in our Winter Palace in Susa. After a joyous and extended celebration of Norooz—when the New Year begins and our honored magi reset the calendar—we will complete our time together with one more feast."

The King grinned as a collective sigh rippled across the guests.

"I know you are all ready to return to your homes and tell your friends and family they should have no fear about the future." He extended his arms wide, "Persia is the greatest Empire in the entire world."

The guests rose to their feet, clapping, cheering, calling out, "Xerxes! Xerxes! Xerxes!"

The King stood quietly, smiling at his guests, clearly enjoying the adulation. Finally, he patted the air to silence them once again.

"Now, I am certain you are as hungry as I. Be seated and let the meal begin."

The guests stood quietly as the King, escorted by the sadfarbod, crossed the pavement, ascended the steps of the dais holding the imperial table, greeted his seven Azam—Karshena, Shethar, Admatha, Tarshish, Merse, Marsena, and Memukan—before moving to the center of the table and sitting in the Throne-like chair with an Immortal on either side. A *shushing* of linen filled the air as the guests settled on the cushions beneath their tables.

After the King was seated, Haman nodded toward the Steward of the Banquet standing near the door. The man picked up a padded mallet and struck a large bronze gong. Within moments, hundreds of servants—arrayed in simple white tunics and trousers—entered the Courtyard bearing trays of meats, breads, parched grain, dates, pomegranates, grapes, figs, lentils, chickpeas, beans, turnips, leeks, cucumbers, lettuce, onions, and garlic. Other servants carried silver amphorae of wine to fill the goblets of gold—each goblet different from the other—set in front of the one thousand guests.

The meal was eaten quietly, each guest focused on their food, but also intent on *not* saying something that might be misconstrued. Once the King had eaten his meal, he nodded to Kurush Tars Dida, his Cup-bearer—whose responsibility was to oversee the servants who tasted the King's wine and food—for his plate to be removed. As this was a signal that the meal was finished, the servants moved to collect all the plates around the Courtyard.

Goblets were refilled as the Royal Entertainers—musicians, actors, dancers, and singers—entered the Courtyard to entertain the King and his guests.

As the hours passed, and the wine flowed, the tone in the

room shifted from restrained to raucous. Men known for being controlled and discreet became boisterous and coarse, exchanging crude jokes. Despite the amount of wine consumed, no one grabbed at the female entertainers; no matter what their status, all servants within the Royal Palace were under the King's protection. To touch one would result in being escorted to the Gate of Eternity.

Haman was not surprised at the guests' drunkenness, nor—he knew—was Xerxes. From his experience with the King, this was exactly what Xerxes expected. From the state of their drunkenness, these men would be unable to lie.

This was the moment for which the King had planned. Xerxes glanced at Haman and gave a single nod of his head.

Haman looked toward the servant standing near the door and gestured; the man picked up the padded mallet and struck a large bronze gong. The music stopped and the Royal Entertainers left the Courtyard.

Xerxes rose. As the guests in the Courtyard stood, he patted the air. "Please sit." He waited until everyone was seated and then smiled. "My friends, I trust you have enjoyed this evening."

A cheer rose from one end of the Courtyard to the other. From his position, Haman saw The Six exchanging subtle glances as the King continued.

"For one hundred and eighty days, you have been my guests as we traveled across our vast Empire. You have seen our opulent capitals, our beautiful cities, the canals, the centers of commerce and the roads which my father, King Darius, built. You saw wagon after wagon carrying supplies and Warriors across the Empire, while royal engineers oversaw large groups of slaves building and repairing roads and canals."

Another round of cheers.

"You have seen our mighty Army."

Haman noticed the cheer from the guests was not as boisterous as before. *They realize what is coming.*

"You—as well as all our citizens—are beneficiaries of the

generosity of our Empire," Xerxes smiled. "As long as our citizens obey the law and are loyal to Persia, everyone is free to pursue their life and their interests, including worshipping the gods of their choice."

Another cheer.

Here it is. Haman's mouth thinned into a smug smile.

Xerxes' smile faded as he dropped his arms. "As much as I wish it were otherwise, there are people within our Empire who are not as loyal as you." His brow furrowed above dark eyes. "These people do not appreciate the power of Persia's Kings nor the generosity of our Empire. These people feel they need to remove themselves from the mighty Persian Empire. These people were those living in Egypt and those now living in Greece."

A murmur rose from the guests.

Indicating the Warriors around him, the King continued, "Our mighty Persian Army crushed the revolt in Egypt."

A cheer.

Now it comes. Haman bit back a smile.

"Now it is time to turn our attention to the rebels in Greece. We must seek vengeance for my noble father, King Darius, and his Army for their defeat at Marathon."

Another cheer.

"In order to do this," Xerxes extended his arms toward his guests, "I need your help."

A cheer rose and then quickly faded.

The smile remained pinned to Haman's mouth. *They realize what the King is going to ask of them.*

"We will crush the revolt in Greece and chastise them," Xerxes extended his fists, "but we need more Warriors and supplies. We," he opened his hands, palms upward, extending them toward the guests, "the Persian Empire, needs your help. We need money and Warriors in order to crush these rebels and return Greece," he lifted his arms wide, "to the control of our mighty Persian Empire."

The Courtyard was silent. Haman looked toward Teresh and

Bigthana and nodded. They, along with other Warriors through-out the Courtyard, moved amongst the tables. A few well-placed nudges with the butts of their spears and another cheer rose from the crowd.

Xerxes smiled, exulting in the apparent adulation of his guests. After a few moments, he patted the air. "I would not wish you to think I care nothing for the thoughts of those who will be con-tributing to our victory." He extended his arms toward his guests, beckoning with his fingers. "Speak. I would hear your questions and your advice."

Haman glanced at the table where The Six sat. Although there were a thousand guests in the Courtyard of the Garden, it was obvious to everyone present that the King was not asking for the advice of all his guests.

All eyes were on the six Shathapavans. In turn, five of these men looked at the Shathapavan of Persepolis. As the oldest of The Six, as well as being Shathapavan of the largest city in the Empire, Agarbayata was expected to speak first.

Agarbayata stood, taking time to smooth his garments before nodding his head, hand opened on his chest. "My Lord King Xerxes," he said. "I believe I speak for all present," he extended his hands to either side, "when I say thanks for your gracious invitation to join you on this *amazing* journey across our great Empire. As you have mentioned, we have seen much of our beautiful country. We have enjoyed your generosity at the banquets held in each of your four capital cities. We will all remember the extended Noorz celebration, culminating in tonight's feast."

Xerxes smiled at the older man. "You are most welcome, Sha-thapavan Agarbayata," he looked at the people seated around the Courtyard, "as are all my citizens."

Another cheer erupted. Haman noticed Agarbayata glancing at those seated at the table with him. Several nodded.

When the cheer subsided, Agarbayata continued. "My Lord King, while we are proud of our mighty Empire and pray Ahura

Mazda's blessings over Persia and over you, there are," he filled his lungs and exhaled, "*some* of us who are... concerned... with the idea of going to war so soon after the subjugation of the Egyptians."

Xerxes' brows lowered as his smile faded. "Oh? What... *concerns*... do you and the others have, Shathapavan Agarbayata?"

Choose your words carefully, Agarbayata. Haman wished the older man would look at him. He noticed the other Six; they were watching Agarbayata as well, their fingers gripping the linen tablecloth. He glanced at General Otanes; his old commander returned his look, slightly lifting his palms off the table in a small sign of surrender. *No one knows what Agarbayata is going to say.*

"My Lord King," Agarbayata filled his lungs again, "it has been three years since your honored father, King Darius, died and you ascended to his Throne."

A murmur of sorrow rippled across the Courtyard. Darius the Great had been a powerful and beloved king.

Agarbayata gestured to those around him. "Your honored father built up the cities of Persia, especially," he straightened, "the beautiful city of Persepolis. He standardized the banking system and coinage across the Empire, introduced the legal code, and oversaw the construction of the Royal Road, six million cubits spanning our great Empire. My Lord King, you inherited much when you inherited your father's Throne."

"Most honored Agarbayata," Xerxes smiled. "You are reciting lessons all present learned at their tutor's knee. My father was indeed a great king and Warrior. Sadly, he did not die as a Warrior would want—leading his troops into battle—but from a lingering illness."

"Lord King, you are new to the Throne," the Shathapavan said. "The Crown of Persia was barely on your head when you left to fight Egypt. Since you became King, you have been *away* from home longer than you have been *at* home. You should focus on establishing your Throne, continuing to build up the country as your father did and not deplete it resources to go to war."

"Shathapavan Agarbayata," Xerxes' mouth was drawn in a grim line, "you speak truth when you say I inherited much from my father. I not only inherited my father's palaces, his citizens, and the wealth of the mighty Persian Empire, I also inherited his battles. Egypt and Greece chose to rebel against my father. I crushed the rebellion in Egypt. Now," he raised a clinched fist into the air, "I will crush the rebellion in Greece."

Agarbayata looked at the other Six, then back at Xerxes. "Lord King, You *are* Persia. Greece is the toenail on the smallest toe on Persia's left foot."

"Most honored Agarbayata," Xerxes smiled at the other Six. "My other honored Shathapavans. If *I* trim the nails on *my* toes, that is *my* choice." The smile remained pinned to his lips, but he continued with more than a touch of acidity. "It is a different matter if someone forcefully trims my nail, no matter how small."

Agarbayata looked at the other Six. Shathapavan Jata sighed and rose, while the Shathapavan from Persepolis sat.

"My Lord King," Jata bowed his head.

"Most honored Jata," the King said, "are you going to give us a lesson in the glory and history of our Empire?"

"No, My Lord King," the Shathapavan from Lydia said. "I am asking you to reconsider." He lifted his hands, "My Lord King, you have all anyone could want. You are King of the greatest empire in the world. You have many palaces, you have many Warriors, many subjects. Your beautiful Queen has given you an heir."

"Ahhh…Queen Vashhhti," a garbled voice said. "She is beautiful!"

Xerxes turned—along with everyone within listening distance—to look at the man speaking; Dojooje tabar Shethar.

Shethar was one of Xerxes' seven *Azam*; his personal advisors. These men were not like The Six, chosen because of their gray beards and years of experience. Of an age with Xerxes, these men seated at the King's table were young nobles of Persia who had been his close companions when he was the Crown Prince. They—along

81

with Xerxes and the other Persian nobles of their age—received training in warfare before Xerxes moved on to study with the magi in the duties of rulers. After their training was complete, Xerxes continued to spend time with these young men. When he became King, he appointed them to be his Azam.

"I have the wisdom from The Six and my other Shathapavans, many whom I do not know," Xerxes had explained his choice for the Azam to General Otanes. "Having the wisdom from men who have been my companions since youth will provide balance."

Shethar and the other six men seated at the King's table, were exactly how Haman told Zeresh Xerxes planned that his other guests would be—drunk to the point they would not have the clarity to lie.

Karshena lifted his goblet. "She is indeed bea-u-tiful!"

"How would you know?" Tarshish retorted. "Since she was crowned Queen, Vashti has never appeared in public."

"My wife has seen her," Karshena retorted. "She says she is bea-u-tiful."

Admatha stood. "My wife—*oooh*," he swayed and grasped the edge of the table before continuing. "My wife has seen her as well. She has seen her every day—and is with her now—during the Queen's Banquet for Women."

"Xerxseeee, you sh-sh-should call for her," Marsena hit the table with his fist. "Then we could all see her."

"See your wife?" Memukan asked.

"No," Karshena nudged Memukan with his elbow, "not Marsena's wife. The Queen." He lifted the goblet to his mouth. "Vashti."

"Yes, Queen Vash-sh-sh-ti," Shethar slurred. "If you could see her, you would agree."

The laughter and raucous comments from the men at the King's table echoed across the Courtyard of the Gardens.

Haman saw General Otanes rise from his cushion, his hand gripping the hilt of his sword, his gaze sharp enough to peel away skin. Though Otanes was often angry at Vashti's lack of care for the young Artaxerxes, she was still his daughter. He would tolerate no one casting aspersions on her. The older man took a step toward the dais when Xerxes' voice stopped him.

"You shall see her!"

The laughter from the King's Azam stopped. General Otanes stopped, foot frozen in mid-stride. All eyes in the Courtyard of the Gardens were on the King.

The General regained his composure first. "My Lord King, what do you mean?"

Xerxes extended his hands to his Azam. "My personal advisors speak the truth. Outside of the women at the banquet—and those who live or serve in the Palace—no one has seen Queen Vashti since she was crowned. Even during our one hundred and eighty day tour, she remained secluded inside our Royal Palaces, our tents, and her palanquin. The Azam believe all present should see Persia's beautiful Queen.

"As King, I am the power and might of Persia. As Queen, Vashti reflects the beauty of Persia." He gestured to his guests. "When all those present see her beauty, they will understand the need to protect not only my beautiful Queen, but the need to protect every cubit of our beautiful Empire.

"Haman," Xerxes commanded, "go to the Courtyard of the House of Women, where Queen Vashti is hosting the feast. Take some of The Immortals with you. Call for Hegai and Shaashgaz—my Chief Eunuchs—no! Call for all the seven eunuchs who serve me—Mehuman, Biztha, Harbona, Bigtha, Abagtha, Zethar and Karkasto—to go with you and escort her here.

"Tell the Queen to come to me, so that all may see her beauty. Now go," Xerxes started to sit and then paused. "Wait. Haman, tell Queen Vashti, 'The King says to wear your new crown.'"

CHAPTER 12

H aman led fifty of The One Thousand Immortals through the corridors of the Palace, their steps echoing toward the Courtyard of the House of Women.

"Sir," Bigthana fell in step at his side. "What are we doing?" he whispered. "Other than the King, it is forbidden for any man to go into the House of Women."

"We are following the advice of the King's *khar* advisors," he spat. He took a quick glance; his cursing the Azam—even if they were behaving as donkeys—could be considered by some as questioning the King's veracity, resulting in a prolonged, painful death. "We will do as the King commands," he added, gesturing for the Warrior to step back in line.

Haman continued walking, his thoughts keeping pace with his steps, examining, and discarding idea after idea, trying to determine how this unexpected circumstance could be turned to the advantage of The Six and—beyond that—of himself. He had thought of nothing by the time they arrived at the corridor leading to the House of Women. He would have to see what opportunity presented itself.

One thing he did know; Vashti would not be pleased to hear Xerxes' command concerning her crown. She made her thoughts on that quite clear last year.

In the days of preparation for the 180-day tour, Xerxes had

sent for her to discuss the trip. Haman, Shaashgaz—the Royal Eunuch in charge of the King's wives and concubines—along with fifty of The One Thousand, escorted Vashti to the Throne Room.

Slender and taller than most women, the Queen's golden tunic fell softly over her womanly curves. There were hints of henna in her thick, wavy hair the color of a raven's wing. Dark, almond-shaped eyes, fringed by even darker lashes above arched brows were set in a face that was a perfect oval. Unlike other women, the rose in her high cheekbones and full lips was not the result of rouges. And unlike other women, Vashti's countenance looked as unmoving as the great Sphinx in Egypt; she claimed facial expressions would cause aging and wrinkles.

After handing her up the steps to the smaller Queen's Throne next to the King's Throne and waiting until Kurush Tars Dida—the King's Cup-bearer—had poured wine for each of them, Shaashgaz bowed and left the Throne Room. Haman made sure the Inner and Outer Courts were filled with guards, before closing the door and sliding a thick bolt across it. With both the King and Queen of Persia in one room, he would take no chances.

He averted his eyes from the royal couple, to provide them some privacy. However, due to the size and construction of the room, even whispered conversations echoed throughout the room.

Xerxes began discussing the coming tour. Vashti responded that she did not wish to go. The reasons she gave then were the ones Zeresh—and the other women at the feast—had heard. *The palanquin is not comfortable. She did not wish to sleep in a tent. The slaves will not be able to keep the insects away. She would be bored.* Then she mentioned a reason of utmost important to her.

"*If I spend the days away from the Palace and in a palanquin, I will not be able to have my oils, my massages, and my other beauty treatments.*"

"*Your beauty treatments?*" Xerxes sounded incredulous. "*Surely you can forego those treatments for a time.*"

"*A time?*" Vashti spewed. "*You are not asking me to travel for a few days to the Palace in Persepolis. You are asking me to travel in a palanquin for one hundred and eighty days.*

"Xerxes, you chose me as your wife and Queen not only because my father is the General of your armies; you chose me for my beauty. As my father attends your armies, I must attend to my beauty with oils and treatments."

"Vashti, take whatever oils and treatments you need with you," Xerxes raised his voice, *"but you* will *accompany me on the tour. Artaxerxes will ride in the palanquin with you so you can watch him."*

"Why do I have to watch him?" she asked. *"I am the Shahbanu, not a nursery maid."*

"As I represent the strength of the Empire," Xerxes' voice was tight, *"the Crown Prince represents the future strength of the Empire. It would be expected for you—as his mother and the King's Lady—not only to accompany me on this trip, but to care for Artaxerxes."*

"Let him ride with your mother," Vashti hissed. *"He likes spending time with her."*

As Malekeh Jahann—the Mother of the World—Atossa dokhtar Cyrus might not have Vashti's beauty, but she had something more. Darius chose her to be Queen not for her loveliness, but for her lineage. Born a Royal Princess, she was the daughter of Cyrus the Great who had conquered Babylon and established the Persian Empire. Later, she became the wife—and Queen—of Cambyses II, then Smerdis, and lastly Darius. After marrying Darius, she gave birth to Xerxes, as well as three other sons—Masistes, Achaemenes, and Hystaspes.

As the King's Mother, Atossa wielded considerable power. Unlike Vashti and the other women of the Royal Harem, she had the freedom to go wherever she wished and do whatever she pleased. She owned Antarrantish, an estate in the satrapy of Parthia, staffed with more than one hundred servants, including artisans from across the Empire and a Greek physician. She had been known to invite Persian nobles of wealth and influence to come to Antarrantish for lavish feasts. She was one of her eldest son's most trusted advisors. When Xerxes was at war—or away from his Palaces for prolonged periods—the Malekeh Jahann stood as Regent for him, fulfilling all of his civil, ceremonial, and religious duties.

Vashti did not care about fulfilling civil or religious duties, nor did she want any more children. *"They ruin your figure."* Once she gave birth to Artaxerxes, she went back to her beauty treatments and relinquished the oversight of his care to his grandmother, not jealous that Atossa had the child's love.

But Vashti *was* jealous about one thing Atossa had; the Crown of the Malekeh Jahann.

Patterned after the King's Crown, both crowns were made of a wide, cylindrical, crenellated band of gold overlaid with lapis. Golden hawks and other imperial symbols were placed around the crown. At the base was a narrower band set with rubies, emeralds, and diamonds.

Although Vashti considered the Crown of the Malekeh Jahann ugly, she was jealous of Atossa wearing it, because it represented the wearer as being the most important woman in the Persian Empire—in the world!

And that was something Vashti could not tolerate.

As Hazarpatish, Haman had heard many heated discussions between Xerxes and Vashti about Queen Atossa. Such as the one on that day a year ago.

"My mother is not accompanying us on the tour."

"Why not?"

"Mother is staying…to oversee the construction in the Palace."

"I was not informed of any such construction."

"You have never expressed an interest in such matters."

"I have an interest now."

"You do not like how hot your rooms get during the warm season."

"No, but what does that have to do with your mother staying in Susa?"

"I have arranged for a master builder to design bagdirs for all the apartments of the imperial, as well as for the House of Women. Not

all of the women of the Royal Harem are accompanying us on the tour. Mother will stay here, to oversee moving these women to another part of the Palace and then oversee the construction inside the Palace. By the time we return to Susa, the work will be finished."

"Well…"

Haman shifted his stance, glancing toward the royal couple. From Vashti's voice, it appeared she was softening. Everyone familiar with the Queen knew her personal comfort was of importance to her.

Xerxes, whose training included warfare, took advantage of this moment to attack from a different direction. *"I commissioned something to be designed for you."*

"Something for me?" Vashti's voice turned sultry. *"What is it?"*

The King picked up a carved wooden box on the table next to the amphora of wine and handed it to Vashti.

She placed the box on her lap and removed the lid. Light from the torches in the room flashed on the mirror resting on top of a silken bundle. Vashti slanted a glance at Xerxes as she removed the mirror and lifted the bundle.

"What can this be?" She hefted the bundle in her hands. Replacing the lid on the box, she set the silk-bound item on top and unwrapped the fabric. In the center of the silk was a golden diadem.

Hundreds of diamonds, rubies, and sapphires flashed from the light of torches around the Royal Thrones. More cap than crown, the diadem was a wide golden band with overlaid leaves of gold inset with the precious jewels. A golden circle set with larger diamonds rose from the front of the diadem and strands of golden beads tipped with diamonds hung around the bottom.

"What…is…this?" she frowned.

"What do you mean?" Xerxes' voice hardened. *"It is a crown."*

"This *is not a* crown," she sneered, dropping the diadem onto the box.

Xerxes reached over to pick up the gift. *"I had one of the royal jewelers design this crown for you."*

"*This is nothing more than a bejeweled cap,*" she snapped, "*perhaps fit as a gift for one of your concubines.*"

"*Silence!*"

Haman stared as Xerxes stood, knocking over his Throne, and stepped to the Queen. The King loomed over Vashti, his fist clutching the delicate diadem.

She leaned back, grasping the arms of the Queen's Throne, speechless.

"*I have* never," the King seethed, "*given any of my concubines a gift such as this.*"

Haman watched as Vashti shrank under the iron gaze of Xerxes. *For once,* he thought, *she remembers the King holds the power of life and death.*

After a moment, the King relaxed. "*Vashti,*" he straightened, opening his fists, "*this is not how I expected this to be.*" He extended the diadem to her. "*Please try it on.*"

Watching him warily, she took the cap, and with trembling hands, set it on her head.

"*It is beautiful,*" Xerxes smiled, handing her the mirror. "*Vashti,* you *are beautiful.*"

She lifted the mirror, turning her head side to side, smoothing a strand of gold beads over an errant curl, examining her reflection.

"*Vashti...*" the King's voice was soft, "*what do you think?*"

"*It is pretty,*" she said. Turning to place the mirror and box on the table, she stood. Lifting her chin to look at Xerxes, her gaze hardened. "*But, you will never again see me wear this.*

"*This. Is. Not. The. Crown.*" Reaching up, she pulled off the diadem and dropped it on the floor. "*This is a token gift which represents nothing.*

"*Until I wear* her *crown,*" she thrust a finger in the direction of the Malekeh Jahann's apartment, "*you will never see me wear any crown.*"

CHAPTER 13

The steps of Haman and the Warriors echoed down the corridor leading to the House of Women. Patterned after the corridor leading to the King's Apartment, it was twenty cubits wide and forty-five cubits high, and the floor was covered in a polished red tile. On the walls were designs of the Shahbaz, the Lamassu, the blue waterlily, the Ten Thousand in full battle array, and—lest anyone forgets whose harem this was—the Kings of Persia. The door to the House of Women was different from the massive doors of the King's Apartment. Here, there was a small door, with a large bolt that locked from the inside and a dozen armed Warriors on either side.

As they approached, the guards lifted their spears. With the penalty being death to anyone entering this door without permission, not even to the Hazarpatish would they lower their weapons. The Warrior standing nearest the door examined the entourage before him before looking at Haman.

"Greetings, Hazarpatish," he bowed his head slightly.

"Greetings, Arsake pur Farrokhzad. King Xerxes has sent me with a message for Queen Vashti. Call his Chief Eunuchs Hegai and Shaashgaz."

"At once, Sir." Farrokhzad turned and crossed to knock on the door.

The door opened and a man stepped into the doorway. "Yes?" his voice was soft and high, like a child. The simple white tunics and trousers he wore identified him as a servant. His voice, along with the hairless skin on his face and body, identified him as a eunuch.

Haman stepped to the servant. "The Lord King Xerxes has sent for his wife, Queen Vashti."

The eyes of every man in the corridor opened wide.

Haman continued, "He commands that Hegai and Shaash-gaz—along with Mehuman, Biztha, Harbona, Bigtha, Abagtha, Zethar and Karkas—escort the Queen to his presence. The King wants Queen Vashti to wear the crown he gave her."

The eunuch bowed his head. "Sir, if you wait, I will relay the King's command to Hegai and Shaashgaz."

"Stay a moment," Haman added as the servant moved to close the door. "My wife, Zeresh dokhtar Tattenai, is attending the Queen's feast. Please tell her I said, 'There is a beautiful sunset; it reminded me of you.'"

The eunuch smiled. "Sir, I will tell her myself." He bowed and closed the door.

Haman turned to see his men gaping. They had never witnessed a soft side to their commander. He stared at them for a moment and turned to Arsake pur Farrokhzad. "I must have had too much wine. But," he grinned, "my wife is as beautiful as the sunset."

The Warriors looked at Haman, then Farrokhzad, and back to Haman, who broke into laughter. The corridor echoed with the men thumping the butts of their spears on the tiled floors, laughing, and sharing the descriptions of their wives and betrothed. When their laughter died, the men resumed their stance, waiting in silence.

After several more minutes, the door opened and an older eunuch stepped into the corridor. The eunuch's white tunic and trousers were of fine linen, and he wore a thick gold chain with a large key on the end, identifying him as Hegai Kouroush Safa, the Chief Eunuch of the Royal Harem. He, along with Shaash-gaz Javed Farrokh—the Chief Eunuch in charge of the Second

House of the Concubines—were more than servants to the women beyond that door. These two wielded extraordinary power, often advising the King.

Walking up to Haman, Hegai bowed his head. "Greetings, Hazarpatish." His voice was high and soft.

Haman nodded his head. "Greetings, Mirza Hegai. Was the King's message delivered to the Queen?"

"Yes, Hazarpatish; My Lady Queen Vashti, received My Lord King Xerxes' message."

"Is the Queen ready to attend the King?"

The eunuch cleared his throat. "No," he croaked. He looked uncomfortable.

"No?" Haman's eyes widened. "No? What do you mean, no? Did the Queen receive the King's message or not?"

"She did."

"And is she preparing herself to obey the King's summons?"

"No, she is not." The eunuch filled his lungs and exhaled. "My Lady Queen Vashti, has a message for My Lord King Xerxes."

Haman frowned. "A message?"

The eunuch looked at the armed Warriors in the corridor and stepped closer. "My Lady Queen Vashti said to tell My Lord King Xerxes," he dropped his voice to whisper, "'This. Is. Not. The. Crown.'"

CHAPTER 14

Haman secured his belt, slipping the sword into its sheath. He crossed to the bed and gently nudged his sleeping wife. "Zeresh..." he whispered, "awake."

She stirred, moaning, and slowly opened her eyes. "Haman...?" She glanced at the shuttered window; streaks of light were peeking through. "I fell asleep...when did you come back to the room?"

"Sometime after the Third Watch," he sat on the bed and reached for his pointed shoes.

Zeresh stretched, "What happened—"

"I do not have time to talk now," Haman cut her off. "Go home. Once I have overseen the guests leaving, I will come home. Say nothing to anyone, not even the children. But Zeresh," he leaned over to kiss her, "it appears we have an opportunity."

CHAPTER 15

The synagogue—located near the Citadel Marketplace—was buzzing when Mordecai and Hadassah entered. Mordecai joined the older men of the Jewish community—dressed in their best garments, prayer shawls tied around their waists—exchanging pleasantries, inquiring after the health of their families, their work, the news in city.

"Hadassah."

She turned to see Miriam waving at her. She and two other young women were standing with her mother at the foot of the stairs leading to the loft. Hadassah moved through the crowd to Miriam.

"Good Sabbath, *Gveret Yintl*. Good Sabbath, Miriam, Keren, Devora. It is a beautiful morning."

"Good Sabbath, Hadassah," her friend responded.

"Good Sabbath, Hadassah," Miriam's mother responded. "Yahweh had indeed blessed us with a beautiful morning."

"Your tunic is beautiful," Keren bat David, daughter of David ben Asher—the fruit farmer—said to her friend.

"It is beautiful," Devora bat Naham agreed. "It reminds me of the soft yellow of Father's bees." Her father, Naham ben Tekoa, was the beekeeper.

"Thank you," Miriam said. "Father received a shipment of

94

this cloth from the caravans. I helped Mother make it. Hadassah, your new tunic is beautiful," her friend touched the sleeve of the soft green linen garment, with cream leaves embroidered on the neckline, sleeves, and hem. "In addition to playing the harp, perhaps you can teach me how to do this delicate embroidery."

"I would love to."

"You did a wonderful job sewing the garment," the older woman said.

"Thank you," Hadassah smiled. "Maman—may her memory be blessed—insisted I learn how to sew." She paused before adding. "I will always miss my parents, but Mordecai and I felt it was time for us to begin moving out of mourning."

"I know your parents—may their memory be blessed—would approve of your decision," Yintl said. "I think your mother would be pleased with your sewing skills." She paused before continuing, "This looks like something you would wear to a...*special day*." She smiled. "Which reminds me; Deagah and I would like you and Mordecai to join us for a meal soon."

"How kind. I will speak to Mordecai," she smiled, "but I am certain he will say yes."

"Mother!"

The five women turned as Kalev crossed the room to join them.

"Good Sabbath, Hadassah," he smiled at her.

Miriam, Keren, and Devora grinned, looking between Hadassah and Kalev.

"Good Sabbath, Kalev," Hadassah smiled shyly. *This might be my last Passover as an unmarried maiden.* For the first time she noticed Kalev not just as the brother of her dear friend, but as a potential husband. His muscles bulged through the sleeve of his cream tunic and dark hair curled around a noble brow.

"Kalev," his mother said. She waited. "Kalev." She laid a hand on his arm and gently shook it. "*Kalev.*"

"Wh-what?" He started and looked at her. "Oh...Mother... what do you need?"

"What do I need?" Yintl grinned at her daughter and Hadassah. "I need to know why you called me so urgently."

Miriam echoed her mother's grin, looking from her brother to her friend.

Hadassah felt heat rising in her cheeks. She lowered her eyes, appearing to study the tiled floor, but slanted a glance at Kalev from under a screen of curling lashes.

"Oh…uh," the color was high in Kalev's face, "Father sent me to…uh…ask you if you needed anything," he finished in a rush.

"How kind," Yintl's voice was flat. "Your father is such a considerate…*husband.*'

Miriam snorted, turning away to study the carved wood on the stair rails.

Before the conversation could continue, the sounds of footsteps echoing in the corridor drew their attention.

"Come Miriam, Hadassah," Yintl turned the girls toward the stairs, "the Rabbi and the Hazzan are approaching. Kalev, rejoin your father."

Hadassah exchanged one more smile with Kalev before she followed the women up the stairs. Yintl was able to find a place for them in the loft before the two men entered the main room.

Like synagogues throughout the Empire, this one was built to accommodate all the Jews in Susa. The main room was large, tiled in blue and white, and had a carved wooden stair leading to the loft where the women and younger children would gather. In the center of the room was a *bimah,* a raised platform with a reading desk where the scrolls of Holy Scripture would be placed during synagogue meetings. The men and older boys would stand or sit on step-like benches placed along the four walls. This arrangement allowed all the people to focus their attention on whoever was reading or speaking, generally Rabbi Omar or the Hazzan, Jerimoth ben Halevi, who always led the people in singing songs worship to Yahweh. Occasionally one of the older men in the Jewish community, such as Mordecai or Mar Deagah, would read the Holy Scriptures during the meeting.

Everyone stood as Rabbi Omar entered, carrying the scrolls of Holy Scripture. Jerimoth ben Halevi followed, carrying a *shofar* made from a long, curled ram's horn. After the traditional presentation of the scrolls, the two men crossed the floor to step up on the bimah. Rabbi Omar laid the scrolls on the reading desk while Jerimoth moved a pace away. The older man smiled, gazing around the room at the assembly of people. Lowering his head, the Rabbi placed his right hand over his eyes and said,

"Hear, O Israel: The Lord our God, the Lord is One. Love the Lord your God with all your heart and with all your soul and with all your strength. Amen."

As the Rabbi spoke the first word, Hadassah—along with everyone present—covered their eyes and joined in speaking the *Shema.* After speaking the "Amen," the Hazzan stepped to the bimah and led the people in a song of praise. As the last note died, he exchanged places with Rabbi Omar.

Looking around the room, the older man smiled. "Good Sabbath, my friends."

"Good Sabbath, Rabbi Omar," the people responded.

The Rabbi unrolled one of the scrolls, looked through the scroll before laying the *yad*—the hand-shaped pointer—across the parchment. Then raising his hands and looking up, he prayed,

"Blessed are you, Yahweh our God, King of the Universe, who has sanctified us with His commandments and has commanded us to engross ourselves in His Holy Scripture. Please, Yahweh, our God, make these Holy Words be sweet in our mouth and in the mouth of Your people, the family of Israel. May we and our offspring and the offspring of Your people the House of Israel, know Your Name and study Your Holy Scripture for its sake. Blessed are you, Yahweh, Who teaches His Word to His people Israel. Amen."

After everyone repeated the "Amen," Rabbi Omar lifted the yad and began reading.

"Praise the Lord, all you nations; extol Him, all you peoples.

*For great is His love toward us, and the faithfulness of the
Lord endures forever. Praise the Lord."*

Replacing the yad on top of the scroll, he looked at the people.
"This reading from the Psalms, speaks of Yahweh's faithfulness to
all nations, and not just to the Jewish people. Whereas we might
feel we are Yahweh's favorites," he smiled, "the Holy Scriptures
speaks of His love and compassion for all people. But," he lifted a
forefinger, "we can say we have…*more examples*," he smiled again,
"of Yahweh's compassionate care."

A soft chuckle rippled around the room.

"The first is Passover, which is a little over two weeks away.
That is when we remember the four hundred years our ancestors
were in bondage to the Egyptians."

Many people around the room nodded.

"We will remember how our ancestors," his voice was heavy
with tears, "cried out for freedom."

A soft moan arose; several older men and women—including
Gveret Yintl—wiped tears from their eyes.

"We also remember," he looked up, "how Yahweh answered
our ancestors' prayers by sending Moses."

"Yes," Hadassah joined the others around the room speaking.
From her childhood, she loved the story of Moses and how—when
he was a babe—Yahweh protected him from Pharoah's edict to
kill all the Jewish male babies.

The Rabbi reminded the people of Moses' mother hiding him
and later placing him in the reed ark and setting it on the river.
How Pharoah's daughter found him and raised him as her son and
a prince of Egypt. How Moses, as a grown man, saw an Egyptian
beating an Israelite slave and he killed the Egyptian. How he left
Egypt and fled to Midian, where he married Zipporah and worked
with his father-in-law tending sheep. How God heard the cries
of the Israelite slaves, and through the burning bush, told Moses
to go back to Egypt.

"We remember how Moses told Pharoah to set the slaves free.

When Pharoah refused, Yahweh sent ten plagues on the Egyptians, until finally Pharoah agreed to set our ancestors free."

"Yes!"

"When Pharoah regretted his decision, he took his Army and pursued our ancestors. When the people saw the Egyptian Army, they were afraid. But Yahweh parted the sea, and they walked through on dry land. When Pharoah and the Egyptian Army followed," Rabbi Omar lifted his arms wide, his voice growing, "Yahweh closed the waters of the sea, drowning Pharoah and his Army."

Hadassah lifting her arms, joined others in the room, "Thank You, Yahweh!" "Yes!" "Praise be to Yahweh!"

After a few moments, Rabbi Omar patted the air. Once the people quieted, he continued, teaching from the Holy Scripture of Yahweh telling Moses how they were to celebrate Passover; sacrificing the spotless lamb, spreading its blood over the doorposts, and eating the Passover meal.

Then Rabbi Omar's beard drooped. "Despite the many years of Yahweh's goodness and care for them, the people—under the Kings of Judah—did what was evil. Yahweh sent Nebuchadnezzar, the King of Babylon, to punish our ancestors. Nebuchadnezzar destroyed Jerusalem and the Temple. He took the wealth of the Temple and the wealth of the Kings of Judah. He took our ancestors into captivity, even carrying some away to captivity in Babylon."

More moans floated around the room.

"For seventy years, our ancestors were in captivity to the Babylonians. But Yahweh did not forget them. He sent the prophets Ezekiel and Daniel with many words of encouragement, including prophecies that the city of David and the Temple would be rebuilt, and one day, Yahweh's Anointed One—the Messiah—would come."

He extended his hands. "Some of these prophecies came to pass when King Cyrus—he who is known as *the Great*—attacked and defeated the Babylonians. It was this Cyrus Yahweh spoke of through the prophet Isaiah." Lifting the yad, he opened another scroll and began reading,

"This is what the Lord says to His anointed, to Cyrus, whose right hand I take hold of to subdue nations before him, to strip kings of their armor, to open doors before him so that gates will not be shut: I will go before you and will level the mountains; I will break down gates of bronze and cut through bars of iron. I will give you hidden treasures, riches stored in secret places, so that you may know that I am the Lord, the God of Israel, Who summons you by name."

He laid the yad on the scroll. "Even the prophet Daniel proclaimed our ancestors would return to Jerusalem and rebuild both the city and the Temple of Yahweh. The prophet lived to see our people freed from captivity when the Gentile King Cyrus overthrew Babylon and established the Persian Empire. After the prophet's death, his memory was honored not only by the Jewish people, but also by the Persians, who buried him near the Shavor River here in Susa.

"The Gentile kings, Cyrus, his son Darius, and now Xerxes, have been gracious to our people, allowing us to worship Yahweh, and to rebuild Jerusalem and the Temple of Yahweh. The work has often been delayed when people tried to stop our ancestors—but each time Yahweh intervened.

"While our ancestors were waiting for Jerusalem and the Temple to be rebuilt, they established synagogues as our houses of prayer," he gestured to the building around them. "This is why we gather in our synagogues to read and study the Holy Scriptures, to pray, and to celebrate the Holy Days. One day we will again offer sacrifices in Yahweh's Temple. Until then, we confess our sins, repent, and—like Father Abraham told Issac—trust God to provide the sacrifice."

Another round of praise echoed, "Thank You, Yahweh!" "Yes!" "Praise be to Yahweh!"

"As we look forward to Passover," Rabbi Omar smiled, "let us remember all Yahweh did to free our ancestors from captivity and to allow us to celebrate Him. Until that day, we stand," he gestured for everyone to stand, "with all the people of Israel everywhere and proclaim:"

Everyone in the room covered their eyes and joined the Rabbi,
"Hear, O Israel: The Lord our God, the Lord is One. Love
the Lord your God with all your heart and with all your
soul and with all your strength. Amen."

Jerimoth lifted the shofar once again and blew a long, great blast.

CHAPTER 16

After greeting those in the loft, Hadassah and Miriam followed Yintl down the stairs to where Mordecai, Deagah, and Kalev were speaking with Hakaliah bar Seraiah and his sons Nehemiah and Hanani.

"Ah, Hadassah," Mordecai smiled. "Good Sabbath, Gveret Yintl, and Miriam."

"Good Sabbath, Mar Mordecai."

The other men exchanged greetings with the three women.

"Hakaliah, Naomi asked me to tell you she would join you soon," Yintl smiled. "Sarai bat Lamech wanted to speak to her."

"In that situation," Hakaliah smiled, "I imagine my wife will linger a little longer."

Born of the line of Judah, and one of the Elders in the Jewish community, Hakaliah was taller than Mordecai and Deagah, yet younger than both. He had hair the color of a raven's wing brushing across a noble brow and dark eyes flecked with amber. A skilled goldsmith, he was known throughout Susa for his beautiful creations. Like Hadassah's father, he received several commissions from Persian nobles and even one from the King. To respect his royal client, the goldsmith would not go into detail, except to smile and say he had crafted a beautiful crown.

Hadassah, along with Miriam and Yintl, returned their

greetings. She glanced at Kalev and caught his gaze. His smile was warm. She returned it with a gentle smile, heat rising in her cheeks.

"I believe you speak truth, Mar Hakaliah," Yintl smiled. "Pray continue with your conversation. We do not wish to interrupt."

"You are not interrupting," Deagah waved his hand. "Our conversation was nothing more than the usual; our families, our work, the Rabbi's words, celebrating Passover."

"Without the Temple," Nehemiah interjected, "how can we properly celebrate Passover?"

The others in their group grew quiet. Hadassah glanced at Mordecai; he shook his head slightly, his lips drawn in a thin smile. Deagah looked at his wife; Yintl arched an eyebrow. Miriam studied the ceiling. A frown creased Kalev's brow.

"Nehemiah," Hanani laid a hand on his older brother's shoulder, "perhaps that subject should not be discussed here."

Nehemiah shrugged off his brother's hand. "When it is improper to speak of the Holy Temple?" Like his younger brother, in appearance Nehemiah was a copy of their father. Unlike his brother, he did not share their father's courteous manner. Hakaliah and Hanani were genteel and careful in their speech. Nehemiah was blunt, speaking what was on his mind without giving thought to his words or to the people around him, as evidenced by his continued diatribe.

"Rabbi Omar mentioned our ancestors establishing synagogues as houses of prayer and for the reading of the Holy Scripture while they were waiting for Jerusalem and the Temple to be rebuilt. Why are we still waiting?"

"It takes time and money to rebuild the Holy Temple," Hanani said.

"Instead of rebuilding the Temple," Nehemiah seethed, "the reports Ezra ben Seraiah sent to the Elders state those of our people in Jerusalem are using the time and money to build their own homes. If I were there, the Temple of Yahweh would have been finished by now."

Hadassah glanced at Miriam and Yintl—the older woman acknowledged her discomfort with a sad smile—before lowering her gaze to inspect the tiles on the floor.

"Son," Hakaliah's voice was soft, but held a touch of iron, "while we honor your commitment to the City of David and the Holy Temple, *this* is not the time to disparage those who are rebuilding slower than you would prefer."

"But Father—" Nehemiah began, when Hakaliah interjected, "*Nehemiah*. This is *not* the time. While Mar Deagah, Mar Mordecai, Kalev, and your brother are accustomed to your brusque speech, you are making Gveret Yintl, Miriam, and Hadassah uncomfortable."

Nehemiah looked from his father to the women, color suffusing his face. He lifted his chin, forcing himself to look at each woman. "Gveret Yintl, Miriam, Hadassah—my father speaks truth. I was wrong to speak as I did." He filled his lungs and blew out the air. "I ask your forgiveness." His lips tightened in a thin smile.

Yintl returned his smile with one of great sweetness. "Of course you are forgiven, Nehemiah. We"—she swept a hand toward Miriam and Hadassah—"honor your concern for the Holy Temple."

"Ah, there you are," Naomi bat Reuben—Hakaliah's wife—called from the stairs. She lifted her saffron-colored garment as she hurried down the stairs and crossed to their group. Of an age with Yintl, she was slender with dark eyes and gray streaks in her black hair.

She greeted everyone before glancing around and lowering her voice. "Sarai bat Lamech stopped me to talk about bread. Yes, bread," she added when her sons lifted their eyebrows. "I realize Sarai misses her mother since she went to Abraham's bosom—may her memory be blessed. I try to be compassionate with Sarai, but," she glanced around once again and huffed, "she must have shared *every recipe for bread* her mother ever baked. So," she blew out air, looking around the group, "what did I miss?"

Hadassah struggled to control her expression as she—along

with those in their group—looked at Naomi and then each other. The silence was awkward.

Until Nehemiah snorted a laugh. Then all eyes swiveled toward the young man as he walked over to hug his mother.

"What is it?" Naomi's eyebrows arched in confusion.

"Maman," Nehemiah chuckled, "Yahweh has blessed you with the gift of timeliness."

Chapter 17

"What happened last night?" Haman asked. He removed his sword and belt, laying them on a table before crossing the floor to sit on their bed. After removing his sandals and gold-trimmed cap, he ran his fingers through his hair as he leaned against a pillow.

It had been more than six months since he had been home. Looking around, he noted the changes Zeresh had made. Although they had not overseen the design of this house, the furnishings and decor were a mix of their own possessions and those from the Jewish master builder they chose to keep.

Larger than his quarters in the Royal Citadel, this bedchamber had a sleeping area, a private wash area, and a dressing area with hooks, chests, and shelves for their garments. A door of double *jali*—decorative pierced stones—opened to a sheltered area of the courtyard. Their furnishings—bed, chairs, tables, washstands, and chests—were carved from the fragrant red wood of the myrrh tree. A thick pallet on the bed frame was covered with ivory linens trimmed with threads of gold and blue. The tapestries on the walls and rugs on the floor had golden Persian lions woven amidst blue curving teardrops.

He and Zeresh had burnt the things from the master builder they did not want; with the exception of a carved marble bench they found in the garden.

"This is beautifully crafted," Haman had said. "We should bring it into the house."

"I do not agree," Zeresh had sniffed. "I do not want cold marble furniture in the house."

"This is embroidered with the royal colors," Haman had run a hand across the cushion. "I will give this to the King. He will remember me whenever he sees this bench."

"That is a good idea," Zeresh had said. "Mention Navjaa when you present it to the King; it will aid our plans."

Plans, Haman shook his head. *No matter our plans, no one could have predicted what happened last night.*

After waiting until the last guest had left the Royal Citadel this morning, he left instructions with his lieutenant before riding home.

"You are going home," Artabanus arched an eyebrow, "after what happened last night?"

Haman nodded. "It was what the Lord King instructed yesterday afternoon."

The King had been in the Royal Apartment, drinking with his seven Azam. *"Even with Zeresh dokhtar Tattenai coming to the Queen's banquets for women,"* Xerxes had said, *"you have been away from your wife, your children, and your home for half a year. Tomorrow morning, after all my guests have left, set whatever Immortals are necessary for protection, and then go home."*

"Zeresh, I ask again. What happened in Vashti's feast for women?"

"First, tell me what happened during the banquet for men," Zeresh smiled, pouring wine from an amphora, and handed a goblet to him. "Knowing what Xerxes said will make more sense of the message he sent to Vashti."

Haman took a sip of wine. "The King waited until after the meal before he spoke." He grinned. "With the amount of wine consumed, I will be surprised if there is a grape left in all of Persia.

"After the meal and entertainment, the King finally spoke."

Haman set the goblet down and extended his arms, imitating Xerxes. "He reminded the Azam, the Shathapavans, and all his guests about the power and might of the Persian Empire. Everyone cheered with each mention of the wealth and the accomplishments, and the King pointing out they were the beneficiaries of the Empire." He laughed. "Xerxes even mentioned that—as long as they are loyal to the Empire—every citizen is free to pursue their life and their interests, even worshipping the gods of their choice."

Haman told her how Shathapavan Agarbayata had spoken, telling Xerxes that he and the other Shathapavans were concerned with the idea of going to war so soon after subduing Egypt. How Agarbayata had gone on to remind Xerxes that he was newly crowned and should spend his time establishing his Throne and building up the Empire, and not deplete the country of the men or wealth in order to wage war against the Greeks.

"He said *that* to the King?" Zeresh gasped, arching a brow.

Haman nodded. "That was not all. Shathapavan Jata stood and asked the King to reconsider. He stated that Xerxes was King of the greatest Empire in the world. He has many Palaces, many Warriors, many subjects. *Then* he added, 'Your beautiful Queen has given you and heir.'

"It was at that point Dojooje tabor Shethar said," Haman pitched his voice higher and slightly unstable, "Ahhh...Queen Vashti. She is beautiful!'

Then, the other Azam began squabbling amongst themselves; demanding to know how Dojooje knew the Queen was beautiful; others stating their wives had seen her; Shethar announcing that *everyone* should see her.

"I thought General Otanes would strike Shethar's head from his shoulders for that comment. Xerxes surprised us all by announcing that everyone *would* see Vashti." Haman took a deep drink before continuing. "The King sent me to the House of Women. I was to take some of The Immortals. We were to tell Hegai and Shaashgaz, along with the King's seven personal eunuchs, to escort

Vashti to the King. The last thing Xerxes said was to tell her, 'The King says to wear your new crown.'

"So," he sat up and set his goblet on the table, "after the eunuch went to inform Hegai and Shaashgaz of Xerxes' command, what happened?"

Zeresh laughed. "It all went according to our plans."

"I sat at a table that allowed me to see the door to the Court-yard and yet be near the Queen." She grinned. "Your arrival with a group of Warriors surprised everyone; it sounded like geese and chickens squawking, 'Why are The Immortals here? Is the Palace under attack?' and other nonsense. After the eunuch approached Hegai and Shaashgaz, he found me and gave me your message about the sunset.

"Vashti called out, demanding to know what was happening.

"I went to the Queen and assured her that—whatever was happening—you and your men would protect her." She laughed again. "You should have seen her countenance when Hegai and Shaashgaz told her she had been summoned by the King and he wanted her to wear her crown."

Zeresh dropped her jaw and lifted her eyebrows and pitched her voice higher. "'What did he say?' The Queen was furious; her face was as red as a pomegranate."

"I have seen her that angry before," Haman laughed. "What happened next?"

"I asked, 'My Lady Queen, why would the King ask you to wear Queen Atossa's crown?'"

"'No. Not that one,' she snapped. 'He had a *little* crown designed for me. It is token gift, a trinket; nothing more.'"

Haman leaned over to kiss her. "What did you say?"

"I said, 'I cannot believe My Lord King Xerxes is asking you to come before his guests wearing a simple crown instead of a royal one. Some might think instead of treating you as the Queen of Persia, he is treating you like a concubine...or worse; he treating you like a slave.'"

Haman covered his mouth, his eyes wide. "You said that?"

Zeresh nodded, smiling.

"That was inspired!" he responded, he kissed her again. "What did she say?"

"Vashti turned to Hegai and Shaashgaz." Zeresh lifted a finger and pointed. "'Go. Go back to Xerxes. Tell the King I am not coming.'

"Hegai and Shaashgaz were shocked. 'My Lady Queen,' Hegai gasped, 'He will demand to know why you are not coming.'"

Zeresh stood, lifting her chin. "'Go back and tell Xerxes... This. Is. Not. The. Crown.'"

CHAPTER 18

11 FARVARDIN
THIRD YEAR OF THE REIGN OF XERXES,
KING OF THE MEDES AND THE PERSIANS

Rabbi Omar glanced down the street in both directions, before closing the synagogue door and sliding the bolt across it.

Mordecai arched his eyebrows, glancing at the other men present: Hakaliah bar Seraiah; Ezer ben Paltiel the tailor; Benayah bar Diklah the carpenter, along with Jerimoth, and Deagah. Only his friend and the Hazzan did not appear surprised by the Rabbi's actions.

One of the older men in the Jewish community, Rabbi Omar bar Anaiah was shorter than most men and of average build. There was more gray than black in his beard and hair that waved above dark eyes. Most of the time, he had a ready smile; but as he turned from the door, his lips were drawn in a somber smile.

"My friends, thank you for coming. I am certain you are curious," he gestured to the bolted door, "as to why I have asked you to come. If you follow me, I will soon tell you." He led the men across the main room, turned down the corridor, and entered a small room.

The room had shelves around the walls on which were baskets filled with clothing, housewares, tools, food, and other items for the poor and needy in Susa. In the middle of the room was a low table with cushions beneath. On the table were two amphorae, cups, a plate of bread, and another of cheese.

"Please sit. Jerimoth brought some bread his wife, Anna bat Yosef, baked fresh this morning," he smiled at the Hazzan. "Whether it is spoken in front of the older women of our community, Anna's bread is delicious."

Everyone grinned at the Hazzan who was pouring cups of milk.

"My wife would be pleased to know you enjoyed her bread." The youngest man present, Jerimoth ben Halevi's lips spread in a slow smile that reached his eyes. He lifted a hand to move the black lock brushing across a noble brow. Newly married, his young wife, Anna, was known as a skilled baker.

After the Rabbi spoke the blessing over their food, the men ate, talking about the recent rain, planting crops, family news, and other simple matters of everyday life.

At length, the Rabbi dusted crumbs from his hands and tunic. "That was delightful. However," he pinned a smile to his lips, "it is time to speak of the reason I asked you here. Deagah told me of something he overheard in his store. It was of serious enough nature, I felt you all should hear it. Deagah, would you share it?"

The men turned to the merchant, who dusted his hands, and reached up to straighten his cream turban.

"Yesterday, a group of people came into my store. From their garments, their jewels—as well as the items they purchased—they were obviously wealthy. Their conversation among themselves—" he held up both palms in front of his chest, "you understand I do not intend to listen in order to pry. However I cannot help but overhear some conversations as I serve my customers."

The men around the table nodded.

"These people were talking about the banquets King Xerxes and Queen Vashti held in the Palace this past week.

112

"From what they said, at one point, something happened that made King Xerxes furious."

"Did anyone say what made the King angry?"

"No," Deagah said. "However, from what the men said, King Xerxes was so mad, he immediately left the room, ending the feast."

"Did anything else happen?" Benayah asked.

Deagah shook his head. "From what these people said, all the guests staying in the Palace left the next morning without seeing or hearing anything more from the King or Queen. Perhaps it was not as bad as these people made it sound. However," he gestured toward the Rabbi, "I felt it serious enough to share with Rabbi Omar and Jerimoth."

"You were right to do that," the Rabbi responded. "As my father—may his memory be blessed—used to say, *Together with the weeds is the cabbage beaten.*"

The men nodded, all realizing that good people often suffer together with a person who does something bad.

"Tell your families what you feel is needed. However," the Rabbi lifted his hands, "until more is known of this situation, everyone in Susa needs to say less and watch more. As the author of the Proverbs wrote, *'A king's wrath is the messenger of death, but the wise will appease it.'*"

CHAPTER 19

"Eggs…honey…rue…garlic…and frankincense," Mordecai checked the piece of papyrus he held against the items on the counter. "I think that is all for today." After a quick barter—Deagah's prices were reasonable, but he knew his friend would be offended if he did not offer a counter-price—they reached an agreement, and coins were exchanged.

"If you have time," the merchant wrapped the honey in a cloth and laid it in the basket, "I have something I wish to discuss with you."

Mordecai arched a brow, remembering the meeting with the other Elders. "I always have time for you, my friend."

"Wonderful. Yintl," Deagah turned to his wife, who was showing some women a selection of combs and brushes, "I will return soon."

She nodded and turned back to their customers. "These combs are made from aloe wood; not only will your hair be smooth, but it will have a beautiful fragrance."

Mordecai followed Deagah through the curtained opening, down the corridor through the door leading to the courtyard. Instead of crossing to the yakhchal, the merchant led him up the stairs, to a large room located over the shop.

Similar to those found in most of their friend's homes, this room stretched the width of the building. It was here the family would gather for meals when the weather was inclement or when they had guests. The walls were swirls of smooth clay, the tile floor was a mosaic of blue and green, and there were lampstands in each corner.

Deagah gestured to the table in the center of the room with thick cushions beneath and on top were two cups, an amphora beading with condensation, and a plate covered with a cloth. "Please be seated, my friend."

After they sat on the thick cushions, the merchant poured two cups of wine and uncovered the plate, revealing cakes made from oats and dates, sweetened with honey.

Wine and Yintl's sweet cakes in the middle of the day? Mordecai controlled his features, as he accepted the wine and sweet cake with thanks.

Instead of speaking of things he might have overheard in the shop, Deagah led the conversation to light matters; the warmth of the Spring weather, humorous encounters with his customers, and new items he had purchased for the shop.

"Allow me to refill your wine, my friend," he lifted the amphora.

"No, I thank you, my friend," Mordecai replied. "I need to have a clear mind. I am to meet Hadassah at Natan bar Chanan's home. His mother, Naibam bat Reuel, continues to struggle with breathing. This is why I purchased more frankincense. I will burn the herb while Hadassah plays the harp to relax Naibam."

"I am sorry to hear that. Please tell Naibam we will be praying for her." Setting his cup on the table, Deagah folded his hands. "You are probably wondering why I asked you to stay."

"I confess I am curious." Mordecai lifted the cup.

"It is about Hadassah."

Mordecai, the cup held frozen to his mouth, stared at his friend. "Oh?" He lifted a brow.

The merchant nodded. "And Kalev," he grinned.

Mordecai set the cup on the table, his mouth stretching into a smile. "Are you saying…?"

"I am speaking on Kalev's behalf. He has asked me to present an offer of marriage for Hadassah."

The two men stared at each other, eyes twinkling.

"Marriage…to my Hadassah?"

Deagah nodded.

"Well…that is…something." *Abihail, Atarah, I have cared for your little Hadassah, and now she has received an offer of marriage.*

"Something?" The creases in Deagah's forehead deepened. "Is that something…*good?*"

"What?" Mordechai shook his head, clearing his thoughts. "Pardon, my friend. I did not mean to…I was thinking of…how happy Abihail and Atarah would be."

The merchant's expression cleared. "Then you mean…?"

"Yes, of course," he reached over to grasp his friend's forearm. "I have spoken to Hadassah about this possibility. Her answer is, *yes.*"

The two men laughed, clapping each other on the shoulders, drinking more wine, and exchanging *mazal tovs.*

"I will of course bring Kalev to your house," Deagah said, "to allow him to speak to you."

"I look forward to quizzing him," Mordecai grinned. He set the cup down. "When should we have the betrothal ceremony?"

"If Kalev had his wishes, it would be tonight."

"I imagine Hadassah would wish for more time, especially with Passover only thirteen days away. I am certain she would wish to sew a new garment wear for the ceremony." He stood.

"I know Yintl would wish to have time to plan a feast," Deagah stood. "Let us wait until after Passover for the betrothal ceremony."

"That is a good plan." Mordecai embraced his friend. "I could not think of anyone else who would be a better husband for Hadassah."

"We will be family," Deagah said.

"Our children will have children," Mordecai clapped his friend's shoulder.

"Your family will grow once again."

"It will indeed," Mordecai's eyes misted. "Yahweh is good."

Chapter 20

Haman rode down the streets of Susa. The air was warm; flecks of golden sunshine mingled with a few wispy clouds in the azure sky.

Passing through the massive Great Gate leading into the Royal Citadel, he rode up to the Palace. Dismounting, he handed his horse over to a groom and crossed to the base of the stairs leading to the Palace. Walking up the flight of sixty-three steps to a landing, he turned and walked up another forty-eight steps to the terrace of the entrance to the Palace of Susa.

Several dozen of The One Thousand Immortals saw him approach. The Warriors nearest him nodded, "Hazarpatish," before returning their attention to the people coming and going through the massive double doors.

Striding through the corridors of the Palace, he paused in the Military Court, where the Warriors would leave their personal belongings, and receive their daily assignments. Here and there Warriors were arriving for the day while others were leaving. The rest were eating, drinking, playing dice, or polishing their weapons. Seeing Haman, the activity stopped as all the Warriors stood, lifted their swords against their chests, and murmured, "Hazarpatish."

Haman returned their salute. "Be at rest." He crossed the room, walked through the far door, down the corridor, passing by the courts leading to the Throne Room, down several more halls, to the Corridor of the Royal Residence. Seeing Haman, the dozen Immortals blocking the Corridor nodded their heads, "Hazarpatish," and moved, allowing him to continue through the Corridor of the Royal Residence to the atrium outside the double doors of the King's Apartment.

Here, as elsewhere in the Palace, the walls were decorated with reliefs of walking lions made from enameled terra-cotta. The floors echoed those reliefs in mosaics of red and gold tile.

The three dozen Immortals standing guard greeted him as had the other Warriors. After acknowledging them, he turned to his Lieutenant. "How goes the watch?"

Artabanus crossed his arms, his mouth thinning. "Not good."

"Oh?" Haman arched a brow. "How so?"

"Let us say," Artabanus stepped closer, "*someone* spent the night...*dispirited*."

"Hmm..." Haman shook his head. "Whenever he consumes the amount of wine he did yesterday, the King normally falls into an exhausted sleep."

"The King did not sleep last night, nor did he send for food, for drink, or one of his concubines. He complained of pain in his head. He called for one of the magi but had him thrown out after only a few moments."

"Truly?" Only the King could bypass punishment for rudeness toward a magus.

Artabanus nodded. "The only person the King has not had thrown out of his apartment has been the Cub-bearer."

"As Kurush Tars Dida was also Cup-bearer to King Darius. Xerxes trusts him almost as much as he trusts Queen Atossa."

"Dida has been in with the King since the Second Watch, reading aloud from the writings of Zarathustra and the Aeorapati Belteshazzar."

"Dida has a soothing voice," Haman said. "His reading has been known to ease the King's headaches, whatever the source of the pain."

Artabanus looked around again before adding, "My aged grandmother would say by choosing to drink as he did, the King, *threw the bouquet into the water.*"

Haman grinned, "An appropriate proverb, although I do not think Xerxes would care to have anyone—even a respected elder—describe his decisions as foolish. Still, it is needful to know of the King's disposition. Artabanus, you are dismissed for the day. Before you leave, send a servant to the kitchen; tell the Royal Chef to have bread and cheese—and a goblet of Egyptian ale—brought to the Throne Room."

Artabanus straightened, lifted his sword against his chest. "At once, Hazarpatish."

Smoothing his garments and straightening his cap, Haman walked over and knocked on the double doors of the King's Apartments. It was answered by two servants, who opened both doors wide and bowed deeply as Xerxes stepped into atrium.

Haman knew, without the King speaking a word, that he was more than—as Artabanus had described—dispirited. Generally, when Xerxes had been away from his Palaces for an extended time, he would wear comfortable clothing—simple tunics, trousers, soft caps, and slippers—for the next few days.

Today—from head to toe—Xerxes exuded an imperial aura. The crenellated Crown of the King of Persia on his black curls, wearing a heavy robe of red linen trimmed with lengths of gold thread, and pointed gold-tipped shoes peeking from beneath the hem, Xerxes was regal. Wide golden cuffs on each wrist, in his right hand he carried the Royal Scepter—made from nine cubits of ironwood, stained red and capped with a golden sphere—and on his left hand he wore his Signet Ring.

As one, Haman and The Immortals in the courtyard lifted their swords against their chests. "My Lord King Xerxes." In the Corridor of the Royal Residence, none of the Warriors would relax their watch to bow, even to the King.

Xerxes nodded to the men before turning to Haman.

"Greetings, Hazarpatish."

Haman saluted, sword against his chest. "Greetings, My Lord King." After two dozen Immortals arranged themselves in front and behind the King, with a dozen staying in the atrium, Xerxes and Haman began walking back through the Palace to the Throne Room.

They walked in silence for several minutes before Xerxes spoke. "Is all well within the Palace?"

"It is, My Lord King." He paused before continuing, "In his report to me, Artabanus tabar Mithradata said you had…an uncomfortable…night."

"I did," Xerxes frowned. "There was pain in my head, but it is almost gone. How was your evening at home?"

"You are kind to ask, My Lord King," Haman replied. "It was pleasant being home with my family. I bring you greetings from my wife and children."

"How is your wi—" Xerxes' mouth tightened. "How is Zeresh dokhtar Tattenai?"

"She is well and will be honored to know you asked about her. *Be careful. The King is only being polite; this is not the time to speak more of wives.* "My sons were home as well."

"Ah, sons!" Xerxes smiled. "Some of your sons are in the Army, are they not?"

"Yes, My Lord King," Haman grinned. "My five older sons are already part of the Army. The five youngest are still completing their training; they look forward to joining their older brothers. They all hope one day become part of the Ten Thousand Immortals."

"With you as their father, I am certain they will become part of The One Thousand Immortals. And your daughter? Is she as beautiful as her mother?"

"Navjaa is beautiful," Haman said.

"How old is she?"

"She is eighteen."

"You no doubt have many young men seeking her as a wife."

"Well…" *Proceed with caution,* "…like other young women, she

120

is ready for marriage. However, with her beauty, her skills, and her family, I will not give her to just *any* man. When she does marry, it will be to a…" he glanced at the King's profile, "*special* man."

"With you as her father," Xerxes grinned at him, "I imagine you have a special man in mind?"

Now! "As to that, My Lord King, I do. If I may speak to—"

As they turned down the corridor, his words were cut off by Xerxes stopping and pointing. "What is that?"

Outside the Outer Court, a circle of Immortals stood, their drawn swords pointing inward. From inside the circle, a cacophony of garbled voices screamed,

"No!"

"How dare you!"

"Stop!"

"Put down the sword!"

"I demand you stop!"

"Do you know *who* I am!"

"There is the King!"

Haman strode forward, drawing his sword while—as one—the Immortals accompanying them encircled Xerxes and turned—swords pointing outward—creating a human shield around the King.

"Immortals!" Haman commanded, "Take these criminals to the Gate of Eternity!"

The Immortals surrounding the circle of men whipped out the black cloths tucked into their belts.

"Noo!" The voices turned to screams. "Please—"

"Stop!"

All in the corridor froze.

Haman turned to the King, his eyebrows raised.

"Haman, these are not criminals," the King pointed to the circle of men. "They are my Azam. They are my advisors—my friends."

"My Lord King," Haman said, "it matters not *who* they are. It is written in the Law of the Medes and the Persians that it is

121

death for anyone to come into the presence of the King without being summoned. As Hazarpatish, it is my responsibility to uphold the Law and protect the King."

The men in the circle screamed. "Nooo!"

"Silence!" Xerxes voice echoed above the screams. "Haman, I am aware of the Law," Xerxes looked at the Warrior standing in front of him. "Lower your sword."

The Immortal bowed his head, lowered his sword, and stepped back.

The King strode to the circle of Persian nobles, some pleading, all weeping.

"Memukan, Shethar," he looked at the advisors nearest him, "why are you all here?" His voice was cold, his eyes colder.

Memukan looked at Xerxes and swallowed. "M-my L-l-ord King," from his slurred voice, it was obvious the Azam was still drunk. "We," he gestured to the others, "each s-spoke with our wives last-t n-n-night." He looked at the others who all nodded. "They told us what happened in the F-f-feast for Women. T-t-they t-told us what th-h-he Q-q-queen said."

The other six men nodded, gesturing for Memukan to continue.

"Our w-w-wives said if Queen V-v-vashti can refuse to ob-bey the K-king, they d-do not have to ob-bey us."

Xerxes' mouth tightened, a vein throbbed in his forehead. "Go on."

"We c-came to a-a-s-sk you to d-do something."

Xerxes stared at his Azam, before turning. "Haman, you know the Law of the Medes and the Persians. Was Vashti's behavior a crime?"

Haman controlled his expression. *Here is it!* "My Lord King, let me answer by asking your knowledge of the Law of the Medes and the Persians. If you had summoned anyone else and they refused, would *you* have considered it a crime?"

Xerxes' gaze turned inward; then it hardened. "Yes," he spoke softly, his countenance darkened. "Yes," his voice grew stronger, the

Scepter trembling as his hand tightened—knuckles white—around the shaft. "What Queen Vashti did *was* a crime. Her actions, her words, were disrespectful to me, to my Throne, and to my Kingdom. However, my Azam's actions, while careless, were not criminal." Turning to the circle, he extended his Scepter between The Immortals to the Azam, the only recourse to save them from death.

First Memukan, Shethar, and then each of the seven advisors reached out and touched the golden sphere of the Scepter, breathing, "Thank you, My Lord King."

Xerxes gazed at the men around the room; the Azam, the Immortals. They lowered their eyes. Xerxes lifted his chin. "Hazarpatish, send for my Cup-bearer and my Royal Scribes."

"My Lord King, it shall be done."

"Come," Xerxes said, turning toward the Outer and Inner Court that led into the Throne Room. "Let us decide—according to the Law of the Medes and Persia—what must be done with Vashti."

CHAPTER 21

"Is it not a beautiful day," Mordecai said.

He and Deagah were walking from Deagah's shop toward the synagogue.

Due to its proximity to the Palace, the street near the Marketplace was generally busy; but with the recent Norooz festival, today it was packed like fish in a net. Beyond the shoppers going in and out of various shops, there were magi in their somber attire, with scarves covering the lower half of their faces, walking toward the Temple of Ahura Mazda; travelers from all parts of the Empire dressed in colorful and exotic attire; nobility leaving Susa on camels and horseback; officials and magistrates walking toward the courts discussing the details of the Law; Persian Warriors armed with their weapons striding through the streets.

That morning, Mordecai had met with Deagah and Kalev; they had settled most of the details of the mohar. Afterwards, Deagah left Kalev in charge of the shop while he and Mordecai joined the other Elders at the synagogue for their weekly gathering.

"Kalev has met with Hakaliah bar Seraiah about a ring to give

124

to Hadassah," Deagah said. "Hakaliah said he would have Nehemiah design and craft the ring, as that will give his son something *practical* to do.'"

"Practical?" Mordecai's brows arched. "Did Hakaliah explain what Nehemiah is doing that is not *practical?*"

"Writing letters," Deagah grinned. "Apparently the young man feels his letters to Ezra ben Seraiah will chivvy those in Jerusalem to finish the Temple and rebuild the city walls. With his drive and passion for the things of Yahweh, I would not be surprised to see Nehemiah go to Jerusalem one day to oversee the work himself."

"That would not surprise me as well," Mordecai replied, "although he would need some means to earn money as I do not think Hakaliah would fund that trip. I imagine most people in Jerusalem would not be as interested in helping Nehemiah as they are in food and fabric or other items such as are found in your store."

"Or in the need of a physician like yourself." Deagah covered a yawn. "Pardon, my friend. I am fatigued from the past week. There are times when not having many customers is a relief. Even though it brought more trade to my shop—" Deagah turned to address two Persian men, dressed in rich raiment, "Greetings, Mirza Alavi, Mirza Bibi. It is a lovely day, is it not?"

After discussing the weather with two of his wealthiest customers, he said, "I must not keep you. I look forward to seeing you soon at the House of Deagah."

Waiting until the two men were out of ear-shot, he turned back to Mordecai. "As I was saying, even though it brought more trade to my shop, I am thankful the Norooz celebration has passed. The walls of Susa were swollen with so many people from throughout the Empire; the door to our shop was never still."

"I am also relieved the celebration for the New Year is over," Mordecai replied. "I saw many people last week who had traveled with the King. They felt unwell." Glancing around, he lowered his voice, "Most of these people's sufferings were due to their excesses during the feasts held in the Royal Citadel. Teas made from the leaves of peppermint plants eased their complaints."

As they reached the Great Gate, the crowds thinned; only those who lived in in the area—or had business there—would have reason to be near the Palace.

"Despite the challenges of the last week, we have much to be thankful for. After Passover, Kalev and Hadassah will be betrothed and," Deagah stepped into the street, "*ieee!*"

"Watch out!" Mordecai grabbed the merchant's arm and pulled him back as a chariot—bells clanging from the horses' harnesses—swept through the Gate, turned sharply in front of them, and stopped.

Besides the charioteer—dressed in a green tunic, trousers, and cap—the chariot held two other men. One was a red-clad Warrior, with a sword at his waist and spear in his hand. The other was a magus. He wore white, but his simple garments and cap, a short scarf draped on his chest to be used to cover the lower half of his face identified him as a *herbad*, a student of the magi who had finished the first level of training. Scrolls, spikes, and a hammer were visible in the basket he carried.

The Warrior jumped out of the chariot and stood, spear resting on the toe of his shoe, watching the crowd who were drawn by the clanging bells.

The magus set the basket by his feet, withdrew a scroll, and turned toward the people. He unrolled the parchment, cleared his throat, and began reading.

"Be it known that on this day—the fifteen day of Farvardin, in the third year of Xerxes, King of the Medes and King of the Persians—the following proclamation is made.

"Two days ago—during the final feast of Norooz—King Xerxes called for Queen Vashti to attend him. She refused."

A gasp rose from the crowd. Mordecai, eyebrows raised, looked at Deagah. The merchant lifted his shoulders and shook his head slightly as the herbad continued.

"Her actions were wrong, not only against the King, but also against all the nobles and the peoples of all the satrapies of King Xerxes' Empire. For when the Queen's conduct becomes known to all, the Persian and Median women will use her actions as a standard and so they will despise their husbands saying, 'King Xerxes commanded Queen Vashti to be brought before him, but she would not come.' Even the Persian and Median women of the nobility will respond to all the King's nobles in the same way. There will be no end of disrespect and discord.

"Therefore, King Xerxes has issued this royal decree, written in the laws of Persia and Media—which cannot be repealed—that..." he paused, *"Vashti is never again to enter the presence of King Xerxes."* The proclamation continues, *"The King has decreed...least to the greatest."*

Another gasp rose around them, followed by buzzing comments, "Is the Queen deposed?" "It sounds as if she is deposed." "What will happen to her?" "Will the King kill her?" "Will he send her into exile?" until the Warrior lifted his spear and thumped it against the chariot.

"Silence!" he yelled.

Once the crowd settled, the herbad cleared his throat and continued reading.

"The King has decreed that her royal position will be given to someone else who is better than she. The King's edict is proclaimed throughout all his vast realm, that all women are to respect their husbands, from the least to the greatest."

Lowering the scroll, the herbad reached into the basket and lifted a mallet and two spikes. Stepping down from the chariot, he crossed to a tall, wooden post near the Great Gate. Smoothing the parchment against the post, he hammered the spikes into the top and bottom.

Turning back to the crowd, he said, "Today, this proclamation is being sent to all one hundred twenty-seven satrapies throughout the Persian Empire, written in the language of all the peoples.

"Thus commands Xerxes, King of the Medes and King of the Persians."

CHAPTER 22

Hadassah held the cup frozen to her lips, her eyes opened wide. "Vashti is deposed?"

Mordecai nodded. "It would appear she is."

"What happened?" Hadassah took a sip of milk and ate several grapes as her cousin related the incidents from early that day.

When he finished, Esther shook her head. "I have not heard much about Queen Vashti, other than she is beautiful and from a noble family." She lifted the amphora to pour more milk into their cups. "What I have heard does not reflect well on her."

"That is my experience as well," he tore a piece of bread in half and used it to scoop some lintels from the bowl on the table.

"What will happen to her?" She bit into a piece of white cheese.

"I cannot say," he shrugged. "As I have no connection to anyone in the Royal Citadel—and neither does Deagah—we have no way of discovering. Disobeying the King—even for someone within his family—is a capital crime. Being exiled to a distant part of the Empire would be the kindest punishment."

"I hurt for Prince Artaxerxes," Hadassah said. "He is so young; being separated from his mother will not be easy for him."

"You speak truth. However, apart from feeling sorry for the young prince, this has no bearing on our lives." He pushed his dish away and dusted crumbs from his hands. "Let us speak of other things."

"What things?"

Mordecai reached into the folds of the wide cloth sash wrapped around his waist and withdrew a small pouch. It *clunked* when he set it on the table in front of her.

Hadassah looked at the pouch and then at her cousin, an unspoken question stamped on her face.

Mordecai grinned. "This is for you."

"For me?" She picked up the pouch. Untying the strings, she upended it, pouring coins onto the table. She looked at him. "Cousin, what is this for?"

His grin softened. "I have always understood young women wish to wear a new garment," he laid a hand on top of hers, "for their betrothal."

Her brows climbed to her scalp; she felt warmth spreading in her heart. "You…" her throat felt parched; she took a drink before continuing. "You mean…?"

"Yes," he smiled. "Deagah approached me on behalf of Kalev with a formal offer of marriage for you. Hadassah, are you still willing?"

Her eyes met her cousin's gaze, but her thoughts were elsewhere. *Maman! Baba! It has happened! Kalev ben Deagah has offered for me. Me! Your estra—your little star—is going to be a bride!*

"Hadassah?" her cousin placed his hand on hers and gently squeezed. "Are you still willing?"

She focused on him, her eyes shining. "Yes," she smiled, "I am willing."

"Wonderful!" Mordecai embraced her. "I felt it was such but wanted to confirm once again. Deagah and I have decided to set the betrothal ceremony after Passover. That will give Yintl time to plan a celebration banquet and you time to sew a new garment."

He embraced her again, "I know your parents would be happy, as I am. Mazal tov, Hadassah. May Yahweh bless you with many children. Because of you, our family will not end."

CHAPTER 23

16 FARVARDIN
THIRD YEAR OF THE REIGN OF XERXES,
KING OF THE MEDES AND THE PERSIANS

"My Lord King," Haman said.

Xerxes did not respond.

The King was seated on the golden Throne of the King of Persia, his hands resting on the heads of golden Lamassu intricately carved onto each arm of the Throne, with a massive tapestry of the Shahbaz woven in threads of gold and red behind him. He wore comfortable clothing; a red tunic and trousers, trimmed in gold, a golden cap on his head, and pointed red shoes on his feet. Yet, the King's dark gaze was focused on something beyond Haman, beyond his Cup-bearer, beyond the Throne Room.

Haman glanced at Kurush Tars Dida standing at a nearby table. He was dressed in a white tunic and trousers like the other servants, but his garments were made from finely-woven linen with gold thread edging the hems. The Cup-bearer was pouring red wine from an amphora into a beaten gold goblet shaped like a long horn of gold resting on a crouching Lamassu.

Kurush lifted white brows, shaking his head slightly. He set the amphora on the table, walked up the steps, and crossed the platform to the Throne. He extended the cup to Xerxes. "My Lord King, here is your wine."

"Huh?" Xerxes startled and looked up at the elderly man and then down at the goblet. "Oh...ah, yes...thank you, Kurush," he took the cup and looked at Haman. "What were you saying, Hazarpatish?"

"I was giving you the morning report. My Lord King, if I might comment, you appear..." Haman paused, "unsettled."

"You speak truth," Xerxes stared into the wine. "I am unsettled."

"May we know the cause?" Kurush asked.

"My son, Artaxerxes."

"Is there something wrong with the Puora Vaspuhr?" Haman asked. "Is he ill? Should I call for the Royal Physicians or the magi?"

"No," Xerxes lifted a hand. "It has nothing to do with his health. Last night I informed him of the proclamation concerning V—" the King's mouth pulled down as if he had tasted a morsel of week-old fish, "his mother. He was quite distraught, pleading for her. I stayed with him until the Second Watch, when he fell asleep."

Haman glanced at the Cup-bearer—who shrugged slightly—and then back to Xerxes. "My Lord King... *she* has been—" he spread his hands wide. "Nothing can be done to undo the Law."

"I know," the King filled his lungs and exhaled. "I tried to explain that to my son, but he is just a child; he did not understand. Despite how she treated him, Artaxerxes still loved her.

"I cannot fathom how...*she*," he spit out the word, "could be so selfish. Even when he was an infant, she did not want to have Artaxerxes around her; she left his care to others. She was his mother!

"My own mother," he laid an opened palm against his chest, "has loved me and cared for me like no other person. When my father, King Darius, was selecting his heir, my mother convinced him I had the best claim to the Throne of Persia.

"Kurush," he turned to the older man, "you remember; you were Cup-bearer to my father. Had it not been for my mother, the Throne would have gone to one of my brothers or half-brothers."

"I do remember, My Lord King." Kurush bowed his head. "Your mother the Queen was quite persuasive."

"My mother was there for me as a prince and now—as King— she has helped oversee the running of my Palaces, offered me advice, and acted as my Regent when I was away fighting the Egyptians. Now, even in her...*confusion*," he frowned, "she loves me still. Artaxerxes needs someone who will love him in the same way."

Haman controlled his features. *Now.* "Queen Atossa is an example to all of a loving mother. My wife is a loving mother to our children. One day, my daughter Navjaa will follow the example of Queen Atossa and will be a loving mother as well."

"Your daughter—" Xerxes said and then frowned, looking beyond Haman's shoulder.

Haman turned to see a Warrior walking into the Throne Room. Grinding his teeth, he walked down the steps and met him. "Teresh pur Ashoor, what is it?"

The Warrior saluted Xerxes and then Haman. "My Lord King," he turned back to Xerxes, "your Azam are in the Outer Court. They said you summoned them."

"I did summon them," Xerxes replied. "Bring them in."

Teresh saluted again. "At once, My Lord King," he turned to walk toward the Outer Court.

Haman resumed his place next to the King. "I was not aware you sent for your Azam."

"I forgot to mention it; I was distracted by..." Xerxes frowned, "the other matters. After yesterday's *incident* in the Outer Court, I wanted to assure my Azam that all was well between us. And I thought to ask their advice on my son's dilemma."

As the Azam walked into the room, Haman moved to the edge of the platform. When the King's advisors reached the foot of the stairs, they bowed, cupped hands in front of their mouths.

"Greetings to my Azam," Xerxes said. "You may approach."

The seven men walked up the stairs and bowed once again.

"My Lord King," Karshena said, "you summoned us. How may we serve you?"

"As my advisors and my friends," Xerxes said, "I wish to speak with you about my son, Artaxerxes." The King retold the story how distraught the young prince was over the loss of his mother. "In a few days, we are leaving for Greece. Without a mother to travel with, Artaxerxes will not accompany us. Yet, I do not want my son to spend the rest of his life without a mother. I need your advice."

"My Lord King," Shethar said, "Prince Artaxerxes has his grandmother, Queen Atossa, to care for him."

"My mother loves my son," Xerxes said, "but she is elderly and not…in full strength. My son needs a mother who is young; one who—when he is King—will sit on the Queen's Throne next to him as the Malekeh Jahann. Beyond Artaxerxes, my subjects need a Queen to represent the future of Persia." Xerxes' brows lowered. "I *need* a Queen."

"My Lord King, you have other wives," Admatha said. "Could you not choose one of your other wives to be Queen."

Xerxes shook his head. "My wives are mothers to my other children. They are caring for *their* own children; none have expressed concern for Artaxerxes. Moreover, I cannot know whether any of them might have been influenced by…*her*. I need someone who will respect me as well as love and care for Artaxerxes—and protect him—as my mother loves and cares for me.

Haman leaned toward the Throne to whisper, "Just as Navjaa would love—"

"My Lord King," Tarshish interrupted, "I have a solution. Let the King send word to the Shathapavans of his Empire to bring all the beautiful young women from their satrapies to the Royal Citadel to enter the Royal harem. Let these young women be placed under the care of Hegai, the King's eunuch, who is in charge of the women. Let beauty treatments be given to them—"

"Azam Tarshish is wise," Panjbaare tabar Merse interjected. "By doing this, instead of choosing from the women in your harem, you can choose from one of these new women to be your Queen. These women will not have had access to V—"

The Azam around him shook their heads, and Merse swallowed hard.

"These women not have been *influenced* by Prince Artaxerxes' mother," he continued. "They will respect the King."

"Azam Merse speaks wisdom," Tarshish said. "When you choose a new Queen from outside the harem, she will set a royal example for all women to honor their husbands."

No! Haman fought to control his expression. *This cannot happen.* "My Lord King—" his words were cut short by Xerxes' lifted hand.

"A new Queen choosen from outside the harem." The King stroked his beard, "Hmm…" he looked at his Cup-bearer, who nodded, and then at his Azam. Then Xerxes nodded. "That is a good idea. Yes," he smiled, "I *will* choose a new Queen. You, my seven Azam, are to arrange this." He pointed to the Royal Scribes seated at a table with writing implements and sheets of parchment. "Let this be written down."

"My Lord King," Haman said, "are you certain—"

"What qualities do you wish for these women?" Marsena asked.

Haman tried again, "My Lord King—" but was cut off when Haftordak pur Memukan said,

"They must be maidens."

Haman opened his mouth again when Shethar added, "They must be pretty."

"Not just *pretty*," Admatha sneered. "Any man can have a *pretty* wife. These women must be beautiful."

"Yes!" Xerxes hit the Lamassu with his fist. "They must be beautiful; even more beautiful than Vashti. My Queen must be the most beautiful woman in the Empire."

Too late, Haman swallowed a sigh, watching control of the situation slip away from him like a boulder rolling down a mountain.

"How do we choose these women?" Yekpeesee asked. "A

proclamation? Do we go to each house in Susa and command them to bring out their beautiful maiden daughters?"

"Why would we need to command them?" Tarshish asked. "What young maiden would not wish to be Queen?"

"Scribes, in the letters to my Shathapavans," Xerxes said, "inform them they are to choose the beautiful maidens in their own satrapies however they wish and send them to my harem here in the Royal Citadel of Susa. You, my Azam," he waved a hand toward the men, "will decide how to select them here in Susa."

"My Lord King," Merse said, "what day are you and the Army leaving for Greece?"

Xerxes turned to Haman, "The date is soon, is it not?"

"Uhm, yes," Haman said. "I have met with General Otanes. The plans are nearly complete; the supply wagons and war towers have already been sent ahead of us. Within a few days, all will be ready for you to lead the Army out of Susa."

"My Lord King, will there be a parade," Marsena asked, "to see you and your Army off?"

"Yes," Xerxes said. "My people will see me in my chariot, as well as the scared Chariot of Ahura Mazda to invite our god to accompany the Persian Army into battle."

"We," Memukan indicated the other advisors, "will be in the streets for the parade. All the people of Susa will be there to watch you and your Warriors pass. We will follow with some of the Warriors who will be left to guard the Royal Citadel, and we will select the young women from Susa at that time."

"My Lord King—" Haman tried once more, but Xerxes cut him off.

"This is a good idea. Let the beautiful maidens from Susa—and the ones from the other satrapies—be placed under the care of Hegai, the King's eunuch who is in charge of my harem.

"I expect it will take about one year for me and my Warriors to travel to Greece, defeat their Army, and return. This will allow Hegai time to make sure these maidens have gone through their twelve months of preparations. When I return," he smiled, "I will begin the process of choosing a new Queen."

CHAPTER 24

"Yes, My Lord King," Azam Memukan bowed to Xerxes, "we will see the Gathering of the Maidens is done as you wish."

Haman escorted him and the other advisors from the Throne Room.

"Sir, if you would stay a moment," he said and beckoned to one of the Warriors in the corridor. "Teresh, once you have escorted the Azam to the door of the Palace, return to me. I need to send a message to my family and messages to The Six."

The Warrior bowed his head, "Yes Hazarpatish."

Haman turned back to the King's advisor, "Azam Memukan, I would speak to you about," he lowered his voice, "...about my daughter, Navjaa."

Chapter 25

18 Farvardin
Third year of the reign of Xerxes,
King of the Medes and the Persians

"Friends, thank you for coming," Rabbi Omar said as Mordecai, Deagah, David ben Asher, Hakaliah bar Seraiah, and Nahum ben Tekoa—the Elders of the Jewish community in Susa—settled on the cushions. "I have called you today because Deagah learned more about the situation between King Xerxes and the deposed Queen Vashti."

Mordecai looked at Deagah, who nodded, as the Rabbi continued.

"He felt this is something might affect us all. Deagah, please share what you have learned."

The merchant stood. "Thank you, Rabbi Omar. My friends, as the Elders of the Synagogue, we believe we are to be diligent with the events within our own community and to stay out of what is happening within the walls of the Royal Citadel. However, Yintl learned something that, as Rabbi Omar said, might affect us all.

"Yesterday, wives of two of the King's Azam came to our shop. Yintl overheard these women discussing the King and the deposed Queen.

138

"It appears the King called for his Azam to discuss this situation. The King was concerned about not having a Queen and how that will affect the Empire and his son, Prince Artaxerxes, who misses his mother and will one day need a Malekeh Jahann."

"I thought," Hakaliah bar Seraiah spoke up, "King Xerxes would select a Queen from one of the women in his harem."

"That is what we all thought," Deagah said. "However, it appears the Azam gave Xerxes other advice." He let out a long sigh. "They advised the King to bring all the beautiful young maidens from across the Empire into his harem here in Susa. Once the King returns from fighting the Greeks, he will choose a new Queen from among these women."

"What?" As one, the men in the room stood, demanding:

"He cannot mean to pick a wife as if she were a pomegranate on a tree."

"How will these women be chosen? When will it happen?"

"Our daughters are Xerxes' subjects, not his slaves."

"I do not want my daughter to become wife to a Gentile, even a Gentile King,"

"What can we do?"

"How can we protect our daughters?"

"Does anyone know somewhere we can send our daughters until this threat is passed?"

"Friends, friends," the Rabbi patted the air, "please be calm." He waited until the men quieted before continuing. "Yintl did not hear details of when or how this will happen. All she heard was, once the King returns, he will choose a new Queen. For now, all we can do is warn our families."

CHAPTER 26

"Hadassah, I have seen many pieces of linen in our family's shop, but I have never seen any as beautiful as this." Miriam smoothed her hand over the fabric. "The color looks like peacock feathers."

"I agree." Hadassah put the fabric in the basket she carried. "I will begin sewing the garment tomorrow. I should have it finished before Passover."

"Just think," Miriam linked arms, "once you and Kalev are married, we will be sisters."

"I always wanted a sister," Hadassah squeezed Miriam's hand. "Soon, my dearest friend will become my dearest sister."

Miriam blinked away a tear. "Did you purchase everything you need?"

"Well, at least most," she tucked a cover over the basket. "I think we can find the rest in the shops on the way back to your home."

The two girls walked through the Marketplace, stopping to buy a comb for Miriam, a bar of fragrant soap and a length of ribbon for Hadassah, until they came to the shop of Hakaliah bar Seraiah. The goldsmith was not present, but Hanani was showing a tray of rings to a young man, and Naomi was wrapping a gold bracelet for a woman. Nehemiah was straightening a display of necklaces.

Naomi finished with her customer. "I hope you will come to our shop again," and turned to the girls. "Greetings, Hadassah, Miriam. It is a beautiful day, is it not?"

After exchanging greetings and commenting on the weather, Hadassah said, "I assume Mar Hakaliah is at the synagogue with the other Elders?"

"Yes, he is with the men," the older woman said, "although the Rabbi's message did not explain the reason for the summons." She frowned. "This is not the regular day for the Elders to meet. I hope they finish soon; we have many customers and could use—what is that?" She cut off her words as the sound of a trumpet fanfare filled the air.

Hadassah and Miriam, along with other people in the Marketplace, turned toward the street.

"*Ooof!*" Hadassah gasped as a group of boys ran past them close enough to jostle her, cheering, laughing, and waving their hands.

Miriam grasped Hadassah's forearm to steady her. "Are you alright?"

She nodded. "I am fine." She smoothed her garment and straightened her head covering.

Another group of boys ran past followed by men and women—some singly, others in groups—all moving toward the Royal Citadel and the growing sound of trumpet fanfare.

Hadassah looked at Miriam, a question on her face. Her friend grinned and nodded. They joined the crowd, arriving near the Great Gate just as six large animals walked through and turned onto the street.

"Baba! Maman! Look!" a small boy near them pointed. "Elephants!"

The elephants had leather straps mounted with spikes wrapped around their tusks. The spikes, along with the *howdahs*—the canopied saddles filled with archers on their backs—identified these animals as trained war elephants.

The crowd cheered as Hadassah realized what they were

seeing; King Xerxes and the Persian Army were leaving Susa to fight the Greeks.

Following the elephants came rank and file of different units of Warriors, all wearing thick, protective clothing, scale armor over embroidered tunics and trousers, and thick caps covering their heads. The archers carried short bows with quivers of arrows strapped on their backs. The *cataphract*—the calvary—followed, the horses covered in thick padding and the Warriors carrying two spears.

Next through the Great Gate marched The Immortals. These legendary Warriors carried thick shields covered in leather, swords, short spears, or large daggers.

Several boys next to Hadassah and Miriam picked up thick sticks and imitated The Immortals marching and then turned to hit each other's sticks, yelling battle cries.

"Baba," a small boy tugged at his father's sleeve and pointed to an elaborate golden chariot, "why is that chariot empty?" Drawn by eight white horses, the charioteer walked behind the chariot, holding the horses' reins.

"Son, bow your head," the man put his hand on the child's head, tipped his face downward, and showed him how to lift a cupped hand to his mouth. "It is the sacred chariot of Ahura Mazda. Dedicated to the creator, it is an invitation for the god to accompany the King and the Army to war. No mortal is allowed to ride in that chariot."

As the golden chariot passed, a trumpet fanfare rang out again. The crowd cried out, "The King! The King!"

Hadassah smiled at Miriam, her eyes wide. She had grown up outside the city walls of Susa and had never had an opportunity to see the King. The two girls turned their gaze back to the street as several dozen trumpeters marched out of the Great Gate followed by the Royal Chariot.

The crowd rippled as people bowed—hands covering their mouths—when the large, scythed war-chariot passed. Drawn by four white horses with bells clanging from their harnesses, it had a golden Lamassu painted on each side of the chariot with a golden Shahbaz emblazoned on the front.

"Hadassah, look at the wheels," Miriam pointed. "Those look like swords attached to the axels. Do you think it is for decoration?"

"I do not think so. Look at how the blades spin when the chariot moves. Anyone near those wheels when the chariot was at full speed would be cut down by the spinning swords."

The charioteer, dressed in red and fully armed, was seated above the turret seat. Behind him stood Xerxes in full battle regalia.

The King's battle-robe was constructed of thick wool dyed red with elaborate golden embroidery and secured by a leather belt. A wide golden band around his head, the Royal Scepter in one hand, and the Royal Sword tucked behind his belt, he looked as fearsome as the battle-hardened Warriors that marched ahead of him.

That is King Xerxes. Hadassah watched as he slowly turned his head from side to side, acknowledging the bows and adulation of his subjects. When his gaze passed over her, she felt a shiver go up her spine. *He looks fierce. What was it like for Baba and Mar Hakaliah to be in the King's presence?*

The boys lifted their stick swords to hold them against their chests in a salute to the King.

On either side of the Royal Chariot was a Warrior on horseback. One Warrior was taller than the King, a hardened expression crowned by gray hair and beard. The other was of average height and build, with dark eyes, a hooked nose, and a frown in a black beard streaked with gray—appeared older than the King. The garments of these two were similar to the other Warriors, but the golden armor around their chests and the tall, pointed golden helmet with a red horse-hair crest on top identified them as officers.

Another unit of Immortals marched behind the Royal Chariot. As the last of the Warriors marched out of sight, the crowd began dispersing in various directions. The boys dropped their sticks and followed their parents, chattering about seeing the

King and one day becoming an Immortal. Some people returned to the Marketplace; others walked away from the Marketplace, carrying their purchases. The street filled with people on foot, on horseback, in carriages, and wagons.

"That was exciting," Miriam said as she and Hadassah turned toward the direction of her family's shop. "I saw the King when he left for his tour of the Empire, but I have never seen so many Warriors. The Army appears able to conquer any enemy."

"I agree," Hadassah nodded. "With so many Warriors and all the weapons of war, I can see how other nations are afraid to face the Persian Army. King Xerxes looked so fier—" her words were cut off by a young woman screaming,

"No! *Manadari*—stepmother—please do not leave me. Let me go. Someone help me. Please!"

Turning, they saw a large wagon near the Great Gate. A man who—from his clothing and sword, appeared to be a Warrior—held a young woman by the arm. She squirmed, trying to wrest free from his grasp, as he led—almost dragging—her to the wagon where stood an older man dressed in rich raiment. Coming from other directions were other Warriors, also leading young women; some screaming for help, others crying.

No one appeared to be responding to the pleas from these women. No one was calling for the Superintendent of Police to help them. Several people approached them—but after a comment from the man directing the Warriors, as well as a glance at the swords in the Warriors' hands—they turn away.

As Hadassah listened and watched, her gaze turned inward. She was no longer near the Great Gate in Susa. She was in the garden near her home, reliving the nightmare filled with angry cries, terrified screams, pleas, groans, and *thuds*.

"No." Her face tightened. "Never again."

"What is happening?" Miriam asked. "Why is no one helping them?"

"I do not know," Hadassah said. "Here," she gave her basket to

Miriam. "Go to the synagogue. Tell my cousin and your father—tell all who are with them—what is happening."

"What are you going to do?"

Hadassah stooped to pick up one of the large sticks the boys had dropped. "I am going to help those women."

"Hadassah, you cannot—"

"Yes, Miriam, I can and I will! Now go!"

Turning, she ran across the street toward the wagon by the Great Gate. As she neared the closest Warrior and the screaming women, she lifted the stick and brought it down on the back of the man's head. Blood gushed from the resulting wound.

"Aieee!" In a single movement, the man dropped the woman's arm, drew his sword, and spun.

Hadassah froze, her gaze fixed on the sword's blade a finger's width from her throat.

The young woman, now free from his grasp, started running but was intercepted by another Warrior who grabbed her around the waist.

"Stop!" the man in the rich raiment shouted.

The wounded Warrior shot hatred from his eyes toward Hadassah as if it were an arrow.

The other man, obviously accustomed to being obeyed, approached. "Lower your sword."

"She struck me," the Warrior growled.

The man stepped between them and faced the Warrior. "I said, *Lower your sword.*"

The Warrior's grasp tightened around the hilt before he saluted, stepped back, and sheathed his sword. But his gaze never left Hadassah. He grasped the corner of a black cloth tucked into his belt and pulled it out to wipe the blood from his face and the back of his head.

The man in the rich raiment addressed Hadassah. "What are you doing?"

"What am I doing?" Her heart was racing. "Who are you and what are you doing to these women?"

145

"Who am I?" The man drew himself up. "I am Haftordak tabar Memukan," he said, "one of the King's Azam. And I am overseeing the Gathering of the Maidens on behalf of King Xerxes. We are taking all the beautiful young maidens to the Palace. Hmm…" He took a step back, his eyes focused on her, studying her face, her figure. "You are a beauty." He turned to the Warrior. "Take her."

Hadassah's eyes widened. "What?" She took a step backwards. "No!"

The Warrior smiled, and not pleasantly. Before she could turn, he grabbed her arm.

"Let me go!" she squirmed as the other young woman had and with as little success. "What are you doing?"

"So many questions. As I explained," Azam Memukan said, "this is the Gathering of the Maidens. We are gathering all the beautiful young maidens throughout the Empire. One more thing," the man added. "Are you a maiden?"

"What?" she gasped, color high in her cheeks. "How dare you ask such a question! Of course I am a maiden."

He dismissed her outrage with a wave of his hand. "You are a maiden and you are beautiful. That is sufficient. You are coming with us."

"No!" she screamed, "I do not wish to go!"

The Azam shrugged his shoulders. "Your wishes matter not." He spoke as lightly as if he were commenting on the weather. "When King Xerxes returns from Greece, he will select a new Queen from these women."

"I do not want to be Queen!" She jerked her arm, trying to twist out of the Warrior's grasp. "I am to be betrothed within a few weeks."

"That will not happen now.

"Stop! Let go of her!"

Hadassah turned to see Nehemiah, followed by Hanani, running across the street. As her friends reached them, one of the other Warriors kicked Nehemiah in the midsection, knocking him down.

Before Nehemiah even hit the ground, the Warrior held a sword to his throat, while another held a sword to Hanani.

"No!" Hadassah screamed.

"Stop! Release her!" She looked to see Mordecai, Deagah, and the other Elders running toward them.

At a gesture from the Azam, another Warrior stepped between the men and Hadassah, the sound of metal singing as he drew his sword from the sheath.

"Nooo!" Hadassah screamed. "Please stop!"

Mordecai froze. "What are you doing? Remove your hands from her!" His fists clinched. "You have no right to do this!"

"As to your last comment, my *right* comes from King Xerxes. I am Haftordak tabar Memukan. Ahhh…" the other man smiled, "so you know who I am."

Mordecai nodded. "You are one of the King's Azam. What are you doing with these other women?"

"They are going to the Palace, along with the other beautiful maidens throughout the Empire. Once the King returns, he will choose one of them as his new Queen."

"What?! No!" Mordecai's eyes blazed. "I demand you release her!"

Memukan lifted an eyebrow. "You…*demand?* Are you her father?"

"No. Her parents are dead. I am—" he glanced from the Azam to the Warriors, "her physician."

"Physician?" the Azam frowned. "Does she have a disease that could be passed on to the King?"

Mordecai shook his head. "It is not a disease. I am a Gyah Pezeshk. She requires special food and herbs to ease her stomach. I have provided them to her since she was a child."

Memukan dismissed it with a flick of his hand. "She will be eating food from the Palace."

"It is not the same. She needs the food I prepare."

"She can ask the Chief Eunuch. Perhaps you will be allowed to continue providing this food."

Mordecai moved to get past the Azam but stopped at the sword lifted to his throat by another Warrior.

"Oh no!" Hadassah screamed.

"Think carefully, Gyah Pezeshk," the Azam frowned. "If you die, who will bring her special food and herbs?"

Hadassah looked at Mordecai—eyes wide—and shook her head.

Mordecai forced his fists open and filled his lungs. "May I have a moment to speak with her…about the foods she should eat until other arrangements can be made with the Chief Eunuch?"

"Certainly," the Azam turned to the Warrior. "Give the woman a moment with her physician, then put her in the wagon with the other maidens."

Mordecai stepped to Hadassah.

"Mordecai!" she gasped. "What can we—"

His upraised hand stopped her. He watched until the Azam walked away. The bleeding Warrior remained within a few paces, waiting. Mordecai turned to her, bending close and speaking in a low voice. "Are you hurt?"

She shook her head. "What can we do?"

"There is nothing we can do now. No—" he said when she sobbed, "we do not have time for tears. You must be careful, so very careful. The King and the Army have only just left. That means Haman is with them, but we have to assume he has people—spies—in the Palace. Say nothing to anyone about who you are or who your family was."

"I do not want to go," Hadassah sniffed. "I am afraid."

His gaze softened, "I know. Do not give up hope. Remember what your parents told you—*You can do hard things.*"

He raised his voice when a Warrior drew near. "*Esther dokhtar Bunyamin,*" he spoke her name using the Persian form, "do not be concerned about what you will eat. I will come every day, to bring you food." Glancing at the Warriors and the Azam, he dropped his voice and spoke quickly. "I *will* bring you food every morning. I will ask the Royal Eunuch, but I do not think they will allow me to see you. Until I know differently, every night, I will stand here, near the Great Gate. I will hold up my lantern. From what I understand, the House of Women is in a position that you should see the light and know I am here and you are not alone.

"Even if Xerxes defeats the Greeks quickly, it will take months—perhaps a year—before he returns to Susa. In the meantime, we will pray for wisdom. Always remember, Yahweh—*The One True God*—is with you."

"We *must* think of something," she said. "I would rather *perish* than be part of the King's Harem."

"Shhh!" Mordecai glanced around. "Do not say that! You are the last of our family. If you perish, your father's house perishes with you."

CHAPTER 27

"What just happened?"

"Was that Azam Memukan, one of the King's closest advisors?"

"Is this what Deagah was telling us about earlier? Were those men selecting young women to be taken into the King's Harem?"

"I need to go home and check on my daughters."

"We need to warn the other families in our community."

"What can be done for Hadassah and the other young women?"

"We can go to the Palace and demand they be released."

"Demand?!" A vein throbbed above Mordecai's eye. He thrust a hand toward Nehemiah. "You saw what happened to Nehemiah and to me. We have no authority; going to the Palace to *demand* anything would result with swords held at our throats…or worse."

"Something must be done!"

The cacophony of questions and demands echoed around the room until Rabbi Omar called, "Friends! Please!"

The men—the Elders as well as Nehemiah and Hanani—turned toward him. Tension pervaded the room.

"Please," the Rabbi patted the air, "I realize this situation is of great concern, not only to Mordecai, but also to—" he glanced at Deagah, *"others*. Please sit; we need calm in order to determine what this means and what can be done."

The men sat on the cushions, clasped their hands—knuckles white—and waited.

The Rabbi turned to Mordecai. "What are your thoughts on how we can help Hadassah?"

Mordecai lifted a hand toward the Rabbi—his throat tight— as he gathered his thoughts. After a moment, he lowered his hand and looked at the men. "Right now, I do not know what can be done. I told Azam Memukan that I am Hadassah's physician— which I am," he added as several men lifted their eyebrows. "I do not know the inner workings of the Palace. I do know *Haman*—" he spit, "ordered the death of Abihail, Atarah, and their servants. That *Amalekite* left with Xerxes this morning, but I am certain he has spies within the Palace. As a precaution, I instructed Hadassah to not use her Jewish name nor say anything about her family or her people."

Chapter 28

Haman lifted the tent flap and walked in, carefully watching the burning fire stick he held as he lit the oil lamps placed inside the tent. Removing his armor and clothing, he set them near his bed; a thick pallet on the ground. After examining and cleaning his armor and weapons, he walked to sit by a low table that held scrolls, a stack of parchment, and writing tools. Even though the Army had been riding since they left Susa that morning, there would always be reports he needed to read and determine whether to share with the King.

After the reports were finished, he reached for a sheet of parchment. Lifting the lid of a small container, he dipped a quill into the ink and began writing.

> *Zeresh,*
> *After traveling seven leagues today, the Army is encamped for the evening. The King, General Otanes, and I are pleased with our speed; moving 150,000 Warriors—in addition to the animals, the supply wagons, and the war towers—is not an easy task. If all goes according to plan, we should arrive in Greece about 12 Mordad. The Persian Navy's triremes sail faster than we can walk; they should reach Greece before the Army.*

As Dalphon will deliver this message to you, you will know I arranged with the King for him and our other sons— Parmashta, Adalia, Parshandatha, and Vaizatha—to carry messages between the King and the Army to those in Susa and the Palace. With other Warriors sending messages to their families, my communication with you and Navjaa will not seem unusual.

I saw Navjaa in the crowd as the Army left Susa today; by now she should be in the Royal Harem. Soon, the young maidens from the other satrapies will begin arriving. As my wife and her mother, you will be able to visit Navjaa whenever you wish. Remind her to become friends with the daughters of The Six and to tell you if she hears of anything unusual happening in the Palace.

I will be responsible for reading the correspondence from the Shathapavans, messages from the Palace, as well as correspondence from Hegai and Shaashgaz concerning the new maidens and the King's family. I will use my messages to direct our plans as I am able. Navjaa will be able do what she can from inside the Harem.

If all goes according to plan, Navjaa will either be friends with the next Queen, or she will become Queen.

Haman

CHAPTER 29

"Maman, Baba," she whispered, "I am alone. I am frightened." Esther drew a shuttering breath. "I cannot believe what has happened."

"I have lost you and our home. I have lost my life with Mordecai and the chance of a life with Kalev. I have even lost my *name* and my *heritage*. I cannot tell anyone I am your daughter, and I cannot not tell anyone that I am Jewish. I know you would tell me not to be afraid and to remember that *Yahweh* is with me, that *you* are with me. But, to speak truth…I feel alone.

"Why is this happening to me? Why did *The One* allow this? What sin did I commit that He is punishing me this way?"

She looked around the apartment assigned to her. Even being the daughter of a wealthy family, this room was more opulent than any she had ever seen. The walls and floors were covered with vibrantly-colored tapestries and rugs. The furniture—chairs, chests, and a low table—were carved from rich wood. Her bed—instead of being a pallet on a wooden frame—was a long, intricately carved divan, with a taller curved arm rest on one side and thick cushion and pillows on top. In the corner was a large cabinet for storing her clothing.

It was all so beautiful, but it was all so foreign; just like the rest of the Royal Citadel.

Born in Susa, she had walked past the Great Gate many times but had never gone through it and onto the grounds of the Royal Citadel. Not until today, when she was placed in the wagon with the other frightened young women.

Including the woman she tried to rescue, there were a dozen like them them in the wagon. All were clutching each other, all were crying. The wagoner had joined a long line of other wagons—each filled with wailing and screaming women—and drove up to the Palace built by King Darius.

White-robed servants waited to hand them out of the wagons and escort them up a long flight of wide steps—passing enameled terra-cotta pictures of towering Warriors dressed in saffron-colored clothing and holding fierce weapons—before turning to continue up another flight of steps, across a broad terrace, to the massive double doors of the Palace. Dozens of Warriors—dressed like those in the paintings and armed with spears and swords—barely glanced at them as they walked through the doors, almost as if it were a common occurrence for throngs of weeping and screaming women to enter the Palace.

Yahweh, help me. She glanced around her, plotting an escape. *There are so many people; help me slip away unnoticed.*

She estimated how far she could run, when armed Warriors stepped in front of and behind each group of young women. One Warrior near her group had a fresh gash on the back of his head; blood still oozed from the wound. Turning, his eyes narrowed when he saw her, his mouth thinned into a smug smile.

Her heart dropped. *There is no escape.* Drawing a shuddering breath, her eyes misting, she followed the other women walking across the Great Hall.

She stared wide-eyed around her, countless lanterns illuminating massive columns and statues that made the tallest Warrior seem like a child, reminding her of the story of King David fighting Goliath.

Before they reached the corridor on the far side, a man's

muffled scream, "No, please no!" echoed through the Great Hall.

She and the other women stared at the wretch—his arms bound, his head wrapped in a large black cloth—being dragged across the floor by two armed Warriors.

Gasps rippled around the room as Esther realized what was happening. Being bound and dragged out of the Palace identified the man as a criminal. The black cloth around his head identified him as having been found guilty of a capital crime. The Warriors were taking him to the Gate of Eternity, a broad field in the center of the Susa Marketplace where public punishments took place. It was common to have dozens of people being executed in various heinous ways, including the most gruesome—impalement.

The Warrior with the gash on his head looked back at her, grinning as his hand slid down to finger the black cloth—now covered in his own blood—hanging from his belt.

She turned from his gaze, her heart pounding, as she continued walking across the Great Hall.

The Palace seemed to never end. Servants and Warriors escorted the groups of women down an interminable corridor past myriad rooms, fountains, and courtyards with countless lanterns illuminating floors inlaid with colorful mosaics and walls embellished with lofty paintings of Kings and Warriors, the royal falcon, the flying lion, and flowers. Reaching the end of one corridor, they turned and continued down yet another Warrior-lined corridor which ended at a small, opened door at the end—at least it appeared small compared to the other doors Esther had seen. On this door was carved the Royal Lamassu.

One side of the door featured a painting of a man wearing a crown accompanied by two servants, one of whom was beardless. Below the painting, a man sat at a table with stacks of papyrus and writing implements in front of him. He was dressed as the other servants, but like the man in the painting, his face and skin was hairless. Although she had never seen one, she believed this man was a eunuch.

The man did not look up from his writing. "Yes?" his voice was high and soft.

One of the men escorting their group stepped forward. "Here is another group of women sent from Azam Memukan."

The eunuch looked up from his writing and glanced at them, his eyes widening briefly when he saw Esther. She felt as if she were a horse being considered for the marketplace. After a moment, he nodded to their escorts, "You may go."

The eunuch drew a new sheet of papyrus in front of himself, lifted his stylus, and dipped it into an inkwell. He gestured to the first woman in their group to approach the table. "What is your name?" he asked.

The woman hesitated and then whispered, "Farah dokhtar Mahboubeh."

He wrote her name, then extended a hand toward the opened door. "Be welcome to the House of Women, Farah dokhtar Mahboubeh."

One by one, the women gave their names then walked through the door, until only she remained. The eunuch beckoned her to approach the table. "What is your name?"

She glanced at the Warriors lining the corridor. Even if she made it passed them, the path throughout the Palace was long and convoluted. *Yahweh help me; I have no choice.* Taking a deep breath, she said, "I am called Esther dokhtar Bunyamin."

He wrote down her name and then extended a hand toward the opened door. "Be welcome to the House of Women, Esther dokhtar Bunyamin."

Esther stepped through the door and into the Courtyard of the House of Women.

Like the other parts of the Palace Esther had seen, this courtyard was massive. Even filled with women, it was larger than any house she had ever been in before. The floor was a mosaic swirl of red, gold, and silver; the ceiling echoed the pattern and was held up by marble columns with capitals carved like leaves. Pots of fragrant flowers edged the walls, and in the center was a pool with divans and pillows around it.

The fourth side opened to an immense, tiled floor with tall columns placed around the edge. Long, white linen curtains were secured to the columns by thick, braided ropes.

"That is where Queen Vashti held her feast," Esther heard someone say.

Turning, she saw the speaker was a young woman with hair the color of a raven's wing cascading to her waist. Unlike most of the other women, her face was not flushed nor her onyx eyes reddened from crying. She was standing with a group of women who, like her, did not appear upset over their situation.

Servants wandered around the courtyard, offering trays of cups filled with wine or milk, bread, cheese, and various fruit. Most of the women turned down the offer, except the group with the woman who had mentioned Queen Vashti. She and the women with her took goblets of wine and selected morsels of food as they chatted about the beautiful room.

The sound of the door closing drew their attention. The eunuch who had taken their name slid the bolt to the main door into place and turned—holding a stack of parchment—as two older eunuchs entered the courtyard from a long corridor to the left.

They walked to a spot where all in the room could see them. The men's bald heads and faces—and the fact they were inside the House of Women—confirmed Esther belief they were eunuchs. The older eunuchs both wore white tunics and trousers made of fine linen. One appeared older than the other; he wore a thick gold chain around his neck with a large key on the end. Their bearing—and the bows of respect from the other servants— identified them as more than simple servants.

They looked over the women in the courtyard and then the older one spoke. "Greetings and welcome to the House of Women," he said. "I am Hegai Kouroush Safa, but you may address me as Hegai." He lifted a hand toward the man standing next to him. "This is Shaashgaz Javed Farrokh, although you may address him as Shaashgaz." He indicated the man standing on his other side. "This is Mehuman pur Abdolhossein, although you may address him as Mehuman."

A hum buzzed throughout the women; although rarely seen, all knew Hegai was the Chief Eunuch of the Royal Harem, overseeing all the women within the Royal Harem, from the newest maiden to the oldest of the King's secondary wives in the Second House of Women. He had no authority over the Malekeh Jahann or over the Queen, but he saw to their personal needs as well as the care of their apartments and possessions. Shaashgaz Javed Farrokh was the Chief Eunuch of the Second House of Women; he oversaw the care of the *harci*, the King's secondary wives and concubines. Mehuman pur Abdolhossein was the Chief Eunuch of the First House of Women.

"From this day, each of you will be known as a *mastoureh*," he looked over the women in the room, "a maiden in the First House of Women.

"Today will be spent getting all of you settled into the First House of Women." He pointed toward a long corridor on the right. "Down this corridor and to the left is another corridor to that leads to the Second House of Women, where the harci—along with their daughters and any sons too young to go into training for the Army—dwell. You are free to go anywhere you wish within the First or Second Houses of Women and all the garden courtyards."

He pointed toward two staircases behind him, one with a thick red braided rope strung across the first step. "The staircase without the rope leads to the rooftop; you are free to go there. I suggest you try it in the evenings during the warm months; you will find it is pleasant and cool."

He pointed toward the other staircase. "This staircase leads to the King's Apartment. You are not to use this staircase unless I escort you. That will only occur when you are summoned by the

159

King. For those who do not know, it is death for anyone to approach the King if they are not summoned." He paused a moment, looking over the women. "Do you understand?"

The women's eyes widened as they nodded.

"Good," he continued, "then we should have no problems.

"Every woman admitted to the Royal Harem undergoes twelve months of treatments," Hegai continued. "The first six months will be for treatments of special oils to soften your skin. During this time, Qabela dokhtar Somayeh and the other Royal Midwives—who have been trained by the Royal Physicians—will examine you to determine your health. We do not want anyone bringing illness into the Royal Palace.

"The final six months will be training in the application of cosmetics and the use of perfumes, as well as The Training of the Bedchamber."

Esther blushed, realizing Hegai was referencing training in *intimate matters.*

He smiled. "For now, rest and eat. This day will be spent assigning each of you an apartment. Your apartment is yours alone; you will not be sharing it with another woman. In it, you will find clothing and other personal items for you. Let one of the other eunuchs or servants know if you require anything else. Meals will be served either here in the courtyard," he gestured toward the outer area, "in the garden, or—if you wish—in your apartment. Also, let us know if you are trained—or wish to be trained—in dancing, singing, or playing an instrument."

A group of servants entered the Courtyard; each carried musical instruments; cymbals, reed-pipes, and—Esther's eyes brightened—several harps.

After Hegai finished, she hurried toward the servants holding the harps. She selected a beautiful, dark wood harp, similar in size to hers, with the top carved and painted to look like the tips of peacock feathers. Lifting it to her shoulder, she ran a finger across the strings; the rich tone lingered in the air.

The harp sat next to her in her apartment. "Maman, Baba," she whispered, "I wish you could hear me play this harp. I wish Mordecai could hear it…wait!" her eyes widened.

"Every night, I will hold up my lantern," he had told her. *"You should see the light and know I am here and you are not alone."*

Lifting the harp, she left her apartment. Hurrying down the corridor on silent feet, she crossed the courtyard to the staircase without the red rope. She walked up the stairs, which opened to the rooftop. A soft rain was falling

Her family's home, as well as the homes of many people she knew, had a rooftop accessed by a stair from a courtyard. She had spent many warm evenings there with her parents, looking at the stars, gazing across the land, and laughing over the cries of the peacocks.

Even in the rain, she could tell this rooftop was as beautiful as the rest of the Palace. She judged it to be directly over the main courtyard in the House of Women. Tables and divans were placed here and there across the roof's expanse, some under wooden pavilions. The air was perfumed from the fragrant flowers; through the rain, she could see their outline growing in deep urns. A carved parapet on the roof's edge provided the women privacy from anyone who might be looking this way. Near one part of the parapet was a small pavilion.

She tucked the harp under the wide sleeve of her garment and hurried to the parapet. Wiping the rain from her eyes, she squinted, staring across the Palace grounds toward the wall near the Great Gate.

"Mordecai," she whispered, "where are you? I do not—wait!" In the distance, she saw a faint light waving back and forth. *It is him!*

Lifting the harp to her shoulder, she plucked a series of rippling chords. As she did with Mordecai's patients, she chose music that reflected the beating of her heart, the sadness she felt. *Yahweh,* she prayed, *why did You allow this? Why did all this happen to me, to my parents, to our servants? My parents loved You and obeyed you, just like the patriarchs.*

A memory washed over her. "*We have faced challenges,*" Maman had said. "*We know when we face them again, Yahweh will be with us.*"

She lifted her chin. *They can take my home, my clothes, all my possessions; but they cannot take my memories. Maman, Baba, you are with me, always in my heart and memories. Yahweh, like my parents taught me, no matter what I face, You are always with me.*

She played a series of running chords and began softly singing the words Yahweh spoke to Joshua. "Have I not commanded you? Be strong and courageous. Do not be afraid; do not be discouraged, for the LORD your God will be with you wherever you go."

She felt something like a waterfall wash over her spirit. She continued singing, "I will not be afraid, I will not be discouraged; for You are with me."

Chapter 30

Mordecai swiped at the rain blowing against his face. Thunder rolled in the distance. "Thank you for coming with me, Kalev."

"You are welcome," Kalev said, "but I did not come for your sake; I came for Hadassah's sake."

"We share the same purpose. Stop," he extended a hand. "This is the place." Mordecai glanced up and down the street; it was not surprising to see it was empty. No one would venture out on such a night.

"I do not see any Warriors guarding the Great Gate," Kalev said.

"They are probably inside, where it is dry. You stay here," Mordecai said, "I will check. They are accustomed to seeing me out at night."

Lifting his lantern, he walked to the Great Gate and looked inside. Four Warriors stood, holding their hands toward a broad urn in which a fire flickered. He stepped inside where the men could see him. "Greetings."

One Warrior glanced up and nodded. "Greetings, Mordecai ben Jair. Are you attending a patient on such a night?"

"Yes, Safa Yazdan Jafari," Mordecai nodded at the other Warriors, "I am. No matter what the weather or time of day, physicians must attend their patients."

"Well, you need not fear being bothered by anyone," the Warrior said. "With this storm, the streets have been emptied since sunset."

"That is good to hear. Hopefully, I will not be long."

Walking back, Mordecai handed Kalev the dome-shaped lantern, while relaying the Warrior's comments.

Kalev used leather straps to secure the handle of the lantern to the curved end of a long shepherd's staff. While Mordecai turned to watch the street, Kalev lifted the staff up until the burning lantern was above the top of the wall. He began moving it gently side to side.

Mordecai began praying. "Yahweh, be with her," he whispered. "Yahweh, be with her. Please be with her."

"Please with her," Kalev repeated.

"Yahweh, please let her see the light and know we are here."

"Let her know she is—"

"Shh!" Mordecai turned, placing a hand on Kalev's shoulder. "Listen."

The street was filled with the sounds of the rain. Then, across the Palace grounds, came the soft sounds of stringed music.

"It is her!" Mordecai squeezed Kalev's shoulder. "I know that song! Thank you, Yahweh!"

Kalev glanced toward the Great Gate. "Why does the music not draw the Warriors?"

"I expect it is common for them to hear music from the Palace. There are many who are trained to entertain the King with harps, lyres, and other instruments." He turned back to watch the streets. "Hadassah," he whispered, "remember what the prophet Isaiah wrote, *Do not fear, for I am with you; do not be dismayed, for I am your God.*"

Kalev waved the lantern, quietly echoing the scripture.

"Remember, Hadassah," Mordecai whispered, "*Do not fear, for I am with you; do not be dismayed, for I am your God.* Hadassah, remember. *Do not fear, for I am with you; do not be dismayed, for I am your God.*"

They stood at the wall, taking turns waving the lantern while whispering prayers and praise. When the lantern flickered out, Kalev lowered the shepherd's hook

Mordecai whispered, "Hadassah, remember."

CHAPTER 31

"I look forward to the oil treatments," a woman said.
"As do I," another said. "I heard they use oil of myrrh and cassia, as well as olive oil. After six months, my skin will feel soft as a doe."

"I look forward to the training in cosmetics."

These two were part of a gathering of more than a dozen women, seated on the far side of a fountain in one of the garden courtyards. They were chatting as if they were hosting a gathering in their homes, rather than having recently been taken into a harem, where their future was at the whim of one man.

Esther was seated on the other side of the fountain in the shade of a blooming pomegranate tree. The breeze—rich with the flowers' musky fragrance—blew across the fountain and over the strings of the harp she held, causing an ethereal, vibrating hum. It sounded sad; it sounded weary, as she herself was feeling. Following the pattern of the hum, she began whispering, "I have become weary from calling out. My throat is parched. My eyes fail while I wait for my God." *Yahweh, when will you hear my prayers? When will you send relief? In this place of elegance and abundance, I am an outcast, I am alone, I am bereft, I am in sorrow.*

"Greetings."

Esther looked up to see the young woman she had tried to

rescue on that fateful day. Dressed in the long, white tunics worn by the mastoura, she was shorter than most women Esther knew. Black lashes fringing dark eyes were set in an oval face the hue of a blushing peach. She fidgeted with the end of a thick, dark braid pulled over her shoulder.

"Greetings," Ether responded. "I am Esther dokhtar Bunyamin."

"I am Farah dokhtar Mahboubeh." She glanced toward the gabble of women and then back toward Esther.

Something about Farah reminded Esther of a skittish fawn. She gestured to the cushion next to her. "Would you please join me?"

Farah released a deep breath and nodded, sitting on the cushion. "You are the woman who tried to help me last week," she glanced around and lowered her voice, "during the Gathering of the Maidens." She bit her lip. "I wanted to thank you. No one else would help me...not even my manadari."

It took Esther asking only a few questions for Farah to share her story.

She was the daughter of Mahboubeh pur Rouzbeh. A tailor, he made beautiful garments for wealthy clients, including the Azam Sekhargoosh pur Admatha. Farah's mother died giving birth to her and—needing someone to care for the infant—her father soon married Mozhdeh dokhtar Zinat. By the time Farah was ten years-old, her step-mother had given birth to seven children.

Although Farah did not state it, it was clear Mozhdeh was not kind to her step-daughter. Even though they had servants, she required Farah to help with the housework, to watch her younger siblings, and was jealous of the affection between Farah and her father. She also insisted Farah address her with the formal *manadari*—step-mother—and not the affectionate *maman*.

Earlier this week, her father had told the family of a commission from Azam Admatha for new garments. While fitting the Azam, her father had learned the King and the Army would be leaving for Greece. "The Azam also told me there was going to be a Gathering of the Maidens."

"What is that?" her manadari had asked.

"You must not speak of it," her father had said. "The Azam have convinced the King to bring all the beautiful maidens in the Empire into the Royal Harem. When the King returns from Greece, he will select a new Queen from among these women."

"Farah should be part of these women," the older woman had said.

"What?" she had looked between her father and manadari, "I do not wish to be part of this Gathering."

"Silence," her manadari had said. "Your wishes do not matter." Turning to her husband, she had continued. "As you have often said, Farah is beautiful. By going into the King's Harem, the matter of her future would be settled. We would not have to pay a dowry for her. Who knows?" she had shrugged, "Farah might become Queen."

Farah had pleaded with her father not to do this to her.

Glancing at his wife, he had shrugged, making vague comments about caring for her and her future.

The following morning, Farah had accompanied her manadari to the marketplace, where—like Esther and Miriam—they watched the King and his Army leave Susa. When Azam Memukan and the Warriors began the Gathering of the Maidens, her manadari had pushed Farah into the path of the Azam.

"I screamed for her to not leave me," Farah wiped a tear from her eye, "but she had already slipped into the crowd and was gone."

"I am so sorry," Esther laid a hand on Farah's arm. "That was terrible for her to leave you that way. You said your father is acquainted with one of the King's Azam? Perhaps he will come to the Palace to get you."

Farah shook her head. "Baba loves me—he says I remind him of my maman—but he is concerned with not making my manadari angry. I imagine she convinced him it is better for the family—and for me—to be here." She sighed. "No one cares what happens to me."

Esther shook her head. *Maman, Baba, I might not have you here, but I have the memory of your love for me.* She squeezed the girl's arm. "I care!"

Farah's eyes widened. "Truly?" she whispered.

Esther smiled. "Truly."

"I care about you too, Esther," Farah said. "You stood for me, you tried to defend me when no one else did. No matter what happens, I will be there for you."

Three servant girls—one carrying a large tray of food and the other two carrying trays with goblets of wine—approached them.

"Greetings, mastoura," whispered the one extending the tray filled with dates, pomegranates, grapes, figs, cucumbers, cheese, and bread. "Would you care for something to eat?"

"These look delicious," Farah selected some grapes, cucumbers, cheese, bread, and a goblet of wine. "Thank you."

"To serve is our pleasure." The servant turned to Esther. "Mastoureh, what would you care for?"

"Thank you. I will take some cheese." Esther set the harp aside.

"You do not wish for more?" Farah asked.

Esther shook her head. "I cannot eat anything else. I have made arrangements for special food."

Farah lifted an eyebrow. "Special food?"

Esther nodded. "I tried food here the first day and was ill that night. I have explained to a eunuch that I can only eat food from my Gyah Pezeshk. He is looking into arranging for my physician to bring food to the Palace. Until that time, I can only eat a little cheese."

A scornful laugh startled Esther. Turning, she saw a tall, beautiful woman accompanied by six other women. These were the women who—on that first day—had appeared unconcerned with being brought into the Royal Harem. The tall woman examined Esther. "You do not wish to eat the food served in the Royal Palace?"

Esther lifted her chin at the woman's disdainful tone. "It is not a matter of *wish*; I cannot eat it."

The woman—and the six others—laughed again.

"This is the Royal Palace of Susa. All the food is wonderful."

"I did not comment on whether or not it is wonderful," Esther said. "I must eat special food."

The tall woman sneered, "They will not make *special food* just for you."

"Yes, they will."

They all turned as Mehuman pur Abdolhossein—the eunuch over the First House of Women—walked up. "This is the Royal Palace. We often have people from around the Empire who require special foods. The Royal Chef is accustomed to arranging food for these people. It is a tradition that goes back to the reign of the Babylonian King Nebuchadnezzar, when the Magus Belteshazzar and three of his friends requested special food."

Esther startled at the mention of the Babylonian name given to the prophet Daniel but quickly controlled her expression, not wanting to draw more attention to herself.

The tall woman arched a brow. "Who were *those* people?"

"Men who were captives under the reign of the Babylonian King Nebuchadnezzar. After King Cyrus defeated Babylon and established the Persian Empire, this man became one of the King's magi. It was discovered he had a special gift of being a seer."

The tall woman *"huffed"* and walked away. The other women followed.

"Who are they?" Farah asked.

"The six other mastoura are daughters of The Six, the governors of the six most powerful satrapies in the Empire. It was arranged for them to be brought to the Palace to be part of the Gathering of Maidens."

"And the tall one?" Esther asked. "Is she also the daughter of a Shathapavan?"

"Ah, no," the eunuch said, "although her father is just as power-ful. That is Navjaa dokhtar Haman. Her father is the Hazarpatish."

Esther stared as the seven women walked away, commenting

that *they* were happy to be in the Royal Palace; *they* were happy to eat whatever foods were presented to them; *they* looked forward to connecting their families with the King. Their conversation changed, resuming their discussions of beauty the treatments.

Esther bit the inside of her cheek to keep from screaming. *That man! He who ordered the killing of my parents and our servants. He who took our home. His daughter is here?!*

Chapter 32

"Deagah, please give my thanks to your wife," Mordecai uncovered the bread, still warm from the oven. "Without her kindness in sending bread, I do not think I would have eaten these past two weeks."

"I will convey your appreciation, but I am certain she will brush it away." The merchant grinned. "She feels as if it is her calling from Yahweh to feed people."

"Will you please come in and have a cup of wine with me?" Mordecai lifted the plate. "We can test some of what I am certain is the best bread in Susa."

"I am always happy to spend time with you, my friend."

He followed Mordecai to the table and sat while his friend collected the amphora and two cups.

"I cannot believe it has been two weeks since Hadassah was taken into the Royal Harem."

"At times it seems like it was yesterday, and at times it seems like it was a year ago." Mordecai poured wine into a cup and handed it to Deagah.

"Thank you." The merchant took a drink. "Have you been able to contact Hadassah?"

"I have, thanks be to Yahweh." Mordecai moved the bread closer to his friend. "Within the first week after she was taken, I received a summons to speak with the Royal Chef. Have you ever been inside the Palace?"

Deagah shook his head. "I might have customers who are guests in the Palace, but I am still just a humble merchant. Hakaliah bar Seraiah told me he has met the Royal Chef. Have you met him? After all, you are a physician."

"Not before this time as I am not a Royal Physician." Mordecai tore a piece of bread and ate it. "I am certain the Palace has a plethora of physicians and magi to attend the Royal Family.

"As I was saying, a Palace courier arrived with a summons from the Royal Chef. I have been inside the homes of wealthy people, but nothing prepared me for the Palace. The kitchen itself was larger than several houses. The Royal Chef wielded the power of a Shathapavan over what appeared to be fifty kitchen staff.

"After discussing Hadassah's dietary requirements," he grinned, "along with a lively conversation of the quality of grain grown locally as opposed to Egyptian grain, I was given permission to bring food to the Great Gate each morning. A servant from the Royal Harem will meet me there and escort me to a spot on the wall surrounding the First House of Women. Hadassah will be on the other side; we will be able to discuss her diet and other things."

"That has to be a relief for you and for Hadassah. I know how she has suffered from stomach issues. At least this way, she will have a connection with you."

"We will have more connection than just food."

"Oh?" Deagah took a piece of bread.

"As her Gyah Pezeshk, I can write down instructions about the food. As I am also a Mantreh Pezeshk, I will be able to include references to Holy Scripture and prayers, although I will have to be vague about the fact the scriptures are from Yahweh."

"I understand. I am certain that will encourage her."

"That is my hope. Passover is next week. I will try to include scriptures for her to celebrate it however she is able," Mordecai sighed. "This will be the first Passover we will not celebrate together.

In the meantime," he set the cup on the table, "I will try to determine what can be done to remove her from the Royal Harem and let her come home."

Deagah grinned. "That will encourage Kalev."

"I am sure it will. Hadassah was looking forward to," Mordecai smiled, "becoming a bride."

CHAPTER 33

I wonder where Mordecai placed the linen I purchased for my betrothal garment?

Esther was seated in the main room of the Royal Harem, playing a soft melody on the harp. She had spent the last two weeks thinking about her betrothal to Kalev. *Maman, I was going to use that peacock linen to make a garment like the one you wore to your betrothal to Baba.* She drew a shuttered breath. *Think of Yahweh's presence.*

She played a rippling melody that evoked a waterfall. "I will not be afraid," she sang softly. "I will not be discouraged; for You are with me." She noticed other women coming her way. Not wishing to talk to anyone, she stood. Lifting the harp to her chest, she quickly wiped her eyes and walked to a doorway into yet another courtyard.

Glancing around, she noted it was as the others in the House of Women, filled trees and containers of flowers surrounding yet another pool. Looking for a private place to sit, she saw a white bench in a corner near a row of fragrant jasmine bushes. Walking to it, she looked down and froze.

The bench was carved from white marble, and on it was a white cushion. Esther took a step toward it, knowing the cushion would have red flowers and twining vines embroidered on it. She sat on the cushion, sighing as the courtyard faded, and she was in her maman's garden, seated with her on this bench, seeing her maman look around and say, *It just feels peaceful.*

Yahweh, thank You for arranging for Maman's bench to be here.

"Look, there is another courtyard," a young woman said.

"Let us see what it looks like," said another.

Esther stood and swiftly moved around the jasmines. The bushes were thick enough to conceal her presence.

The first woman said, "Oh, what a pretty bench."

"You think it is pretty?" a third woman said, her voice smug. "Navjaa, you do not?"

Navjaa! Esther gnashed her teeth.

"This bench was in the garden of the house King Xerxes gave to my pedar as a reward for faithful service," Haman's daughter sounded smug. "My madar thought it ugly."

She laughed. "She suggested my father give it to King Xerxes, which he did. Pedar later told us the King gave it to Vashti. She apparently did not like it either, as it is here, in a small garden in the First House of Women, and not in the Queen's Apartment."

Esther clinched her fists. *You think Baba's gift to Maman is ugly?* She spit out a curse that would have made her mother blush. Turning, she walked to the edge of the planting of jasmines, but stopped at the sound of a woman crying.

"Where is he? He is gone, and I cannot find him!"

CHAPTER 34

Gently moving aside some of the jasmine branches, Esther watched as Navjaa and the other two women left the garden courtyard before stepping from behind the bushes and walking to the entrance to the Courtyard of the House of Women. She saw Farah waving to her. Holding her harp against her chest, Esther walked around the clusters of women and joined her friend.

"I heard a woman crying out," she whispered.

Farah nodded her head toward the two staircases. An older woman, dressed in a green linen tunic and wearing only one slipper, was standing near the staircase leading to the King's Apartment. Shorter than most women, her face showed the ravages of time, dark eyes set beneath a noble brow, dark braid heavily streaked with gray. She ignored the women in the room, wringing her hands, and repeating, "Where he is? Someone please help me. He is gone and I cannot find him."

The courtyard buzzed as the mastoura and harci discussed the old woman.

"Who is she?"

"She is missing someone; perhaps she is one of the servants."

"She is not wearing the garment of a servant."

"Maybe she is someone important to the King; perhaps his old nursery maid. She came down the staircase leading to his apartment."

"Whoever she is, she appears to have been touched by a *daeva*, an evil spirit," one woman laughed. "She should pray to Ahura Mazda to chase away this evil spirit."

At the laughter of the women, the elderly woman drew back, pulled trembling hands against her chest, repeating, "Someone please help me. I cannot find him."

The beating of blood in Esther's ears drowned every sound. *She is old and confused. Instead of helping her, they are laughing at her.* She crossed the floor to the elderly woman.

Seeing her approach, the woman drew back again, as if she were a frightened animal. "I cannot find him," she repeated. "He is gone."

"Shhh…" Esther set the harp down next to a bench and took a step toward the woman, her hand extended. "Please," she pitched her voice low and soft, "let me help you."

The woman stared at Esther, glanced at the women in the room—as if noticing them for the first time—and then back to Esther. "Where is he? He has not been to see me in several days."

The door to the Courtyard opened; a young boy entered and crossed to the elderly woman. His blue tunic and robe, trimmed in silver, and the silver cap on black curls, were not that of a servant. "*Madarbozorg*—grandmother—there you are!" From his height and voice—along with the fact he was here in the Palace and not training for the Army—Esther guessed he was younger than twelve.

"I came to see you after my lessons. Darya and Roshanara were distraught at your disappearance. I joined in searching for you."

The woman grabbed the boy's shoulders. "*Pesarbozorg*, where is he? He has not visited me in days. I went to his apartment, I looked everywhere, but I could not find him." She began crying.

"She is just a crazy old woman," a boy sitting with one of the concubines laughed.

The young boy speaking to the older woman pivoted toward the laughing boy and lifted his chin. "*Havou*," his voice and expression took on an authority and distain above his age, "you will not speak thus to the Malekeh Jahann."

A collective gasp rippled across the courtyard.

Esther's eyes widened. The younger boy had named the older boy 'havou,' a child born to a concubine and therefore inferior. Beyond that, he identified the older woman not only as his madarbozorg, but as the mother of King Xerxes. This distraught, weeping elderly woman was Queen Atossa and the young boy was the Puora Vaspuhr Artaxerxes Kiapur Xerxes, the son of King Xerxes and the heir to the Throne of Persia.

Esther—and all present in the courtyard—bowed to Atossa and Artaxerxes. The other boy's mother nudged him, instructing him to apologize to the Queen.

The conversations of the women in the courtyard continued in hushed tones, including the women with Navjaa.

"That is the Mother of the World?"

"She hasn't aged well."

"Look at her face. She was probably ugly as a young woman. Why would King Darius choose her as his Queen?"

"Because she was a royal princess, the daughter of Cyrus the Great."

Atossa ignored the women and continued speaking to her Pesarbozorg. "Where he is?"

"Madarbozorg," the boy looked toward the people gathered in the courtyard. He lowered his voice, yet Esther was close enough to hear. "Father is away. Remember, he came to see you before he left."

"He has left?" Her voice was tinged with fear.

"For a short time. He is fighting the Greeks. Do not worry, he will return." Artaxerxes straightened. "He instructed me to care for you while he is away."

Hegai entered the courtyard, with two other eunuchs and a servant, and approached Queen Atossa and the Prince. "My Lady Queen," he bowed, "here you are. Allow us to escort you to your apartment." The servant carried what appeared to be the missing slipper.

"I should accompany them," Navjaa left her group of friends and approached them, bowing again to the Queen and the Prince.

Hegai turned to her. "Navjaa dokhtar Haman," it was obvious the Chief Eunuch knew who she was, "why should you be the one to accompany Queen Atossa and Prince Artaxerxes?"

"Uh," Navjaa took a step back, glanced at her friends and the other women in the room. She lifted her chin, "I am the daughter of the Hazarpatish. I am certain my father would wish me to act as his representative."

Before Hegai could respond, Atossa said, "No! I do not want you." She pointed to Esther. "I want this young woman to come with me."

Esther slanted a glance at Navjaa through lowered lashes. Spots of scarlet burned high on the other woman's cheeks.

Navjaa bowed to the Queen and Prince, lifted her chin once more, and turned to rejoin her group of friends.

The Queen turned to Esther. "I am hungry and thirsty. Would you get me something?"

"Uh," Esther looked from the Queen to Hegai, "I am certain something can be brought to you."

Hegai snapped his fingers. "Bring wine for the Malekeh Jahann," he said and turned back to the Queen. "My Lady Queen, I have arranged for a meal for you and Prince Artaxerxes to be served in your apartment."

"I would like to eat with you *Mamanbozorg*," the boy addressed her with the informal, *Grandmama*. "I can tell you about my morning lessons." He grinned. "I am certain you will know more than my *Erbed*—honored teacher—does."

The Queen's face relaxed. "*Javansher*—young lion," she smiled, wagging her finger, "I will know if you make a mistake."

"I am certain you will, Mamanbozorg. Now, let the servant put on your slipper." He led her to a bench to sit.

Another servant brought a goblet to Hegai, who handed it to

Queen Atossa. While she was drinking and talking to the Crown Prince, the man turned to Esther.

"Come aside. I would have a word with you."

Esther controlled her expression—*What would Hegai wish to say to me?*—but nodded and followed the Chief Eunuch to a corner of the courtyard.

Hegai looked around before speaking. "What is your name?"

Esther swallowed, remembering Mordecai's final hurried instructions. *"Say nothing to anyone about who you are or your family."* "I am Esther dokhtar Bunyamin."

"Esther dokhtar Bunyamin, you would not be aware of this," his voice was low, "but the Malekeh Jahann has been caring for Artaxerxes while the King is gone." He slanted a nod toward the young boy and his grandmother. "And Artaxerxes has been caring for her.

"As Queen Atossa wishes you to attend her, I must tell you she has a..." he met her eyes, "unique condition only few know about."

Esther paused, realizing what the eunuch was telling her. "I understand." She spoke in a lowered tone. "Some of the honored elders I have known had this same...condition."

Chapter 35

Walking through the corridors of the Palace, with an escort of six Immortals, Esther tried to control her expression at the opulence around her. *How long before I will no longer be surprised by all of this?*

She had been surprised when Queen Atossa insisted she—a simple mastoureh—accompany her to her apartment.

Esther had tried releasing the Queen's hand, but the older woman had tightened her grip.

"I need someone to help me."

"I will help you, Mamanbozorg." The young Prince had taken the Queen's other hand.

"Yes, I know you will, Javansher," the Queen grinned, "but I also wish…" she turned to Esther, "what is your name?"

"Uh," she glanced at Hegai, who nodded, "I am Esther dokhtar Bunyamin, My Lady Queen Atossa."

"Ah, yes," turning to her Pesarbozorg, the older woman continued, "I also wish Esther dokhtar Bunyamin to help me."

From that point, the surprises continued, as the older woman kept up a steady stream of conversation as if Esther were her guest, pointing out courtyards and reception rooms, introducing her to white-clad servants, dignitaries visiting the Palace, as well as other Immortals lining the corridors.

After walking through what felt like half of the Palace, the Queen turned and stopped in front of a wide corridor blocked by a dozen Immortals.

From the expression on the Warriors' faces, it was obvious they were surprised to see the elderly Queen here. Queen Atossa arched an eyebrow at them and waited. They returned her gaze, unwavering as if they were the Warriors painted on the corridor walls.

Hegai approached the Warriors, speaking to the one in the middle. "Greetings, Artabanus tabar Mithradata. The Malekeh Jahann visited the House of Women today, where she met," he indicated Esther, "Esther dokhtar Bunyamin. She will be visiting with Queen Atossa today."

"She will be visiting with me *today*," the older woman's voice exuded imperial authority, "and whenever I wish to see her."

The Immortal bowed his head. "It will be as the Malekeh Jahann's wishes." After appointing six Immortals to accompany the Queen, the Prince, and their guest, he nodded to the other Immortals. As one, they moved back—allowing the group to enter the corridor—before stepping back to their previous position, the butts of their spears placed on the tip of their pointed shoes.

Once in the corridor, Atossa released her Pesarbozorg's and Esther's hands, and strode regally ahead of them.

Artaxerxes stepped to Esther's side. "I have never seen Artabanus tabar Mithradata, the lieutenant of the Hazarpatish, discomposed." He suppressed a laugh. "Having my mamanbozorg wander from her apartment was almost worth seeing the disarray she caused." He glanced at the Warriors. "Do not think they distrust you." The young Prince indicated the corridor in front of them with two Immortals standing guard at each of the doors. "This is the Corridor of the Royal Residence, which includes my baba's apartment, my mamanbozorg's apartment, as well as my apartment."

"It also includes the apartment for the Shahbanu," the Queen added casually over her shoulder, "but she is gone. My son sent her away," she flicked a hand, "which was a wise choice; Vashti was a terrible wife and mother."

Esther slanted a glance at the boy; he had turned his head to lift a hand to wipe his eyes. It was obvious that in her special condition, Queen Atossa was unaware of the pain her words caused her Pesarbozorg. However, the gossip Esther had heard in the House of Women echoed the older woman's comments; Vashti *had* been a terrible mother.

"Ah, here we are." Atossa stopped in front of a large double door on which was carved two golden griffins with curved leaf-shaped tails; the imperial symbol of the Malekeh Jahann. The Immortals' eyes widened at seeing the Queen in the corridor. They controlled their expressions and opened the doors, bowing as the Queen and Crown Prince passed them. Esther was startled when they briefly bowed to her. *They do not know who I am, but surely my garments identifies me as one of the mastoura.*

Two women turned as they entered the Queen's Apartment. Dressed in blue linen, with delicate embroidery across the front, these women appeared as old as Atossa and as frantic as the Queen had been when she wandered into the First House.

"My Lady Queen!" They gave a quick bow and rushed across the room.

"Greetings, Darya and Roshanara," the Queen smiled.

"What happened?" one of the women said. "We left you in the courtyard garden while we oversaw the servants cleaning your apartment. When we came back, you were *gone*. We have been looking for you everywhere!"

"There was no need to be distraught. I wanted to visit my son, so I went through the courtyard to his apartment."

"There is a wall surrounding the King's courtyard and the gate is locked," the other woman said. "How did you get through?"

"I was the Shahbanu of three Kings of Persia," Atossa grinned. "I was made aware of where the key to the gate was located. I am also familiar with the *special* corridor from the King's Apartment to the Queen's Apartment."

Hegai turned to the Warriors. "I will relay this information to the Hazarpatish. He will need to assign additional Immortals to guard that passage."

"When I did not find my son in his apartment," the Queen continued, "I sought him elsewhere." She extended a hand toward Esther. "This young woman is Esther dokhtar Bunyamin. She was helpful to me, so I invited her to accompany me to my apartment. Look," she pointed to the instrument in Esther's arms, "she even plays a harp." The Queen walked to a chair and sat.

Esther paused, not knowing how to address the other women.

Hegai stepped to her side. "This is Darya dokhtar Niloofai," he bowed his head to the first woman and turned to bow to the second woman. "This is Roshanara dokhtar Nahid. They are the Queen's *Sarkar Khanums*."

Esther copied Hegai's bow. "It is an honor to meet you." As *Sarkar Khanums*—the Queen's personal ladies—they were more than simple servants. They were women of noble families, who attended the Queen as personal companions.

"They have been with me since I was Darius' Shahbanu," Atossa added. "I had more Sarkar Khanums, but they are gone." She frowned, squinting her eyes in deep thought. "I do not know why they left." As quickly, she smiled. "Sit, Esther," she indicated a chair near her. "Darya, Roshanara, Hegai told me you have food and drink for me."

The other women bowed. "Yes, My Lady Queen. At once." Crossing to a back table, Darya lifted a tray which held silver plates and bowls of cheese, olives, pomegranates, and bread. Roshanara lifted a tray that held an amphora and silver goblets. They offered the food and wine to the Queen, then to the Prince, before turning to Esther.

"Thank you," she set the harp on the floor next to her chair. "I will have some wine, please. I have already had my meal."

After handing her a goblet, the two Sarkar Khanum moved to sit with Hegai at the far side of the room.

While Atossa and Artaxerxes ate, Esther sipped her wine and looked around the room. She had expected the Queen's apartment to be beautiful, but she had to bite the inside of her cheek to avoid gaping at the grandeur around her.

This room alone was larger than Esther's apartment in the First House of Women. Divans, tables, chests, and throne-like chairs placed around the room were delicately carved and gilded with flowers, vines, and imperial symbols. The cushions on the chairs and the rugs on the floor were thick and woven to complement the furnishings. Lamps on the tables and lanterns hanging on the walls were of bronze finely carved to look like lace. A large fireplace—sculpted with lotus flowers—was set in the wall nearest the main doors. On each of the side walls were closed doors. *They must lead to the Queen's bedchamber and bath area.* On the wall opposite the fireplace, two double doors opened onto a courtyard garden.

In the outer corner, she squinted at something that looked familiar; a carved box in the wall, with slanted vents. She gasped, choking on the wine, her eyes widening.

"Is something wrong?" the Queen asked. "Shall I send for a physician or magi?"

"Uh, no, My Lady Queen," Esther took a deep breath. "I was surprised by this," setting down the goblet, she stood, crossed to point at the box. "I believe I have seen these before."

"That is a bagdir, a wind catcher," Artaxerxes stood and walked across the room to join her. "My baba commissioned these to be made for the Royal Palace. The master builder was kind enough to allow me to watch him construct it and to explain how it works.

"He built a tall tower," he lifted a hand over his head, indicating height, "that has windows at the top with slanted vents like these," he pointed to the box. "The wind is caught by the slats in the tower and flows down through one of our yakhchals." He looked at Esther. "Do you know what that is?"

"I believe I do," Esther smiled. "It is a domed structure with a storage room beneath the ground where blocks of ice are placed near shelving to keep food and wine cold."

"You are correct," the Prince smiled. "There are yakhchals and bagdir throughout the Palace, including the Royal Apartments. As the wind from the bagdir flows through one of the yakhchals, it is cooled before going through smaller channels to boxes with vents like this one."

In the upper corner of the box's frame was a small multi-pointed Persian star. Esther did not need to get closer to know that, in the center, was the Hebrew letter A. *Thank you, Yahweh, that, even here in the middle of the Royal Palace, I find my father.* She smiled, blinking away the sheen of tears that gathered in her eyes as the young Prince continued discussing the bagdir. *Baba, you would have been proud of this young boy, explaining your work as if he were your son and not the Crown Prince of Persia.*

"Javansher," Atossa said, "if you are finished explaining the bagdir, perhaps we can learn more about Esther dokhtar Bunyamin."

"Of course, Mamanbozorg. Please forgive me," he smiled at Esther. "I hope I did not bore you."

"I was not bored at all, Your Royal Highness," she smiled. "I enjoyed learning more about the bagdir."

Crossing to sit in the chair next to the Queen, Esther folded her hands and waited.

"Tell me about yourself," the Queen said.

"What would you wish to know, My Lady Queen?"

"Tell me about your family. Who are your parents?" Atossa took a sip of wine. "Of course your father will not be permitted to visit the First House of Women, but your mother will be allowed to visit you."

Esther drew a rugged breath. "My Lady Queen, I will never see my parents again," she said, wiping away a tear. "They are no longer in the land of the living."

"I am sorry, Esther," the elderly lady said. "I did not intend to cause hurt."

"There is no need to apologize, My Lady Queen, as you did not know."

"May I ask how long it has been since you lost them?"

Esther nodded. "It was one year on the last day of the Norooz celebration."

"How sad to lose your parents during the celebration of life. Enough," the Queen waved her hands. "I will cause you no more pain. Might I ask if you would please play music for us? The harp is my favorite instrument."

"Certainly, My Lady Queen." Esther picked up the harp and rested it against her shoulder. Plucking a series of chords and ripples, she glanced at the elderly woman, noting her response to the music, adjusting the chords until she saw the Queen close her eyes and lean her head against the back of the chair. Esther continued playing the soothing melody. After a few minutes, the Queen's breathing slowed; at one point, her jaw opened against her chest as she softly breathed, "*Whhhooo.... mmmmm.... zzzz.*"

"Mamanbozorg is snoring," Artaxerxes whispered.

She nodded, "I believe you are correct." She played for a few more minutes, before quietly ending the tune and lowering her harp.

Hegai stood. "Esther dokhtar Bunyamin," he spoke softly, "it is time for you to return to the First House of Women."

Esther stood. "Of course." After bidding farewell to the Sarkar Khanums, she turned to bow to the young Prince. "Thank you for your kindness, Your Royal Highness. Please give my farewell to your honored grandmother Queen Atossa."

"I will tell her." Artaxerxes grinned. "I would say farewell, but I would wager a gold daric she will call for you again."

"A gold daric? The amount a Warrior earns in one month?" Esther returned the boy's grin. "I could not take that wager, as I do not have any money."

"Well then, we will see you again, Esther dokhtar Bunyamin."

Esther bowed. "I hope we do, Your Royal Highness."

"One more thing."

"Yes?"

The Prince looked at the eunuch and the Queen's personal ladies. The three turned away. He stepped closer to Esther. "I am sorry about your parents. I know some of the sadness you feel." He frowned, "I cannot ask anyone about my madar. My baba refuses to speak of her and my grandmother only speaks ill of her. I do not even know if Madar is alive or dead. Like you, I only know I will never see my mother again."

CHAPTER 36

SEVERAL DAYS LATER

"Greetings, Safa Yazdan Jafari," Mordecai nodded to the Warrior. "You are no longer attending the Great Gate during the night?"

"Greetings, Mordecai ben Jair. You are correct," the Warrior grinned. "Praise Ahura Mazda, I am now assigned to tend the Gate during daylight hours. And you? You have a patient in the Palace?"

"I do." He lifted the basket covered with a cloth. "One of the mastoura, Esther Dokhtar Bunyamin, requires special foods. As I am a Gyah Pezeshk, it was arranged with the Royal Chef that I bring her these foods each day."

"Ah, I understand," Jafari said. "If you will wait but a moment. As this is my first time attending the Gate during the day, I need to confirm the details with my superior."

"Of course," Mordecai pointed to an empty bench at the far end of the Great Gate. "I will wait for you there." Crossing to the empty spot, he sat, setting the basket next to him. He noticed a symbol on part of the gate; a multi-pointed star with a Hebrew letter A in the center. It was his cousin Abihail's master-builder mark. He smiled. "Cousin, I am still watching over your daughter. If *The One* wills, someday she will come home."

190

"I do not know why we were not chosen to accompany the King to Greece," a man's voice said.

Mordecai slid toward the center of the Gate, not wishing to be in a position to listen to another's conversation.

"I do not know either," replied another man. "Warriors earn more in battle than guards do watching this gate."

"However, Bigthana, we have an advantage other Warriors do not have."

"What would that be, Teresh?"

At hearing those names, Mordecai straightened, his eyes widening. *Surely it cannot be those two!* He leaned, carefully tilting his head toward the voices.

"We might not be killing Greeks," Teresh's voice dropped, "but we were left here to guard the new mastoura. I have seen several of them; they are beautiful."

"How have you seen these maidens? They are in the First House of Women. It would be death to get near them."

"I said nothing about getting near them. I said I *saw* them."

"What do you mean?"

"Last night I was walking the perimeter of the wall surrounding one of the courtyards of the House of Women. I found a small hole in the wall on the far side that is shielded by tall jasmine bushes."

"You found a break in the stone wall in the middle of some jasmine bushes," Bigthana snorted. "Are you sure you did not *cause* this hole?"

"Possibly," Teresh laughed. "However this hole was created, it provides a clear view of the courtyard. The moon was shining brightly, and it was easy to see the courtyard. As I said, these women are beautiful.."

"You should show me this hole. We might need to *report* it." The two men laughed.

Mordecai stood and walked away. It had been over a year since he heard those voices, laughing as they murdered Abihail,

Atarah, and their servants, but he knew it was them. *I need to warn Hadassah, but someone needs to know what these two are doing.*

"Mordecai ben Jair." Safa Yazdan Jafari was walking toward him. "I have confirmed you are allowed to bring food for Esther dokhtar Bunyamin whenever you wish. As you are her Gyah Pezeshk, you may give her instructions concerning this food."

"Thank you," Mordecai said. "I do have some instructions for her. Is it possible for me to speak with her?"

"It is. I will have someone escort you to the wall surrounding the House of Women. There is a section where the wall is a jali with benches on the inside for the mastoura and on the outside for their guests. You will have to sit with your back against the jali, as you are not allowed to see her, but you will be able to speak with her."

Several minutes later, Mordecai was seated on the bench, his back against the wall, watching for any sign of anyone approaching.

"Mordecai?" a voice said from beyond the wall. "Is that you?"

He smiled, hearing her voice. "Yes, Had—uh, Esther; it is me.

"Praise," her voice dropped to a whisper, "*The One*! I have longed to speak to you."

"I have longed to speak with you, too. However, we do not have much time. I brought food for you. It has been delivered to the Royal Chef. He will see it prepared according to my instructions. I have been given permission to bring you food each day."

"I am certain it will taste wonderful. I wish I were at home, eating with you."

"I wish for that too and pray for," he glanced both directions, "*The One* to bring it to pass. I am not giving up hope. How are you?"

"I am well." She told him about finding the white bench her father made, meeting Queen Atossa and Prince Artaxerxes, and seeing the bagdir.

"That is amazing. I am thankful *The One* allowed you to find things that remind you of your maman and baba. I see his master-builder mark each time I walk through the Great Gate."

"It makes me feel close to him and to Maman," he heard her sigh. "So, how are you?"

"I am well."

"How are our friends?"

"They are well. Miriam sends you her love, as does her..." he grinned, "family. They send you their greetings and affection."

She laughed. "Send my greetings and affection to them, as well. How is the rest of our community? I miss seeing everyone each Sabbath, even when Nehemiah was being...brusque."

"He is still brusque and still corresponding with Ezra. From what Hakaliah tells me, Nehemiah is not interested in becoming a goldsmith. It appears he would prefer to be a builder and move to Jerusalem. He does not seem to believe the City of David and the Temple are being properly restored.

"However, we cannot speak further of *friends*. I do not have much time and there is something important you must know." Mordecai told her about overhearing Teresh and Bigthana's conversation.

Esther gasped when she heard of their peeking at the women. "I will report what you have told me to Hegai."

"No. You cannot report this as coming from me."

"Why? What these men are doing is improper. Beyond that, they," she hissed, "*murdered* Maman and Baba and our servants without any repercussions. They deserve to be punished for something."

"We will leave their punishment for murder to *The One*. For now, you must find this opening in the wall."

"I will locate it and bring it to the attention of Hegai. He will see the wall is repaired."

"Good." He saw a Warrior walking toward him. "My escort is coming. Farewell, Esther. I will come every day to see you and will continue praying for you."

"I look forward to your visits. And Mordecai..."

"Yes?"

"I will pray every night not only for you but that *The One* will punish these two and that," she spat a curse, "Amalekite Haman for what they did to our family."

CHAPTER 37

"Esther dokhtar Bunyamin, you should know the wall has been repaired," Hegai's brow furrowed. "Thank you for bringing it to my attention, although, it is a mystery to know what happened to create such a hole."

"I am glad to hear it was repaired." Esther controlled her expression. "The privacy for myself and the other mastoura is important." She paused. "Hegai, may I ask a question?"

"Of course," the eunuch nodded, "although I cannot promise I will be able to answer."

"I have been honored to have you as my escort to and from the Malekeh Jahann's apartment over these last few weeks," Esther smiled. "But surely someone else can escort me. The Chief Eunuch of the Royal Harem must have more important tasks to attend to than escorting a simple mastoureh through the Palace."

"Greetings, Mehuman pur Abdolhossein," he nodded to the eunuch at the door of the First House of Women. Hegai gestured, indicating Esther should precede him. "What you say might be true, *if* the simple mastoureh was visiting a common part of the Palace. In this case, the simple mastoureh is visiting the Malekeh Jahann and the Puora Vaspuhr in the Queen's private apartment."

"Yes, I understand. I have enjoyed my time with the Malekeh Jahann and Crown Prince. Queen Atossa's attention to Prince

Artaxerxes—listening to his lessons, sharing stories of their family—reminds me of my own mother, may her memory be blessed."

"From what her Sarkar Khanums tell me, the Queen has enjoyed her time with you. Ah, here is Farah dokhtar Mahboubeh."

Esther's friend was standing next to a closed door, biting her lip as she exchanged a smile with the eunuch.

"Greetings, Farah," Esther looked from her friend to the eunuch and then back to Farah. "Why are you here?"

"We are waiting for you."

"We?"

Instead of answering, Farah opened the door and stepped aside, gesturing for them to enter.

A frown creased Esther's brow as she walked passed the eunuch into the room.

At first glance, it was clear the room was an apartment, obviously bigger than hers. The rugs and tapestries were woven with flowers in vibrant hues. There was a sitting area with several divans, chests, and tables. A door opened to a small courtyard with plantings of flowers and jasmine bushes.

What drew her attention was the group of women bustling about the room. Dressed in the white tunics of Palace servants, these women were placing amphorae and goblets and trays of fruit on a table, lighting the wood in a fireplace, and carrying baskets filled with what appeared to be clothing and linens though a door into what Esther assumed was a bedchamber..

At their entrance, the women stopped and bowed to the eunuch, "Greetings, Mirza Hegai," and then to her, "Greetings, Khanum Esther."

Esther turned to Hegai and Farah, her brows arched. "*Khanum?*" This was the first time since she was brought to the Royal Harem that she had been addressed with the title of respect.

The eunuch and Farah grinned—obviously enjoying the moment. Hegai swept a hand toward the room. "Welcome to your new apartment, Khanum Esther dokhtar Bunyamin."

"My…new," she looked around, "apartment?"

"Yes!" Farah hugged Esther. "This is your apartment!"

Hegai nodded. "Farah is correct; this is your apartment. And these," he indicated the women, "are your personal attendances. This is Banafshe, Laleh, Orkideh, Golshan, Irida, Liana, and Anemos. They will be responsible for caring for your apartment, for your clothing, your food, and anything else you require."

Esther greeted the women before turning back to Hegai. "I do not understand. Why have I been moved to *this* apartment? Should it not go to a daughter of one of the Shathapavans?"

He shook his head. "Assigning apartments in the Royal Harem is my decision, and it is not dependent upon the mastoura." He smiled again. "I chose to move you to this apartment because of your concern and kindness for others."

"Such as your concern and kindness to me," Farah embraced her again.

"You were concerned for the Malekeh Jahann and to the Crown Prince," Hegai said, "and were kind to them *before* you knew who they were. You have continued to be kind to them, even with Queen Atossa's special condition. She asks for you each day and you go without complaint. Her Sarkar Khanums tell me she is getting better, and her personal physician agrees. As for Prince Artaxerxes, I—as well as many within the Palace—are aware he misses his mother. Until you, no one commiserated with his sorrow."

"He might be the heir to the Throne," Esther said, "but Prince Artaxerxes is still a child."

"Your kindness has not gone unnoticed," Hegai extended his hands, "which is why you have been assigned to the best apartment in the First House of Women.

"Queen Atossa's Sarkar Khanums inform me she sleeps late each morning. I have arranged your treatments with oils to be moved to first in the morning, so you will be free to spend the afternoons with the Queen. After you finish the treatments with oils, you will begin the training in cosmetics and perfumes and the Training of the Bedchamber—" he paused, studying her face. "Esther, something is wrong."

"Ah," Esther felt herself blushing to the roots of her hair. She glanced at Farah and the other women in the room; their faces were suffused with color.

"Hegai, I am honored to attend the Queen and the Crown Prince and to play my harp for them. I am accustomed to being productive and would rather be with the Queen and Prince than lying around the pools in the courtyards doing nothing. I have never before had treatments with oils and find they are pleasant and soothing to my skin. However…" Esther looked away, unaware how to proceed.

"However? Esther, please continue."

She looked at her friend and then the eunuch. "I prefer not to go through the last training you mentioned," she said in a rush.

"What?" Hegai raised his eyebrows significantly. "Why would you refuse this training?

"Hegai Kouroush Safa," Esther filled her lungs and blew out the air, "I am a maiden, not," she lifted her chin, "a courtesan. My maman—may her memory be blessed—explained that once I was married, my husband would be the one to teach me about," she blushed again, "such things."

CHAPTER 38

Haman smiled at the sight of the Warrior riding toward him. "Ah, Parmashta; you are back."

"I am, Pedar," his son dismounted. After giving a groom instructions on the care of his horse, Parmashta removed a heavy bag from the horse's saddle and turned to hand it to his father. "Here is the correspondence from the Palace and Shathapavans. I also have a message from Madar." Reaching into the folds of the sash wrapped around his waist, he withdrew a small scroll secured with a ribbon. "I helped her write it."

"Good," Haman tucked the scroll into his sash. "Your madar is beautiful," he grinned, "but her skill at writing and reading is poor. Now go greet your brothers and rest. Come to my tent and share the evening meal with me." He hefted the bag of correspondence. "I will have read the messages by then and can you ask any further questions."

Haman walked to a large metal urn in which a fire burned brightly next to a table holding baskets of sticks. Selecting a stick, he lit it and walked to his tent. Once the lamps inside his tent were burning, he poured a cup of wine and carried the bag of correspondence to the low table. Reaching into his sash, he withdrew the message from Zeresh. He unrolled it and held it next to a lamp.

Haman,

Parmashta arrived today with your letter for me.

I was glad to hear of the Persian Army overwhelming the Greeks at this place called Thermopylae, as well as the burning of Athens. I do not understand the details of warfare, but it is good to hear of the Persian victories.

Our son showed me the wounds he sustained during the battles. He said you and his brothers also received wounds, but none were serious. From Parmashta's explanation, it sounds as if the Warriors have been proudly displaying their wounds. I was proud when he told me that he—along with our other sons—have been added to the Ten Thousand Immortals.

Your letter said King Xerxes is leaving General Otanes with the rest of the Army to continue the subjugation of Greece. Parmashta said that you—along with the Ten Thousand Immortals—will accompany the King back to Susa. If Ahura Mazda blesses your travels, and the weather remains dry, you could be home by Azar or Dey at the latest.

I go to the Palace to see Navjaa several times each week. She is doing well and has followed your instructions by making friends with the daughters of the Shathapavans as well as the daughters of other Persian dignitaries.

She told me that some of the mastoura became ill with pains in their stomachs and were unable to keep food down. One of the maidens died. Navjaa said for you not to worry, as she was not affected by this illness.

The other mastoura were examined by Qabela dokhtar Somayeh, but no cause of the distress was discovered.

Rather than expose King Xerxes or the Royal Family to potential illness, Navjaa said Hegai Kouroush Safa decided to release the maidens who were ill and send them back to their families. Each of these women received a dowry as a gift from the King to be given to a future husband.

*Navjaa says there are two mastoura she has issues with;
Esther dokhtar Bunyamin and Farah dokhtar Mahboubeh.
Navjaa said when the Malekeh Jahann wandered into the
First House of Women—confused and appearing to not be
in her right mind—this Esther pretended to care for her.
Now Queen Atossa sends daily for this Esther to come to
her apartment.*

*As a result of this Esther's care for the Queen Mother,
Hegai gave her the best apartment in the First House of
Women and assigned seven women as her attendants.*

*Navjaa tried to befriend this Esther, but she rejected her
friendship. Navjaa tried to befriend this Farah, or some of
Esther's attendants, but without success. Navjaa is furious;
she has been unable to learn anything about this Esther and
is determined to discover something that will be of use in
this situation.*

*As to Navjaa, she has finished the six months of treatment
with oils and has begun the training in cosmetics. She is also
going through the Training of the Bedchamber. She should
be finished with all her training by the time you and the
King arrive in Susa.*

Zeresh

Haman twisted the scroll and pushed it into the fire, watching as the flames consumed the parchment. He was not concerned with Navjaa contracting the illness that struck the other mastoura. *Zeresh may not be skilled at reading and writing, but she knows how to create poisons.*

"Navjaa," he whispered, "you cannot remove all your competition in this way. You must work to win Xerxes over with your beauty and *womanly skills*. If that does not happen, we might have to rethink our plans."

CHAPTER 39

Esther played a quiet tune, smiling as Queen Atossa listened to her Pesarbozorg lessons on their family history.

"My baba's grandfather—he who was known as Cyrus the Great—defeated the King of Babylon and established the Persian Empire," Price Artaxerxes lifted his chin, "and became the ruler of the greatest Empire the world has ever seen."

"That is correct," Queen Atossa smiled. "My father was known as a mighty Warrior, but do you know what else he was known for?"

"Uhm…" The young prince closed his eyes, lifting his chin toward the ceiling. "Wait!" he snapped his fingers. "King Cyrus was known for his mercy."

"Yes," the Queen said. "Instead of being cruel as other kings, my father was merciful. Do you remember how he displayed this mercy?"

"Uhm…" the Prince tapped his chin, "It had something to do with the Jewish people, correct?"

Queen Atossa nodded, "Yes. Father not only freed the Jewish people from captivity in Babylon, but he allowed them to return to Jerusalem, the city they considered holy."

"That is right!" Artaxerxes bounced on his toes. "He allowed them to rebuild Jerusalem and their Temple and he returned the sacred items the Babylonians had stolen from their Temple."

Esther began singing softly, *"Who says of Cyrus, 'He is My shepherd and will accomplish all that I please; he will say of Jerusalem, 'Let it be rebuilt,' and of the temple, 'Let its foundations be laid.'"*

A voice came from behind Esther, "This is what the Lord says to his anointed, to Cyrus."

Startled, Esther grabbed the harp strings; a *twang* resonated in the air. Turning, she saw a man standing in the doorway. His garments—long white tunic, simple cap covering gray-white curls, and a scarf resting on his chest in preparation to cover the lower half of his face—identified him as a magus. The pendant on his chest of a Faravahar—the winged sun disk with a seated male figure in the center—identified him as an *Ostad*—a learned teacher.

"Erbed Saeid!" Artaxerxes crossed the room to the magus. "You have returned!"

The man bowed, lifting a hand to cup his mouth. "Greetings, Your Highness. Yes, I arrived from Persepolis just this morning." He crossed the room to repeat the bow to Queen Atossa. "Greetings, Your Majesty. I trust you are in good health?"

"Greetings, Saeid Mogh Elaikim," she responded. "I am well, as you can see, much thanks to my new friend." She extended a hand to Esther. "This is Esther dokhtar Bunyamin. She is one of the mastoura."

The older man folded his hands in front of his chest and nodded. "Greetings, Esther dokhtar Bunyamin."

Esther placed a hand on her chest and bowed her head. "Greetings, Erbed Saeid Mogh Elaikim."

The Queen continued, "I have known Saeid all my life. He was a young magus when my father was King. Saeid is now one of my Mantreh Pezeshk, and he is one of Artaxerxes' *erbeds*, his honored teachers. He is also one of the magi in charge of the Royal Treasury. He has been in Persepolis with the other magi to inspect the Royal Treasury before the next Norooz Festival."

The magus dismissed the Queen's praise with a wave of his hand. "I am certain Esther does not care to hear about the simple duties of a magus." He looked at her. "You play a harp?"

"The Malekeh Jahann is kind. Yes, I am honored to play my harp for her," she lifted the instrument, "and hope she finds it pleasant."

"This is a beautiful instrument, and you are a skillful harpist. From reports I have received from My Lady Queen's other physicians, your harp playing is quite beneficial to her. Were you trained by a Mantreh Pezeshk?"

She ran her hand over the neck of the harp. "Why would you ask that?"

He studied Esther. "In your song, you were singing from the writings of the prophet of Isaiah ben Amoz. How do you come to be familiar with the writings of a Jewish prophet?"

"Oh, uhm," Esther placed the harp against her shoulder. *Think.* "My family has been in Susa since King Cyrus the Great conquered Babylon and established the Persian Empire." She began playing. "I grew up hearing about Cyrus the Great, including this quote from," she looked at him, "the prophet you called Isaiah?"

"Esther," the Prince said, "you must have heard of me speak of the words Isaiah ben Amoz wrote about my great-grandfather." Artaxerxes said. "Or you heard my mamanbozorg speak of him."

She breathed a sigh. *Thank you!* "You are probably correct, your Royal Highness." She turned to the magus. "And you? How did you come to hear of this prophet of the Jews?"

"I trained in the Eastern School. My Erbed was the *Aeorapati Magi*—learned teacher—Belteshazzar, although his true name was Daniel ben Judah. He was a Jewish man who had been taken captive by the Babylonians when he was young. Despite his youth, he was a wise man and became an advisor to King Nebuchadnezzar. I met him shortly after Queen Atossa's noble father," he bowed to the elderly lady, "defeated Nebuchadnezzar's descendant Belshazzar. I was honored to study with Aeorapati Belteshazzar for a year before he passed."

"Each week, on Sanb, Saeid Mogh Elaikim speaks about this Daniel and Isaiah," the Queen said, "and reads from the Jewish

204

Holy Scriptures. I attend it, as these are the prayers and holy words he uses when he treats me." She looked at Esther. "You should come too."

"Your Royal Highness," Saeid turned to the boy, "what do the Jewish people call the day Sanb?"

"Uhm…it is their Sabboth—no wait—it is Sabbath." He smiled at his teacher. "It is their one of their Holy Days."

"You are correct, Your Royal Highness." The magus turned to Esther. "I would be honored to have you come to my Sabbath meetings." He gestured to her harp. "I would also be honored if you brought your harp. I am certain reading the Jewish Holy Scriptures while you play would sound beautiful."

Esther filled her lungs. *To hear Your Holy Words spoken once again!* "I would be honored to come and will certainly bring my harp." She smiled. "I would love to hear more of the Holy Scriptures of the God of Belteshazzar."

CHAPTER 40

"Several women have been ill over this week. They experienced pain in their stomach and were unable to keep their food down. One woman," Esther whispered, "died. Hegai called in Qabela dokhtar Somayeh to examine these women. She found nothing that would cause this illness. Rather than risk infecting the Royal Family, Hegai sent the other women back to their homes."

"I am sorry to hear of this illness." Mordecai looked around. Over the months, the Palace servants and Warriors at the Great Gate had grown accustomed to him speaking with Esther through the courtyard wall each day. However, he still watched, knowing that Teresh and Bigthana were in the Palace. "How are you?"

"I am fine. Whenever I see Navjaa dokhtar Haman, I cannot but wonder if she were somehow responsible for this illness. I saw her going into some of the mastoura's apartments. I had thought of eating a small portion of their food, so I would be sent home too."

"No!" Mordecai clapped a hand over his mouth and glanced around before whispering, "You cannot do this. With your own special condition, whatever caused these women to become ill might be worse for you. Even if you did not get ill, should it be discovered you did something intentionally in order to be sent home, it might be considered treason and punishable by death.

No," he cut the air with his hands, "we will continue to trust *The One* to bring you home.

"Esther, I have little time left before I must leave. Let us speak of other matters." He took a breath, "Are you continuing to enjoy your new apartment and attendants?"

She laughed. "It was challenging at first. I have had servants before, but never this many and never just for me. For the first few weeks, I was getting in their way, trying to help them.

"Still, I do not need seven women attending me all the time. After speaking with Hegai, we have arranged a schedule. Every day, two of them tend to my apartment and clothing; two bring the meals you send to the Royal Chef; two women stay with me. They are standing at the door to the Courtyard, where they can see me, and I can speak with you privately. The last woman has a day to rest and see her family. We rotate it so all seven have a day of rest."

She chuckled, "Even with this arrangement, I think they are happy that Queen Atossa sends for me every day. I am too. I have finished the twelve months with oils and cosmetics. As I have… refused…the other training, I have nothing else to do"

Mordecai frowned; although Esther had not explained it, he had heard of this *other training*. Thankfully, it did not appear Hegai was going to force her into it. "How is Queen Atossa?"

"She is well and—according to her physicians and to Erbed Saeid—she is getting better. I am thankful *The One* has allowed me to minister to Queen Atossa and to Prince Artaxerxes." She drew a shuttering breath. "The Prince tries hard, but it is obvious he misses his mother and his father. He is a unique young man. To speak truth, I have enjoyed listening to his lessons, especially about their family history. Were you aware that Queen Atossa was responsible for King Xerxes being crowned and not his older step-brother?"

"I have heard that. It had to do with her being the daughter of King Cyrus and Xerxes being Darius' first child *after* he became King."

"Yes. Queen Atossa has mentioned many times how she has protected King Xerxes and now protects Prince Artaxerxes. She frequently tells the Prince to take care of his family. Recently, she has begun telling me the same thing. 'Esther dokhtar Bunyamin,'" she pitched her voice to sound regal, "'family is important. Do whatever you must to protect your family.'"

Chapter 41

2 Bahman
Fourth year of the reign of Xerxes,
King of the Medes and the Persians

"Deagah, you said Yintl feels it is her calling from Yahweh to feed people," Mordecai smiled, "but she does not have to provide me with bread each week. I have funds to buy food."

"Mordecai, enough," the merchant raised his hand to stifle further protests. "I know what my wife's response would be if she learned you purchased bread from the marketplace instead of accepting the bread she baked. If for nothing other than peace in my home, please take the bread."

Mordecai patted the air. "I would never wish to offend your wife. Once again, please give Yintl my thanks." He took the cloth-wrapped bread from Deagah. "Beyond eating delicious bread, her weekly gifts allow me to spend time with a close friend. Please come in; I have wine and cheese to eat with this bread."

For several minutes, their conversation centered on common matters; "This morning, Rabbi Omar told me the roof of the synagogue leaks."

"The Elders will need to speak with the Rabbi and the Hazzan.

With the rainy season upon us, and the Norooz celebration just weeks away, we will need to attend to that quickly."

"Speaking of the Hazzan, the Rabbi informed me that Anna bat Yosef gave birth last night. Yahweh blessed them with a son."

"Ahhhh…how wonderful! I will have to wish Jerimoth and Anna mazal tov. Speaking of mazal tovs, I saw Hakaliah yesterday." Mordecai smiled. "He informed me of some news concerning your Miriam and his son Hanani?"

"Yes," Deagah smiled. "Hanani wishes to become betrothed to my daughter. We are discussing the details of the mohar now and hope to have the celebration soon."

"Mazal tov, my friend. May Yahweh bless Miriam and Hanani with much joy and many children. I must say that it is rare," Mordecai took a drink, "for a younger son to marry before the older son."

"Well," Deagah lifted his hands in front of his chest, "we know Nehemiah."

"You speak truth; we do indeed know him. Hakaliah tells me Nehemiah is too busy corresponding with Ezra about the reconstruction of the Temple to think about a wife." Mordecai grinned. "Perhaps one day he will; but not now." He lifted the amphora, "May I pour you some more wine?"

"Thank you, no," Deagah wiped the crumbs from his hands and then clasped them. "Mordecai, my friend, as much as I enjoy spending time with you, I confess I came to see you on…another matter."

Mordecai lifted an eyebrow. "Oh?"

"My friend," Deagah heaved a sigh, "there is something we must acknowledge."

"And what is that?"

"It is time to accept that we will not become family."

Mordecai blinked. "What?"

"My friend, it has been almost a year since Hadassah was taken during the Gathering of the Maidens. Kalev realizes she is not coming home."

"What? Of course she will come home! Kalev just needs to be patient—

"Mordecai," Deagah interrupted him. "Kalev wishes to become betrothed to Devora bat Naham."

"Devora?" He shook his head, certain he had misheard. "The beekeeper's daughter?"

"Yes. Kalev spoke to me last night. He realizes I must speak with you first before approaching Naham with his offer of marriage."

"Well," Mordecai snorted, "how kind of Kalev to have you to speak with me first." He spread his hands wide. "May they be blessed with many years and many children. I assume Kalev will use the ring he purchased from Hakaliah to give to Devora."

"I had thought you would understand Kalev's desire to marry and have children."

"I had thought Kalev cared about Hadassah, but apparently I misunderstood."

"My friend," Deagah laid a hand on Mordecai's forearm, "I know you are shocked and hurt."

"I am shocked and hurt, for Hadassah. Deagah, you asked me to understand. I will try. However, you need to understand something." He tapped the table with his finger. "Abihail and Atarah left Hadassah in my care. She is the last of our family. Whatever it takes, however long it takes," he pounded the table with his fist, "I will never give up hope of bringing Hadassah home once again."

CHAPTER 42

"Artaxerxes, what has Erbed Saeid taught you today?" Queen Atossa glanced between her grandson and the magus.

The young prince grinned at his teacher before turning to his grandmother. "He told me part of what I will learn about Ahura Mazda and my position as Puora Vaspuhr. As Ahura Mazda represents all light and truth, I am to always be truthful, to be courageous, and to have self-restraint." The boy straightened his body. "I am to be wise, just, prudent, and brave."

Esther smiled listening to the young Prince recite his lessons. *How wonderful it would be to have a son like Prince Artaxerxes.* Her smile slipped. *That will not happen to me. Bless Miriam and Hanani with many years and children.* Her heart ached realizing her dearest friend got married last week and she had been not there to celebrate. She sighed. *And bless Kalev and Devora with many years and children. I cannot fault him for not wanting to wait for me. What man would wish to marry an outcast?* Her heart ached. *I will never go home.*

Esther felt tears stinging her eyes. She turned away from the Queen and Prince to wipe the tears from her cheeks. Lifting her harp to her shoulder, she played softly, plucking the strings singly, to echo the loneliness, the melancholy, the sadness she felt. In a soft voice, she sang, *"Out of the depths I cry to You; hear my voice. Let*

Your ears be attentive to my cry for mercy. I cry to You. She repeated, *Please hear my voice. Let Your ears be attentive to my cry for mercy. Please hear my voice.*"

"Esther dokhtar Bunyamin, are you sad?"

She startled, turning to see the magus standing next to her. "Uhm…I am sorry Erbed Saeid. I did not hear you approach. What did you say?"

"Forgive me for startling you," the elderly man glanced beyond Esther's shoulder, to where Queen Atossa was still quizzing Artaxerxes, before moving to sit near her. "You were singing the lament written by the Jewish King David. He was the one I spoke of during the last Sabbath meeting. Your words and your music sounded sad. Are you sad?"

"Oh, uhm, yes, Erbed Saeid; I am sad. Several of my friends recently married, and I was not able to attend the celebrations. It made me feel…lonely. I remembered you talking about this King and remembered a few of the words of one of his poems; they fit how I felt."

"I am sorry you missed your friends' celebrations." He glanced again at the Queen before lowering his voice. "You were using the same technique on yourself that you use on the Queen; to play music that echoes how you feel. Then you slowly change the music—"

The sound of the door opening behind them, followed by Artaxerxes' cry, "You are back!" cut off the Mangus' words.

Esther looked toward the young boy. Eyes bright, the Prince dropped his tablet and stylus, and jumped up, crying, "Baba! You are home!"

All in the room turned toward the door, where several men stood amongst the Warriors guarding the Queen's Apartment. Artaxerxes ran across the room and embraced the man standing in the middle. "Baba!"

Esther eyes widen. *The King!*

The magus stood and bowed, hand covering the lower half

213

of his face, as did Sarkar Khanum Darya and Sarkar Khanum Roshanara.

Setting her harp down, Esther stood, copying their bows. She kept her face lowered but slanted a glance at the King.

Still in his battle-robe, the same wide gold band around his head, the Royal Sword tucked behind his belt, King Xerxes looked as fearsome as he had a year ago.

Several Warriors had accompanied the King, including the one Esther had seen riding next to the King's chariot on the day the Army left; on the day she was taken during the Gathering of the Maidens.

She glanced at the magus and the Sarkar Khanums. They had straightened from their bows, but remained standing, eyes averted. Esther straightened and clasped her hands in front of her, studying the rugs at her feet.

"Baba! I heard you won the war against the Greeks! *Sadbas*—congratulations—what was it like? Did you bring me a trophy of war?"

Esther bit the inside of her cheek, to keep from laughing at the unbridled joy and enthusiasm of the young boy.

"*Pesar*—Son—slow your words. Allow me a moment." Turning to the man next to him, he said, "Haman, set whatever guards you deem necessary, but go home. Give your wife my greeting, tell her your sons are great Warriors, and she can be proud of them."

Haman? Esther looked up, stunned by the nearness of the man who had murdered her parents and her servants. She clinched her fists, digging her nails into her palms, forcing herself to not run across the room and attack him.

"My Lord King," Haman said, "Navjaa—"

"Haman," the King interrupted him. "We will speak more of your daughter later."

Haman bowed, "Yes, My Lord King." He bowed to Queen Atossa, "Your Majesty," and to Prince Artaxerxes, "Your Highness," before turning to the Warrior next to him. "Artabanus, come with me." After bowing to Xerxes once more, they turned and walked down the corridor.

"Baba! Did you…"

Xerxes laid a finger across the boy's lips. "Pesar, proprieties must be observed." Turning his son, the King led him across the room to Queen Atossa. Xerxes, then Artaxerxes, bowed to her and kissed her hand. "Greetings, Malekeh Jahann," the King smiled.

The Queen smiled and bowed her head. "Greetings, my pesar and My Lord King." Within a breath, her regal smile changed to a grin. Standing, she embraced him. "Praise Ahura Mazda for your safe return! We did not know you and the Army would arrive today."

"In my desire to return home, I forced the march. As we did not take time to bathe and change our garments," he patted his tunic; dust wafted the air, "I decided against having a parade through the streets of Susa. It also allowed me the pleasure," he grinned at his son, "of surprising you and Artaxerxes."

"Will you have a meal with me?"

"I would be honored," he bowed his head and then grinned. "Will you ask the Royal Chef to make his sweet bread? The bread the Army ate tasted like our horses' saddles."

Artaxerxes and the Queen laughed. "Of course, I will send Darya and Roshanara to arrange for it."

Turning, the King spoke to his mother's elderly attendants, asking after their health. After they left the apartment, he turned to greet the magus. "Erbed Saeid, thank you for your letters concerning my mother and my son. They were a pleasant change from messages of battles and supplies."

"You are most welcome, My Lord King," the magus said. "I was happy to send good reports."

"I was encouraged to read them." Turning, the King looked at Esther. "And who is this?"

Esther bowed again, feeling the flush heat her cheeks.

"This is Esther dokhtar Bunyamin," the Queen said. "She is

one of the new mastoura in the First House of Women. She plays the harp—and she is my friend."

"Baba," Artaxerxes tugged at his father's robe and crooked a finger.

The King lowered his head so the Prince could whisper to him.

"Esther's playing has helped Mamanbozorg…feel better. Baba, Esther has lost both of her parents. She understands…" he lowered his voice even more, "how I feel."

"I see." The King straightened and looked at her. "Greetings, Esther dokhtar Bunyamin."

Esther glanced at the magus; he gestured that she rise. She straightened, lifting her eyes to look at the King. She had heard many describe him as intimidating, powerful, even fearsome. The first time she saw him, she would have agreed. He looked and sounded like the King of the largest Empire in the world; but now…there was more. He looked…weary.

"Thank you for your kindness to my mother and my son," the King said. "I have received reports from my mother's physicians and from Erbed Saeid. They confirm what my son tells me; that your playing has been," he smiled at his mother, "beneficial for her." He paused. "I would hear you play."

Esther took a breath and nodded. "You are welcome, My Lord King. I would be honored to play for you." She glanced at Queen Atossa and smiled. "The Malekeh Jahann is a kind and wise lady; she reminds me of my own mother, may her memory be blessed. The Puora Vaspuhr is an intelligent and insightful young man." Out of the corner of her eye, she saw the boy straighten and lift his chin. "He will be a wise king," she looked at Xerxes, "like his father."

Xerxes bowed his head once. "Thank you for your kind words about my mother and my son. Well, Esther dokhtar Bunyamin, it appears you have learned much about my family." The King regarded her, a smile hovering around his lips. "I look forward to learning more about you."

Chapter 43

"Ahhh…" Haman set the goblet on the table. "The meal was delicious, Zeresh; much better than the food served to the Army." He grinned. "The Immortals are mighty Warriors, but terrible cooks."

She lifted the amphora to refill his goblet. "I am certain most food taste better at home than in camp."

"You speak truth. When in camp, or on the march, Warriors are generally focused on the coming battle. At some point, however, you need food. For most of the time, I was able to ignore the source of the meat and just eat. However," he grimaced, "there were some times when I doubted even a starving dog would eat it." He laughed. "There was this one meal when Arida and Aridatha were unable to keep the food down."

"Ugh," Zeresh wrinkled her nose. "However," she shrugged, "they *are* twins. I would expect the two of them to get sick at the same time. I wish our sons had come home with you."

"Well," Haman selected a cluster of grapes, "they are Warriors. They comported themselves with honor during the battles and wanted to celebrate with their comrades. They will come home tomorrow."

"I will have Cook prepare another meal to celebrate with them. So, the war was a success?"

He shrugged. "As far as Xerxes is concerned, we accomplished his goals. We killed the Spartan King Leonidas, along with his Warriors at a pass known as Thermopylae. We marched on to Athens and destroyed the city, burning it to the ground. Xerxes was ready to return to Susa. He left General Otanes and his son Mardonius to continue the subjugation of Greece.

"Enough about the Greeks. What about you?" Haman looked at his wife over the edge of the goblet. "What have you been doing while we were gone?"

"I did not spend it here," she sneered, "tending to the gardens. I realize you wanted this house for the seclusion it provided for you and The Six."

"Shhh…" Haman lifted his hand. "Do not speak loudly."

Zeresh snorted. "The servants know better than to listen to our conversation. Those who do not know," she looked at Haman, arching an eyebrow, "are no longer with us."

"I trust you were careful in…*dismissing* those servants?"

"Of course," she selected a piece of cheese. "To continue, once your goals are accomplished, I want to move to the Susa; especially if Navjaa is Queen."

"In your letters, you said you have regularly seen Navjaa."

She nodded. "I have seen her almost daily."

"How is she?"

"She has followed your instructions." She lifted a hand to tick off her fingers. "She has made friends with the daughters of the Azam, the Shathapavans, and other noble families. She has also… *dealt*…with the women she considered likely rivals."

Haman frowned. "She needs to be careful with the frequent use of poison."

"I agree," Zeresh nodded, "and I cautioned her on that point. She has finished the treatments with oils, learned about cosmetics, and completed the Training of the Bedchamber. She is anxious for the King to send for her. She wants to know when that will be."

"I am the Hazarpathish," he snapped, "not the Chief Eunuch

of the Royal Harem. Xerxes mentioned looking forward to celebrating the Norooz with his mother and his son. Once the festival
is over, I imagine he will speak to Hegai about Navjaa and the
other mastoura.

"Whenever the opportunity arises, I continue to mention our
daughter to Xerxes," he stood. "But I have no control over which
woman is sent to him."

CHAPTER 44

"You actually met," Mordecai looked around, before continuing, "King Xerxes?"

"Yes. I was in Queen Atossa's apartment yesterday when he came to see her. He had just returned from Greece."

"What was he like?"

"Regal. He looked much as he did on the day the Army left for Greece; on the day I…was taken. This time, there was something more."

"More? What?"

"Gentleness." She described Xerxes leading Artaxerxes over to bow to Queen Atossa. "There is respect and love, between him and his mother, between him and his son. To speak truth, I was not expecting the King," she paused, "to love anyone."

"It is difficult to know someone from afar. With Xerxes in the Palace, perhaps you should avoid going to Queen Atossa's apartment. If the King continues to see you, he might decide to summon you."

"I would draw attention to myself if I refused her summons. If she did not send one of her Sakar Khanums for me, I am certain Hegai would inquire. The other day, he spoke to me about finishing the…*training*. Of course I refused it."

Even though Mordecai could not see Esther, he could hear the embarrassment in her voice.

"I am thankful Hegai did not insist. I am beginning to wonder what happens if I do not complete the training. At the least, I am certain I will not be summoned by the King."

Chapter 45

15 Esfand
Fifth year of the reign of Xerxes,
King of the Medes and the Persians

"My Lord King," the King's Cup-bearer said, "you look different."

Haman's eyes widened. He glanced at Kurush Tars Dida standing at the table next to the Throne. The Cup-bearer poured red wine into a gold goblet and handed it to the King.

"And how," Xerxes accepted the goblet, "Kurush Tars Dida, do I look different?"

"You look," Kurush shrugged, "happy."

"Happy?" The King arched a brow. "Is being happy a rare occurrence for me?"

"Well, My Lord King, " Kurush lifted his hands—palms together—to his chin, studied the King, and then grinned, "it is."

The King looked at Haman, Hegai—even his Royal Scribes—before throwing his head back in laughter.

Haman joined the others in quiet laughter. *Beyond his mother and his son, only Kurush can make the King laugh at himself.*

"Kurush, you are correct. I am happy." The King lifted his goblet high. "I have struck a mighty blow to the Greek rebellion

222

and have left my father-in-law and brother-in-law to finish the task." He lowered his hand. "I arrived in Susa to find my mother and my son are well and contented. It has been a while, but yes," the King smiled, "I am happy." He took a drink and set the goblet on the table next to the Throne. "Now, let us finish this meeting." He looked at the Royal Scribes, "What is next on the list?"

The two Scribes consulted their scrolls. "The upcoming Norooz festival."

At length, the details of the festival—the feasts, the displays of athletic and military skills, the hawking and falconry—were discussed and finalized.

"Well, praise Ahura Mazda this Norooz will not include a lengthy tour of the Empire," the King frowned. "That was fatiguing even for me."

Memories of the tour are not causing his frown. He is thinking of Vashti.

"Now, it is time," the King lifted his chin, "I choose a Queen. Hegai, I would hear your report on the mastoura."

"My Lord King," the Chief Eunuch bowed his head. "On the day you left for Greece, Azam Haftordak tabar Memukan oversaw the Gathering of the Maidens here in Susa. Within the next month, the mastoura from the other satrapies arrived in Susa. With the help of Shaashgaz, Mehuman—and the other eunuchs—all the mastoura were settled into the First House of Women and began their treatments and training."

"Good," the King said. "Who has completed these?"

Hegai unrolled a scroll and began reading a list of names. Haman recognized most as daughters of the some of Shathapavans, a few daughters of the King's Azam, some daughters of wealthy nobles, and Navjaa.

When the eunuch lowered the scroll, the King commented, "You did not name Esther dokhtar Bunyamin."

"I did not name Esther dokhtar Bunyamin," Hegai replied, "because she has not completed the preparation."

223

"What?" Xerxes frowned. "Has she been examined for illness? She has been with my mother and my son daily."

"Yes, My Lord King," Hegai nodded, "Esther has been examined by one of the Royal Midwives. She requires special food—which has been arranged with the Royal Chef—but that is nothing that would cause illness to you, to Queen Atossa, or to Prince Artaxerxes. She has completed the six months treatments with oils as well as the six months training in cosmetics."

"What has she not completed?"

"The Training of the Bedchamber."

Haman felt his cheeks grow warm, noting that Kurush, the Royal Scribes, and even Xerxes were flushing. Hegai's expression remained unchanged, as if he were discussing the choice of wine and not the training of women on intimate techniques.

"Well," the King coughed, "Esther has been with my mother and my son almost daily. Surely time can be arranged for her to complete the training."

"My Lord King, a lack of time is not the reason."

"Oh?" Xerxes raised his eyebrows. "What is the reason?"

"My Lord King," Hegai said, "Esther dokhtar Bunyamin has requested to not have this training."

"What? She refused?" Haman spoke without thinking.

Xerxes ignored Haman's interruption. "Why has she declined this training?"

"My Lord King, when I asked her," Hegai said, "Esther replied she was a maiden, and not a courtesan. She added that when her madar was still among the living, she told Esther that once she was married, her husband would be the one to teach her such things."

"This is disrespectful!" Haman said. "Does this mastoureh expect the King to send for an untrained woman? To refuse the training should be considered treason—"

"Peace, Haman." Xerxes stroked his beard. "Kurush," he turned to his Cup-bearer, "What are your thoughts?

224

"The King wishes to know my opinion?"

Xerxes nodded. "I do."

"Well," the elderly man carried the amphora to refill Xerxes' goblet, "the Training of the Bedchamber is not written into the Law of the Medes and the Persians. It is simply tradition.

"From what I have heard of this Esther, from what Queen Atossa and Prince Artaxerxes—as well as what Hegai—tell me, it does not sound as if her actions are disrespectful nor treasonous. It sounds like something one would expect a *maiden* to say."

"But My Lord King," Haman sputtered, "to refuse—"

"No," Xerxes' raised hand cut off Haman's words. "No. She is not refusing *me*." He smiled softly, his gaze turned inward. "She is honoring her madar's teaching and loving memory." He looked at the men in the room. "I understand that kind of love and honor.

"Hegai, set a schedule for the women you have named to be sent to me."

"Offer Esther the Training of the Bedchamber once more. If her answer remains the same, so be it." He lifted the goblet. "Either way, send her to me."

CHAPTER 46

"Where do you wish to eat?" Farah asked.

"Not here," Esther said. "Let's go to the rooftop courtyard."

Walking toward the stairs in the House of Women, they passed mastoura and harci, eating the morning meal and talking about matters of important to them; their daily beauty treatments, the warmer weather, and Xerxes being back in Susa.

Esther led the way up the stairs and through the double doors onto the roof. Like other courtyards in the House of Women, it was edged with jali screens interspersed with tall jasmine in containers set around ornamental pools and small pavilions shading couches and tables. They walked to a pavilion on the side facing the city. After setting her plate and cup on the table, she looked out over the Palace grounds.

"Ahh…this is nice." Farah joined her. "Even with it being the month of Khordad, the air is soft and cool."

"It is," Esther nodded. "Thankfully, today it is not raining. Look, butterflies," she pointed toward several of the lovely creatures—wings of blue, edged with black—flittering on white jasmine blossoms. "Are they not beautiful?"

Farah agreed. "However, where there are butterflies," she walked back to the table and waved away a group of flies gathering over their plates, "there are also other creatures that would love to share our food."

Over the meal, their conversation turned to the topic of most importance.

"Esther, you continue to see the King?"

"Yes. Not every day, but he came to the Queen's apartment yesterday."

"Imagine seeing the King of Persia. Before being brought here, I thought it was common for people living in the Palace to see the King every day. I know the harci see him, at least when they are," she blushed, "summoned, but you are the only mastoura to have seen him."

"I believe you are correct," Esther selected a grape. It was obvious that Farah, like many of the other mastoura, was bored. For the women in the First House, each day was the same: they woke up; they ate; they went to their beauty treatments; they learned how to play an instrument, sing, or dance; they bathed, ate, and then went to sleep. Talking about the events in the Palace—especially now that the King was home—was part of the daily routine.

"I have not seen some of the mastoura lately," Farah tore a piece of bread in half. "I have also noticed Mehuman overseeing apartments in the First House being cleared. Do you think the King has begun summoning them? After all, it has been over two months since the King and the Army returned from Greece."

"Possibly," Esther waved away a fly interested in her plate. "Like you, I noticed several mastoura are gone, including Navjaa. That is a relief."

"Praise Ahura Mazda for that gift!" Farah grinned. "At least we do not have to be concerned about her."

Esther echoed Farah's grin. "I agree."

"It will not be long," Farah's grin faded, "before you are summoned."

"What? Me? No!"

"Yes, you. You are beautiful, and unlike *other* beautiful mastoura and harci, you are kind. If the King calls you, he will certainly select you as Queen. If you become Queen," she paused, "would you please select me as one of your attendants?"

"Farah, I cannot be summoned. I have not completed all…" Esther looked around before continuing, "the training. Hegai offered it to me again this morning. He did not appear concerned when I refused.

"If I do not complete the training, I cannot be summoned. My hope is Xerxes will choose a Queen—hopefully not Navjaa—and they will release the mastoura in the First House. We will be able to go home."

"I cannot go home," Farah sighed. "My baba and manadari would not want me."

"Then you can come and live with me." Esther laid a hand on Farah's shoulder. "We would be like sisters."

CHAPTER 47

Haman secured the tooled leather belt around his tunic, and slipped the short, double-edged sword into the sheath. He crossed to the door of his bedchamber, opened it, and stepped into the corridor. He walked toward the Throne Room, passing soldiers of The One Thousand Immortals lining the corridors. The Warriors flicked their eyes toward him, before returning their gaze to watch the corridors and courtyards of the Palace.

He turned into the Outer Court, lined with a dozen Warriors, who snapped to attention, swords against their chests, murmuring, "Hazarpatish."

"Be at rest," he said and turned to the table where his lieutenant was standing.

"Greetings, Artabanus. How goes the watch?"

"It was quiet." He handed Haman several scrolls. "Even the Malekeh Jahann remained in her apartment."

"Truly?" Haman lifted a brow. "That is a rare occurrence."

"It is indeed." Artabanus tilted his head toward the Throne Room. "The Puora Vaspuhr is with the King now."

"That is good to know. I will wait until the Prince leaves before checking in with the King. Once you have overseen the changing of The One Thousand, you are dismissed for the day." He nodded to the Warriors and stepped into the Inner Court.

Crossing to the table, he set the scrolls down, and then made a quick survey of the room. Even with Warriors protecting the Outer Court, Haman would not simply assume it was secure. He could hear muted voices beyond the door; clearly it was the King and his son.

Moving back to the table, he sat, unrolled the first scroll, and began reading Artabanus' report. As he finished the first report and picked up the second, he heard—

"Baba, please, do not do this!"

Haman frowned. Standing, he crossed the floor and turned to lean against the closed door to the Throne Room. No one would question his position; being Hazarpatish, he frequently heard conversations between the Royal Family.

"Pesar, I do not understand,"

"Please, Baba!"

"Artaxerxes, stop. Take a breath." The King's voice was firm, but gentle. "Good. Now tell me, what is wrong?"

"Baba, please do not send for the other women."

"What? Artaxerxes, how do you know about these *other* women?"

"One of the havou in the House of Women told me. He said you were sending for the all the mastoura. Baba, please do not."

"Pesar, you do not understand."

"I do understand. You want to find another queen."

"And," the King softened his voice, "a madar for you."

"They want to be *your queen*, but they do not want to be *my madar*. They love the position, but they do not love you—and they care nothing for me. Just like my madar did not love me. Please Baba; no one loves me except you, Mamanbozorg, Pedarbozorg Otanes, and…" the boy started sobbing, "Esther."

"Artaxerxes," the King said, "pesar. Please, do not cry."

Haman moved away from the door and sat at the table. Lifting an amphora, he poured some wine into a goblet.

I did not realize Artaxerxes wielded such influence over Xerxes.

Something might need to be done about him. He frowned. *Otanes cannot be involved in our plans anymore. The boy is right; the General loves him. Nor can I involve any of The Six; several have daughters in the First House of Women.*

"Pedar."

Haman looked up to see his son Dalphon. He raised a questioning eyebrow. "Why are you here?"

"I brought a report for Artabanus," he lifted a scroll, "but learned he had already left for the day. The Warriors in the Outer Court said you were here. Do you wish to have the report?"

"Yes, I do," he stood and took the scroll from his son and indicated a chair. "Sit for a moment. I have a question to ask." He moved his chair so he could see the doors to the Throne Room and the Outer Court. Lowering his voice, he asked, "Have you seen Navjaa?"

Dalphon nodded. "I saw her this morning when I was guarding the Corridor of the Royal Residence. Hegai was escorting her from the Royal Apartments to the Second House of Women. She seemed..." he grinned, "pleased with herself."

Haman scowled. "She needs to focus on the King's pleasure and not her own."

Dalphon snorted. "Have you ever known Navjaa to consider anyone's pleasure before her own?"

"If she is to be Queen, she will have to raise Prince Artaxerxes. She will need to learn to care for him as her own child."

"Navjaa has never cared for children. If she conceives, she will turn the babe's care over to the nursery maids. Why would she care for Prince Artaxerxes?"

Haman glanced around before telling Dalphon about the Prince's conversation with Xerxes. "If Xerxes listens to Artaxerxes, Navjaa might not be chosen Queen." He clinched his fist. "We need to deal with the child," he hissed. "Find Teresh and Bigthana."

Dalphon sneered. "I can handle a boy."

"And if you get caught? The punishment for killing the Puora Vaspuhr would be death, and it would not be over quickly. Xerxes would see you lingered for days in great agony."

"What is your plan?"

"I do not know yet, but we will think of something. Find Teresh and Bigthana. We need them to get rid of anyone who might influence the King, whether it is Artaxerxes, Atossa, or Dida."

Dalphon glanced around before whispering. "The Prince, the Queen Mother, and the Cup-bearer? And if Teresh and Bigthana fail?"

"If they fail, we can report them to the King." Haman filled a second goblet and handed it to his son. "Xerxes will *appreciate* our dedication to him and his family. If he does not, then something else can be done." He grinned, "How would you like to be the Puora Vaspuhr?"

CHAPTER 48

Farah answered the knock at the door. After a brief conversation, she closed the door and walked to Esther. "Hegai is here to see you."

"Invite him in." Esther stood, brushing the breadcrumbs from her tunic. "He is here to escort me to Queen Atossa's apartment."

"I do not think so." Crossing the floor, Farah opened the door and stood aside. "Please, come in."

Hegai entered the apartment. Mehuman was with him, his arms extended holding clothing sewn from a beautiful white linen, embroidered with gold thread. On top were a white cap and slippers trimmed with gold thread.

"Greetings, Hegai; greetings, Mehuman. I am ready to go to Queen Atossa's apartment. Let me get my harp."

"You are not going to see the Malekeh Jahann this morning."

"I am not?" Esther's eyes widened. "Is she ill? Has Saeid Mogh Elaikim examined her?"

"Forgive me; Queen Atossa is not ill."

"Hegai," she frowned, "I do not understand."

233

"Esther dokhtar Bunyamin," the Royal Eunuch said, "I will ask once again. Will you finish the training?"

Esther blushed, glancing at Farah and her attendants, before looking back at the Royal Eunuch. "I am sorry, Hegai Kouroush Safa," she lifted her chin. "I will not."

"So be it." Hegai turned to indicate the clothing Mehuman was carrying. "You will wear these."

Esther exchanged looks with Farah, who shrugged, and then looked at the eunuch. "What is this?"

"After you bathe and apply cosmetics and perfume, you will wear this tunic and cap and these slippers. Your other things will be moved."

"Moved?"

"You may take whatever you wish for tonight," Hegai said. "I suggest your harp."

"Please forgive me, Hegai," she extended her hands to either side. "I still do not understand."

"Esther dokhtar Bunyamin," the Royal Eunuch folded his hands in front of his chest, "you have been summoned by King Xerxes."

Chapter 49

"Greetings, Safa Yazdan Jafari," Mordecai said. "It is a beautiful day, is it not?"

"Greetings, Mordecai ben Jair," the Warrior smiled. "While I am thankful Tishtar has blessed us with rainfall, I am also thankful that Oromazes blessed us with sunlight."

"As usual," Mordecai lifted the covered basket, "I am here to bring food for Esther dokhtar Bunyamin."

"You will be escorted to the Palace Kitchen. You can leave the basket with the Royal Chef."

"I also wish to speak with Esther."

"I am sorry," Safa said, "the daily report states she is not available today."

"What?" Mordecai frowned. "Is she ill? I am her Gyah Pezeshk; I should at least speak with someone who is caring for her."

"I was not given an explanation, but we," he indicated the other Warriors in the Gate, "have been making wagers."

"Wagers?" Mordecai frowned. "I do not understand."

"The odds are," Safa grinned, "that Esther dokhtar Bunyamin has been summoned by the King."

Chapter 50

Esther kept her eyes lowered, grasping the harp to her chest, focused on following Hegai's steps through the corridors of the House of Women to the Courtyard with the two staircases.

It seemed like years since she was first brought to this room on the day of the Gathering of the Maidens. It was here she met Farah dokhtar Mahboubeh. It was here she first saw Haman's daughter, Navjaa. It was here she hurried to help a confused old woman, only to learn she was the Malekeh Jahann. It was here she met the Puora Vaspuhr Artaxerxes. She kept her gaze low as they walked passed other mastoura and harci, not wanting to see their knowing gazes.

At length, Hegai stopped at the foot of the double staircases. Esther stopped, staring at the mosaic swirls of red, gold, and silver tiles, knowing from the sounds that he was removing the thick red braided rope.

"*This staircase leads to the King's Apartment.*" Hegai had informed them on that first day.

"*You are not to use this staircase unless I escort you. That will only occur when you are summoned by the King.*" He had added, "*For those who do not know, it is punishable by death for anyone to approach the King if they are not summoned.*"

"Esther."

She startled and looked up to see Hegai standing to the side of the staircase, his hand extended for her to precede him.

She stared at him, tears trembling on her lashes. *This cannot be happening. I refused the training, I cannot do this. It is too hard.* As she looked at Hegai, her gaze turned inward. Instead of standing in the Courtyard of the House of Women, she was at home, listening to her maman.

"And if this is so hard that you perish?" Maman had asked. *"We have faced challenges. We know when we face them again, Yahweh will be with us. And one day, if we perish,"* Maman had shrugged her shoulders, *"we perish. But then Yahweh will take us to Abraham's bosom."*

"Esther..." she faintly heard her name. She shook her head, clearing her thoughts, and looked. Hegai was still standing by the staircase, his hand still extended. "Esther." His countenance was stoic, but in his gaze, was a hint of kindness. "Come. It is time."

Drawing a shuddering breath, she nodded. Lifting a hand to wipe away the tears, she placed her slippered foot on the first stair. *If I perish, I perish.*

At the top of the stairs, she followed Hegai as he led the way through a series of convoluted corridors and courtyards. *How did Queen Atossa find her way through this maze?*

"I was the Shahbanu of three Kings of Persia," Queen Atossa had told her elderly Sarkar Khanums on the day she had wandered through the Palace. *"I know about the special entrance from the King's Apartment to the Queen's Apartment."*

At length, Hegai stopped in front of an atrium. At the end was a set of double doors carved with the Royal Lamassu and guarded by a dozen Warriors. The walls on either side of the doors had a painting of a man wearing a crown accompanied by two servants, one who was beardless. It was the same as the painting next to the small door leading to the House of Women

A Warrior next to the door approached them. "Greetings, Hegai Kouroush Safa."

"Greetings, Mehrab pur Kalantari." Hegai lifted a hand toward her. "This is Esther dokhtar Bunyamin. She has been summoned by the King."

The Warrior nodded. "I will inform the Cup-bearer." He crossed the floor to knock on the one of the doors.

It was opened by an elderly man dressed in a white tunic and trousers of finely-woven white linen edged with gold thread. "Greetings, Hegai Kouroush Safa."

"Greetings, Kurush Tars Dida." Hegai extended a hand to Esther. "This is Esther dokhtar Bunyamin. She has been summoned by the King."

"Greetings, Esther dokhtar Bunyamin." The Cup-bearer stepped to one side of the opened door. "Please come in. The King is waiting for you."

Esther looked at Hegai, not sure what was expected of her. *I did not take the training.*

"Come," the eunuch said. "Let us greet the King." He walked through the door.

After a quick glance around her—*I could not outrun the War-riors*—Esther followed Hegai into the King's Apartment.

Once inside, Kurush gently closed the door and turned. "Hegai, the King is still not feeling well," he spoke in a whisper. He looked at Esther. "He often suffers from severe pains in his head."

"Oh...I am sorry to hear that." Esther glanced between Hegai and the Cup-bearer. "Perhaps I should come another day."

"I suggested that to the King," Kurush said. "He refused, saying he wanted to see you." He led them through a short corridor into the sitting room of the King's Apartment.

Esther and Hegai waited near the entrance of the corridor while Kurush approached the King.

She controlled her expression, not wanting to appear to be gaping at the King's sitting room. *Will I ever grow accustomed to the size and lavishness of the rooms in the Palace?* From a quick glance, she judged this room to be twice the size of the one in Queen Atossa's Apartment. The room was square, the floor covered in polished red tile with twelve tall marble columns— crowned with a capital of two kneeling bulls—holding up the ceiling. A set of doors on the far wall opened onto a garden courtyard. On the third wall were two closed doors; Esther assumed these led to the King's bath area and—*she blushed*—his bedchamber. On the wall closest to them, a fire burned brightly in a fireplace carved to look like the opened mouth of a Lamassu. In front of the fire were two Throne-like chairs, the arm rests carved to look like Lamassu and padded with red cushions. Tapestries of the Kings of Persia hung on the walls, with divans, tables, chests, bronze lampstands, and hanging lanterns placed around the room.

In the corner of the room next to the garden, Esther saw a bagdir. She bit back a smile. *Baba, even in the sitting room of the most powerful man in the Persian Empire, you are here.*

All of this flashed through her mind in the time it took Kurush to approach the man seated in one of the chairs near the fireplace. Dressed in soft blue linen trousers and tunic and wearing leather slippers, the King was leaning against the thick cushion, eyes closed, one hand rubbing his brow.

"My Lord King," Kurush bowed, his voice low, "Hegai Kouroush Safa and the mastoureh Esther dokhtar Bunyamin have obeyed your summons."

His eyes still covered, the King beckoned with his other hand.

Kurush turned to them. "You may enter."

Esther followed Hegai into the sitting room. Once near the King, they bowed low, right hand covering their mouths, remaining in that position until the King spoke.

"You may rise."

Esther waited, allowing Hegai to rise first, which she assumed—given his position—was the correct thing to do. When she straightened, she met the King's eyes. She felt uncertain and shy as he regarded her, a smile hovering around his lips.

He turned to the other two men. "Thank you, Hegai. Thank you, Kurush, I have no more need of you tonight."

"My Lord King," the Cup-bearer said, "your headache—"

"—is getting better," the King finished. He smiled. "Kurush, I appreciate your concern and dedication to my health and comfort. I speak truth before Ahura Mazda when I assure you I have no further need of you tonight. You are free to go."

"As you wish, My Lord King." The elderly man bowed, "Have a restful evening," and walked to the door.

Esther's heart flew up in her throat and beat there wildly. *This cannot be happening. This cannot be happening.* She looked at Hegai, eyes wide and pleading.

He turned to her. "Esther dokhtar Bunyamin, I will return for you in the morning."

She watched the Royal Eunuch bow to the King and cross the room to join Kurush. Both men bowed deeply once more and left the King's Apartment. The doors closed with faint but dreadful, *click.*

She stared at the closed door until the King spoke, "Greetings, Esther dokhtar Bunyamin."

Drawing a shuddering breath, she turned. Just as the first time she met him, he looked weary, and—from a sudden grimace—in pain.

Noting the amphora and goblets on the table, Esther set her harp on the floor near the other chair, poured a goblet of wine, and handed it the King.

"Thank you. That is a kindness." He took the goblet and indicated the other chair. "Please sit."

She smoothed her tunic and sat, folding her hands in her lap. She knew, as a mastoura, she should avert her eyes from the King, but due to her training with Mordecai, she watched as he took a sip and set the goblet on the table, grimacing. *He might be the King of Persia, but he is suffering.*

"My Lord King, are you in pain?"

"I am." Covering his eyes, he rubbed his brows. "I have had

240

pains like these since I was Artaxerxes' age. As I told Kurush, it is better. There are times when it feels as if I am hit between my eyes with a hammer."

"What methods of treatment have the Royal Physicians recommended?"

He opened an eye to peek at her. "Erbed Saeid said you had the skill of a Mantreh Pezeshk and a Gyah Pezeshk." He smiled. "I have never met such a one among the House of Women." He took another drink. "The Royal Physicians have tried the methods of healing; some have helped in the past, but not tonight."

She hesitated—*Hegai, is this why you recommended I bring my harp?*—and said, "My harp music might help."

"It might indeed. Your playing has helped my mother."

Lifting the harp, she settled herself in the chair where she could see him through the harp strings. She began playing a series of single notes, creating the lulling sound of a gentle waterfall. She watched him, adjusting the music until she saw the grimace ease and his breathing slow. *Perhaps he will relax and fall asleep, and I can sit quietly until Hegai comes for me.* She continued playing, altering the music to a lower key.

She began humming softly, thinking of a psalm from David. *Whoever dwells in the shelter of the Most High will rest in the shadow of the Almighty.* She sang the phrase in her mind over and over before switching to another of David's psalms, *Let the morning bring me word of Your unfailing love, for I have put my trust in You.* She closed her eyes, playing the waterfall on the harp, and repeating the scriptures that resonated in her. *I will dwell in the shelter of Your shadow. I will look for Your unfailing love. I put my trust in You.*

"Thank you."

Esther stifled a gasp and looked at the King.

He was sitting upright, his eyes free of pain. "I did not mean to startle you," he smiled.

"Oh, forgive me, My Lord King. I was not startled." She moved

her hand across the neck of the harp. "It is common for me to be…
drawn into the music myself."

"I can see how you could be. You play beautifully, and my
pain is gone."

"I am glad to hear that, My Lord King. Would you like
more wine?"

"I would. Pour some for yourself."

"Thank you, My Lord King." She felt his eyes on her as she
refilled his goblet and poured one for herself.

Xerxes took a drink. "I would get to know you better."

She stared at the wine.

"My maman and pesar," his voice held affection, "speak much
of you."

Be careful what you say. She looked at him and smiled. "The
Malekeh Jahann and Puora Vaspuhr speak of me?"

"Yes," Xerxes ran his thumb on the edge of the goblet. "They
tell me you have lost your parents."

"I have." She set the goblet on the table and picked up the
harp. She began playing chords, slowly moving toward the strings
at bottom of the instrument.

"How long has it been?"

"Nearly two years. It feels like forever." She switched to single
notes, sad, echoing the pain in her heart. "It feels like yesterday."
She lifted a hand to wipe a tear.

"Are you still in mourning?" His voice was soft, caring.

"I will always mourn their loss."

" I understand. It has been five years since my father died." He
set the goblet on the table. "Do you recall Marathon?"

Esther nodded. All knew of the Persian Army suffering a
defeat at the hands of the Greeks in the valley of Marathon.

"After Marathon, my father began planning another campaign against the Greeks, only this time, he was determined to
command the Warriors." He looked away, his gaze as if he were
seeing through the years. "Father spent three years preparing for

242

the war, when a revolt broke out in Egypt. Soon after this news reached him, he grew ill. The physicians were unable to do anything for him, not even to alleviate the pain. He suffered for a month before dying.

"Many people throughout the Empire think I wanted to wage war on Egypt and Greece for power. That was not the reason." Xerxes tightened his hand into a fist. "It was in retaliation for my father's death." He relaxed his hand, letting out a long breath. "I feel the pain of his loss as if it were yesterday."

She looked at him, empathizing his sorrow. "Grief is like a splinter deep in every fingertip," she whispered. "To touch anything is torture."

He nodded. "It is indeed. So, Esther dokhtar Bunyamin," he lifted his goblet, "tell me about your family."

"My family?" *Watch your words. Speak truth, but watch your words.*

"Yes. Your family."

"My family has lived in Susa since your noble ancestor, Cyrus the Great, established the mighty Persian Empire."

He grinned. "I am certain my maman told you about my pedarbozorg."

"She did indeed." She smiled. "Queen Atossa is obviously proud of her father."

"She always has been," he nodded. "So, your family has been in Persia for three generations. What were your parents like—if it does not cause pain to speak of them."

She controlled her surprise. *He cares whether I am hurting.* "Maman was beautiful."

"As is her daughter."

Esther smiled. "She was skilled at many things, but Maman truly loved gardening." She pointed to the courtyard garden. "She would be able to walk into any garden and tell whether the plants were healthy or suffering."

"It sounds as if she could have been a Gyah Pezeshk."

"It was not uncommon for Maman to have," she grinned,

"*heated discussions*...with our Gyah Pezeshk over various herbs and plants."

"So your mother loved gardening. What did your father love?"

"Maman," she smiled, looking at the King. "And me. He loved Maman and gave her many beautiful things." She laughed, "One time, my maman told me she had to be careful of saying, 'I wish I could have a particular item,' because Baba would get it for her."

He smiled. "And you? Did you wish your baba and maman would give you things?"

"As a child, yes," she laughed. "There were many things I wanted. But as I grew older—no." Her eyes misted. "Now they are gone, and I have come to realize Maman and Baba gave me something more valuable than anything in all of Persia."

"And what is that?"

"Their love." Her gaze turned inward, her voice softened. "My parents loved each other, and they loved me. There is nothing more valuable for a child than that."

"No one loves me," Xerxes whispered, "except you, Maman-bozorg, Pedarbozorg Otanes, and..."

"Forgive me, My Lord King," Esther's brow wrinkled, "I did not hear what you said."

"It is nothing," the King said. "I was thinking of something my son told me." He looked at her. "I agree; to have parents who love each other is a rare gift. Do you have siblings?"

"Sadly, no. Maman lost several babies before I was born." She sighed. "I always feel my parents' presence." She glanced at the bagdir. "Every day I see things that remind me of them. I honor them by honoring their memory, by honoring their teachings."

"I too understand honoring a parent's memory." He looked at her over the rim of the goblet. "Hegai told me of your desire to honor your mother's teaching concerning...the relationship between a husband and wife."

"My Lord King," Esther stared at the floor, her cheeks burning, "I...you see..."

"Esther," his voice was soft, "there is no need to explain." He set his goblet down and stood. "Come."

Setting her goblet down, she picked up the harp and stood.

"Leave the harp. You will not need it."

"I do not understand."

"It is time," Xerxes extended a hand to her, "for your training to begin."

Chapter 51

Esther lay still, listening for any sounds from the sitting room. It was quiet.

She opened her eyes, squinting against the morning sun streaming through the windows, illuminating the gold inlays on the bedframe, the side tables, the woven rugs on the floor, the imperial Shahbaz emblazoned on the walls, even the threads of gold in the overhead canopy and in the simple white tunic on a nearby chair.

Everywhere she looked in this opulent bedchamber was evidence of wealth and power beyond imagination.

Yet, she wanted none of it.

Not that…*he*—she could not bring herself to even think his name—had been harsh or unkind.

This was not what she had wanted; this was not what she had dreamt of.

I will never have it.

Never will I have a betrothal ceremony. Never will I watch for my betrothed husband to come for me. Never will Rabbi Omar, Mordecai, and Deagah speak the blessings over us. There will be no mazal tovs from our families and our friends. I will never go home. Mordecai would not want me. No one would want me. I am an outcast.

She covered her mouth with her hands as moan rose from deep within, erupting from her lips as a sobbing wail.

PART TWO
SHE WAS AN OUTCAST

Chapter 52

"Rabbi, it was kind of you to bring bread. As I told," Mordecai's lips thinned, "others, I am capable of preparing meals."

"Ah, but if I did not bring bread," the Rabbi smiled, "I would not have the opportunity to have time with a friend."

"You speak truth, Rabbi." Mordecai smiled. "While I welcome spending time with you, I imagine there are more reasons for your visit."

The Rabbi smiled. "Mordecai," he shook a finger, "your skills as a Mantreh Prezesh give you insight. Yes, I came to see how you are. You have missed some of the gatherings of the Elders."

"I am sorry." He looked away, "I have been *distracted* by other matters."

"How is Hadassah?"

Mordecai smiled at the other man. "Now who has insight? To answer your question," he lifted his shoulders, "I do not know. Shortly after she was first taken, it was arranged for me to daily bring her foods and to speak with her.

"Several weeks ago, I was told I would not be able to speak to her." He looked away. *"The odds are,"* Safa had grinned, *"that Esther dokhtar Bunyamin has been summoned by the King."*

He shook his head and looked at the Rabbi. "I continue to go to the Palace every day, and I receive the same answer; she is not available. I confess; I am worried, and there is nothing I can do."

"Ah, but there is something we can do."

Mordecai looked at the rabbi, his brow furrowed. "What?"

The Rabbi extended a hand. "We can pray."

CHAPTER 53

"Kurush Tars Dida's breath is labored," Behrouz pur Mansour said. "He refuses wine and eats little."

"He sleeps most of the day," Khodadad pur Arman added. "When he is awake, he speaks things that…cannot be."

"What?" Xerxes stood, his voice echoing across the Throne Room. "I summon my Royal Physicians in to examine my Cup-bearer," he seethed, "and you dare to accuse him of the crime of lying?" He snapped his fingers, "Haman."

Haman drew his sword, stepping toward the two physicians standing at the foot of the King's Throne.

"Oh no, My Lord King! No!" Khodadad gasped. Holding the scroll in front of his chest, he stepped back, staring wide-eyed between Xerxes and Haman. "That is not what I meant."

"Stay," Xerxes lifted a hand to stop Haman.

"Khodadad pur Arman," the King's voice was soft and deadly, "you have one opportunity to explain what you meant about *Kurush speaking of things that cannot be?*"

"Forgive me, My Lord King," the physician wiped his brow. "I was trying to explain that the Cup-bearer speaks as if things from long ago are happening now and people who are no longer living are in the room with him."

"Ahh…I see," Xerxes took a deep breath and sat. "What is

251

causing Kurush's weakness and confusion? What medicines do you suggest?"

Khodadad nodded at Behrouz.

"My Lord King," Behrouz said, "from our examinations, we can find only one thing to cause his weakness and confusion…age. Kurush Tars Dida is not ill; he is old. He is preparing to pass across the Chinvat Bridge into the presence of Ahura Mazda."

"Kurush is dying?"

The two physicians nodded.

"He was fine a week ago. How long does he have?"

"We cannot say," Khodadad said. "It could be days, weeks, perhaps longer."

Haman looked across the Throne at Hegai. The eunuch shook his head, frowning.

"How can it be *days*?" The King shook his head. "Since I ascended the Throne, Kurush has been like a father to me. I thought I would lose my mother first." He looked at the physicians. "No one else is to tell the Malekeh Jahann of this news. I will. Hegai," he turned to the Royal Eunuch, "bring Esther to me and have her bring the harp. We will go together to visit the Mother of the World. I am certain she will want to hear Esther's music."

"My Lord King; Esther dokhtar Bunyamin cannot come."

"What?" Xerxes frowned. "Why can she not come?"

"Shaashgaz Javed Farrokh informed me is ill."

"What?" Xerxes stood again. "Send for Qabela dokhtar Somayeh."

"It has already been done. Qabela is examining her now."

"Behrouz, Khodadad, you stay with Kurush," the King started walking across the Throne Room. "I will go to Esther."

Chapter 54

"Here, Khanum Esther," Qabela dokhtar Somayeh held a cup to her lips, "drink this tea. It is made from mint and ginger. It will help ease your discomfort."

"I cannot," Esther pushed the midwife's hand away. "The smell is causing my stomach to roil. *Ooph!* "She clasped a cloth over her mouth and lifted a hand to Farah. "Bowl…please."

In quick steps, Farah moved the midwife out of her way and placed a bowl in front of Esther just as she vomited.

After several minutes, Esther fell back on her pillow, moaning.

Farah removed the bowl as Irida dipped two cloths in water, handing one to Esther to wipe her mouth while she used the other to wipe her brow. Liana waved a fan over her face. "Better?"

Esther took a shallow breath. "A little."

A gentle knock from the other room drew their attention.

"Who can that be?" Qabela stood. "Shaashgaz knows you are not feeling well."

Farah walked to the bedchamber door. After a brief conversation, she closed the door and turned to Esther. "Hegai Kouroush Safa is here to see you." Farah's eyes were wide.

"Hegai?" Esther laid a hand on her brow. "Let him in."

The eunuch entered the room. "Esther, how are you feeling?"

"It has eased some."

"You have a guest."

"A guest!" Qabela stood, placing fists on ample hips. "She cannot see a guest."

"She will see this guest," Hegai turned to open the door and stepped aside as the King entered the bedchamber.

As one, the other four women bowed.

"My Lord King!" Esther gasped, throwing off the linen sheet, "Forgive me for not receiving you," she stood. *"Ohhh..."* the room went dark.

Esther crept towards consciousness as someone caught her, lifted her, and laid her on the bed. She felt a cool, wet cloth across her brow. Then she became aware of voices.

"Esther, Esther, wake up." It was Farah voice; she sounded worried.

"Is she all right?" Liana also sounded concerned.

"Hegai Kouroush Safa," Qabela was angry. "I cannot believe you would surprise her in this manner."

"Do not blame Hegai," a third voice said. "I could not wait to see her."

The third voice—a man's voice—brought Esther back to full consciousness.

She opened her eyes slowly, looking at the people around her. Farah stood on one side of the bed, a damp cloth in her hand; next to her was Liana, holding a cup; and Irida was waving a fan in her direction. Qabela was next to Hegai, who stood at the foot of the bed, stoically ignoring the midwife's whisperings about the impropriety of disturbing her patient. Esther turned her head to the other side of the bed. There...his arm beneath her shoulders, his breath soft on her face, his gaze worried was...*the King!*

"Oh, My Lord King, forgive me," Esther tried sitting up, "I did not mean to be disrespectful, *ohhh...*" She collapsed against his chest. She looked up into his face.

"*Shhh…*" A finger moved the lock of hair from her eyes. "I was told you do not feel well. Qabela Somayeh," he turned to the midwife, his tone hardened, "do you know the reason?"

The woman bowed, "I do, My Lord King."

"I know the cause," Esther tried sitting up again; Xerxes arm held her tight. "My stomach has always been unpredictable. This is nothing more than what I have experienced all my life."

"Not this time," Qabela said.

"What do you mean?" Xerxes asked.

"She has not experienced *this* before." The midwife gave the King a knowing look, nodding when he lifted an eyebrow.

"I do not understand," Esther said.

Qabela looked from Xerxes to Esther and grinned. "You are with child."

CHAPTER 55

Haman entered the Throne Room the next morning. The King was talking to Hegai. "See to it."

"It shall be done." The Eunuch bowed and walked out of the Throne room.

The King turned to Haman. "Greetings," he smiled.

"Greetings, My Lord King," he bowed, controlling his expressions. *Yesterday he was concerned over his Cup-bearer. Now he is smiling?* "My Lord King, how is the harci Esther dokhtar Bunyamin? I heard she was ill."

"She is still weak, but the Royal Midwife expects her to be better soon. I will escort her to visit with my mother and my son later this day."

"My Lord King," I am happy to hear the harci—"

"Her name is Esther dokhtar Bunyamin, not *the harci*."

Haman bowed his head, "As you say, My Lord King. I am happy to hear *Esther dokhtar Bunyamin* is expected to recover, but until she does," Haman spread his hands, "do you think it wise for you—or the Malekeh Jahann or the Puora Vaspuhr—to be around her?"

Xerxes laughed. "What has caused her discomfort will not harm us. Haman, you will be one of the first to hear the news."

No! "News, My Lord King?"

"Yes, news! Scribes, write this proclamation." Xerxes lifted a goblet and took a drink while the scribes set out the parchment and their writing implements. When they nodded they were ready, he declared, "Let it be proclaimed throughout all the satrapies of the Persian Empire that I, Xerxes Kiapur Dairus—King of the Medes and King of the Persians—have chosen Esther dokhtar Bunyamin to be my Shahbanu."

He lifted his goblet, "Long live the Queen!"

CHAPTER 56

22 ORDIBEHESHT
5TH YEAR OF THE REIGN OF XERXES,
KING OF THE MEDES AND THE PERSIANS

"Mordecai!"

He turned to see Hakaliah bar Seraiah waving at him from their shop. Mordecai crossed to the road. "Greetings, Hakaliah," he nodded to the goldsmith's wife, "Greetings, Naomi bat Reuben."

"Greetings, Mordecai," Namoi said. "Pardon me, I must tend to a customer." Turning, she nudged her husband's side before walking to a lady inspecting a tray of bracelets.

Hakaliah glanced back at his wife, turned toward him, and smiled. "Mordecai, Naomi and I would…uh…be honored if you would take supper with our family one night."

Mordecai smiled. "I would be honored to have supper with your family. It appears I am becoming quite popular among our community of late. I have received," he grinned, "many invitations to come for meals."

He exchanged looks with the goldsmith. They broke into laughter, clapping each other on their backs, until a clanging of bells drew their attention.

A chariot—carrying the charioteer, a Warrior, and a herbad—
was pulling up to stop at the side of the Great Gate. A crowd was
already gathering as a herbad and a Warrior stepped out of the
chariot. The herbad followed, carrying a basket filled with scrolls,
spikes, and a mallet. Setting the basket on the ground, the magus
selected a scroll and turned toward the people. He unrolled the
parchment, cleared his throat, and began reading.

"Be it known that on this day—the 22nd day of Ordibehesht,
in the fifth year of Xerxes, King of the Medes and King of the
Persians—the following proclamation is made.

"King Xerxes Kiapur Darius is happy to announce that he has
at last selected a new Queen."

The crowd started whispering, "Who do you think it is?" "Probably one of the daughters of a Shathapavan or one of the Azam."

The Warrior lifted his spear and thumped it on the road.
"Silence!" he yelled.

Once the crowd settled, the herbad cleared his throat and
continued reading. "Be it known that King Xerxes has selected
Esther dokhtar Bunyamin to be the Shahbanu, the King's Lady,
the Queen of Persia.

"In honor of Queen Esther, the King has proclaimed a holiday
throughout all the satrapies of Persia. There will be celebrations
held across the Empire. In one week, everyone within Susa will
be invited to come to the Palace, to greet Queen Esther and to
accept a gift from her and King Xerxes."

Lowering the scroll, the herbad picked up a mallet and
two stakes, crossed to the tall, wooden post near the Great Gate.
Smoothing the parchment against the post, he hammered the
spikes into the top and bottom.

Turning back to the crowd, he said, "Today, this proclamation
is being sent to all one hundred twenty-seven satrapies throughout
the Persian Empire, written in the language of all the peoples.

"Long live King Xerxes; Long live Queen Esther."

Part Three
She Was The Queen

CHAPTER 57

Esther looked at her reflection in the tall mirror set in a carved wooden frame adorned with gold.

She ran a hand along her garment. Woven from silk and dyed the blue of a peacock's feather, it was embroidered with threads of silver and gold, from the Imperial Lamassu and Shahbaz sewn into the cloth, to the wide ribbons edging the neckline, sleeves, and hem. Her slippers were of golden leather edged with diamonds.

Farah set the brush down and turned to a pillow on which was resting a golden collar set with diamonds and sapphires. From the center, a single large, blood-red ruby hung in an oval gold setting. On either side of the collar were matching earrings. Farah secured the jewelry around Esther's neck and in her ears, and then stepped back.

Esther stood, looked at her reflection once more, and turned.

Farah, along with all seven of her attendants, lowered their heads, their right hands covering their mouths. "My Lady Esther."

Esther's eyes widened at their bows. "Farah," she looked at the others, "Banafshe, Laleh, Orkideh, Golshan, Irida, Liana, and Anemos; this is me. I am just Esther."

"I mean no disrespect," Farah said, "but you are no longer *just Esther*. Today, you will be crowned. You will become the Shahbanu, the King's Lady, the Queen of the Medes and the Persians."

Esther placed a hand on her stomach. *And mother of our child.* Xerxes had insisted on having this ceremony quickly because of her pregnancy. *"I do not want anyone to think of our child,"* he had told her privately, laying his hand on her stomach, *"as a havou."*

A knock at the door interrupted her thoughts. It was Hegai. Dressed in his court robe, he wore a white turban with a large diamond set in front.

"Greetings, Hegai Kouroush Safa," she smiled.

He bowed. "My Lady Esther."

"Is it time?"

He extended his hand. "It is time."

She turned to Farah and embraced her. "Thank you for everything," she whispered.

"Thank you," Farah said, " for being my friend. We will," she looked at the other women and then back at Esther, "await you—in the Queen's Apartment."

Esther nodded and turned to Hegai. "I am ready."

Esther followed the Chief Eunuch through the door at the entrance of the House of Women. Stepping into the corridor, they were surrounded by a sadfarbod. Hegai had explained what would happen that day, but it was still unbelievable to be escorted by one hundred Warriors.

They walked through the corridors of the Palace, until they reached the Inner Court of the Throne Room where they were approached by Haman's lieutenant.

"Artabanus tabar Mithradata," Hegai extended a hand toward Esther. "This is Esther dokhtar Bunyamin. She has been summoned by King Xerxes."

The Warrior nodded. "King Xerxes awaits." He stepped aside, bowing as she walked passed him into the Throne Room of the King of Persia.

Esther had never been in the Throne Room, but she did not look at the room nor at the throngs of people gathered, nor the countless Immortals stationed around the room.

Her gaze was on the platform on the far end, where was located the golden Throne of the King of Persia. Seated on the Throne, dressed in his Royal Court robe, holding the Imperial Scepter in his right hand, wearing the Imperial Signet Ring on his left hand, and the Crown of the King of Persia set on his head, Xerxes Kiapur Darius waited for her.

When she reached the foot of the platform, Esther bowed. "My Lord King Xerxes."

"Rise, Lady Esther dokhtar Bunyamin."

As Esther straightened, Hegai handed her up the steps to stand before the King's Throne. She bowed again to Xerxes.

Behind the King and to his left was Haman pur Hammedatha. Lifting her chin, she met his gaze. *Never will I bow to you.*

She noticed movement. Seated behind the King, also dressed in Royal Court robes with the Crown of the Malekeh Jahann on her head, was Queen Atossa. The elderly lady grinned, waving at her.

Esther smiled at her and turned as Erbed Saeid Mogh Elaikim, in white ceremonial robes, stepped over to escort her to the Queen's Throne.

After she was seated, the ceremony continued as a dozen magi escorted Prince Artaxerxes, dressed in his Royal Court robes and carrying a red pillow on which was set a crown and a ring. When he reached the platform, the Prince climbed the steps, bowed to his father, and extended the pillow.

Xerxes picked up the ring and stood. Crossing to Esther, he held out his hand. She laid her left hand in his, blinking back tears as he slipped the ring on her finger. "My Shahbanu," his eyes were gentle.

"My Lord King," she smiled.

After Xerxes sat down, Artaxerxes turned to extend the pillow to Saeid.

The magus lifted the crown—diamonds, rubies, and sapphires flashing from the torches in the Throne Room—and turned to place the golden diadem on Esther's black curls, speaking the words that would officially acknowledge her Queen of the Medes and the Persians.

Turning to the crowd in the room, Saeid lifted his arms. "Long live King Xerxes. Long live Queen Esther."

The Throne Room reverberated with a fanfare of trumpets and cheers of the people crying, "Long live King Xerxes. Long live Queen Esther."

After the people quieted, Xerxes stood. He thanked them for witnessing this momentous event and looked forward to introducing his Queen to each of them during the coming festivities. He turned and gestured for Haman. "See the room is cleared," he lifted a finger, "respectfully but quickly."

Esther was relieved this ceremony had not been lengthy. Xerxes had explained not only did he know she needed to rest, but he was also concerned for his mother. "This is the first imperial event she has attended in years. I would not want…something to happen."

She nodded. "I understand." She looked at the ring on her finger—a smaller replica of Xerxes' Signet Ring—and reached up to feel the band of the crown.

"Would you like to see it?"

She smiled. "I confess I would. I only caught a glimpse of it when Erbed Saeid lifted it from the pillow. It looked beautiful."

"I will send for a mirror."

"My Lord King," she smiled, "I did not mean now."

"Ah, my Shahbanu," he smiled, "you will need to learn to be careful what you ask for. I will give you anything, even up to half my Kingdom." Within minutes, he handed her a mirror.

Esther turned her head from side to side, looking at the wide gold diadem, the overlaid leaves of gold. She ran a finger along the golden circle set in the front and the strands of golden beads tipped with diamonds on the bottom. On one side, she saw letters H and S intertwined with leaves. *Hakaliah's goldsmith's mark.* "This is the most beautiful thing I have ever seen."

"It looks beautiful on you," Xerxes said.

"Javansher, help me up." Atossa called.

Artaxerxes hurried over to help his grandmother out of the chair and escorted her to his father.

Releasing her grandson's arm, Queen Atossa bowed to Xerxes. "My Lord King," and then turned to Esther, "My Lady Queen."

Esther smiled, acknowledging her bow. "Malekeh Jahann."

After bowing to his father, Artaxerxes turned to her, "My Lady Queen."

Esther smiled, acknowledging his bow. "Puora Vaspuhr."

Artaxerxes turned back to Xerxes, leaned over, and whispered, hand cupping his mouth.

Xerxes smiled. "We will have to ask Queen Esther."

"Ask me?" Her eyes widened. "Ask me what?"

The King looked at Artaxerxes, "He wants to know," he turned his gaze back to her, "if he may call you, *Maman.*"

Blinking away the sheen of tears that gathered in her eyes, Esther smiled and nodded. Standing, she opened her arms.

The young boy stepped across the platform into her embrace. She felt his shuddering breath, "My maman."

She tightened her arms. "My pesar."

CHAPTER 58

E sther's lips were sore from smiling.

The celebration was larger than any Norooz festival she had ever seen.

Over the last week, displays of athletic and military skills, dancers, singers, and theatrical performances were held on the grounds of the Royal Citadel.

Inside the Palace, people waited in long lines to meet the new Queen.

Xerxes told her Haman had questioned this idea. "The Hazarpatish was concerned with so many unknown people inside the Palace. He said it presented a potential threat to the Royal Family.

"I told him to do whatever was necessary to protect us. I said, *Esther is not Queen of only the wealthy and powerful,*" he grinned, "*but of all the citizens of the Persian Empire.*"

In response, Haman called for the Ten Thousand Immortals to be stationed across the grounds of the Royal Citadel and throughout the Palace.

Every day during the celebration, Esther sat in the Queen's Throne next to Xerxes. Erbed Saeid would ask each citizen's name and then turned to introduce them to the King and Queen.

"Mordecai ben Jair."

Esther controlled her expression as the King acknowledged her cousin's bow.

Turning to her, Mordecai bowed. "My Lady Queen."

"What is your profession?" Xerxes asked.

"My Lord King, I am a Gyah Pezeshk and a Mantreh Pezeshk,"

"That is an honorable profession, Mordecai ben Jair," she smiled.

"Thank you," he smiled at her, "My Lady Queen."

Esther watched as he left the platform.

"Hakaliah bar Seraiah," Erbed Saeid intoned, "his wife Naomi bat Reuben, their sons Nehemiah and Hanani and their *dokhtar-zan*—daughter-in-law—Miriam bat Deagah."

Esther turned to her friends. *Do they still consider me their friends?*

"Rise, Hakaliah bar Seraiah," Xerxes turned to Esther. "This is the goldsmith who created your crown."

She lifted a hand to touch the band of the diadem. "It is beautiful," she smiled. "You are a skilled craftsman, Hakaliah bar Seraiah."

"I am honored My Lady Queen thinks so."

"And this is your family?" Xerxes smiled. "Are your sons following in their father's footsteps?"

"Hanani is following in my footsteps, My Lord King. Nehemiah…has yet to determine his path."

"And what," Esther looked at the young man, "does he wish to do?"

"He is a man of letters," Hakaliah smiled at his son. "He writes many, many letters."

"Perhaps he should train as a scribe," Xerxes said. "We always have need for more scribes."

Nehemiah bowed, "I would be honored to serve the King and Queen however I may."

"We will mention your name to our Royal Scribes," Xerxes said, turning to Miriam, "And this is your dokhtarzan?"

"Yes, My Lord King. Miriam is Hanani's wife. They are newly married and," the goldsmith smiled at Esther, "Miriam is carrying our first grandchild."

"Sad-bas!" Xerxes smiled.

"Yes, sad-bas," Esther smiled at her friend. "May you be blessed with many years and many children."

"Thank you, My Lady Queen," Miriam smiled. "May you also be blessed with many years and many children."

Chapter 59

5 Aban
Fifth year of the reign of Xerxes,
King of the Medes and the Persians

Haman tightened the leather belt. "What does Navjaa say?"
"She has not seen Xerxes of late. Hmm…" she inspected
the garments the maid held out for her, "should I wear
the green tunic or the yellow one?"

"I care not what color you wear," he seethed. "What do you mean?"

"Marjaneh, leave the green one," Zeresh flicked her fingers to
the maid. "You may leave."

"Yes, my Lady," the servant laid the robe across a bench, bowed,
and left the room. "If you must discuss our plans," she turned to
Haman, "perhaps you should wait until we are alone. Marjaneh is
a new servant; I have not determined whether she can be trusted."

"If she is not trustworthy," he slid his double-edged dagger
into its sheath, "dismiss her or kill her; I care not which. Now, what
do you mean Navjaa has not seen Xerxes of late?"

"Navjaa said since Esther was crowned Queen, the King has
not been calling for her—or the other harci—as frequently. When
she suggests the things you have instructed to Xerxes, the King
dismisses them, saying he will consult with those closest to him."

271

"Who are those people?"

Zeresh shrugged. "I assume it is Queen Atossa, Kurush tars Dida, or Queen Esther. She also mentioned the King boasting about how wise Prince Artaxerxes is becoming."

Haman spit out a curse. "I have worked too hard and too long to have two old people, a child, and a woman influencing Xerxes. We might have to," he lifted the sword, running a finger along the edge, "do something about them."

CHAPTER 60

"He is handsome," Atossa stroked the infant's cheek, laughing softly when he grabbed her finger, "and strong. Just like his father and grandfather. Sad-bas, Xerxes. Sad-bas, Esther."

"Thank you, *Madarzan*," Esther smiled, feeling bemused. *I am addressing the Malekeh Jahann as my mother-in-law. A mother-in-law who had spent time teaching me how to be Queen.*

She looked around at her apartment, the Queen's Apartment. Smaller than Xerxes' apartment, hers was similar in design to Atossa's. She was not surprised to see a bagdir in the room. She had Hegai arrange for Maman's white marble bench from the Courtyard in the House of Women to be placed in her private courtyard garden. Now, whether she was inside or in the garden, she felt her parent's closeness.

Here I am, in my apartment—the Queen's Apartment. I was an outcast, without a home, without a family. Now I have a home and family.

"Thank you, Maman," Xerxes chuckled the baby's chin. "He looks like Father, does he not?"

"He does indeed," Atossa smiled.

"Then he shall be named after my father." Xerxes lifted the child from Atossa's arms. "Prince Darius Kiapur Xerxes. Dar-i-us, Dar-i-us," he cooed, rocking the babe as he crossed the sitting room to Artaxerxes. "Here, Artaxerxes, do you wish to hold your younger brother?"

"Oh, I, uh," the older boy lifted his hands in front of his chest, "Baba, uh…I do not know how… I do not wish to harm…"

"Sit," Xerxes laughed. He waited until his older son was seated before handing the baby to him, demonstrating how to support the infant's head.

Atossa crossed the room to sit by Esther on the divan. "How are you feeling?"

"Better. I do not," Esther glanced at Xerxes and Artaxerxes and lowered her voice, "*hurt* as much. Farah dokhtar Mahboubeh found some herbs to *ease* the discomfort."

"Ah, yes," Atossa laughed softly. "It is a surprise the first time you give birth. Are you planning to nurse the babe?"

Esther nodded. "I am. I realize some might think, as Queen, I should have a wet nurse care for him, but he is *my baby*. I want to take care of him. Xerxes agreed with me. He said he would have a door installed to connect my apartment with with the Royal Nursery." She pitched her voice lower, *'I will give you anything, even up to half my Kingdom.'* She smiled. "He even agreed to my request to allow Farah to become my Sarkar Khanum."

Atossa smiled. "Why does he need other women when he has you?" She looked at Xerxes and grinned. "If I were to tell anyone—even my two Sarkar Khanums—that King Xerxes was playing with a baby, they would think my mind was wandering. But it is not," she glanced at Esther, "at least not at this time."

Esther turned to the older Queen, her eyes wide. "Madarzan… I…uh…"

"Esther," Atossa patted her arm, "I am aware my mind often confuses the past with the present. But not today. No, not today." She looked at Xerxes and Artaxerxes with the baby. "This is good."

"Yes, it is good," Esther said.

"Take care of them. Xerxes, Artaxerxes, baby Darius. Take care of them." Atossa looked at her. "Always remember: Family is important."

CHAPTER 61

Mordecai was walking to the synagogue when he noticed some people staring at the Great Gate. Crossing the street, he waited until the others left, before stepping up to the Gate, to see what the parchment announced. Below the Royal Seal of the Persian Empire, it read:

King Xerxes Kiapur Darius
and Queen Esther dokhtar Bunyamin
wish to announce the birth of their son,
Prince Darius Kiapur Xerxes
on 3 Dey.
May Ahura Mazda bless the new Prince with long life.

Mordecai smiled. "Mazal tov! Esther. Mazal tov."

275

CHAPTER 62

"Zeresh! Where are you?" Haman walked through the house and found her in the last place he expected; in the kitchen with their Cook

"Why are you here?" he laughed. "You never prepare food."

"I may not cook, but I have to approve purchases from the marketplace."

"When you are finished, come to our sitting room." Haman walked through the house, up the staircase, to their private sitting room. It was arranged similarly to his bedchamber in the Palace.

Removing his weapons, he hung them on the wall before crossing to the table to pour two goblets of wine.

A few minutes later, Zeresh joined him.

"Why are you home in the middle of the day?"

Haman frowned. "I came to tell you to prepare to leave."

"What? Leave?" Her brow furrowed. "I do not understand. Why are we leaving?"

"We are leaving," he studied the wine in the goblet, then grinned, "because we are moving."

"What? Moving?" Zeresh smiled. "Wait." She picked up a goblet of wine, crossed to a chair and sat. "Now, what is happening? Why are we moving?"

"The Cup-bearer is needed closer to the Palace."

276

"The Cup-bearer already lives in the Palace..." Zeresh's brows climbed to her scalp as realization set in. "*You* are the Cup-bearer?"

Haman grinned, nodding.

"What happened to Kurush Tars Dida?"

"The croaking old frog finally died this morning."

"Haman!" Zeresh set the goblet down. "You did not—"

"No! Shhh—" he crossed to room, checked the corridor, and closed the door. "Kurush died a natural death from age, and the King appointed me to be his new Cup-bearer.

"I will need to live closer to the Palace. Go to Susa today; choose whatever house you want. Arrange for our things to be moved there."

"What about this house? Are we going to sell it?"

"We will keep it for now. This has been a good place for our *meetings*. Once we are settled in, I want you to become friends with Queen Esther."

"Why would I want to become friends with her? I thought that was Navjaa's task."

"Because Queen Esther does not care for Navjaa," he laughed. "Perhaps she is jealous of any of the harci in the Second House of Women. For some reason she also appears to distrust me. I do not know why; I have always attempted to be pleasant when I am around her."

He frowned. "Navjaa is correct, Xerxes' focus is on his mother, Queen Esther, and the young Princes. I have worked too long trying to influence the King to discard it now. We will have to do something to weaken their influence." He stroked his beard. "Perhaps I can draw the King's attention to the remaining mastoura in the Harem. It worked with Vashti. If that does not work, there is always poison."

"From what Navjaa hears, certain foods make Queen Esther ill. No one is allowed to bring her food except her attendants."

"When the time comes, you prepare the poison," Haman emptied the goblet. "I will find a way to use it."

277

CHAPTER 63

ordecai set the leather bag of herbs, tonics, and supplies next to the basket, leaned back against the stone wall, and closed his eyes, taking time to enjoy the cool relief in the center of the Great Gate. Mordad was especially hot and dry this year.

After a few minutes, the sound of feet crunching across the pavement caught his attention. *It is probably Sarkar Khanum Farah coming for Esther's food.* He sat up, tucking the cover over the bread.

"From what I have heard, the Malekeh Jahann is growing weaker."

Mordecai stopped, wrinkling his brow. *I have heard that voice before.*

"That is what I have also heard," another man said. "If she dies, our task will be easier."

"But our wages should not change."

Mordecia's eyes widened as the men laughed. *Teresh pur Ashoor and Bigthana tabar Farrok!*

Standing slowly, he glanced toward the other opening of the

Gate before slipping off his leather sandals and creeping toward the edge of the shadow. *Yahweh, please let this darkness hide me.* He listened as the two Warriors continued talking, pausing now and then—Mordecai assumed—to watch for anyone's approach.

"Why does," Teresh paused, "*he* want to do something now?"

Bigthana laughed." Possibly because…the recent second gathering of mastoura in the First House of Women did not draw the King's attention."

"They would draw my attention," Teresh laughed, adding a crude comment.

"*Shhh*…we do not have time…*He* wants us to…*deal*…with the King's mother, Queen Esther, and her new baby."

"There is no way to deal with Queen Esther and the baby. They are carefully guarded. Even her food is handled by her personal attendants.

"We can deal with personal attendants." Bigthana laughed, "We can deal with *all* the family."

"You mean…" Teresh hissed, "the King and the Puora Vaspuhr?"

"Yes. *He* will be happy with the results."

"*Shhh*…someone is approaching…come on."

Mordecai leaned into the darkness, waiting until the men's footsteps could no longer be heard. He hurried back to open his leather bag, digging through until he found a piece of parchment and writing implements. Sitting, he began writing a note.

"Greetings, Mordecai ben Jair." Farah entered the Great Gate. "I am sorry I was delayed."

"That is just as well," he folded the note and stood. "Hide this note within your garments," he turned away to allow her privacy. "Do not let anyone see you give it to Queen Esther. It is imperative that you follow my instructions. Do you understand?"

"Of course, but why—"

"No questions. Take the food." He handed her the basket containing Esther's special food. "I must go; no one should see us talking."

CHAPTER 64

"My Lady Queen," Hathak bowed, "My Lord the King is here."

Stepping to one side of the door, the eunuch bowed as Xerxes entered and crossed the room to her. "Esther," he grasped her shoulders. "You sent for me? Are you ill? Is something wrong with Darius?"

"My Lord King," she bowed, not wanting the Immortals or her attendants to see her face. "I wanted to see you," she glanced at him through her lashes, "*alone.*"

Xerxes relaxed, drawing her into his embrace, "Ah, My Lady Queen." His voice was warm.

"I have something to tell you," she whispered into his chest. "Please send everyone away."

She felt him nod. "Whatever you desire, up to half my Kingdom." He looked up. "Everyone leave. Artabanus, set guards in the corridor, but give us privacy."

Xerxes held her until the door closed. "They are gone." He stepped back, his hands on her shoulders, "Esther, what is it?"

She reached into the girdle wrapped around her waist and withdrew the piece of wrinkled parchment. "Farah gave this to me. She received it from Mordecai ben Jair."

"Who is this Mordecai ben Jair?" he frowned.

"You met him during the celebration of my being chosen Queen. He was the Gyah Pezeshk, but that does not matter." She pointed to the parchment. "Read what he wrote."

She crossed to sit in the chair nearest the bagdir.

at the Great Gate...two Warriors named Teresh and Bigthana.
He looked at her, "They are part of The One Thousand Immortals," He continued reading,

...spoke of a plot to...
What!? Artabanus!"

Within moments, Esther's apartment and private garden were filled with Immortals, weapons drawn.

"Set The One Thousand throughout the Royal Residence, including the courtyards," Xerxes said. "Send Warriors to bring Artaxerxes here; he is training with the Army in the fields outside the west wall of Susa. Call for a Royal Scribe and send for my Cup-bearer. I believe he is at their new home.

"Artabanus," Xerxes' face tightened, his eyes kindled. "Find Teresh pur Ashoor and Bigthana tabar Farrok."

Within minutes, the Immortals were dispersed and the Scribe was seated, parchment and stylus ready.

Xerxes handed the Hazarpatish the parchment.

"Let it be recorded in the Book of the Annual of the Kings of Persia," he said, "that Teresh pur Ashoor and Bigthana tabar Farrok conspired to kill the King. For this crime, let them be impaled.

"Artabanus, take the two criminals to the Gates of Eternity."

"Yes, my Lord King," Artabanus saluted and whipped out a black cloth tucked into his belt.

"Artabanus," Xerxes' gaze darkened, "make them linger."

Chapter 65

The sky was dark as kohl, save for occasional light from a blood-red moon. She ran, tripping over rocks, running into tree trunks. The night echoed with the cacophony of squawking peacocks, *thuds*, terrified screams, screams cut short and *thud...thud...thud.*

"Maman! Baba! Where are you?" She stumbled and fell, hitting her head on something cold and hard. The clouds shifted; the moonlight illuminated a white marble bench. Rolling over, she looked into the eyes of Maman; Baba was next to her. Their eyes were fixed; blood poured from gashes. Beyond her parents was Mordecai, his skull crushed beneath a boulder.

"Hadassah," Maman looked at her. "You must go."

"No," she shook her head. "I will not leave you."

"You cannot stay. You must go." Maman wheezed. "You must protect *them.*"

"Who?" She shook her head. "Maman, who do I need to protect?"

Her mother drew a ragged breath, "...family. You...must... protect...your...family," she sighed, breath leaving her body.

"Nooo!" Hadassah threw her head back, screaming! "Do not leave me! Please do not leave me. I cannot do this! I cannot!"

"Esther...Esther," she felt hands on her shoulders. "Wake up."

She woke with a gasp. "Where am I?"

A tinder flared; illuminating Xerxes' face. He turned to touch the tinder to a lamp next to the bed. "You are in your bedchamber."

She looked around, noting the decorations, the tapestries, the linens on her bed. "It is my bedchamber." She looked at him, her eyes wide as memories of the dream came flooding back.

"I was in a garden. It was dark, and I could not see. My parents were there…they were," she brushed the tears from her eyes, "dying. Someone had attacked Maman, Baba…and other people I loved." Trembling, she told him about the dream. Her parents dying, her mother's last words—*You must protect your family.*

"Family! Xerxes, what about Darius? Your mother? Artaxerxes?"

"Esther, shhh…" he drew her into his embrace. "They are all safe in their apartments, with Immortals standing guard. We are safe. You are safe."

"Safe," she drew a shuddering breath. "How can I feel safe when those men wanted to…*kill* you?"

"They are gone." She felt his arms tighten around her. "They cannot hurt me, or you, or any of our family. Remember what my mother always says."

She leaned against his chest. "Fight for your family."

"Esther," he lifted her face, wiping her eyes with the edge of a linen sheet. "I will always fight for you; for our family."

She looked at him, her smile tremulous. "Family is important."

CHAPTER 66

5 AZAR
SIXTH YEAR OF THE REIGN OF XERXES,
KING OF THE MEDES AND THE PERSIANS

"Haman," Xerxes said. "My mother is slipping away. Her physicians do not think she has many more days before," he drew a rugged breath, "she passes across the Chinvat Bridge into the presence of Ahura Mazda."

"My Lord King, I am sorry to hear that," Haman handed the King a goblet. "What may I do to help?"

"Be my Regent."

"What?" Haman's eyes widened. "Your Regent?"

"Yes. Until she…" Xerxes paused to take a drink, "my family and I will be spending our time with her. For now, you are my Regent."

"My Lord King, I am honored. But surely one of your Shathapavans, one of your Azam—"

"No," Xerxes cut him off. "You. As my former Hazarpatish, you understand the Army. As my Cup-bearer, you understand me and my thoughts on ruling the Empire."

"My Lord King, I will do my best, but your Shathapavans, the Azam—even your nobles—are accustomed to seeing me as

284

a Warrior. They barely know me as your Cup-bearer. Will they recognize me as your Regent?"

"Hmm," Xerxes said. "You might be right. Then let us do something they will recognize." He turned to the scribes. "Write a proclamation."

CHAPTER 67

"Greetings, Safa Yazdan Jafari." Mordecai patted his garments, shaking off some of the rain, before stepping over to the Warrior.

"Greetings, Mordecai ben Jair. You are out in a storm like this?"

"Whatever the weather," Mordecai lifted the basket, "I must bring food for the Shahbanu."

"Courier, take word to Sarkar Khanum Farah to come for the Queen's food." After the young man left, the Warrior turned to Mordecai. "You will have time to obey the new proclamation."

"Another proclamation?" Mordecai arched his brow. "What is it this time?"

"Something none of us expected." He pointed the side of the Great Gate where a piece of parchment hung. "Read it for yourself."

Mordecai walked to tall wooden post near the Great Gate and noted the parchment was barely wet. *Must have been recently hung.* Wiping the rain from his eyes, he leaned in to read:

Be it known that on this day,
the 5th day Azar, in the fifth year of Xerxes,
King of the Medes and King of the Persians,
the following proclamation is made.
From this day, my Cup-bearer,

Haman pur Hammedatha,
will act as my Regent.
In this position, he is second only to me.
Anyone coming through the Great Gate
—even the royal officials—
must kneel and pay him honor.
Thus commands Xerxes,
King of the Medes and King of the Persians.

Pay honor to Haman! Mordecai's eyes narrowed. *I will never honor that,* he turned his head and spit, *cursed Amalekite.*

Walking to Safa, he handed the basket to the Warrior. "Give this to Sarkar Farah."

Turning, Mordecai walked away.

CHAPTER 68

4 DEY
SIXTH YEAR OF THE REIGN OF XERXES,
KING OF THE MEDES AND THE PERSIANS

The air in Atossa's apartment was filled with fragrant smoke from burning incense. Erbed Saeid Mogh Elaikim, along with a dozen magi, stood around the sitting room, intoning prayers.

"May the Guardian Fravashi guide Malekeh Jahann across the Chinvat Bridge into the House of Song," Erbed Athornan Mogh Moallem intoned, "where she will dwell in the presence of Ahura Mazda forever."

In the Queen Mother's bedchamber, Xerxes was seated next to his mother's bed with Artaxerxes at his side. Xerxes' three younger brothers stood on the other side of the bed. On the far wall, her two elderly Sarkar Khanum stood, weeping quietly.

Esther sat on a chair, quietly humming as she rocked the sleeping Darius.

Atossa stirred, lifting an eyelid. "Xerxes?"

"I am here, Maman," he took her hand. "We are all here."

She crooked a finger. "I wish—" she drew a ragged breath.

"What do you wish, Maman?" Xerxes leaned closer, listening

to his mother whisper. "Yes, Maman. It will be done." The King stood and crossed to at Esther. "Maman wishes you hear you play your harp."

Esther's eyes filled with tears. "Yes, of course. Perhaps Darya or Roshanara would hold Darius?"

"I will hold our son." Xerxes lifted the baby from her arms.

Within minutes, the harp was brought to her. Artaxerxes drew a chair for her near Atossa's bed.

Esther sat, placed the harp against her shoulder, and drew a deep breath. Lifting her hand near the top of the harp, she plucked a string; a single note—clear as the dawn—echoed in the room. She plucked another, following with a series of rippling chords, like a waterfall. Esther began humming, singing a silent prayer—the psalm of King David walking through the valley of the shadow of death.

As the last note faded, Atossa turned her head to look at her. "Esther...that was...beautiful."

Esther nodded, tears washing her eyes.

"Xerxes..."

He crossed to the bedside. "I am here, Maman."

Esther set the harp down and joined him, taking Darius from his arms.

"Xerxes...Esther," Atossa looked at them. "Remember...take care of your family." She whispered, "Fight for your family." Her breathing grew labored. "Family is important." She sighed as breath left her body.

"Maman?" Xerxes whispered. He looked at Erbed Saeid. The magi stepped over, laid two fingers on Atossa's neck, paused, and then looked at Xerxes. He shook his head.

Tears caught in Esther's throat as Xerxes bent over to kiss his mother's cheek before Saeid laid a white linen cloth over the Queen Mother's face.

Xerxes heaved a ragged sigh. "Farewell, Maman," Standing, he lifted his chin. "Atossa dokhtar Cyrus, the Queen of Persia, the

Malekeh Jahann, has passed. Let the Malekeh Jahann be buried with all honors. May her body be placed beside her husband and my father—Darius the Great—where together they will dwell in the light of Ahura Mazda."

Chapter 69

"Sh..sh..sh...Darius, *sheeren am*," Esther whispered, "*my sweet one*, do not cry."

The baby looked at her, tightened his face, and wailed, arching his back and waving little fists.

"Does your stomach hurt?" Esther lifted her son against her shoulder and gently rocked him, humming, until his cries eased and he fell asleep.

Stepping quietly to the cradle, she kissed his check and laid him down, covering him with a blanket of wool. She left the Royal Nursery and crossed to sit on a divan in her sitting room.

Farah brought her a cup of hot tea. "My Lady," she whispered.

"Thank you," Esther took a drink. "Darius has been crying since the Second Watch of the night."

"Poor little one."

Esther shook her head. "It might be caused from the pain of his new teeth, or he might have the same issues with food I have. I need to discuss my diet with my Gyah Pezeshk. I have not seen him since Queen Atossa died. Farah, arrange for a courier to summon Mordecai ben Jair to the Palace."

"At once, My Lady."

Farah returned a short time later.

"When will he arrive?" Esther asked.

"My Lady, the courier has taken the message. However," Farah paused, "the Gyah Pezeshk will not be able to come."

"Why not?"

"He is not allowed past the Great Gate."

"What?" Esther shook her head. "Why is the Queen's Gyah Pezeshk not allowed to come to the Palace?"

"I asked the same question, My Lady," Farah lifted her hands in confusion. "All I was told is that Mordecai ben Jair refuses to bow to the King's Cup-bearer."

CHAPTER 70

"Safa Yazdan Jafari, Queen Esther has summoned me."

"Mordecai ben Jair," the Warrior shrugged, "you know what I am going to ask."

"And you know," Mordecai frowned, "what my answer will be."

The Warrior shook his head. "You cannot enter the Great Gate unless you bow to Haman pur Hammedatha."

"The Queen has summoned me. Surely King Xerxes—"

"—the King is in deep mourning for the Malekeh Jahaan," Safa interrupted him. "He has set Haman as his Regent."

Mordecai clinched his fists, "I will not bow."

"Why?" the Warrior asked. "Why will you not bow? Then you can go to the Queen."

"Safa Yazdan Jafari," Mordecai seethed. "I am a Jew of the tribe of Benjamin. I worship Yahweh. Haman is an Amalekite, an enemy of my people. I will *never* bow," he turned his head and spit, "to him."

CHAPTER 71

H aman rode a circuitous route through the streets of Susa. He did not choose the longer path to enjoy the beautiful day, but rather to see the people throughout city kneeling and bowing to him, the murmur of "Haman pur Hammedatha," floating on the air. *This is what I have worked for,* he smiled. *This is what I deserve.*

Riding past the Citadel Marketplace, he reached the Great Gate. He smiled as those in front of the entrance to the Palace dropped to their knees and bowed, acknowledging him.

All save one. Standing in the midst of people honoring him, stood a man, fists on his hips.

Haman stopped his horse, frowning at the man.

Meeting Haman's gaze, the man lifted his chin—showing no respect, no awe—and turned to walk away.

Gnashing his teeth, Haman rode into the Gate.

The Warriors bowed to him, murmuring his name; it would not be expected for Warriors guarding the Great Gate would lower their guard by kneeling.

Haman dismounted. "Safa Yazdan Jafari," he pointed to the man walking away, "who is that?

"Mirza Haman pur Hammedatha, that is Mordecai ben Jair."

"He does not obey the King's command to bow to me."

294

"Nor will he."

Haman frowned. "Why?"

"Mordecai refuses to bow," Safar paused, dropping his voice, "to you."

"What?" The word echoed within the Gate's stone walls. "Why does he refuse? Tell me!"

Safar stood to attention, looking over Haman's shoulder. "Mirza, Mordecai ben Jair said he is a Jew and he would not bow to an Agagite."

"Another Jew!" he growled. *I will have this Mordecai bound, drug to the Gates of Eternity, and killed. No, that is not sufficient! I will kill his family, his friends, all of his people. Yes! I will have him watch the annihilation of all the Jews in Persia before I kill him myself. The question is…when?*

"Safa, give me some dice."

"Dice, Mirza?"

"Dice!" Haman held out his hand. "All Warriors carry dice. Give me your dice!"

Safa reached into the sash wrapped around his waist and drew out a pouch. He opened it and poured several dice into Haman's palm. "Mirza, may I ask why you need them?"

Haman smiled, and not pleasantly. "I wish to ask the gods on which day my enemies will be destroyed."

Haman stood in the King's sitting room. "My Lord King," he bowed.

Dressed in dark clothing, with a goblet and several empty amphorae on the table at his side, the King glowered. "Haman, why are you here? I made you Regent so I could be left alone to mourn the loss of my mother and my Cup-bearer. Has something occurred you cannot handle?"

"My Lord King, it has. If it were just one person—or even ten people—I would not approach you with it. However, it is more.

"There are a certain people within the Empire who do not respect our customs—and worse—they do not obey the King's laws. As your Cup-bearer and Regent, I believe it is not in the King's best interests to tolerate them."

Xerxes lifted his hands—palms together—to his chin. "Go on."

"If it pleases the King, let a proclamation be sent to the one hundred and twenty-seven Shathapavans throughout the Empire instructing them to destroy these people. I realize many of the governors are still feeling the weight of paying for the war against Greece. Therefore, out of my own monies, I will give ten thousand talents of silver into the Royal Treasury to pay for this task to be accomplished."

Haman's years as a Warrior gave him strength to stand under the force of the King's stare.

"Keep your money." Xerxes pulled the Signet Ring from his hand, extended it to Haman, then brushed his hand toward him as if shooing away an irritating fly. "Do with these people as you please."

"It shall be done according to your command, My Lord King," Haman bowed. He slid the Signet Ring on his finger and turned to leave when the King called his name.

"When will this cleansing occur?"

"On the thirteenth day of Esfand." He bowed and left the King's Apartment.

As he walked toward the Throne Room, Haman's lips twisted into a cruel smiled. *In two months' time, the enemies of my people will be destroyed. Hate and Revenge are twin wolves; they never perish, and they are always hungry.*

Chapter 72

The cries of the people echoed within the Synagogue.

"The King wants to destroy *all* Jews throughout the Empire?"

"Not only does he want to destroy us, but he has also chosen to do it three weeks before Passover?"

"Why? What happened?"

"We are good citizens of the Persian Empire. We have done nothing to justify the King ordering our destruction."

"What can we do?"

The sound of a shofar silenced the voices. They all turned as Jerimoth ben Halevi lowered the horn.

"Friends," Rabbi Omar extended his hands, "please sit." He waited until everyone settled before continuing. "We do not know what happened to make the King pronounce this sentence of death on our people. Please, please," he patted the air as the cries and wails resumed.

"We have no answers for why this is happening. As to what we can do…" he lifted his hands, palms up, "we can that pray Yahweh will deliver us."

Part Four
And She Was Born
For Such A Time As This

CHAPTER 73

5 BAHMAN
SIXTH YEAR OF THE REIGN OF XERXES,
KING OF THE MEDES AND THE PERSIANS

"My Lady Queen," Hathak said, "all of your instructions have been carried out."

Esther nodding, staring at the pieces of parchment she held.

"Is there anything else you require?"

"No, thank you," she exhaled a deep breath. "There is nothing more anyone else can do." She looked at the eunuch. "That is all for tonight. And Hathak…keep what has happened to yourself."

"Of course, My Lady Queen," he bowed and left the apartment.

Farah came through the door that led to the Royal Nursery. "Prince Darius is sleeping."

"Good, good. Thank you. Farah," she looked up from the notes, "please come early tomorrow morning. I will need you to help me prepare to," she exhaled a deep breath, "go to the King."

Farah bowed, "I will rise before the dawn, my Lady Queen."

After the door closed behind her friend and Sarkar Khanum, Esther stared at the notes she held—notes that had been written

301

over the last week; the ones from her to Mordecai and the notes he had written in response.

> *Mordecai, I have heard reports that you—and many of our people—are in great distress, crying and weeping, and wearing sackcloth and ashes. With the King and all the Royal Family still in mourning for Queen Atossa, I have not heard what the cause is. I am sending Sarkar Farah and Mirza Hathak with new clothing for you, as you cannot go beyond the Great Gate wearing torn cloths or sackcloth. Please come soon, I am most anxious to learn what has happened.*

She set that note on a table and read the next one.

> *My Lady Queen, I am not able to come to you, as I refused the offer of clothing which you sent. On your behalf, Hathak asked for an explanation of what has caused such distress among the Jews. I told him of the King's proclamation and have sent a copy for you to read what Xerxes has decreed for our people.*

She glanced at the scroll Hathak had brought to her. It was still incredulous to read the decree.

> *"Xerxes, King of the Medes and of the Persians,*
> *To all the Shathapavans throughout my Empire*
> *They are to be ready on the thirteen day of Esfand. On that single day, they are to destroy, to kill, and to annihilate all the Jews—young and old, men, women, and children—and to plunder their goods."*

She shook her head. *That did not sound like Xerxes.* She continued reading Mordecai's note.

> *Yes, I write 'our people' because it was necessary to tell*

Hathak about your family. You must go to the King and plead on behalf of our people.

Hathak told her everything Mordecai had told him, including the exact amount of money set aside in the Royal Treasury for the destruction of the Jews. He also returned the notes she had sent, explaining Mordecai wanted to keep this as private as possible until she acted. Esther looked at her response to Mordecai's previous note:

> *For the last month, the King—and the entire Royal Family—have been in deep mourning for the loss of Queen Atossa as well as Kurush Tars Dida. The King will not see anyone.*
>
> *All the King's officials and the Shathapavans throughout the Empire know that if any man or woman approaches the King in the Inner Court without being summoned, they are to be put to death, unless the King extends the golden Scepter to them and spares their lives.*
>
> *The King has not called for me during this last month.*

She moved her note to the table and read Mordecai's response.

> *Do not think that because you are in the Palace, you alone of all the Jews will escape. For if you remain silent at this time, relief and deliverance for the Jews will arise from another place, but you and your father's family will perish.*
>
> *And who knows but that you have come to your royal position for such a time as this?*

"You and your father's family will perish." She realized through Xerxes, little Darius was descended from Persian Kings. She lifted her chin. *Through me, Darius is of the tribe of Benjamin and descended from King Saul. My son has royal blood on both sides.* She looked at the note: *For such a time as this.*

She had sent a note to Mordecai, telling him to have all the Jews in Susa fast for three days, praying for her, and she and her attendants would fast and pray. She ended the note, *I will go to the King, even though it is against the law. And if I perish, I perish.*

For the last three days, she and her attendants *had* fasted and prayed. She had played her harp, singing Scripture: of Yahweh loving them and being with them; of His being is a fortress, a stronghold, a deliverer, their refuge, their shield, and their strength, that He cared for those who trust in Him.

She had prayed for the strength of the patriarchs Moses, Joseph, King David, of Aeorapati Belteshazzar and his friends, Shadrach, Meshach, and Abednego. *The God we serve is able to deliver us from the furnace and from Your Majesty's hand*, Daniel's friends had said, *even if He does not, we will not serve your gods or worship the golden idol.*

But by this morning, Esther had received no word from The One, no assurance of deliverance...nothing. She knew only one thing: She had to see Xerxes, even if her actions angered him. She had heard people speak of the King's anger, but from the first time she met him in Queen Atossa's apartment, she had never seen his anger directed at her. "This will be hard," she murmured.

"You can do hard things."

She had walked to the corner of her room, to touch her father's bagdir, before going into her private garden to sit on Maman's white bench. Looking around, she remembered the times she had sat with Maman in their garden, snuggling for warmth, eating handfuls of almonds. She remembered her parent's teachings.

"Trust Yahweh. Remember the patriarchs."

"Maman," she had asked, *"why would Yahweh allow the patriarchs to suffer and—even some—to die?"*

"If they perished," Maman had said, *"it was because Yahweh was calling them to Abraham's bosom. We have faced challenges. We know when we face them again, Yahweh will be with us. And if what you face is so hard that you perish...?"*

"Yahweh, give me strength," Esther whispered.

"And if I perish," Esther looked up, lifting her hands to the sky, "I perish."

CHAPTER 74

Esther stood silent as her attendants dressed her. Laleh smoothed the Royal Court robe. Banafshe secured the bejeweled golden collar and Anemos the matching earrings. Golshan held her hand for balance while Orkideh slipped the golden leather slippers on her feet. After Irida finished pinning her hair, Farah set the Queen's Crown on her head.

Esther looked at her reflection in the tall mirror. *Will Xerxes remember the first time I wore these, the day I became his Queen? Will he remember that I am his Shahbanu? Will he remember I am madar to Darius and Artaxerxes?*

Yahweh, be with me. Let me find favor with Xerxes.

She took her sleeping baby from Liana, kissing his brow, whispering, "I love you, sheeren am. Love your brother, love your father. Trust Yahweh. Farah, do you have my letters for Prince Artaxerxes and Prince Darius? If today does not go well, I want my sons to one day understand the reasons for my actions."

"I have the letters, My Lady Queen," Farah lifted a hand to wipe her eyes. "I will keep them safe." She gestured to the other attendants. "We will pray for you, that your Yahweh will protect you and these notes will not be necessary."

Esther nodded, "Amen," her throat constricted with tears. She handed her baby to Farah. "Thank you."

She looked at her other attendants. "Thank you all,"

She lifted her head and took a deep breath. "It is time."

The Warriors outside her apartment and in the Corridor of the Royal Residence had been informed the Queen was going to the Throne Room. They did not question why they had not been informed of the King summons; they arranged themselves in front and behind Esther, escorting her through the Palace. With each step, she reminded herself of Yahweh's promises:

Because of the Lord's great love we are not consumed. His compassions never fail; they are new every morning. Great is Your faithfulness. From the ends of the earth I call to You, I call as my heart grows faint. Lead me to the rock that is higher than I. You have been my refuge, a strong tower against the foe.

When they arrived at the Outer Court of the Throne Room, she turned to the Warriors. "You are dismissed," she said. "The King will arrange an escort to accompany me back to my apartment." She turned and walked through the Outer Court to the Inner Court, where Artabanus tabar Mithradata, along with several dozen Warriors, stood. The doors to the Throne Room were open revealing the King on his throne with the Cup-bearer standing beside him.

Artabanus bowed. "My Lady Queen. How may I serve you?"

"Greetings, Hazarpatish." Esther fixed her eyes on the Warrior and filled her lungs. "I would see the King."

"My Lady Queen," the creases in Artabanus' forehead deepened, "the Cup-bearer has not informed me that you have been summoned."

"I am the Shahbanu; I am the Queen," Esther looked at him and lifted her chin. "I would see the King."

"My Lady Queen, perhaps there has been a mistake. I will send word to the Cup-bearer."

"What is the issue?"

Esther turned to see Haman walking down the center aisle of Throne Room.

"My Lady Queen," he bowed, his presence blocking her view. On his right hand was the Royal Signet Ring.

Esther's fists gripped skirts to restrain the desire to attack him. "Haman pur Hammedatha."

He turned to the other Warrior. "Artabanus, what is the issue?"

"My Lady Queen wishes to see the King."

Haman turned back to her. "My Lady Queen; you have not been summoned." His voice dripped condescension, as though speaking to a child. "You know the Law—if *anyone* comes into the presence of the King without being summoned, that person is," he eyes narrowed, "to be put to death."

Her heart was pounding. "I am aware of the Law." *If I perish, I perish. Yahweh, protect my sons.* She lifted her chin, her voice picking up strength with each word, "I would see the King."

Haman slowly raised his eyebrows, a gesture that was sarcastic, arrogant, and dismissive all at once. He opened his mouth—

"My Lady Queen."

Esther looked around Haman to see Harbona Karim Masoud —one of Royal Eunuchs—stepping into the Inner Court from the Throne Room.

"Harbona," Esther acknowledged his bow. "I would see the King."

"Indeed, my Lady Queen. My Lord the King saw you standing in the Inner Court."

Esther looked over the Harbona's shoulder, and saw Xerxes sitting on his Throne with the Royal Scepter extended. Even from the distance, she saw him smiling.

"My Lord the King commands the Queen be escorted to him."

Esther swallowed a sigh of relief. *Thank you, Yahweh.*

Haman grimaced and took a step into the Throne Room, but Harbona stopped him. "The King instructed me to tell the Cup-bearer that he is dismissed for now."

Esther locked eyes with Haman…and smiled.

His face tightened. "As My Lord the King commands." He stepped to one side, bowing his head. "My Lady Queen."

She lifted her head regally, as Atossa had taught her. "Thank you, Cup-bearer." As she followed the Eunuch through the doors into the Throne Room, she heard Haman speak to the Artabanus. "My plans are completed. On 13 Esfand, all the Jews in the Empire will be destroyed."

Esther stopped, her eyes widened. *Haman is responsible for the decree to kill my people?* Remembering where she was, she quickly relaxed her expression and continued walking. *Does Xerxes know who the people are in the decree?* Her heart raced, keeping pace with her thoughts. *What do I do now? Do I speak with the King now in the Throne Room or should I request to speak with him privately?* By the time she reached the platform, she still did not know what to do. *Yahweh, help me.*

Xerxes looked at her and smiled. He extended the Royal Scepter. "My Lady Queen."

Esther stepped up to the Throne, bowed, and reached out to touch the Scepter. "My Lord King," she smiled.

Xerxes stood, took her hand, and escorted her to the Queen's Throne.

"Greetings, *atashe del-am;* the fire of my heart."

She relaxed as the King addressed her by his term of endearment.

"Greetings, *delbar-am;* he who holds my heart."

"You were brave to come here," he said, stepping back to his Throne. "Why did you risk it? You could have sent a note, requesting to see me."

She lowered her face and slanted a glance at him under thick lashes. "I missed you. I want…" her voice trailed off. *What do I want? Time. I need time to think, to learn what has happened, and to discover how Haman is involved in this decree.*

"Ah, my Queen, what is it?" the King jumped on her words. "What do you want? I will give you anything," he smiled, "even up to half my Kingdom."

Anything. I must be careful about this. "If it pleases the King," she said, "let the King—together with Haman—come today to the Banquet Hall in the Courtyard of the Royal Residence. I will have a banquet prepared for you."

Xerxes turned to Harbona. "Go to the Inner Court; see if Haman is still here."

"At once, My Lord King." A few moment later, he returned with the information that Haman had left the Palace to return to his home."

"Go at once to Haman's house. Bring him back to the Palace," the King turned to smile at her, "that we may do what Queen Esther asks."

CHAPTER 75

"Zeresh, it is settled," Haman lifted a goblet. "The plans to kill Mordecai ben Jair—along with every Jew in the Empire—are complete."

"That is good news," Zeresh lifted her goblet to touch his. "We should plan a celebration with our friends and family. Obviously, Navjaa cannot attend, but our sons are with the Army in Susa." She frowned at the servant who entered the sitting room. "Aziz, what is it?"

"My Lady," he bowed, "Harbona Karim Masoud, along with other eunuchs from the Palace are here."

"Harbona is here?" Haman's eyes widened. "That is strange, as I left the Palace not an hour ago." He set the goblet on a table. "Aziz, escort them in."

Within moments, Haman was greeting the eunuchs.

"Zeresh," Haman turned to his wife. "Harbona is one of the Royal Eunuchs who attends the King."

Zeresh bowed her head. "Welcome to our home."

"Lady Zeresh."

"Harbona, why are you here?" Haman asked.

"My Lord the King has sent us to take you back to the Palace."

"What?" Haman frowned. "Why?"

"My Lady Queen Esther is having a banquet for My Lord King Xerxes. You have been invited to join them."

"Who else is attending this banquet?" Zeresh asked.

"No one," Harbona said. "The banquet is for King Xerxes, Queen Esther, and the Cup-bearer. It is to be held in the Banquet Hall of the Royal Residence. My Lord Haman, you must come now."

"Of course." Haman set his goblet down and stood.

Standing, Zeresh crossed to him to dust his robe and tunic. "Thank the gods your garments are appropriate for a private banquet with the King and Queen. Remember all that happens."

"I will," he said. "I will return later. In the meantime, send for our sons and invite our friends to a celebration."

CHAPTER 76

"My Lady Queen," Xerxes wiped his mouth with a linen napkin, "that was delicious."

The Banquet Hall in the center of the Garden of the Royal Residence was small, seating only one hundred people. Patterned after the larger Courtyard of the Garden which Xerxes had built several years ago, this banquet hall had the same mosaic pavement, the same white and blue linens fastened to the walls with silver rings. The table was laden with intricately carved gold platters of roasted chicken and fresh bread, along with silver bowls of cheese, dates, pomegranates, grapes, leeks, and cucumbers. There were a dozen amphorae of a variety of wine to fill their silver goblets.

"I am happy you enjoyed it," Esther refilled his goblet, "but I cannot accept the compliment. All I did was speak with the Royal Chef about what food and wine to serve."

"You are Queen," Xerxes sipped his wine. "No one would expect you to know how to prepare food."

"And they would be wrong," Esther moved her plate away. "My maman—may her memory be blessed—taught me to cook, to sew, and to take care of a house."

Xerxes raised his eyebrows. "Truly?"

She nodded. "Maman was training me for when I became a wife."

"I have often wondered," Xerxes said, "what it would be like to be an ordinary man with a wife and children." He grinned. "My maman did not know how to prepare the simplest food."

"Your maman—may her memory be blessed—was the Malekeh Jahan; she was an amazing woman," Esther said. "My maman taught me how to be a wife; your maman taught me how to be Queen and Shahbanu."

He drew a deep breath. "I miss her."

"I miss her too." Esther glanced at Haman, who appeared focused on consuming all the wine in Persia. She laid a hand on Xerxes' arm and lowered her voice. "How are you?"

"I still grieve, but it is not so deep." He looked into her eyes and smiled sadly, "Grief is like a splinter deep in every fingertip…"

"…to touch anything is torture." *Switch the topic,* she told herself, *something that will make him think on happy things.* "You spoke of children. Have you heard from Artaxerxes?"

"I have," he grinned. "He is doing well. He is with my brothers, looking forward to starting his military training. And you? How are you? How is Darius?"

"I am well, but Darius has been in pain."

"What?"

She held out her hand, palm facing him. "I do not believe it is anything to worry about; it is probably just his new teeth. It might also be that our son has inherited the same stomach issues I have. I have been speaking with the Royal Chef and rubbing medicinal oils on his gums."

"I am glad to hear that. I will have to come see him."

"He would enjoy seeing you," she smiled. "I know he loves me, but I think he grows weary just seeing me and my attendants all day." She laughed, "This is the first time in weeks I have left my apartment."

"And the first thing you did was come to the Throne Room," Xerxes touched her cheek, "to see me."

She smiled at him. "I am glad I found you there."

"It was my first day back in the Throne Room," Xerxes took a deep breath. "I need to look to the care of my Empire."

"I have looked af-f-fter the Empire for you, My Lord King," Haman lifted his goblet, not noticing his wine sloshing onto the table linen. He took a drink and raised the goblet again, "In the K-King's name, I have corresponded with the Shathapavans, discussed the coming Norooz celebration with the magi, and arranged to kill all the Jews th-th-throughout the Empire."

"The *Jews?*" Xerxes asked. "*Those* are the people you spoke to me about for that edict?"

Xerxes did not know?! Esther's eyes widened. *Haman took advantage of Xerxes' grief to arrange the destruction of my people?*

"Yes-s-s," Haman slurred like a viper. "Within a few weeks, we will anni-il-late every Jew in the entire Persian Empire."

Esther flinched and closed her eyes. *Haman treats killing my people with no more concern than he does spilling wine on the linen.*

"Haman," Xerxes said, an edge had crept into his voice that the Cup-bearer did not seem to notice, "I need to learn more about what you have been doing in my name, but now is not the time. Queen Esther did not invite us here to speak of government matters."

Turning to her, he picked up her hand, "My Shahbanu, I need to know; what do you want?"

What do I want? Time. I need time to think.

"My atashe del-am, tell me; I will give you anything," he kissed her palm, "even up to half my Kingdom."

"My Lord King," she filled her lungs, "delbar-am, you wish to know what I want? I will tell you," she looked at him, "tomorrow.

"As your *atashe del-am*, I have one request. Please come tomorrow—you and Haman—to the banquet I will prepare." She smiled. "Then I will answer My Lord King's question."

CHAPTER 77

"I am the King's Cup-bearer and his Regent. After Xerxes, I am the most important person in the Persian Empire. I have wealth, I have ten sons serving in the King's Army, and a daughter living in the Palace. I spent the morning at the Queen's Banquet; she invited only the King and me to this banquet. She has also invited me to come with the King tomorrow for another banquet.

"Yet, all of this gives me no satisfaction when I ride out of the Great Gate and see that Jew Mordecai there, boldly refusing to bow to me. I have to restrain myself to not have the Warriors take his head off, but to wait for the 13th of Esfand."

"Haman," Zeresh refilled his goblet, "why wait? Have him killed now." She turned to their guests. "What say you?"

"Kill him," the wine merchant, Jata pur Zurakara said.

"Kill him," the Magi Nohpanguan agreed.

The other guests nodded, echoing, "Kill him."

"How should I do this?" Haman asked.

"Haman," Zeresh answered, "when you were Hazarpatish, you told me the Gate to Eternity had stacks of long poles prepared for impaling criminals."

"Yes," he drew out the word, and smiled. "There is one pole that is fifty cubits."

316

"Send Aziz and our other servants to get this pole," Zeresh said, "and have them set it up here by our house. Tomorrow go to the King and ask him to have this Jew impaled on it. Then you can enjoy yourself when you go with Xerxes to the Queen's banquet."

Something about Zeresh's smile reminded Haman of a crocodile.

CHAPTER 78

The sound of voices drew Esther from her sleep.

She pushed her hair away from her eyes and looked about the room; the King's bedchamber was empty. The voices—one obviously Xerxes'—came from the sitting room. *Who is Xerxes meeting with at this hour?*

Noting the slant of the sunlight on the floors, she gasped. *I have to get back to my apartment.* She sat up and threw off the linen bedcovers. *I have to check on Darius, and then plan for today's banquet.*

Dressing quickly, she crossed the room and opened the door wide a finger's width. "My Lord King?"

Within a moment, the door opened, and Xerxes came in, barefoot and dressed in a red sleeping tunic. "Esther, I am sorry. I did not intend to awaken you." He stretched, yawning. "I woke during the Second Watch of the night and could not get back to sleep.

"I kept thinking about the things Haman said about being my Regent. I realized I have been so focused on my grief since my maman's death, I did not know what has happened in my Empire.

"I went into my Sitting Room and summoned the Royal Scribes to bring the Book of the Annual of the Kings of Persia. I have been listening to them read about the events in my Empire, when they came upon the story of Mordecai ben Jair, the man you introduced to me, who had overheard the two Warriors plot to kill me."

"Xerxes, I am so sorry you had to hear that again."

"I was not upset hearing that story. What did upset me was realizing that nothing had been done to honor this Mordecai for saving my life."

There was a tap at the door. "My Lord King," Harbona said through the wood. "Your Cup-bearer wishes to speak with you."

"Xerxes, I must get back to my apartment. What do I do?"

"You can go through the back corridor."

"What?"

"Did my maman not tell you there is a," he grinned, "*special* corridor between the King's Apartment and the Queen's Apartment?"

Chapter 79

"Haman! Why are you here and not at the Palace?" Zeresh asked. "And why is your head covered?"

"Because," he pulled the scarf off, "I did not want anyone else to see me." He pulled the dagger from his belt and slashed the scarf. "This should have been Mordecai!" He dropped the pieces on the ground and stepped on it, grinding the cloth beneath his foot. "This should have been Mordecai!"

"Haman," Zeresh crossed to take his arms. She screamed when he lifted the dagger over his head. "Haman, stop!"

He froze, looked at Zeresh, looked at their friends in the room, and then threw the knife down. "I…am…" he shook his head, walked to the table, poured wine into a large goblet, and downed it in a single draught before throwing the goblet across the room. He grabbed the hair on both sides of his head and screamed, cursing, calling on all daevas to drag Mordecai into the grasp of the demon god Angra Mainyu and be dropped into the House of Lies to suffer eternal torments.

Zeresh calmly poured a goblet of wine, turned to her husband, and tossed it into his face.

"Enough," she said as he gasped and sputtered. "Aziz," she looked at the servant, "go fetch fresh garments."

"Now, Haman, my love, you do not have much time before

the Queen's banquet," she handed him a linen napkin. "Tell us what happened."

Haman wiped his face as he told them about going to the King's Apartment. He was surprised to see Xerxes sitting with the Royal Scribes, one who held the Book of the Annals of the Kings of Persia.

"Xerxes asked me," Haman pitched his voice lower, "*What should be done for the man the King delights to honor?*"

"Of course I thought he was talking about *me*; after all, I have been his Hazarpatish, his Cup-bearer, and now I am his Regent.

"So I said, *For the man the King delights to honor, have servants bring a royal robe that you, My Lord King, has worn, and a horse that you have ridden, one with a royal crest placed on its head. Once this man is dressed in this royal robe, let him sit on the King's horse, and have one of the King's most noble princes ride ahead of him throughout the city streets of Susa, proclaiming, 'This is what is done for the man the King delights to honor!'*"

"I waited for the King to tell the Royal Scribes to write down that this honor was to be bestowed on me. But no!" Haman grabbed another goblet and drank. "That was *not* what Xerxes said."

"Haman, no!" Zeresh's eyes were drenched with horror.

"Yes," he spit. "Mordecai. That Jew! The King told me—*me!*—to get all I had listed and do everything I had just described for Mordecai ben Jair.

"From the first hour to the sixth hour, I rode through Susa, proclaiming this *Jew* as *the man the King delights to honor.* People lined the road, cheering for *him*, while many were pointing at me and," he paused to take the fresh tunic from Aziz and exchange it for the soiled one, "*whispering.*"

He looked at Zeresh—then suddenly noticing his friends gaping at him. He extending his hands wide and asked, "What can be done?"

Their guests looked at each other, then at Zeresh and Haman. They shook their heads.

"Nothing," said one.

Several echoed him.

"Mordecai ben Jair has won."

"You cannot stand against him."

"You will never recover from this," Jata pur Zurakara declared. "You and Zeresh should leave Susa—today."

"Haman, your reputation is ruined," Erbed Nohpanguan stood and moved toward the door.

"No!" Haman stood in the middle of the room, turning in a circle. "I am not ruined! I planned it all. Mordecai and all the Jews were to die. I had planned it all. Mordecai was supposed to die. Mordecai was supposed to—" He stopped, his mouth open in horror.

Standing in the doorway was Harbona Karim Masoud and the other two Royal Eunuchs. From their gaze—intent enough to peel away his skin—Haman knew they had heard all.

"Haman pur Hammedatha, you are summoned by King Xerxes to attend him at the Queen's Banquet. You will come with us now."

CHAPTER 80

Esther ran her hand over the cool marble of Maman's bench remembering the times she had sat on the bench with Maman in their garden. Hearing her claim it as her favorite place. *"It just feels peaceful."*

"Esther…"

Fingering one of the red flowers on the white cushion, she remembered Baba pointing out the colors on the cushion were reserved for the Royal Court. Maman responded there were no chances King Xerxes would ever see it, adding that their family was of the tribe of Benjamin and descended from King Saul.

"Esther…"

Maman is gone, Baba is gone, and now the Amalikite Haman *wants to kill all my people!*

"Esther…" A hand touched her arm.

"What?!" She turned to see Xerxes, a frown creasing his brow.

"Esther, my atashe del-am, are you alright?"

"Oh, forgive me, delbar-am," she smoothed her garments and smiled. "I was distracted."

"You are fatigued," Xerxes said. "You have been caring for our son. You have spent two days preparing a banquet for Haman and me."

Esther slanted a sideways glance at Haman. The Cup-bearer

was staring at the table. Unlike at the previous banquet, he had eaten little, had drunk little, had said little.

"While I have enjoyed being with you, I ask again," Xerxes lifted her hand, "Queen Esther, what is your petition? It will be given." He smiled. "Even up to half my Kingdom, it will be granted."

She filled her lungs. *Yahweh, take care of my sons, my family, my people.* "What do I want?"

"Yes, my Shahbanu. What do you want?"

"I want my life—and the lives of my people."

"What?" Xerxes shook his head. "Esther, I do not understand."

Slipping from the bench, she knelt before Xerxes. "If I have found favor in your sight, My Lord King, and if it pleases you, grant me my life—this is my petition. And spare my people—this is my request. For I and my people have been sold to be destroyed, killed, and annihilated."

"What?!" Xerxes' word was as sharp as a blade.

She laid her head on his knees, weeping. "If we had merely been sold as male and female slaves, I would have kept quiet, because no such minor distress would justify disturbing the King."

"Esther, rise," Xerxes helped her up to sit next to him. "Esther, tell me," he wiped her eyes. "Who is he? Where is he—this man who has *dared* to do such a thing?"

"There!" Esther stood, pointing. "There is my adversary and enemy! This vile Haman! He would destroy my family!"

"Haman?" Xerxes' hissed.

Haman froze, his mouth stretched around a silent scream.

The King stood, swiped his arm across the table, sending plates crashing and amphorae spinning. In quick strides, he left the Banquet Hall and stomped into the garden.

Esther moved to sit on Maman's bench. She watched Xerxes pacing through the garden, knocking over statues, wrenching branches off new trees, kicking bushes. All the while cursing, spewing venom, devising pain and death for the man dared to threaten his Queen.

"My Lady Queen," Haman fell to his knees before her. "Please...*please!* It is a mistake. I would never hurt you, I would never hurt your people. I would never hurt your family." He grabbed the edges of the bench and bowed his head, almost touching her lap. "Have mercy!"

She leaned over. "Haman, did you hear my mother's pleas for mercy? Did you hear my father's pleas? Or our servants?"

He shook his head. "I do not understand."

"You speak truth," she hissed. "You did not hear them because you were not there. But you ordered their deaths and took our home as your reward."

Haman's eyes widened in sudden recognition. He reached up and grabbed Esther's shoulders. "Please," he begged, "have mercy!"

"What...is...happening?!" Xerxes stood in the door, his voice echoing across the Banquet Hall. "Will you even molest my Queen while she is with me in the Palace? Immortals!" he roared.

Within a breath, Warriors filled the room, swords drawn. Behind them stood Harbona with the King's personal eunuchs.

Haman shook his head. "No! Please, My Lord King. I am innocent. I would never attack the Queen or her family!"

"My Lord King," Esther said, "Haman has already attacked my family. He hired men to kill my father, Abihail ben Shimei, the master builder who built the bagdir throughout the Palace, and who build this bench for my mother. He hired men to kill my parents and all our servants. I was not there when the attack happened. I was helping my cousin," she turned to look at Haman, "Mordecai ben Jair."

"No!" Haman shook his head. "I would never—She is a Jew! She lies—"

"Haman," Xerxes seethed. "Now you accuse the Queen of *lying!* Artabanus," he turned to the Hazarpatish, "remove him from my sight."

"At once, My Lord King."

The Immortals surrounded Haman, whipping out black cloths,

to tie them around his face, cutting off his screams. Xerxes grabbed Haman's hand and pulled off his Signet Ring.

"Now, take him to the Gate of Eternity."

"My Lord King," Harbona bowed. "When we went to Haman's house today, there was a tall pole in his yard. We heard Haman boasting to his wife and friends that he would impale Mordecai ben Jair on it."

The King said, "Impale him on it! And Harbona; take a scribe with you. Before he is allowed to taste death, see that he tells you all."

The Eunuch bowed. "He will be drained, My Lord King."

CHAPTER 81

"My Lord King, you have met him before, but I want to introduce you to my cousin, Mordecai ben Jair."

"Greetings, Mordecai. I am pleased to meet my Queen's cousin once again."

Mordecai bowed. "I am honored, My Lord King."

Xerxes looked at Esther. "I have given the estate of the criminal Haman to my Queen."

"Mordicai," Esther said, "As the King's Cup-bearer, you will need to live closer to the Palace. But I also want you to oversee this estate." She smiled, "I want you to oversee my parents' home."

"I am honored with My Lord King's trust as your Cup-bearer," Mordecai bowed. "It will take time to find other physicians to tend my patients."

"You do not need to give up your patients," Xerxes said. "Esther has a suggestion."

"What is that?"

"You should appoint Nehemiah bar Hakaliah as your assistant." Esther smiled. "I hear he writes many, many letters."

CHAPTER 82

"My Lord King," Mordecai said, "the couriers have been sent, carrying the edict to all of the Satrapies across the Empire."

"Xerxes," Esther wiped the tears, "will they arrive in time? I could not bear the thought of Haman's plan succeeding after his death, for disaster to fall on my people."

"It will not succeed," he said, "While the decree Haman wrote in my name—and sealed with my ring—cannot be revoked, your cousin has written an edict that will circumvent it."

"Esther," Mordecai lifted a scroll, "this edict allows the Jews throughout the Empire to assemble and protect themselves. It is written as a law, so every Jew will be ready on the 13th of Esfand, the day Haman chose by lot to annihilate our people."

"My Lord King," Esther said, "I will pay for this with the inheritance from my parents."

"Keep your inheritance for our children," Xerxes smiled. "I will pay for it. Now, Cup-bearer, has Haman's family been located?"

Mordecai glanced at his scroll. "His ten sons are nowhere to be found in Susa. There are Warriors scouring the Empire, looking for them."

"And Zeresh and Navjaa?" Xerxes asked.

"Dead."

"What?" Esther gasped.

"How?" Xerxes asked.

"Poison," Mordecai said. "They were found by a sadfarbod, as they were trying to escape to Greece. Before the Warriors even dismounted, Zeresh pulled two containers from her bag. They both drank. The mother and daughter were dead within minutes."

CHAPTER 83

"I have received reports from all the Shathapavans in the Empire," Mordecai said. "As a result of the King's edicts, all the Jews were saved."

Xerxes looked up from the scroll, "Mordecai, is seventy-five thousand the full count of the dead?"

"It is, My Lord King, including the ten sons of Haman who died and their bodies impaled."

Esther frowned, "Their impaled bodies will serve as a warning to anyone who might seek to harm the Jews."

"And the plunder? What did it amount to?"

"Nothing, My Lord King."

Xerxes frowned. "Nothing?"

"Nothing. Our people were not fighting for wealth and plunder." Mordecai looked at Esther. "We were fighting for our lives, for our freedom."

"I believe this calls for a celebration." Xerxes lifted his goblet. "With games, feats of strength, artists, food, everything. Mordecai, you will plan it."

"I will do so at once," Mordecai bowed. "My Lord King, My Lady Queen."

After the Cup-bearer left the Throne Room, Xerxes turned to hand the scroll to Esther. "Well, My Shahbanu, your request is complete. Your people are saved."

"Thank you, My Lord King," she sighed.

"Thank Me? No, no, no," Xerxes shook his head. "I am not responsible for the saving of your people. That honor falls to you," he lifted her hand to kiss it, "my Lady Queen. You were willing to sacrifice your own life to save your people."

She smiled. "As your honored maman always said, *Fight for your family*. As my maman always told me, *If we overcome, it is a victory, a gift, from Yahweh*."

EPILOGUE

28 FARVARDIN
THE TWENTIETH YEAR OF ARTAXERXES,
KING OF THE MEDES AND KING OF THE PERSIANS

"Why does my Cup-bearer look sad?" the King asked. "Are you ill?"

"No, My Lord King Artaxerxes," Nehemiah said. "I am not ill."

"Then this is sadness of the heart."

Nehemiah looked at the Queen who was sitting next to the King.

She nodded. "Speak what is in your heart."

"My Lord King, why should I not look sad when the city where my ancestors are buried lies in ruins, and its gates have been destroyed by fire? When another year has passed and our Holy Days are not celebrated in the Temple?"

"This city is Jerusalem," Artaxerxes looked at the Queen and then at his Cup-bearer, "is it not?"

"It is, My Lord King."

"Nehemiah, what is it you want?"

The Cup-bearer closed his eyes for a moment. The Queen saw his lips moving, as if in prayer.

After a moment, he opened his eyes. "If it pleases My Lord King, if your servant has found favor in his sight, let him send me to Jerusalem, where my ancestors are buried so that I can rebuild it."

The King looked at the Queen. She nodded.

"Nehemiah," Artaxerxes said, "I know this city is as important to the Malekeh Jahann as it is to you. Yes, I will send you to Jerusalem."

"Thank you, My Lord King Artaxerxes," the Cup-bearer bowed. "My Lady Queen Esther." As he turned to leave the Throne Room, the Queen stopped him.

"Nehemiah bar Hakaliah, you have always felt called to rebuild Jerusalem and the Holy Temple. As my mother—may her memory be blessed—always said, *What you do in this life will remain after you are gone.*"

She smiled. "For we are all born for such a time as this."

Persian, Jewish, Georgian Dates

PERSIAN - JEWISH - GEORGIAN

	PERSIAN	JEWISH	GEORGIAN
1.	3 Farvardin	Nisan 1	March 23
2.	3 Ordibehesht	Iyar 6	April 27
3.	6 Khordad	Sivan 7	May 27
4.	5 Tir	Tammuz 7	June 26
5.	4 Mordad	Av 8	July 26
6.	3 Shahrivar	Elul 8	August 25
7.	2 Mehr	Tishrei 9	September 24
8.	3 Aban	Heshvan 9	October 24
9.	2 Azar	Kislev 10	November 23
10.	2 Dey	Tevet 11	December 23
11.	2 Bahman	Shevat 29	January 22
12.	2 Esfand	Adar30	February 21

GLOSSARY

Ahura Mazda: The supreme god of the Zoroastrian religion, Ahura Mazda was the creator and god of light and truth.

Ashoo Pezeshk: A physician who oversaw the well-being of the city, preventing the spread of disease, overseeing the maintenance of the city's sanitation system.

Atashe del-am: *The fire of my heart.* Term of endearment from a man to his beloved.

Bagdir: A wind catcher. A tower on top of houses, designed to funneled wind down to the basement, where the air is cooled before being channeled through a series of canals to vents throughout the rooms to help cool the house.

Dad Pezeshk: A physician similar to a modern-day pathologist/coroners who examined the dead to help find cures for future cases.

Daric: A gold daric is the amount a common warrior earned each month.

Delbar-am: *He who holds my heart.* Term of endearment from a woman to her beloved.

Erbed: Honored teacher.

Gyah Pezeshk: A Physician who used food and herbs to treat conditions, similar to a modern day nutritionist.

Havou: A child born to a concubine and therefore having inferior status compared to a child born from a wife.

Hazarpatish: The Captain of the King's Bodyguard of 1,000 Immortals.

Herbad: A student of the magi who had finished the first level of training.

Kard Pezeshk: The surgeons of the time.

Lamassu: The deity in the shape of a flying lion.

Madarbozorg: Grandmother.

Malekeh Jahaan: Mother of the World, a title assigned to the Queen Mother of the Persian Empire.

Mantreh Pezeshk: A physician who used readings from holy scriptures, poetry, prayers, and music for their patients.

Mastoureh: A maiden in the First House of Women.

Pesarbozorg: Grandson

Norooz: Persian New Year is celebrated on what is March 23–28 in the Georgian calendar.

Sadfarbod: 100 Protectors of Glory, elite Warriors selected from The One Thousand Immortals.

Sarkar Khanums: The Queen's personal ladies in waiting, typically more than simple servants, they were women of noble families.

Shahbanu: The King's Lady, the Queen of the Medes and the Persians.

Shahbaz: The royal falcon, representing the strength and aggression of the Persian Empire.

Shathapavan: Governor of one of the Persian Empire's 127 Satrapies (provinces) who levied and collected taxes, maintained the peace, punished criminals, and provided soldiers for the King's military campaigns.

Yakhchal: A tall, ceramic, domed structure with a storage space beneath the ground where great blocks of ice were stored next to their food and wine for preservation.

Acknowledgments

I have a confession.

In the past, I have read books and closed the cover without reading the author's acknowledgements. After all, I didn't know the people and didn't care whether they had any part in the creation of the book. All I wanted to do was flip past the page and move on to the story.

Now that I have been on the other side of the book creation process, I realize a book is one child that takes a village. The story might be birthed in the author's imagination and fingers, but it takes a team of behind-the-scenes people to carry it through to the published state. Not to mention the author's family, who selflessly sacrificed so he or she could craft their story.

Therefore, please take a moment to allow me to publicly acknowledge and thank these people.

Thank you to everyone who read my *Sisters of Lazarus* series and *The Carpenter and His Bride* and then encouraged me to write more biblical novels. Your enthusiasm, your kind comments, and readers' reviews—as well as your recommendation to your acquaintances—were a blessing and balm to my heart. I wish I could list each of you by name, but alas, there is not sufficient space.

Thank you, Malcolm Down. Even though we no longer work

together professionally, your belief in my writing and your comments made me realize that it was possible for me to become an author.

Thank you, Rick Larson, for sharing from your research about the Star of Bethlehem. Your research led me on a path that sparked ideas for this novel about the Magi of the Eastern School who trained under the prophet Daniel.

Thank you, Tracy H. Sugg, for urging me to write Esther's story and for suggesting I include a harp.

Thank you, Kim Kohut, for sharing the sweet dream you had of Mama and the white bench. I know your intention was to comfort me after the loss of my mother, but your dream birthed ideas that I added to the story.

Thank you, Katelyn Nelson and Annette Woolf, for explaining your experiences with food allergies.

Thank you, Donna Williams, Holly McClure, and Tracy H. Sugg for your humbling endorsements of this book.

To my mother, Helen Jones. You always believed in me and my ability, sharing my books with many of your friends. You were on this side of Heaven when I began writing this novel; I am certain you are looking down and cheering me on. To Fred and Jean Parker, you are also looking down from Heaven; thank you for your encouragement and for being the best in-laws ever.

To my children: Rachael, Anna, Joshua, Bethany, and Mary; my three sons-in-law: Nathan, Billy and John; my daughter-in-love Wendy; and my grandchildren: Isabella, Penelope, Aubrey, Harrison, William, Charlotte, Eleanor, and Josephine. You are everything I have ever prayed for and one of the reasons I do what I do.

To Mike, my best friend, the father of our children, the best husband a woman could ever have, and now my publisher. Thank you for listening as I discussed various tidbits from my research, for suggesting things that added a new dimension to the story, and for taking over the housework and cooking so I could finish the book. You are my biggest fan and my best editor. Thank you for designing this stunning cover. Thank you for the love, support, encouragement, and courage to pursue our dreams and chart a course into untested waters.

Of course, I cannot end an acknowledgment page without thanking the One who loves me more than anyone in the world, Who sacrificed His life for me, Who daily reminds me I am worth so much more, Who reminds me that I am here for such a time as this, and Who holds my life in His hands; my Lord and Savior, Jesus Christ.

Author's Notes

When I read stories in the Bible, I wonder about how or why the people said or did certain things. How did Noah gather the animals into the ark? Why would Rebekah and Isaac favor one son over the other? Why did Balaam not run screaming in terror when the donkey spoke to him? Why did Mordecai tell Esther not to reveal her name and her family? What did Mary think when Gabriel appeared to her? What did Joseph think when Mary told him she—a virgin—was to give birth to the Son of God? What did Peter think when he was walking on the water? Who could afford perfume that costs a year's wages?

Perhaps because of their "moment in time" nature, the people in these Bible stories are often viewed as iconic figures on a stained-glass window. David was a courageous young boy. Solomon was the wisest of all. Peter was brash and impulsive. Mary had an uneventful pregnancy. Joseph had no concerns over raising the Son of God. Esther was the brave queen who risked her life to approach the king. Martha fretted over a meal while Mary sat peacefully at Jesus' feet. People misunderstood Who Jesus of Nazareth truly was.

But these people were more than a boy with five stones; a man with a floating zoo; parents who played favorites; a queen of the largest empire of that time; a couple with an unexpected—albeit unique—pregnancy; a disciple who acted before thinking; a woman with an expensive bottle of cologne; or people following the teacher from Nazareth. They had flaws and strengths, likes and dislikes, favorite foods, challenges, hopes and fears, pride, and insecurities.

Just like us.

One reason I like writing biblical novels is—for me—when I view these people as simple humans, when I research their time period and culture, the Bible stories come alive, and I glimpse possible answers to some of my questions.

Including questions about Hadassah, a young Jewish woman who would become the Queen of the Persian Empire and go on to rescue her people from an ethnic cleansing.

To be honest, I have never been drawn to the book of Esther. It is such a sad story, from Hadassah being an orphan, to risking her life to save the Jews from annihilation.

The encouragement to write *If I Perish* came from my dear friend Tracy Sugg. She and I were having an afternoon tea, catching up on our family and our work; Tracy is an amazing artist and sculptress. She had read my latest novel *The Carpenter And His Bride* and suggested I write the story of Esther. Knowing I like to give my characters unique giftings—and because I play the harp—Tracy suggested I should write Esther as being a skilled harpist.

I told Tracy the challenges I had with the story of Esther. She continued to encourage me to think and pray about it. I agreed.

I started by reading the book of Esther, making notes, and listing questions I had about this story. From there, I went through my stack of Bible commentaries, books on biblical archeology and cultural archeology before moving on to continue the research online.

The things I learned about Esther, as well the Persian (Achaemenid) Empire, were nothing short of astounding. I knew I had to write her story.

Whenever I write a biblical novel, I want the characters to be ordinary people chosen by God for an extraordinary task. In addition, I wanted them to have traits a modern reader would understand and empathize with. During my ponderings, one question I had was, after Esther was in the harem, why was Mordecai allowed to visit her, especially as they could not identify each other as relatives? Then it occurred to me; Mordecai would be allowed to visit her if he was her physician. Another friend of mine, Katelyn Nelson, has a plethora of food allergies, some of which are anaphylactic. I thought that would be an interesting trait for Esther, as it could require frequent visits from her doctor. I spent time chatting with Katelyn, and her mother Annette, about Katelyn's allergies, their symptoms, and their management. I began researching physicians during the Achaemenid Empire and discovered the ancient Persians had multiple different types of doctors, including physicians who would use herbs and food—rather like a dietitian—and they had another type of physician who treated patients with readings from holy scriptures, praying, and listening to music. This not only provided the answer for Mordecai being allowed to speak with Esther, but it also provided for Tracy's suggestion that Esther should play the harp.

If you would like to learn more about the research I used for different aspects of this book, visit my website:

www.paulakparker.com

or scan the QR code below:

Under the "Resources and Reviews" tab you'll find some fascinating information including a Biblical Fiction Glossary, Research, and a fun "Real vs. Hollywood" section that talks about actual historical people, places, and events, and their fictional counterparts.

Finally—and this is a big request—if you liked this story, would you please consider leaving a review on your favorite online bookstore, social media platform, or blog? I now love Esther's story and want as many readers as possible to discover it; your voice can reach people I cannot. Leave a review and tell a friend. The best compliment you can give an author is to recommend their book to your friends and family.

Thank you, dear reader, for giving your time to read this book. Stories need an audience. It means a great deal to me that you trusted me to entertain—and hopefully inspire—you with this story.

Blessings,

Paula K. Parker

Milton Keynes UK
Ingram Content Group UK Ltd.
UKHW040259291024
450401UK00021B/270/J